Stealing You

MOLLIE GOINS

To the black cat that is secretly soft, the golden retriever that's faking it, and everyone who puts on a front for others— It's okay to be unapologetically you.

Boston Blues

Stealing You primarily takes place during the off-season so the core group our the primary mentions throughout this book. For the full 26 man roster and teams in their division, please see molliegoins.com

Dex Larsen #53 | P

Adam Reyer #04 | C

Tripp Pierce #11 | 3B

Will Anderson #24 | P

Beck Daines #36 | 1B

General Manager: Jim Olsson | Team photographer: Callie Reyer | Emma Olsson: Team Secretary

Author Note

I'm so excited for you to read Stealing You! As always I love author's notes as I feel they are so important to the reader's experience. Stealing You does end on an HEA but there are some content warnings I would love to mention. Potential spoilers may be noted minimally.

Stealing You does cover some very deep and personal topics that may be sensitive for some readers. Topics of note include: On page loss of a parental figure, off-page loss of a family-like relatives during childbirth, mental health aspects such as anxiety, depression, and on page panic attacks from the MMC. Grief is heavily discussed throughout this book as Beck navigates his mother's diagnosis of Early-Onset Alzheimer's.

Thank you for reading Stealing You Please see the Dick-tionary chapters with explicit content.

Dick-tionary

Listen, I'm not here to judge, so whether you're here to find those spicy chapters *wink wink* or skip over them, I'm so happy you're about to spend time with Beck and Jensen!

Explicit content is mentioned throughout the book. Stealing You is intended for a mature audience only. Chapters of high sexual content are listed below.

Chapter 18

Chapter 21

Chapter 23

Chapter 28

Prologue – Beck
Midseason - July

"Alright, I've seen your slutty thigh tattoo, but there's no fucking way you're pierced." Jensen pins me with a look that makes my very-much pierced dick twitch.

We may be surrounded by all our friends for a game of poker, so hell, I'll call her hand. She's the one who started this conversation—not to mention, she's a licensed piercer and a soon-to-be licensed tattoo artist—as if I would let this opportunity pass me by.

I give her a cocky grin. "Want to find out, Jennie? I'll show you all my slutty tattoos and piercings if you ask nicely."

Jensen clenches her jaw as she grits out, "In your fucking dreams, Beckham."

Oh, they are, Jenni-cakes. And while she might play like she's not interested, I'm pretty positive I'm in her dreams too.

The rest of the table takes her words like the dismissal she wanted, but I don't miss the rise and fall of her chest with the breath she takes. I don't miss the flash of her eyes down and immediately back up. Almost as if she wanted to picture it but wouldn't allow herself to.

My best friend, Dex, sits across from me with his former nanny, Lucie, who he's head over ass for, and she leans on the table. "Anyway! Miles and I have been trying to talk Dex into playing again."

All my attention switches over to Dex, because what does Lucie mean "*trying*"?

"Why the hell have you not immediately agreed to this?"

"I second Beck. Actually, turning up the aggression, why the *fuck* not?" Our newest starting pitcher, Will, backs me up. Which is slightly surprising, considering Dex is his pitching coach. But Lucie is his sister and if she wants it, then I guess he knows it's better to just be on board.

Tripp, our third baseman, starts snapping his fingers at Emma, our general manager's daughter and the new team assistant. "Ems, get your dad on the phone."

Emma doesn't even seem fazed by the demand because, apparently, they're friends, which was a major shock to everyone here. We knew Olsson had a daughter, even though she hadn't really been around much since he took over as our GM. When she started as our new team assistant, I half expected Tripp to hit on her, not tell us they've actually been close friends for a couple years now.

Dex sends Lucie a look with a deep sigh. "No, for fuck's sake, can you all chill out? I'm perfectly happy where I'm at. You all can drop it now."

The fuck I will. He's lost his mind if he thinks I'm going to drop this now.

"Nah." I wave my hand dismissively. "Hate that. Next option."

Jensen's eyes meet mine for a brief moment before she

nudges our team catcher, Adam. "Wait, can he even come out of retirement?"

Adam shrugs. "I mean, yeah. Olsson, I'm sure, would extend him a contract easily."

"I'm not above forgery," Lucie adds.

This time it's me snapping my fingers at Emma. "Great. Emma, get your dad on the phone."

Callie, our team photographer, hits my arm and whips out her phone. "Quit snapping at her, this is her first game night. I'll do it."

"Okay!" Dex yells. "I'll tell you what—you guys win the World Series and I'll play again."

Our table goes silent. I don't love the idea of waiting to have Dex play with us again, but if he wants to make it a challenge so be it. Just ask Jensen, I love a challenge.

I extend my hand. "Alright, Dad, bet?"

Dex begrudgingly shakes it before turning to pull Lucie's chair closer and starts whispering in her ear. There's a tug in my chest when she smiles back at him. I can't seem to think of anyone who deserves happiness quite like Dex and Lucie do.

When Dex leans in to kiss her temple, I relax back in my chair and let my eyes wander over to Jensen—I can't say I want that love from her. I don't want a relationship from anyone, really.

I love my team. I love my friends. I love seeing my friends all happy and in love. However, I don't want it, and I don't exactly know how to explain why without someone trying to rationalize with me.

The pull I have toward Jensen I can't really understand, and I know I should let it go, but something in me hasn't been able to stop thinking about her since the night I met her.

Callie technically met her first—something to do with some weird "dating-not-dating" thing—I don't really know nor care how it happened. But when Callie brought her to the bar, I nearly choked on my drink.

Her silky black hair falls over her shoulders. Red and black tattoos start from her fingertips then up to the Marigold tattoos on her collarbone which are my personal favorites. When I asked her about them, she talked about their callback to her Mexican heritage, and I think that might have been our first conversation where she didn't completely blow me off.

As the night comes to an end, I keep one eye on Jensen as she talks to Lucie and Dex in the living room as I help Callie clean up the poker chips.

"She's going to knock you on your ass, Beck," Callie says under her breath.

I snort a laugh. "I can't wait. Think it'll bruise?"

"Gross." Callie tosses a chip at me. "She's about to leave, so hurry up and help me so you can follow her out like the lovesick puppy you are."

Eh, here we go.

Outright saying "I just want to fuck her" will likely earn me a slap from Callie, and I wouldn't blame her...but there's more to it than that. I may play the field in baseball, but I'm picky as hell when it comes to sleeping with someone. So damn picky that I haven't even entertained the idea of anyone except Jensen since the moment I laid eyes on her. Not to mention, the ones before Jensen were very few and way far between.

Unless it was abundantly clear it wasn't going to turn

into anything more than a one-night stand—it wasn't happening. The smallest hint—I mean the tiniest gut feeling—that the other person's thinking *maybe I could change his mind*—nope, not happening.

I don't entertain the reasons for being so hung up on Jensen. Could be that she seems to hate our palpable chemistry, and what better match-up than with someone who doesn't want anything to do with me other than getting some orgasms out of it?

Maybe it's once and out of our system... Maybe it's friends with benefits... Maybe it's just chemistry that will die out on its own and we'll still be left with this friend dynamic.

"At the risk of sounding like a complete asshat, I'm going to trust you love me enough to know what I mean when I say you know that's not what this is." I have my reasons and they're mine alone. I love Callie like a sister, but this just isn't something I can tell her, or anyone else for that matter.

Callie hums and her lips form a thin line. She does that every time she's dying to say something but chooses not to.

"Spit it out. *You know you wanna.*"

Callie shakes her head. "No, I have nothing to say."

I snort. *Yeah fucking right.* "Well, that would be a first."

She sends me a smart-mouthed grin. "Watch it, or I'll only submit shit photos of you for the rest of the week."

I let out a low whistle. "The injustice." I note Will making his way over to us and send Callie a wink. "You know I love you most anyway, Callie Bear."

Will wraps Callie up in his arms all possessively. "Okay, time's up. Get out of my house."

The tug in my chest comes back as Callie rests her head back on his chest. "You're interrupting our girl talk."

Will laughs, loosening his hold. "Yeah, well, Jensen just

walked out, so who am I really doing the favor by kicking him out?"

I toss the last of the chips in the lid of the case. "Sorry, Callie Bear, gotta do what the man says."

"Yeah, yeah, go on." She waves me off, and I plant a quick kiss to the top of her head to really get under Will's skin.

Racing down the hall, I grab the elevator just before it closes. As I step in, I see my Jennie all cute and angry.

"Desperate much?" she huffs out.

"Oh, come on, don't act like you're not happy to see me. It's the same look you get when I meet you for our Tuesday runs."

The joy I felt when I randomly ran into Jensen running with her dog a couple months ago and realized that we both loved a long ass run. I do that route every Tuesday my schedule allows—and the kicker, *she* still does too.

We may seem to be polar opposites, but sometimes I think we might have a little more in common than it appears.

Jensen gives me an eye roll. "Oh, my desperate, delusional stalker."

Ah, the insults and name calling. I turn to face her. "So possessive with your little 'my.' If you want me to be yours, Jenni-cakes, all you have to do is ask."

Jensen chokes on the air as she snorts a laugh. "You're not mine, Beckham. I'm not yours. Those titles have very little appeal to me."

"I get it, I might be a romantic for other people, but I don't need the label in order to hear you scream my name."

Jensen cocks her head. "Will I be screaming from the trunk of your car, some secret room in the basement...abandoned cabin, maybe?"

I step closer to her. "God, I love when you flirt with me."

Her nostrils flare as she lets out a deep breath. "You're exhausting."

Exhausting... Not, "get lost." Not, "leave me alone."

The corners of my mouth turn up. "I could exhaust you in other ways if you're tired of this one?"

This sexy grin comes to her face as she turns to face me, then meets my step. "Maybe you do have a pierced dick, you talk like you do..." Her inked hands brush against my chest before landing on my shoulders. "Let me see."

In a flash, Jensen's hands grip my shoulders, and her knee connects with my dick just as the elevator dings.

"Still can't tell. Maybe next time," she says, then walks out as I crumple to the floor.

The pain isn't enough to distract me from the "next time" comment.

I let out a breath and find a little strength to grit out, "Next time it is, Jenni-cakes."

Chapter 1
Beck
Three months later

"Out!" the umpire calls.

I can't decide what I like more, the sound of the ball hitting my glove paired with the "out," or the fact that this was the last out of the game to land us in the postseason. One step closer to the World Series. It might just be the look on my team's face as they realize what we just accomplished.

Our last season was a shit show...this one—this one has been incredible. Has to be one of the best seasons I've ever played in the major leagues and best team as a whole. We're going in as the second seed in the postseason which is a complete fucking 180 from last year.

With the entire team riding an absolute high from the field to the dugout, and back to the clubhouse, I take in this moment. Dammit, I love this team, I swear it's all I need in life.

Turning, I find Dex pinning me with a glare. "You just had to make that last out, didn't you?"

As if he should be surprised—we made a bet that night playing poker, and there was no way this team was going to lose it. We get that trophy and Dex signs a new contract—I want this asshole to pitch again, we all do.

"Sure as shit did. Tell Lucie her favorite player's about to come out of retirement."

"You don't have a trophy in hand yet. Best not to get too cocky." He shakes his head but claps my shoulder as he walks past me toward our general manager.

"Hey, I like to think I'm the perfect amount of cocky," I toss over my shoulder.

When I turn back around, Tripp's making his way to my cubby. "Think you can be cocky enough to be my wingman this weekend to celebrate? I love Ems, but if I ask her again, I'm afraid she'll paint my apartment pink in retaliation."

I snort a laugh. "As she should."

"You have got to stop roping Emma into being your wingwoman." Will joins our conversation. "The poor girl is a chronic people pleaser who doesn't know how to tell you no."

Tripp brushes him off. "Hey, Emma tells me no. We've been friends for years, she's told me no plenty of times."

Will looks to me with raised eyebrows and mumbles a sarcastic, "Okay."

Will's got a point, over the past couple months I don't think I've seen Emma tell anyone no. She'd bend over backward for her dad, hence her becoming our team assistant during the middle of the season, and with Tripp, it's just as bad.

Tripp opens his mouth to argue, but I decide to cut him off. "Count me in for this weekend. We can all go out, maybe *someone* could be a wingman for Emma this time around?"

The look that comes to Tripp's face lasts maybe two seconds, but it doesn't go unnoticed. "I could do that."

Will shakes his shoulders. "Don't worry, Callie is an excellent wingwoman, in case you can't. Count us in."

Tripp *humphs*. "Good to know, maybe I'll bring her next time. How do you feel about sharing?"

I chuckle when Will's face falls at Tripp's flirty tone. "Fuck off."

"You first," Tripp mocks.

"Both of you better fuck off, the girls practically run this team now—ain't no way I'm getting on their bad side."

Will tilts his head. "Fair point. Just text Callie where we're going and we'll be there."

I know where we're going if I get to pick, but just nod. Looking at Tripp next, I pin him with a stare. "*Ask* Emma if she wants to come, don't tell her."

Tripp sends me the middle finger while mumbling some additional curses under his breath as he walks off.

Digging out my phone from my bag, I send a text that will probably go unanswered.

> Saw you in the stands tonight with Lucie. I must have missed your fan sign for me. Maybe next time.

After our postgame meeting and dinner in the clubhouse, I'm walking into my townhouse. I toss my bag on the floor and fall back onto the couch. I'm not typically one for silence—I'm all for some background noise or music, but after screaming coaches, teammates, and fans for several hours, I welcome it.

I take two deep breaths to reset then reach for my phone, knowing it's about to ring. With the first feeling of it vibrating in my hand, I answer. "Hey, you catch the game?"

My dad's gruff laugh comes through the line. "As if we ever miss one. Isn't that right, Mils?"

"It was so good, there's one player that I really like—oh, what's he play? He stands on one of the sides..." My mom's voice starts out chipper, but as she tries to remember, I know it can turn to frustration quick.

"I think it's first base, honey. Beck plays first." Dad's voice is calm and reassuring. It kills me to know that without being there, my mother can't place me. I know it's not her fault, but the guilt of it threatens to eat me alive.

We're coming up on year five of her early-onset Alzheimer's diagnosis. She was fifty-fucking-two when all this started, but by year one she had already moved into the middle stage of her prognosis. They said that stage was supposed to be the longest, and I did everything in my power to slow the progression down, but it seemed to be nothing but fast. This past year we've officially moved into private end-of-life care that keeps her comfortable at home.

It guts me I'm not there with her, but Dad reminds me constantly that it's because of what I do that she gets the best care imaginable. It never feels like enough.

"Right, he has red hair like you do. I like his name too— Beck. It reminds me of someone...Beck...I think my dad was named Beckham, is that right?"

I can't seem to swallow the baseball-sized lump in my throat, so I let my dad continue to answer her.

"That's right, he was. Do you know someone else with that name? He—"

"Dad," I snap, finally finding my voice.

He knows I hate when he tries to make her remember. She hasn't remembered I'm her son for nearly two years. Sometimes she brushes off the idea of a son, but other times she gets so upset and frustrated. I get what he's trying to do, but I'll take being a player she likes to watch on TV over forcing her to remember.

"Right. Sorry, son."

"Son? You have a son?" Mom's words cut me deep.

There's a pause, I can tell he's struggling to not remind her it's also her son on the phone, but she rarely remembers Dad too. He lets out a small breath. "I do, he's really great. I think you would love him."

"Dad," I state my warning calmly, but he ignores it.

"We can talk about him more when I get back if you want. Or if you're ready for bed, I'll let Nurse Jamie know."

I hold my breath as I wait for her to answer.

"Oh, I'm ready to sleep," she says. "Just watching those boys run round and round made me tired."

I let out a pained laugh as I imagine the look on her face. She would say that to me after every game all the way from little league to now. These are the moments I need. It's more than enough to hold on to.

"Alright, I'll have Jamie come in to help. I'll be back in just a few." I wait in silence as I imagine the kiss to the back of my mom's hand and the smile she'll give my dad in return, like they would do every single time they parted ways. Didn't matter if Dad was simply grabbing something from the fridge...every single time. I know that's not actually happening now, but the memory of it helps.

My romantic side comes from watching them growing up. It's the reason why I hope to see every single one of my friends happy and in love. The love my parents have now is the reason I don't want to find it for myself.

The kicker with early-onset is that it's familial. Especially with my grandfather passing away with it, we had to have the genetics conversation. It was enough to have my head spinning, but I clung to the words that even though my chances of having it weren't definite, and there were things I could do to help encourage my brain function, the bottom line was...there was no guarantee I wouldn't.

I hear a sliding door open then close. "Alright, I'm outside, you can lecture me now."

"You know I don't want you forcing her to remember me."

"I did no such thing, but you know the doctors have encouraged us to help keep her memory up—it doesn't hurt to gently remind her about the son she loves very much. We both took those classes on how to talk to her during these later stages...we ought to put that to use, don't ya think?"

I pinch the bridge of my nose. "I know what the doctors and all the nurses say, I have all their personal numbers and much to their dismay, I use them quite frequently. I know you know, it's just...I'm not there. It's a lot easier—"

"Ah, so it's that bullshit again. You're just as stubborn as your mother," Dad cuts me off, his tone becoming a lot less calm than it was a minute ago. "Get this through your head, Beckham—you are providing round-the-clock care along with the best doctors and medications. We no longer have to go out for appointments that leave both of us disappointed. She's comfortable, and had a good day today so some memory-jogging is encouraged. You are the first person we always start with, end of discussion."

I let out a deep sigh. "I'm coming down a few days after the postseason ends. If we don't make it to the final game, maybe I can come sooner."

"That's fine, son. You know we always want to see you, but we also couldn't be more proud of you. You know good and well that your mom would lose it if she saw how much weight you carry in this."

Silence hangs as I let his words run through my brain.

Before I can respond, he clears his throat and asks, "So, any chance you'll bring someone special with you this time?"

I muffle a laugh. "Not this time." *Or any time.* "I'm perfectly happy being on my own."

He mumbles another curse. "No, you're not. You were practically Velcro growing up, even as a teenager. You hate being alone."

Correction, I used to hate being alone. I have my team, my friends—that's all I need. Not that I can tell my dad that, I can't even begin to think of how to explain to him why I don't want a relationship anymore, but at the end of the day it's my choice.

"If I stop feeling guilty about not being home, will you stop bringing up me finding someone?"

Another beat of silence passes. "I'll give you the, what, two weeks you'll be here—no questions unless you start acting guilty."

I barely form a chuckle. "I'll take it."

The silence hangs heavy on the line for a moment. "We just want you to be happy, you know that?"

"For fuck—" My hand grips my phone tight. "What about our deal?"

"I said during the two weeks," Dad snaps. "Actually, screw that deal. I need to know you're happy. Show me that, I don't care how it looks. Alone. With someone. I don't care if you become your own version of a cat lady, just show me that you're happy when you're here, and I'll never ask again."

"Fine, I can do that." *I think.*

"I'm serious, Beckham. There's not much I can threaten you with anymore. All I've got is parental guilt."

My laugh comes without a thought. "I think you could still kick my ass if you really wanted to, old man."

He lets out a *humph*. "Kick your ass in pool, maybe, you might have gotten better since we played last."

There's a small ache in my chest. "We'll see about that when I get there."

"Sounds good. Get some sleep, you deserve it after that game."

"Will do, Dad. Call when you can."

"Of course. We love you."

"Yeah, I love you guys too."

Ending the call, I let out a string of curses. Each phone call has me looking up red-eye flights out to them. With my phone in hand, I can't say I won't do it this time, but then I see a text.

JENNI-CAKES

Didn't think Olsson would appreciate "Beck Daines is a stalker" on a giant poster board. Next time.

Chapter 2
Jensen

Therapy Dupe

JENSEN

Alright, the first person to bring me an
energy drink and protein bar to Winedown
gets their first drink on the house.

LUCIE

Have you eaten any actual food today?
Sips of water at least?

JENSEN

Okay, Mother, I didn't ask for a lecture.

REAGAN

Sorry, I've been running around Boston all
day looking for a new storefront for the
floral shop. I'm beat and need to go
scream into my pillow for a bit.

CALLIE

Boo, for no rental property under a million
dollars.

Jen, what if Emma and I bring one of
each? Will that qualify us both for the free
drink?

EMMA

Goodness knows I'm going to need one if
Tripp ropes me into being his wingwoman
again.

LUCIE

Dex and I are doing a movie night in with
Miles tonight, but I'll still bring you actual
food, Jen.

JENSEN

If it's not highly caffeinated and something
I can shove down in two minutes then it's
a no.

CALLIE

I got you. Beck won rock-paper-scissors,
we're coming to Winedown.

LUCIE

I'll come over in the morning with breakfast
and an IV.

JENSEN

Wait Callie... What?

Thirty minutes into my shift, a pink Red Bull and about
three different granola bars hit the bar top in front of me.
The kicker—the wrong redhead brought them.

"Dinner's on, Jenni-cakes," Beck beams. I never considered red curly hair and the freckles on his face that meet his slight facial hair to be my type, but Beck has made it my type.

My stomach turns in knots when I meet his bright green eyes. It really wouldn't hurt for this man to be a little less attractive. What's a girl got to do around here for him to lose some teeth with a fly ball?

I mask my attraction with a snarky look. "I didn't ask you to bring me those—you don't get the free drink."

Beck raises an eyebrow as he slides onto the barstool. "Didn't realize that was the prize for bringing you treats. I was more thinking of the company."

Callie takes the last empty seat next to Beck, and Emma stands behind her as each of them drop another Red Bull and a jerky stick.

Callie clocks Beck's stuff and hits his arm. "Hey, I didn't know we had competition."

"Yeah, he can afford his own drinks, he doesn't count," Emma adds.

I look at Beck, his smile bright, like fucking usual. "I don't have to count, but I would like to."

I slide the granola bars back to him, not having the complete strength to let go of the Red Bull. "He doesn't count," I parrot Emma's words. Nothing Beck does counts because no matter how hot he is, I don't want to date him— kind of, more like, I won't *allow* myself to date him.

Beck slides the snacks back toward me. "See, I went by Dex's place on my way here. When I noticed Lucie had started a breakfast casserole, I had some questions. So, you're going to take both drinks and eat at least two of these, or I call her and she'll bring a whole-ass casserole to the bar. Your choice."

Callie folds her lips into a thin smile while Emma snickers.

Of course, Lucie's the mole. I love her immensely, but she's been Team Beck since the start. I snatch them off the bar top as a man a few seats down calls for me. "I'll take them, but when I get back I'm only serving Callie and Emma. You and the rest of the guys can order from Mia for the night."

Beck stands up with a wink. "Eat, and we have a deal."

Emma slides into the now empty seat. "*Eat, and we have a deal,*" she mocks. "Whatcha gonna do, Jen? If you don't eat them, you won't have to see Mia flirt with him all night."

I hate how right she is. I don't like watching anyone flirt with Beck, let alone Mia, who's wicked smart and the soon-to-be owner of this freaking bar. Granted, I don't hate his dismissals of her. It's petty, but true. He never flirts back, never has second glances. He gives polite responses and tips, but nothing more.

The man a few seats down snaps at me again. I groan, what I wouldn't give to quit this job. I'm damn near counting down the days. One more shift with my apprenticeship. Eight measly hours until my sleazy bosses can sign off for me to get my tattoo license, and then I'm out of there.

I may not be able to jump ship here just as quickly if I want to afford my rent for the shitty apartment I have, but hopefully I can cut back on some hours until I get my clientele up past the piercings I do.

I shove the bars and jerky into my apron and set the drinks on the back bar before going back to my friends.

"Listen, if you want those free drinks, then no more Beck talk. I'll be right back."

While thinking of the potential tip, I force a smile to my face. "How can I help you?"

Despite his impatience, the man takes his time looking me over before speaking. "Sorry if I interrupted you and your little boyfriend, but some of us have been at the office all day and would love a Manhattan."

Swallowing every snarky remark I can think of, I take my time looking back at this asshat. He looks so familiar...I'm positive I've watched him slide his ring into his pocket before. I clock his hand and see the ring.

Alright, customer service voice, let's push through. "One Manhattan coming up. Do you want to start a tab?"

The man sets his card on the table as his answer and barely spares me another glance. I guess with his first look over, he found I'm not his type. *Poor me.*

After starting his tab, I grab a short glass and some rye whiskey to start throwing his drink together.

"Ooo, the Blues men are here tonight," Mia all but purrs as she comes up behind me. "Makes this double I'm working completely worth it."

I roll my shoulders back and exhale. "Yeah, they're ready to order when you are. I've got the girls in the middle of the bar."

"Got it. Beck's still single, right?" she asks.

I grit my teeth as I drop the toothpick of maraschino cherries in the glass. "Yep."

"Perfect." Mia tugs at her auburn hair in her already high ponytail. "Wish me luck."

I very much don't do that. In fact, I bite the inside of my cheek to the point that I'm sure I've drawn blood. I like Mia, I truly do, but I don't want her flirting with Beck. I don't want him to realize how cool she actually is, then agree to go on a date with her...

This is ridiculous, how did I get here?

Just a few months ago, Beck was annoying and had that overly cocky persona that I loathe...but somewhere along the way, the asshole pulled some voodoo magic because I actually look forward to spending time with him now.

Setting the Manhattan in front of the tool in a suit, I finally let go of my cheek when I realize this man's ring is now mysteriously gone. And shocker, he's talking to the woman who has, unfortunately, sat down next to him.

My blood starts to boil. You know what? I'm not going to get a decent tip from this dipwad anyway.

"Here we are." I slide the drink to him then turn to the woman. "What can I get you?"

She flashes a small smile to me then the secret pig next to her. "I think I'll have a dirty martini, two olives."

I wait for it.

"On my tab," he adds.

I fake a smile. "Perfect." Without question, I ring up her drink on his tab, per his request. When I slide the drink back, I hold my smile. "And here you go. While you are sipping on this, ask him about the ring he has in his pocket," I say, not waiting for any response and heading back over to Callie and Emma.

"Okay, give me your orders before I change my mind on those free drinks."

"I'll take a glass of merlot, please," Callie says.

"How uncool is it of me to order a Shirley Temple?" Emma asks with a scrunch on her nose. "I was thinking I could finish this painting tonight, and I'm on my fine line details that will require Sober Ems."

I snort a laugh. "Not uncool, but I thought you said you needed the drink to be wingwoman of the year?"

Emma's eyes nearly roll out of her head. "I'm off duty tonight. Thank god."

Callie rests her head on her shoulder. "I, however, am on duty for our Ems because she needs to move on from our playboy of the century."

I slide Callie's glass of wine in front of her then reach for a new glass to start Emma's. "You sure you don't need a shot of courage for that?"

Emma lifts her shoulder to shake off Callie. "No, I don't, because she's just been fired. And I've moved on from Tripp, thank you very much."

When Callie and I give each other looks that say *yeah, right,* Emma whines. "It's true! I have."

Callie pats her shoulder. "Of course you have."

I slide the drink across the bar top and match Callie's sarcastic tone. "We so believe you."

Emma tosses her hands up. "There's truly nothing to move on from, we've only ever been friends."

Callie waves her off. "Been there, done that. It's better to get the orgasms out of it."

I give Callie a wink because, gah, I love how happy her and Will are. What I don't understand is Tripp and Emma. "Okay, I really need more details, because you keep saying you guys became friends in college, but that doesn't make sense to me. How are you two 'college' friends...isn't Tripp older than us? Did *he* even go to college?"

Emma all but shrinks in her chair. "It's a long story."

More people filter in around the bar, and I let out a sigh. "Give me the highlights as I pass by." Taking two steps over, I take some drink orders before popping the tabs on two Modelos, then bring a bottle of champagne in front of Callie and Emma to uncork.

"Go."

"I really don't—" Emma starts, but between my evil eye and Callie's shove, she groans. "Okay, highlights. We met my sophomore year of college and we just were quick friends. I don't know how to explain it...we sort of hit it off."

I raise an eyebrow. "If you guys 'hit it off,' you'd be dating. Leaving out some context, Ems. But hold it." I put the bottle into a bucket of ice and grab two empty flute glasses. I pass that off then I'm back in front of my girls. "Shoot."

Emma's cheeks turn bright red before she even speaks. "I was dating his brother, okay."

"What?!" I did not see that being a part of this equation.

Callie sits up and turns in her chair to face Emma. "*Tripp has a brother?* How did I not know this? I feel like I should know a lot more about these guys than I do."

"That's because you and Will are practically glued together."

Callie shrugs. "Alright, fair. Sorry, continue."

Emma winces slightly. "It's his estranged brother. They don't talk—haven't talked since the beginning of my senior year— Right before he broke up with me, it all blew up."

"Oh, my word," Callie squeaks. "This is so much more than I was expecting! What happened? Why don't they talk?"

"Look, I don't have all the details, but Tripp promised it wasn't about me." Emma shakes her head. "His brother hated our friendship and accused me of cheating with him constantly. Which never happened, but you'll call me out if I didn't acknowledge the small, teeny-tiny attraction on my end."

I barely get my *pah-ha* out before Emma jumps on me. "Hey, what about you, Mrs. Daines? Let's talk about how Beck just brought you all your favorites—completely unprompted."

I grab her Shirley Temple back before she can reach it.

"Talk of He-Who-Shall-Not-Be-Named and lose your drink."

Callie snorts a laugh. "Here we go."

"No, I'm not starting this right now," I say before Emma can counter. She'll have too many good points considering we give her the same crap about liking Tripp, but at the same time it's different with Beck. Granted, her and Tripp seem a lot more complicated than I previously thought, but still.

As hot as Beck is—as good in bed as I'm sure he is—it's not going to happen. I push the uninterested bit the best I can, but my girls have seen through that facade enough. I like him, and they know it. Well, Lucie, mostly, but Emma and Callie seem to have caught on over these past few weeks.

I've used time and other priorities as my excuse to not explore whatever this is between me and Beck for the most part. It's usually enough to get them off my back, but the reality still stands, and as awful as it is to admit—I have a fucking crush on Beck.

There are many reasons I haven't acted on it and two of them are sitting right across from me.

Callie takes a drink of her wine and twists slightly back and forth on the stool. "Okay, new topic. You're almost done with your apprenticeship, right? We're on our final week?"

"Yes, thank god. Eight more hours and one signature from my ass of a supervisor and I'm out of there. For the past month, I've been envisioning the insults I would tattoo on Hank's forehead, but I'm running out of words for the bastard."

Emma snags her Shirley Temple back. "How creative have you gotten?"

"Pretty out there. I started with Spanish curse words to make my mama proud, reimagined them in English, then took a little inspiration from Lucie and tried to think of non-curse words. Some were satisfying—most were not."

Callie snorts. "I can only imagine. But you're almost there and then you can tattoo your favorite one on his forehead legally."

"The options are endless." I glance over to the guys at their table. Mia hovers over Beck while everyone places their orders. Fighting the eye twitch, I scan the table to see who all came out tonight. There's Beck, and of course, Tripp, then Adam and Will across from them, then two empty seats meant for Callie and Emma.

I swallow down some of my pride. "You two can go hang with the guys, I'll be here all night."

Callie slides off the stool with a small smirk. "I'm not against feeling up my man for a bit, but I'll be back. I only want my drinks coming from the hot tatted bartender."

"Don't flirt with me, Cals, or I'll give Will a run for his money," I joke.

Emma hops off her seat next. "Do it. Giving Will shit is my and Adam's favorite pastime...ya know, minus baseball."

I shake my head with a laugh. "Go have fun with the guys, just come see me when you need a refill."

"Will do," Callie hollers over her shoulder. "Unbutton your top a bit, and I'll tip you better next time."

I roll my eyes with the shake of my head, then realize half of the guys sitting at the bar are now looking at me in a completely different way. For fuck's sake.

I push another hour before I spot Beck staring at me from across the bar. I note his empty drink and Mia nowhere in sight. There's a small pull to walk over to him, but I fight it off. Beck is a no-go zone, no matter how much of a hopeless romantic I am at heart—my brain is smarter. And my goals are my priority right now.

It's a play I've been the star of before. A girl likes a boy—girl tells boy she wants a career and not his babies...girl moves to Boston with a broken heart and no friends.

I know deep down that this group is different, but if Beck and I were to have a nasty ending, it would be me who gets left out of the mix. Callie is just as close with him as she is with us girls. Lucie is all but married to Beck's best friend, and Emma works for the team now too.

One-night stand or friends with benefits has crossed my mind several, *several* times, but it all loops back to that stupid heart of mine. A crush I can move past, but full-on feelings is a whole different level. I can manage what I feel for him now, but it all goes back to us wanting the same things.

I can't truly know what Beck wants from me. He flirts constantly and meets me every Tuesday for a run together, but he has never exactly asked me out either.

Whatever we are works for now, and maybe one day this attraction will simmer down. All I know for certain is that I can't hear how I'm not doing my womanly duties for not wanting to have kids right away, and I definitely don't want to lose my girlfriends.

I set an old-fashioned and glass of chardonnay down on the bar top for the older couple in front of me. "Shall we start a tab?" I ask.

The man looks at his wife and nods with a bright smile. "That would be great." He slides his card to me. "Any chance we can take these to the upstairs bar?"

The lady shakes her shoulders. "Oh, he's actually going to dance with me tonight."

See, this—I love this. As the husband kisses the back of her hand, I can't help but smile. There are things I do and don't want in a relationship, but love...true, obsessed with each other, love? Yeah, I want that...eventually, at least.

Sometimes, I really do think Beck would be this great guy to have that with but it's not like I can ask him *"Hey, so I know you flirt, and I act like I don't enjoy it, but quick question...how do you feel about kids?"*

When I return with the card, they raise their glasses to me as they get up from their spot. I watch as they walk hand in hand for a moment, but movement in front of me catches my eye.

"What can I—" I start, then stop when I see Beck's moved to the spot the couple just vacated. "I thought I said I wasn't serving you tonight."

Beck takes the seat with a smirk. "I don't need a drink. I told you I came for the company. Have you eaten yet or should I call Lucie?"

"Call Dex, actually. Tell him you want his girlfriend to bring food downtown when they're supposed to be having family night."

Beck opens his mouth then shuts it. "Touché," he mumbles as he leans forward on the bar. "Just tell me if you're about to pass out so I can look real heroic and catch you."

I start to respond when a new person hollers at me from across the bar. "Just let me hit my head, you'd be doing me a favor."

Beck tilts his head with a smirk. "Don't let me keep you from working, ignore me like you pretend to do all the time."

I bite my cheek again as I walk away. This will go away eventually, he'll move on and my crush will fade. If my sister were here, she'd probably slap me for not telling Beck to move on after she helped snap me out of the last relationship I was in.

But she's not here, and I've gained some serious strength since then. My hard exterior can keep Beck at bay, my heart will catch up eventually and we can just be a part of the same friend group.

I make some more drinks and refill Callie and Emma a few more times before I catch a small break.

I might be testing my restraint a bit, but I find my way in front of Beck again and open up one of the granola bars. "So, World Series?"

Beck leans over on the bar with a small smile. "We still have to play in the division series, but I feel good about our odds. You want to come watch?"

I snort a laugh and look around at anyone but him. "I'm not coming as one of your little groupies."

"Oh, come on, you'd look so cute with my face printed on your shirt."

I think I'd look pretty cute sitting on your face. Hell, that's the wrong thought.

"Beckham," I deadpan.

"I'm kidding, relax. I'm sure Lucie would love the company. If you want to come, it'll just require a simple poster with 'I love Beck' written in big block letters."

"*Dios mío*, does your ego need stroking on a daily basis? Or is it an hourly thing?"

Beck leans back from the bar with a shrug. "Depends. I start every morning with positive affirmations about how amazing I am. Then the rest filter in naturally from strangers. I'm charismatic, what can I say?"

I meet his emerald eyes. "You're insufferable."

Beck gives me that cocky grin. "Stroke my ego, or somewhere else for the tickets, Jenni-cakes."

"Not happening." Can't. Won't. And every negative contraction there is.

"I guess you'll never know if I'm truly pierced or not..."

"That's easy—you're not." At least, that's what I'm forcing myself to believe. There are many things about Beckham Daines that I do not need to know, and at the top of the list is knowing whether his dick is pierced or not.

It's been months since that damn game night where the topic was brought up. Just the idea of it was enough to bring an already ten-out-of-ten man to a freaking fifteen. Confirmation of what he could do with it would bring him up to a twenty.

Me kneeing him that night in the elevator was a cheap shot, but it was either that or call his bluff.

I take the last bite of my granola bar and toss the wrapper in the trash. "Thank you for the snacks," I mutter, against my better judgment.

Beck's shoulders drop slightly and an eyebrow raises.

"What? What's that look for?"

The corners of Beck's mouth turn down with a bemused smirk. "Just wasn't expecting all this gratitude. Is that why you fight me so much? Are you just hangry?"

Instant regret. "I'm going to spit in your drink," I mumble.

"Is that supposed to be a threat or a good time?" Beck folds his arms and leans closer on the bar top.

Dear lord, and I have a crush on this guy? Really? How the hell did this happen?

I catch Mia in my peripheral before leaning forward to

meet Beck with a smirk then tilt my head toward my regret-table escape. "Hey, Mia, Beck needs a refill, and I think your phone number."

"You little fucker," Beck mutters before I walk away.

Chapter 3
Jensen

T-minus fifteen minutes left in my hours required. Nine hundred seconds, and I'm fucking counting. Sitting on my tiny stool, I watch as Hank drags his tattoo gun against one of his regulars then wipes with a paper towel.

I hold my breath with each rotation because half the time he pauses and something stupid comes flying out of his mouth.

"You know, Jensen, I'm going to miss having you watching me. Maybe I should pull all your timecards before I sign off on your hours. I'd hate to miss an opportunity to have you *learn* something."

"*Puerco*," I mumble under my breath. *Pig.*

He's been stretching out my last eight hours for over a week already. "All my time has been properly recorded. I hand them over to Tally for her to double-check every week."

At the mention of the owner and his *wife*, Hank goes back to the phoenix he's supposed to be finishing.

How Tally stays married to this asshat is beyond me. I've thought about bringing up his beyond inappropriate commentary and wandering eyes...recently, hands...many times. But Hank's smart— it's always small touches, and everything he says he flips around as if he's simply joking. Not to mention, Tally thinks he's the funniest guy in all of Boston—her doing something is a long shot, and I'm too close to the end of this to ruin it.

"I suppose it won't be all that different when you start working here," Hank says over the buzz of his gun.

Yeah, in his dreams—my nightmares—will I stay at the same shop as him, and part of me thinks Hank knows that.

Something about his demeanor this week has made me even more uneasy. I'm not usually one to take shit like this, but sometimes it's more about knowing when to step in it or step over it.

"Interesting choice of bird," I say to Hank's regular, Charlie. He's fruit from the same tree, but that's not even the worst part about him. Charlie is my freaking landlord. Shall I reference the metaphor again, because I've been stepping over shit that really feels like it should qualify as a landmine.

Another reason for my hesitation to tell Tally is that she's the one who sent me in the direction of these apartments. I can't tell if she's oblivious to their bullshit or into it.

Charlie glances down his arm and his face lifts like he's just now remembering that he's getting a phoenix. "Yeah, I thought it was the perfect tattoo to get since my divorce from that bitch is final. Rebirth. New *experiences* to be had."

Charlie's eyes trace down from my black hair to my feet. Ugh. *Perverito, perv,* and for Lucie, *sleazebag.* Yep, all of those, right on his forehead they go.

"Well, that...that is what the tattoo typically symbolizes. Rebirth," I mutter.

Charlie and Hank give each other a look that I can't, nor

want, to understand. At the end of the day I need Hank's signature, and Charlie provides my place to live, but each come with expiration dates. I just need to be smart enough to make sure one doesn't fuck up the other.

"Well, this sure is something." Blake, the other artist in this shop comes up behind me.

Now, Blake, I like. He's never once crossed over into creepy territory. No insults imaginarily tattooed on his forehead. He even covered for me a few months back so I could tattoo some turtles on Lucie's arm.

"You know, I hate to steal Jensen, but I believe her time is officially fulfilled, and I've got someone up front wanting a nose piercing."

Thank god. Thank god. Thank god.

I hold myself back from completely jumping out of the stool. "I'll go take care of that, then loop back for that requirement form."

Blake gives me a nod to lead the way to the front, and I gladly go because I know what he's doing—he's blocking the two with *perv* tattooed on their foreheads from checking me out as I walk away.

"Saved by the rebellious teenager wanting to disappoint her parents," Blake whispers.

I wave him off. "A nose piercing is mild. They could do much worse."

"God knows I did." Blake keeps his voice low. "Just know, I'm betting she's going to be a crier."

"Joy," I mutter, but I'd take an indecisive, low-pain-tolerance client over sitting for a second longer with those two.

And that is exactly what I get. Half an hour of *yes*, then *no*, then finally convinced the poor girl to just get her second ear piercing as a compromise.

"Think she'll be back for more?" Blake turns slow circles in the office chair behind the desk tossing a ball mindlessly in the air as he goes.

I glance at the entry door where the freshly eighteen-year-old, parent-pleaser just walked out of. "Eh, another bad breakup or two and she might be back. Didn't seem like she gets to make too many choices on her own merit, so I gotta give her some credit for at least following through with something."

"Heads-up." Blake shrugs then tosses the ball to me when the front door chimes again. "Well, double heads-up, Tally's going to offer you a spot to work here. She's coming up." Blake hurries to stand as he whispers quickly. "If you don't take it, I understand, but if you do, I'll help run inter-ference."

"Jensen," Tally sings behind me. "We're officially up on your apprenticeship. I should've brought champagne!"

"Yep, all done." I turn around with the best customer service, happy to see you, bullshit face I can manage. My smile bares a little authenticity when I take in Tally's outfit. Cheetah print tank top, tight leather pants, and truly kick-ass boots. She ties it all together with oversized hoops, and chunky brown highlights in her bleach-blonde hair.

Her outfits are always over the top and tacky, but she loves it. And, in an odd way, it suits her so well that I don't think any other style of clothing would look right on her.

"Here's that letter stating you completed your require-ments. You can just take your cute ass down to the health department so you can be all legal and what not. I was thinking you could start next week, maybe match your walk-in hours to Hank's in case you need any help."

Wonderful. Not a job offer, a job told. With Tally's blunt

personality, I can't quite tell if this is just her being her, or a form of bullying to get me to stay here, but it's not happening. I refuse to work next to Hank a second longer.

"I appreciate the offer, Tally. I really do, but I'm going to have to pass on this position right now."

Tally's overdrawn eyebrows pull together. "You don't want to work here? After all the time you just put in?"

"Not what I said. It's nothing personal." *To her, technically...just her husband.* "I think it would be good for me to branch out, that's all." *Not a complete lie.* "You all have fully booked clientele—I've been here two years and the only walk-ins we get are for piercings and the occasional drunk who stumbles in with a random tattoo idea."

Tally starts to nod in an overly exaggerated way. "I hear you, I hear you—don't want to work here, that's fine. You got what you needed. Enjoy figuring it out on your own." Tally walks toward the back, not giving me any option to respond.

Not that I was going to. I don't need her approval, I just need this paper and my "cute ass" is out the door.

I click my tongue and bend down to grab all my files. "Could've gone worse," I say, because I know Blake was listening.

"Yeah, could have told her you hated her outfit." Blake sits back down in the office chair. "What'd you do with my ball?"

I let out an amused huff as I bring my plastic file organizer up on the counter, then toss his ball back. "I'm sure she's telling him everything now, so I'm going to make a quick escape before it gets worse. If you find anything of mine, can you—"

I trail off as Blake waves me off. "I got you, now go on. Run while you still can."

Hank and Charlie's voices start to echo. I'm not sure what's coming out of their asses, and I don't care. I throw on my denim jacket and grab my stuff before mouthing a *thank you* to Blake, and I'm out the door.

As soon as my feet touch the concrete of the sidewalk, I feel this weight off my fucking shoulders. Ugh, I'm free of that place! I can't wait to tell the girls.

When I reach my apartment floor, my phone starts to vibrate in my bag. Setting my stuff down, I dig it out near the last ring and answer, assuming it's Lucie or my sister.

"Hello," I answer with a bit more enthusiasm than normal.

"Jenni-cakes, you answered!" Beck's chipper voice comes through the line. "And you sound...dare I say...happy?"

Wonderful. I pin the phone between my ear and shoulder to dig out the keys to my apartment. I flatten my tone the best I can. "Beckham, why are you calling me?"

"Well, see, I have some tattoos I need done...you know to go with my slutty thigh tattoo. And I know someone who just finished all her required hours—I want to get on her books before she's too busy for little ol' me."

I bite my cheek to stop the smile. Of course, he knew I was finishing today. "One, I'm already too busy for you, Stalker. And two, I'm finished with my hours, but I still have to get my professional license and find a place to work."

"Tally's doesn't want you to stay there?"

Not about to explain that situation to him. "They could —they offered, but I think it's good for me to find a new place. Be pushed out of my comfort zone."

"Do you have a comfort zone? I pegged you as more that 'free spirit' type."

Finally pulling out my keys, I work on unlocking my

door and can hear the clicking of my border collie, Dottie, prancing on the other side.

"What in the hell gives you 'free spirit' vibes?" I nearly laugh at his words as I kick my box of papers into my tiny apartment, and Dottie circles my body, tail wagging a mile a minute.

"First, give Dottie love from me," Beck says. "Second, free spirit, as in has no boxes or comfort zones. More of a 'I can take what life throws at me' person."

My silence feels near deafening. This is how I got in this mess—why does he always have to do sweet shit like this? It should be annoying. I've never once felt this attraction to the goofy, sweet guy. Romantic at heart, yes, but cheesy? No, never...until Beckham.

"I'd donate five hundred dollars to whatever charity you want if you lie to me and say you don't have a tapestry up on your wall. Really round out my free spirit feeling."

I look up at the wall completely covered by the thin cloth my sister had custom made with one of my first designs. "It was a gift," I grit out.

"I fucking knew it. Let me know the charity, Jenni-cakes."

"I thought I was supposed to lie for that donation." Dottie paws at my side. "I've got to take my dog out, Beckham. Pick a charity on your own. Bye."

I click the End Call button immediately, then toss my phone on my bed with a sigh. Scratching Dottie's head, I do what I know I shouldn't. "Beck says hi," I tell her...like a crazy person.

No, talking to her doesn't make me crazy, but telling her about Beck sure does.

Clicking on her leash, I grab the fanny pack I have ready

by the door that I take every time I take her out, then pick up my phone.

STALKER

*A donation was made to the Animal
Rescue Shelter - Boston in the amount of
$1000.*

I doubled it for the truth.

Of course he would follow through and still be extra about it. Sliding my phone in my back pocket, I don't bother giving him a response.

A sharp knock comes to my door then a piece of paper is flying from under the crack.

"What the hell?" I mutter to myself, or Dottie, I suppose.

Picking up the paper, my fingers tense, crinkling the bullshit in my hands with every word I read.

Monthly rent raised to thirty-five hundred dollars.

Motherfuckers work fast.

Chapter 4
Beck

Today's the day. Our final game in the World fucking Series. We all handle game days differently. Some of us have strict game day superstitions and others are a little more lax with it, but today is different. Everyone seems to be on edge...well, except me.

Nerves? Yeah, those don't exist for me on the ballfield. Outside the game, they definitely do, but not here. Not in my uniform. It's been six grueling games of equal wins and loses that's led us to game seven, but frankly I've never felt more confident.

Adjusting my hat outside the guest locker room, I can already hear the crowd. Then I hear the flashes of a camera.

"I think you're the only one giving me decent candids today," Callie says with a laugh.

"Oh, I'm so telling Will. Have your camera ready, I want candid pictures of his reaction."

"Trust me, my man's plenty photogenic." Callie lets her camera hang on its strap as she walks up to me. "I meant you're the only one not looking like a robot about to take over the world."

Humph. She's not wrong. My lax attitude might come off as cocky or uncaring, but anyone who thinks that is wrong.

"We deserve to be here. I'm not too stressed about something I know we earned the right to have."

Callie hums. "You know, I couldn't have related to words less at the beginning of this season, but now—"

"Now you see how fucking awesome you are."

Callie hits my shoulder. "More like how awesome I am when I'm with the right people. People who actually care."

"Crazy concept, isn't it?"

"It sure is, but also quite simple when I think about it." Callie looks at her watch. "I'm going to go talk to Will in the bullpen before I head to the field. Don't forget, Luce is counting on you guys to win this bet to get Dex playing again."

I let out a *humph* in amusement. "That fucker's gonna play whether we win or lose."

"I thought the same thing. So maybe we win for us instead?" Callie holds up her hand for a high-five.

I lightly clap my hand to hers. "Hell yeah, we will. Now, go, or you'll be late for your and Will's not-so-secret pregame closet make-out session you think we all don't know about."

Callie waves me off then turns to walk away. "Oh, we know you all know, we just don't care."

Yeah, I should've figured that. "Have fun," I holler over my shoulder.

"I will!" she yells back.

I shake my head as my phone vibrates in my back pocket. Shit, I've got to put that away before I head to the dugout. Pulling it out, I see I have the best texts.

DAD

Mom's had a great day. We're sitting down now to watch and she's so excited.

JENNI-CAKES

Don't make me regret this.

picture of poster with writing in all caps: My Stalker is Playing in the World Series

My thumbs type and erase several messages to Jensen, teasing her for not coming to LA with us first before ultimately switching to respond to my dad.

Happy to hear. Now wish me luck and call me tomorrow when you can.

Walking back in the locker room, a few of the players are still psyching themselves up, while others have already made their way to the dugout.

I pull up Jensen's message thread one more time. Scrolling back, I see the many texts from myself and the occasional response from her. I should probably take the hint, but then I pull up the picture of her sign again. Is that... a heart for the exclamation point?

Well, that's interesting.

"Hey." Tripp comes up behind me with a shake to my shoulders. "You ready for this?"

I toss my phone in my bag without responding. "When am I ever not ready for a game?"

"You have got to be one of the weirdest people I know. Do you ever get stressed?"

"Fuck off, of course I do." I shove him as I turn around to walk out to the dugout. "Just not about this. Hey, a hundred bucks says I can hit a home run this game."

Tripp lets out a *tsk*. "You should be studied."

"Can't say I disagree with ya."

And eight innings later, I may not be a hundred dollars richer, but I'm still on fire. I've had beautiful line drive after beautiful line drive. Best believe I've started dedicating every one to Dex.

I'm pretty sure he gets a wave of regret for this bet—and our friendship—each time.

By the bottom of the ninth, I've all but considered our win locked down. We're up 4–2, and even though the Rays bat last, I'm pretty sure they've already accepted their defeat with their first batter striking out.

The second out is a pop-up caught in outfield. The only thing standing between us now and our World Series win is one more out, and I'm going to be the one to get it.

My eyes find Dex in the dugout, and the fucker already knows.

A ground ball is hit, but that's fine, nothing we can't handle. Our shortstop, Mateo, scoops it up with ease then sends it my way.

My favorite sound of the ball connecting with my glove comes, followed by the ump yelling "out."

That's game.

Now this is a fucking high. From the fireworks shooting off, the confetti falling, and countless beers being sprayed, we're all on cloud nine.

I let Dex have his time with Lucie and Miles on the field, but he can't escape me in the locker room.

"What'd I tell you, asshole?" I shake his shoulders as I come up behind him.

Dex turns around with a small shove and a chuckle.

"Can't say I doubted you, but ya know, you could not be so cocky about it."

"Everyone says cocky, I say confident—and fucking right, mind you. I want a copy of your signed contract framed on my wall."

"You and Luce both." Dex shakes his head, then makes his way over to his duffle. "Come on, I want to show you something." He searches through it for a minute before pulling something out. "Now, don't fucking saying anything."

I cross my finger over my chest then hold my hands up. "Okay, Dad, chill."

Dex rolls his eyes, but then holds out the ring box. "Gonna ask Lucie to marry me when we get back to Boston. Figured since you were rooting for us the most—"

You know, I didn't think tonight could have gotten better, but I stand corrected.

"Fuck, man, I'm so happy for you. You deserve another shot at playing, with someone in the crowd actually cheering for you. I mean, I always cheer for you, but you know I'm not the pretty blond."

Dex gives me a small punch before putting the ring back. "I do prefer Lucie's cheers to yours, but I appreciate you. Thanks for always being there."

"God, Lucie's turned you sappy," I joke but recover quick before he hits me again. "I appreciate you too. And really, so happy for you and Luce. You guys gonna come out with us to bar hop our winning?"

"Nah, Luce said she isn't feeling too great so we're just gonna go back to the hotel." Dex pulls his bag on his shoulder and claps my back. "Have fun and don't call me for bail. You all figure that shit out on your own."

"Eh, your brother-in-law can handle that," I say with a shrug as he starts to the door.

I expect him to flip me off, curse me out, or something, but he doesn't. Simply tosses his hand up with a wave. "Sounds good to me."

Hell, Lucie really has made him a softie.

We make our way back to the hotel to clean up, and I feel so much fucking relief when I take my contacts out of my eyes. Nothing makes me happier than switching to my glasses after a game.

Pulling out my phone, I bring up Jensen's message again. She's bound to be asleep, I'm sure, but frankly, I never truly expect a response from her even when she's awake.

> Can I hang your poster in the Blues clubhouse? I think it should be my new good luck charm.

Much to my surprise, she replies.

JENNI-CAKES

> Funny I was sure that all the looks you gave Dex during the game meant he would be your new good luck charm.

> Should someone tell Lucie you have a crush on her man?

> First Lucie is well aware. Second YOU WATCHED ME?!

> Maybe you have a crush on me

> Don't let your win get to your head Beckham. I'm still out of your league.

I've made it from little league to the majors. Don't underestimate my game.

Don't undermine my ability to file for a restraining order.

Looking forward to stalking you when I get back to Boston.

Goodnight Beckham.

Hope your dreams are full of me.

And tell Dottie goodnight from me.

Chapter 5
Jensen

"I'm going to lose it, really, I think I just might lose my actual shit." I stare at the three messages that have all come through this morning. How in the hell do I get three rejections back-to-back? I just sent inquiries for these shops yesterday. Not to mention, Ink Envy literally just posted they were looking to add another person to their store.

"What does the second one mean by 'current informa-tion'?" My sister Stella huffs over the line. I sent her the screenshot of each message, then called her, ready to rant the moment she answered.

"Hell if I know. The only clear thing about their messages is that they don't want me. The last one freaking posted on their Instagram story yesterday that they were looking to add another person. I filled out their request form within an hour of them posting."

"See, that feels weird to me," Stella hums softly. "I just keep rereading them all and something isn't sitting right in my gut."

"Not sitting right with you? My rent's been raised an extra eight hundred dollars. My gut is in knots and my face is breaking out from stress." I fall back on my bed with a huff. "Maybe I should just move back home."

"No! Have you lost your mind? After everything we went—"

"*We?*"

"Oh, yes, *we!* If it wasn't for me, you'd be miserable playing Suzie Homemaker with one, if not two babies, and more on the way. Rent, we can figure out. No place hiring, fixable. But so help me, I'll rip out your nipple piercings if you step foot in the same city as him."

"Ow, Christ's sake, Stella." I wrap my arms protectively around my boobs. Just the thought makes me cringe. "And people think I'm the aggressive sister."

"You're outwardly aggressive, but soft on the inside. I, however, am a narcissist's worst nightmare. I look gullible, but hard on the inside."

I snort a laugh. "That sounds wrong."

"Well, it's true! I may be just a girl who loves bright colors and frilly dresses, but I take no bullshit, and neither should you. You're incredible at what you do! Anyone would be lucky to hire you!"

My internal groan is definitely shown on my face, but thankfully this isn't FaceTime, or else I'd be hearing Stella's power speech she says when she wants to hype herself up.

"It's not that I'm taking anyone's shit, more I just want to live the life I came here to live. I didn't think it would be easy but after all of Hank's shit, following Travis's...I wouldn't mind one thing to not be so complicated."

"Oh, Jennie, that's too much to ask for," Stella says in the most sweet and sarcastic tone. "Remember my adoption process? There was practically no one to contest it and we still had issues."

That one hits me in the chest. After losing her mom and younger brother during childbirth, Stella's dad essentially gave up on taking care of her. The adoption may have officially made her my sister, but our moms raised us that way from the start.

The loss of Stella's mom and brother affected all of us, and for a while we all went to therapy. My mom lost her best friend. I developed a horrible phobia of pregnancy. My dad practically forced Stella's dad to every session, but ultimately Dad stopped forcing him and put all his energy into Stella.

"You're right, thanks for the perspective reminder."

"You know, I just imagine if you had a little angel and devil on your shoulders that they would look like me. It's not your own subconscious, it's me in there."

I try to stifle my laugh. "That checks out, honestly. Here I am calling you, angry at the world, and you've taken me on a full trip of pep talks, humbling me and giving me a reality check."

Stella hums. "I did do all that, didn't I? I didn't even bring out my tarot cards yet, let me get those!"

"No!" I yell, shooting up off my bed. "I feel better, please save those for next time. I've had you be my *la angelita y la diablita*, Stella, save *bruja* Stella for another day."

The silence tells me that she's not super happy about it, but she sighs. "Fine. Next phone call, though."

"Deal." *Thank goodness.*

"Even though I think they would be a super great tool to help process these messages a little bit more—"

"Stella."

"Fine, fine. I'll go off my intuition alone. I definitely think there's something going on with those messages. Three in a row is crazy enough, but you said things didn't go over well when you turned down Tally's offer to work there. Do you think...possibly..." Stella trails off with what I've already suspected but don't want to believe.

"It seems highly probable. Ugh," I groan. "I'm going to have to go down there, aren't I?"

"You've stepped over Hank's shit enough, sis. I think it's about time it came to a head. Shall I start my 'you're an absolute badass' pep talk?"

My laugh comes again. "As good of a speech as it is, I'm gonna have to pass. Everyone's back from Los Angeles now, so we're having a celebratory dinner at Dex and Lucie's house tonight. I'll go by Tally's before, and at least there'll be a possibility that a drink will greet me after."

"I love how you're so casual about this. '*Oh, my friends are back from Los Angeles,*' like they're not pro baseball players who just won the World Series. I still can't believe you didn't go."

"You know why I couldn't go, Stel. I thought you would

be proud of me for not going. With you-know-who in mind, a relationship is not currently in the five-year plan we mapped out."

"Oh, *the plan*." My sister all but gags. "I still can't look at a Red Bull without feeling queasy."

I, however, smile at the memory. I was mid-crash out following the aftermath of breaking up with Travis, but then Stella busted in my room with a pack of Red Bulls, a fresh journal, and yes, her tarot cards.

"It's just..." she continues on, "that would have been a freaking bucket list opportunity. But I get why you said no, I do. I'm proud of you, I guess."

"Clearly," I huff out as Dottie puts her front paws on my bed with a whine. "Alright, I gotta take Dottie out. I'll let you know what happens with Hank."

"Okay, I'll be sure to accept any collect calls from jail. Not that I'll be close to pick you up, but still."

I push off my bed with a smile. "Excuse me, I'm not the one with a record."

"It was one time! One little shoplifting incident! I have a big girl job where I clean up other people's scandals, and yet my one fuck up from nearly ten years ago is still brought up! Will I ever live that down?"

"Nope, sorry, Stel, it's just too funny. I'll let you know how it goes at Tally's."

Stella snorts. "Don't worry, I'll have my tarot cards charged up and we can make any adjustments to the plan if we need."

I can barely fake excitement with a dragged out, "Greeeeat."

"You're welcome in advance. Love you, byeeee."

I find a smile. "Love you, bye."

Putting Dottie's leash on, I grab my coat and we head down the stairs.

> Hey you there alone today?

BLAKE
> Yeah and we need to talk.

> Glad we're on the same page. On my way.

After walking Dottie around the block a few times, I run her back upstairs and give her two of her favorite treats. "Sorry, I know that wasn't much of a walk, but I'll be back."

Hopefully. I could have Lucie coming to get Dottie while someone else bails me out of jail.

I exhale what I can of my frustration—maybe it's not that bad. I know leaving Tally's was the right move to make, and whatever dick move Hank is playing I should be able to put an end to. Granted, my only play seems to be telling his wife everything he's done in heavy detail.

The chime to the front door rings as I walk in. Trusting Blake's word, I don't bother worrying about someone else being here and head straight for the back.

"Blake?" I call, walking farther in the shop.

"Back here, Jen, I'm just finishing up," Blake hollers back.

Walking through the curtains, I find Blake at his station wrapping up a girl's arm with plastic wrap.

"Okay, keep that on until you get home, and here's the printout going over the aftercare instructions we discussed."

The girl blushes as she looks down at Blake's hands taping off the wrap. "Great, and if I have any questions, I can call..." She trails off, clearly hoping he finishes with his number.

I partly understand her blush and interest to some extent —Blake isn't exactly bad to look at, and from what I've come to know, he's not a douchebag. I personally have zero interest because he's not a redhead who plays first base for the Blues, doesn't give me cheesy nicknames, and doesn't follow me around like he's obsessed with me.

Good god.

"You can call the shop if you want," Blake says, completely oblivious to her intentions.

"Great, thank you." The girl feigns a smile and starts to walk out with a shake of her head.

"You're welcome, have a great rest of your day," Blake says, still not picking up any vibes. He looks to me and waves. "Hey, come on in, we can talk while I clean up."

I look back to make sure the girl is out of earshot before speaking. "You know she was asking for your number, right?"

Blake lifts an eyebrow as he sprays his chair down. "No, what does she need that for?"

Ugh, men.

"Are you serious? She was asking for your number so you could go out. You know, like, date, and other fun things."

Blake tears off a paper towel then stops as he processes what I said. "Well, even if I did actually realize what she was asking, I wouldn't have given it to her. I don't mix business with pleasure. Anything involving this place is strictly business."

"That's fair. Speaking of, does your 'need to talk' text have any links to my three rejection messages from tattoo shops this morning?"

"Unfortunately, yes."

Dammit. I knew it. Well, Stella spoke it first, I guess I should give some credit to her.

"First, Charlie raises my rent and now—"

"Wow, wait, Charlie raised your rent?"

"Yep, I'm now paying thirty-five hundred dollars for that shitty studio apartment. And before you ask, I researched it, he can raise it. It's the beginning of the month, so at most I could get away with a small extension because his only requirement is to give a thirty-day notice."

"Fuckers aren't going to let you go, Jen. That's insane."

"It's outrageous, I'm aware. My lease ends at the end of January so I can try to find a new place, but I have to make ends meet in the meantime. Which is much harder to do, considering I can't even get my foot in the door to work outside of the wine bar." I throw my hands up in frustration. "Fucking Hank and Charlie."

"You forgot Tally," Blake adds.

"What? What's she doing?"

"Jen, you seriously don't know? You think Hank and Charlie are smart enough to know the requirement and timing for raising rent legally? That they would know how to get lies about you spread out to nearly every tattoo shop downtown in the span of a week?"

My jaw hangs. "Tally's doing this?"

Blake gives me a pity smile. "I've tried to calm things down the best I can. I didn't know about the rent being raised, but I think I've gotten Tally to at least stop black-listing your name for now."

"All because I don't want to work here? This is insane! Her husband is an asshole who hits on anything and every-thing. You know how he is, how he treated me! Maybe Tally needs to be clued in on all that."

The pity only intensifies. I don't have a good feeling about this.

"She's well aware of Hank's behavior, Jen. She doesn't care—they have an open marriage and frankly, I think she's just as bad."

"Of fucking course," I grit out. Some part of me knew she wouldn't care if I told her about Hank, but I didn't want to believe it. "What lies is she telling people?"

Blake gives me a pointed look. "You really want to know?"

"I need some sort of idea. I can't disprove her lies if I don't know what they are."

The pause Blake gives me only makes his next sentence worse. "She's got a few circulating. One that you were having an affair with Hank."

"Oh, fuck off, you just said they're in an open marriage!"

Blake snorts a laugh. "You just found that out yourself, not every tattoo parlor in Boston knows that."

Dammit.

"He's repulsive!"

"Again...Boston, Jen. They don't care, they just know they have another tattoo place calling saying bad things about a person looking for a job. No sane person wants unnecessary drama in their place of work."

I crane my neck back. "Keep 'em coming. What else is she saying?"

"That you didn't actually complete your requirements. You stole from the shop on several occasions, and now, bear with me—she apparently found out about me supervising Lucie's tattoo. She's spinning it that she was underage."

"*Ay,* wonderful. That's just perfect."

"Listen, don't give in. I've stayed here way longer than I need to, and you telling Tally 'no' was the nail on the coffin for this place. I hate that it comes at your expense, but I see I'm going to have to play my exit smartly."

I damn near want to laugh. "Glad I could show you what leaving gets you."

I want to scream and rage break everything in this place, but they aren't deserving of that reaction from me. I refuse to give them any more ammunition, especially one that would be true.

"I'm going to continue trying to run interference for you the best I can in the meantime. Maybe lie low on the tattoo places for a bit, let them get their fit out. If you need a place to stay while finding a new apartment, I can offer up my couch. Gotta warn you, though, I have shit roommates."

"Thanks, I'll keep that in mind. Might be my last resort."

Blake sits back on his rolling stool. "Hey, as long as working here isn't above that. I'm serious, Jen, don't back down. I should have left a long time ago."

"It's not on the table, I swear. Thank you for sticking it out while I was here."

Blake shrugs. "Don't mention it, I would want someone to do that for my sister."

"I know the feeling. I owe it to my sister to keep going, so I'll figure it out. Lies will only get them so far, I think completing this apprenticeship is proof that I'm patient enough to outlast their bullshit."

Blake hums. "There's a silver lining if you want to look at it this way, but they have to lie to ruin your hard work and reputation. Truth would ruin theirs, and there should be peace in that."

"Bad fruit falls from every tree eventually, doesn't it?"

"Sure does." Blake clicks on his phone. "You might want

to head out, Hank's got someone coming in half an hour. I wouldn't want to risk—"

I hold my hands up. "Consider me gone. Hope your exit goes smoother than mine."

Blake chuckles. "Plotting and planning it as we speak."

I muster up every bit of strength I have left to make it to Lucie's dinner. I wanted so badly to cancel, but Lucie sent out a "no bailing" text to the group chat with about five different threatening emojis.

If this had been anyone else's party, I might not have cared about canceling, but Lucie is my girl. I love Callie and adore Emma—Reagan is just as aggressive as I am, but Lucie is my favorite. We all have favorites, whether we admit it or not.

After my talk with Blake, I called my sister and we worked out an extreme budget for me to be able to make my rent. Granted, it also calls for me to up my hours at Wine-down, but thankfully that job is practically locked in place. Tally wouldn't get ahold of a person in charge through the phone to save her life, and if she showed up, I think Mia would laugh her lying, tacky ass out the door.

We made small adjustments to my five-year plan. When she pulled out the tarot cards, I was practically begging her to hold off on them. Diving into anything of my past, present, and future after the day I've had really might've sent me over the edge.

Walking in Dex's penthouse, I know I'm bound to be the last one here, and with the sound of all the voices coming from the living room, I'd say that's a pretty accurate assumption.

I hang my bag and coat on the racks by the door when it swings open.

"Well, if this isn't perfect timing," Beck says with a smile.

"Hey," I grumble. I don't have it in me to be anything but tired with him right now. All my energy is being reserved for faking it around Lucie. She's already Stella's twin flame, just take out the burn. I don't need her mother-henning me. If she knew, she'd have already sent me an astronomical amount of money or moved me in.

Before I can even make a full turn to the living room, Beck lightly grabs my arm. "Whoa, Jensen, you good?"

Beck softly rubs his thumbs back and forth. I can see the genuine concern written all over his face. For a solid two seconds, I consider unloading everything, but by the third second, I come to my senses and pull my arm tight.

"I'm fine, Beck. Just a long day, and I don't have the energy to entertain you on a normal one, so..."

The corner of Beck's mouth turns up. "I guess you can call me on a lazy day then."

Don't smile. Don't smile.

That should not have made me feel anything. It was a cheesy one-liner that borderlines stupid, but it wasn't him pushing me to talk. It wasn't him calling me out for being a bitch. It was what I needed his response to be without me even realizing it.

I meet his green eyes. "I don't have lazy days, Beckham. Now, come on, they're probably waiting on us."

Following the sound of all the voices, Beck and I find everyone circling around Dex's massive island full of home-made pizzas.

Lucie spots us first and her eyes light up. "Beck and Jensen are here!"

I guess Lucie's threatening text worked. We're met with a chorus of greetings from our whole group, and Miles all but launches himself at Beck.

Beck catches him with ease. "Hey, All-star, you make any of these pizzas?"

A small pit forms in my stomach watching Miles recount every detail of making these with his dad and the completely captivated look on Beck's face.

Yep, that's enough of that. Breaking away from them, I move toward Lucie. "Hey, sorry I'm late."

"That's okay, it seems to me like you had perfect timing." Lucie beams, and I swear my eye starts to twitch.

Callie leans over from behind Lucie. "She means we're so happy you're here. Don't hurt her today. She gets a pass."

She gets a pass?

Before I can ask, Dex swoops in, pulling Lucie to his chest, and kisses the top of her head. She looks up to him with freaking hearts in her eyes.

I love how happy they are and while seeing Beck with kids might form a pit in my stomach—Dex and Lucie only make me feel happy.

"Okay, everyone, listen up," Dex says. "Lucie and I were going to wait to say anything, but considering you guys are the nosiest fuckers on the planet—"

Will tosses his hands up. "Heaven forbid a guy ask about his sister when she's been sick."

Callie takes his hands and pulls them around her. "He's done."

Dex shakes his head with a sigh. "Between that, and the fact that Callie, Emma, and Miles now know—"

"Lucie's growing me a baby brother or sister!" Miles yells from the other side of the island, still being held by Beck.

Dex hangs his head with a laugh. "Yeah, what Miles said."

While we're all still processing, Lucie pulls a ring out of her pocket and slides it on her finger before flashing it to us. "And we're engaged!"

At that, everyone cheers and moves to crowd them. Beck, Adam, and Tripp go for Dex first, while Callie, Will, Emma, Reagan, and I steamroll Lucie.

My head is slowly wrapping its way around the baby announcement, so I reach for her hand first to get a look at the incredible marquee diamond. "Holy shit! Lucie!"

Callie comes around to the other side. "Ah, I didn't know he was going to ask you!"

"But you knew she was pregnant!" Will scoops up Callie and takes her place. "I'll deal with you later."

"Ooo, lucky me." Callie wiggles her eyebrows while I snort a laugh.

"Relax, Will, I needed a pregnancy test. Callie and Emma were just helping."

Reagan squeezes in the front and puts her hand on Lucie's stomach. "What do you mean you have a baby in there and I didn't immediately know about it!"

Emma pops up from behind Lucie. "Let me see the ring, I knew about the baby, but not that rock on your finger."

Before Lucie can respond to anyone, Dex is pulling her out of our huddle. "Give her space, for fuck's sake."

Miles jumps in front of Lucie with his arms spread wide. "Yeah, fuck's sake—"

"Miles!" Lucie, our never-cursing princess, squeals.

I fold my lips together to keep the laugh contained, but mostly everyone else loses it.

"Okay, but that was his dad's fault." Beck's voice comes from right behind me.

My body betrays me because I immediately look over to him and...smile. *Shit, shit, shit.* Why did it do that? It was just an impulse, I'm happy for Dex and Lucie and too tired to control my inner softie.

Beck sends me a wink, then goes back to Dex. "Father of the year, really, think you can teach this one's first word to be 'fuck'?"

Dex opens his mouth to give what I'm sure is a well-deserved comeback, but Lucie places her hand on his chest.

"Why don't you explain to Miles why he doesn't need to say that word, while I go throw up real quick. Everyone, please start eating the pizza so the smell goes away."

As Lucie races out of the kitchen, Dex scoops up Miles then stops the herd of hoverers this group is from following her. "Jensen can go check on her, the rest of you guys need to chill and eat."

Oh, goody.

I swallow every bit of nerves I have and give Dex a nod. As I walk out, I hear Will say, "Come here, Miles, I have several new words to teach you."

Waiting outside Lucie's bathroom, I hesitate. It's not at all that I'm afraid of pregnant women, I've had enough therapy discussions about it that it usually only links back to me never wanting to be pregnant. But if I really sit and think about it—I don't want to lose my best friend like my mom lost hers.

I take a deep breath and knock. "You okay, Princess Peach?"

At first, my only answer is the sound of Lucie getting sick, then I hear the toilet flush with what barely qualifies as a laugh. "Can you make me stop throwing up? I thought morning sickness was supposed to be in the morning!"

I turn the handle, walk in, and plop right down next to her on the tile floor. "So, Daddy Dex must really like his title."

A hint of a smile comes to Lucie's face before she gives me a weak shove. "Shut up."

I force every hint of worry way down. My fear isn't one I need to force on to Lucie. I know she wanted this eventually. People have babies every day. Everything is going to be fine. I'll just channel my inner Stella, force positive thinking, then believe it.

"I'm so happy for you, Luce. You're going to be a kickass mom."

Lucie tilts her head back onto the wall. "Thank you, even with my new bestie being the toilet, I'm really excited. It was a relief that Dex is so happy too. I wasn't too sure how he'd take surprise pregnancy number two."

A laugh bubbles out of me. I wouldn't have even thought for a second that that man would be upset about anything to do with a life with Lucie, but remembering that Miles came from an accidental pregnancy and now this one... "I hope I get his name for Secret Santa. I'm going to get him a pamphlet on all the different kinds of birth control."

Lucie fails at another shove and ultimately rests her head on my shoulder. "Being pregnant is weird. I'm suddenly exhausted and I keep throwing up...but I'm also so freaking happy."

"You deserve to be happy. Just be prepared, Will

might've been teaching Miles some new bad words after Dex let me in here to check on you."

She snorts. "I'd expect nothing less from my brother. I guess I should probably go back out there."

The sigh I let out is heavy from the impact of what a roller coaster of a week this has been. My exhaustion hits like a freight train, and I'm pretty sure I could fall asleep right here on Lucie's bathroom floor. "Yeah, probably so, or we could hide out in here for a few minutes longer."

Lucie lifts her head. "What's wrong?"

Dammit. "Don't worry about it, Luce, I'm just tired."

"Well, yeah, you're constantly running on hope and a prayer that is an energy drink and varying power bars, that's your normal. You just said you wanted to stay on this cold, hard title floor after I got sick. Try again."

"God, you're already such a mom. I'm fine, I have everything under control."

"What's under control?"

I turn to look at her with a mischievous smirk. "Ask me again and I'll go get you a huge slice of pizza with all the toppings."

Lucie's nose crinkles. "Ugh, just the thought makes me want to throw up. This sucks, I love pizza!"

I lay my head on her shoulder. "I know you do. I'm sure it's just a first trimester thing."

"And the worst part, I can't even have concession stand hot dogs. Do you think if Dex grills them they'd be okay?"

My laugh comes and I instantly feel a little lighter. It's not something that happens often, but my sister and Lucie seem to have this ability to make me feel better without hardly doing anything. It's as if their energy alone fills my cup even just a smidge.

"Poor pregnant Princess Peach, you ready to start cussing more now?"

"Thinking about it," Lucie mumbles.

I find the courage to pick myself off the floor then hold out my hand to help Lucie. "Come on, your kid's probably working on that right now, and I fear Daddy Dex might not be enough to get them to stop."

Lucie takes my hand. "And you think I will?"

"Luce, you're marrying and knocked up by their grumpy coach—I think you might out rank Callie on the fear factor scale now."

Lucie laughs. "Dex isn't grumpy anymore, or their coach either, technically."

"Only helping prove my point. Your sweetness is scary."

"Goodness, you all really need to toughen up." Lucie waves me off and starts back out toward the party. She looks back over her shoulder and drops the pitch of her voice. "If I was really that scary, I would have you giving Beck a chance by now."

"And if you weren't pregnant, I'd kick your ass."

"But I am. Oh, do I have a nine-month pass for being pushy? Think I could push you all the way to a date with Beck?"

"I don't know...we could have a double date. Do you want green olives or banana peppers on your pizza? Maybe both with some artichokes—"

Lucie puts her hand on her chest and makes a gurgling noise. "Okay, stop, please."

We walk into the living room, and my eyes immediately find Beck completely captivated by what Miles is telling him. "Right back at you, Luce."

Chapter 6
Beck

Ah, Tuesdays, a.k.a. the day Jensen and I go on a run together. Or, well, we usually run together.

For the past several weeks I've gotten used to finding Jensen stalling with stretches until I get there. She claims she's not waiting on me, but she doesn't seem to stretch for much longer after I arrive.

But today there was no Jensen stretching. No Dottie to bark in excitement when I get there. Whether she wants to blame it on exhaustion or not, I could tell something was off with her last night...

Maybe she started without me? It wouldn't be the first time, I guess, even though it hasn't been our normal lately.

By my third mile, I'm starting to think she outright ditched me. I push harder for one more mile and still no Jensen. Fuck.

Cooling down, I call Callie.

"Hey, Beck, what's up?" she answers with an exasperated breath.

Dear god. "You know you don't have to answer the

phone when you and Anderson are going at, right? Or is he that boring in bed?"

"We're done, actually." Callie laughs while Will yells a threat I can barely make out in the background. "And don't mess with me, Beck, you know I have zero filter. I'll recount it in heavy detail."

My laugh comes next. "I'll pass. I have a different favor to ask you."

Will's voice comes through the line next. "Answer it and hang up, baby, or your phone is going in the shower with you."

"You heard the man, whatcha need?"

"Think you can track Jensen down for me? She bailed on our run this morning."

"Okay?" Callie pauses for a second. "Is Jensen bailing on you really that surprising, though?"

Normally I'd hate to say no it's not, but something isn't sitting right. Between the look on her face last night and the fact that we've done this every Tuesday I can make for months now...

"I just want to make sure she's okay, and if she's not meeting me here then I doubt she'll answer any call or text."

"Well, she hasn't replied to our group chat at all this morning, which isn't crazy unusual, but I did check her location. Looks like she's at Winedown."

"Winedown?" I parrot back. "She doesn't work Tuesday mornings and it's barely ten a.m."

"I don't know what to tell you, that's what her location says. Hey, I thought you were leaving for your parents' house today anyway?"

"I am—not till later, though. Might've planned a later

flight because of this little standing running date we've got going."

"You're hopeless." Callie chuckles softly. "Let the group chat know when you land safely in Virginia, okay?"

"Yeah, yeah, I will. Thanks for checking on Jensen for me."

Will replies this time. "Okay, time's up, she's hanging up now." Just as soon as the words leave his mouth the call ends.

Asshole. Not that I entirely blame him, but still—asshole.

I click on my watch and start a map to Winedown. Another three miles and I get to see Jensen? Sold.

I take the first open seat I see at the bar, despite the fact that it's November and fucking freezing—after seven miles I've worked up a bit of a sweat.

"Oh, well, good morning, Beck." The bartender that Jensen always pushes me off on, comes up in front of me. "You look like you need a drink."

I check her name tag again, because despite the many interactions I can never seem to remember it. "Hey, Mia, is Jensen here?"

I feel like a huge dick for asking her after my clear "no" to her offering her phone number last time I was here, but it needed to happen. I don't want a relationship, and while I can't tell what has me so hung up on Jensen...it's never going to be Mia and she deserved to know it's not on the table.

Mia doesn't seem to take my words to heart though, she actually...smiles? "Yeah, she's here. There was a bridal brunch that rented out the upstairs bar. Jensen's working it."

"Any way I could sneak up there?"

Mia laughs. "They're two mimosa towers and at least two rounds of shots deep—they'd change your career from baseball player to stripper so fast."

Yeah, can't say Olsson would love that news. "Right, well, I just wanted to check on her, we usually run together on Tuesdays. It's no big—"

"Ugh, stop talking. You're too good looking to be caring and thoughtful."

Uh... "I'm sorry?"

"You should be." Mia walks to the side then rounds the bar. She points to a waiter walking in. "You, perfect, watch the bar. I have to go cover for Jensen for a sec." She points to me next. "You, follow me."

The waiter and I make eye contact, but neither of us dare to question her. I catch up to Mia as she heads up the stairs. "I thought me going up here was a bad idea?"

"Oh, it is. You're going to wait here." Mia points at the ground, and I fall in line. *Damn, when did she get so bossy?* "I'll send Jensen out here and cover for her for a few minutes."

"Yeah, well, don't tell her it's me or she won't trade with you."

A scoffed laugh comes from Mia. "She won't have a choice."

I look at her and I can't say my face is doing a very good job of hiding my emotions right now. "You're scaring me."

Mia scrunches her nose. "Oh, we definitely wouldn't have been a good match up."

"Nope, don't believe so." I lean against the wall with a shrug. "I prefer Jensen's snarky hard-to-get attitude."

Mia sends her braid to her back with a shrug. "Hey, I respect the honesty—plus, Jensen's the best employee I have. I'm not afraid to shoot my shot, but I'm a girl's girl first. Consider all my interest gone." She scrunches her nose. "I swear I didn't mean that snobbish...I'll send her out."

As Mia disappears through the door, I pull out my phone to check the confirmation on my flight to my parents' place later today. I'll be gone for two weeks, and I hate that when I get back it will most likely be too cold for these runs together.

"You've got to be kidding me, Beckham."

Ah, yes, that's the tone I like. I slide my phone back in my pocket to give Jensen all my attention.

"You're such a stalker! Making Mia come cover for a few minutes, have you lost your mind?!"

Well, it does make me feel better that she seems to have the energy to be feisty today.

"Okay, first, what the hell is up with her? Have I really paid her so little attention that I didn't realize how bossy she is?"

Jensen fights her smile so fast I nearly miss it. Her lips fold into a thin line and her eyes widen just a smidge before she goes back to her mad face. "She's bossy because she's about to be *the* boss. Her parents own Winedown, and they want to sell it, but Mia wants to take it over. She's been learning every working position here for the past several months."

Alright, respect back to her.

"Ah, so that's why you came out here. I was sure you'd put up a fight on leaving your post. Hey, since I have an in with your boss now, think I can get her to never schedule you for Tuesday mornings so you don't ditch running with me?"

Jensen tilts her head up to the ceiling and mumbles words in Spanish too quickly for me to try to understand. "Beck, you came here and interrupted my workday because I didn't meet you to exercise?"

I give her a pointed glare, because I mean, come on, what kind of question is that?

"Right, I should have known better." She sighs. "Listen, if you've microchipped me, just tell me."

I push off the wall with a laugh. "No, just a breach in girl-code. Callie ratted you out."

Jensen mumbles several more words, and just a hint of that stress she was wearing last night shows again.

"Jen, is everything okay? You never work on Tuesdays, and with how you were last night...I just wanted to check on you."

Jensen meets my eyes. It doesn't happen often, but in an instant her face softens. "Thanks for checking. I'm fine, really. Someone needed to cover, and I was available. I'm sorry I didn't tell you I wasn't going to meet you today."

Holy shit, did Jensen just apologize? I feel her forehead and she swats at my hand.

"Beck!"

"Hold on, you must be sick—I'm checking for a fever."

There's a pain in my chest because then Jensen starts to laugh. "God, you must need to go to the hospital—I didn't know you could laugh."

"Beckham!" Jensen continues to hit my hands away. "You're pissing me off again."

"There's my Jenni-cakes." I step back, satisfied at the bite back in her tone. "Since you brought it up, here is my official heads up that I won't be able to go running for the next two weeks."

Jensen holds up a hand. "Don't touch me when I ask this —but why not?"

Oh, I'm smiling so hard right now. "I'm visiting my folks in Virginia. Don't worry, I'll miss you too."

The clench in Jensen's jaw has to hurt. "I will knee you in the balls again."

I hold my hands up, letting her have free reign. "If that's how you need to express your love, then so be it."

Jensen's knee doesn't raise but she does give my chest a shove. "You came and checked on me. Please leave now."

"Alright, I'm going, but...hey, are you sure you're okay?"

"I'm fine," Jensen huffs with a sharp tone.

I hold out my pinky with a smile to really piss her off. "Pinky promise?"

Jensen's eye twitches. "You're pushing it. I appreciate the check in, but I don't have to pinky promise you anything. I said I'm good, so take my word."

"Fair." I retract my hand, and honestly I'm happy with her answer. Whatever chemistry we have aside, there's a level of friendship at its core—I needed to see her bad attitude and go-to-hell look. The softness and laugh she gave me will probably haunt my dreams in the best way possible, but leaving tonight without seeing this bite from her felt wrong.

I take a step back. "See you in two weeks, Jenni-cakes?"

"Something tells me that won't be too long of a separation, Stalker."

I pause at the top of the stairs going down, she's yet to move, and I swear she's biting her cheek. "Just call me if you're having a lazy day and find the energy to be around me."

"Bye, Beck." Sarcasm laces her tone, but there's the slightest hint of a smile on her face.

Despite telling my dad that getting a rental car was not a hassle for me, he insisted on picking me up from the airport.

My argument for him staying with Mom was only met with the fact that I already pay for around-the-clock nurses, therefore it's his "fatherly duty" to pick me up.

I, however, think that term is bullshit and he wants to spend the maximum amount of time together in order to prove his point that I'm not "happy."

Which I am, it just looks different now.

Before I even reach baggage claim I spot him with a huge ass sign that reads: MY SON JUST WON THE WORLD SERIES.

I can't help the laugh. "Subtle, old man, I think the size of this poster is a little too braggy."

"Good, you got my point." Dad drops the sign and meets me with an equally big hug. "Happy you're home."

The guilt of it being so long between visits takes over and practically knocks the breath out of me, but just as quickly relief washes over me because I'm also so happy to be home.

I clap his back as I return his bear hug. "Me too, thanks for picking me up."

"Of course, that's the response I was looking for when I brought it up. Not that bullshit about getting a rental." Dad shakes my shoulder before releasing his hold. "Come on, let's get this show on the road."

With a nod, we head over to baggage claim where I stand tight-lipped to keep the five million questions I have about how Mom's actually doing to myself. All those questions can come out on the drive home. Or better yet, to the nurse who won't sugarcoat anything for me.

"So, you remember our deal? I need to see you happy, and you're not off to a good start," my dad says with zero regard to discretion.

"Christ's sake, we haven't even made it to the parking lot.

I just got off a plane, most people aren't exactly rays of sunshine immediately after traveling."

"They are when they fly first class."

The twitch of an eye roll starts, but I stop it. I can't and won't give him any sort of ammunition. No negativity. Nothing.

I roll my tense shoulders back and relax. "I would love for it to not include you psychoanalyzing every tiny move I make. We're standing around waiting for bags to start rolling out and praying that it didn't somehow get lost, so maybe we can hold off on the accusations for a bit."

Dad waves a hand. "Alright, fine. I'll wait...but everything about you feels melancholy, and I don't like it."

"Maybe it's the fluorescent lights?"

He snorts. "I suppose you're right. Could just be how much we missed you." He holds his sign back up. "Very proud, but missed you."

I'm not one to really feel embarrassment, you get over that pretty fast when every fuck up in a game is analyzed by sports commentators, but I wouldn't mind passing on less attention right now.

"I'm right here, I think you can put your sign down now."

"You must have missed the part where I said *proud*—I almost wore my T-shirt too, but the not-fun nurse is on shift today and she said it was too much."

Thank god for that.

I pat his chest as the conveyor belt starts up. "Cheesy, old man."

Once we get my stuff in his truck, I send out a text to the team chat first.

(Blue) Balls for Life

BECK

Made it to my parents

CALLIE

Yay!! Tell everyone we said hi!

LUCIE

Dex said to text him if you need him outside of the group chat because he has it muted.

CALLIE

Daddy Dex that's rude!

WILL

Please don't say that again.

ADAM

Cals, I beg you, please don't respond with something even more inappropriate.

TRIPP

Please do.

EMMA

Can I order Dex's new jersey with "Daddy Dex" on the back.

BECK

PLEASE FUCKING DO

Switching out of that chat, I immediately go to my chat with Jensen. Texting her feels like a dangerous game with my dad hovering. I don't want to explain what she is to me, because really I don't know that answer fully either.

Eh, fuck it. One quick text.

I know you aren't as keen on stalking as me so I thought I'd help you out. I made it to Virginia safely.

I should put my phone away. I'm practically on borrowed time as it is on the questioning-my-life-choices front. My thumb rests on the lock button for a solid five seconds and I nearly click, but then the dots pop up.

JENNI-CAKES

Enjoy your break from following me
around.

It takes a whole lot of effort to swallow down my chuckle. Dropping my phone into my pocket, I know I'd be smiling like a fool with my comeback and that's just not about to happen around my dad.

"So, how's Mom actually doing today?" I ask, hoping I can steer our conversation for at least the drive back to the house.

Dad scratches at his chin. "She's okay. It's not exactly what I'd call a good day, but not bad either. She's quiet today, no real desire to chat, but loved watching you play in that final game. She's chattiest after games."

I don't know what emotion comes over me at that. I feel a little bit of pride because this was always her hope for me, I just fucking wish she remembered how important this game was to us.

I guess, on some level, she does considering it seems to spark something in her. More accurately, I wish I could experience it with her fully.

"Stop making that face. Hell, you're not even going to make it home before you seal your fate on this deal."

"Okay, excuse me for not jumping up and down." I exhale. "Can't you just give me the tiniest bit of grace, please? I get updates through text and phone calls. Sometimes I might look sad because, guess what, I'm fucking sad that my mom is going through this and you're here alone dealing with it."

Dad's mouth opens with what I'm sure is an argument, but I'm not done. Hell, so much for being cool, calm, and collected.

"I get that I'm providing all the treatment and care. I know that I'm doing what I can, but feeling sad about the situation doesn't make me lose this bet. I'm happy with my career. I have great friends, and hobbies. But, yeah, I'm still sad about what's happening, and that's okay!"

Dad huffs. "First off, I'm not 'dealing' with it all. I get to take care of your mom. It's a fucking privilege."

That one hits. Hits hard.

"I'm sorry, I didn't mean it like that."

He nods but holds his hand up. "Second, you're right. You are allowed to be sad. I get it, I'm sad too. But you're lying to yourself if you think you're the same happy kid your mom and I raised."

The argument that I am, in fact, not a kid anymore hangs on the tip of my tongue, but I know that's not how he means it.

Deep down, I knew convincing him I'm doing fine was going to be an uphill battle with all the time we spend apart now.

"You know I'm allowed to change, right?"

He sighs, scratching at his chin again. "Yeah, then maybe you need to show me that the change isn't eating you alive. From where I'm looking, you're letting this consume you."

Chapter 7
Jensen

It's been a week from hell, but a hell that pays. I even dropped off my rent check a few days early to be a little bitchy about it. As if this raise didn't nearly knock me on my ass.

My back and feet may be killing me, but at least I made it work. I've looked thoroughly through my lease agreement, and unless I want to pay the next three months' rent up front then I'm stuck here until the end of January.

I'll most definitely continue my search of finding a new place, and hopefully Tally will find a new hyperfixation and leave me the fuck alone so I can actually start tattooing.

With today being my one and only day off, I fall onto the back of my bed. My eyes fall shut for a few seconds before all forty-plus pounds of Dottie climbs on top of me to snuggle.

I chuckle, scratching behind her ears. "I know. I've missed you too. All this work sucks, but I swear it's short-term."

Dottie paws at my chest. "Ow, come on now, what's that

for?" I get a whiny grumble from her, and I know what she wants. A run.

"Dottie," I groan.

If I could sink deeper into this mattress I would. With me still not getting up, she lets out a bark. Ugh, she's right. I'm punishing her by not taking her out.

"Alright, you win."

With the small lift of my head, Dottie jumps off me and starts turning circles until it gets so out of control that she runs into one of the kitchen chairs.

I snort a laugh and pat her head. "I get it, you're excited. I know I've been slacking, but let's calm down."

Throwing on my fleece workout set and running shoes, Dottie's excitement starts up again, but she does her best to contain it—she knows I won't fight her on the leash.

As I click it on, she loses it, turning circles again in full force. Bless her, I really need to make sure I stay on top of her runs. I pull out my phone to record her joy as my reminder, but the moment I stop, my thumb clicks on the share button and before it even registers, I've sent the video to Beck.

Shit. Shit. Shit. Why is it when I'm exhausted I always slip up with him?

BECK

Way to break my heart. Poor girl must miss me so much.

It's Monday, she's not expecting to see you today.

Oh so it's you that misses me?

Apparently so, and against my better judgment.

Semi-lazy day I guess. Found the tiniest bit of energy for you today.

Shame I'm missing it.

My thumbs dance over my screen but I ultimately lock my phone and slide it in my pocket. "Okay, girl, you ready?"

Dottie lets out a few barks as her response.

"Alright, let's do it."

I have a bit of a rough start, but by mile three I hit my high, and Dottie pushes me for another three. With our cool down walk back, Dottie practically prances, and as much as I didn't want to do it, I feel so much better.

"You were right, this was a good idea." I pat her head as we start back up the stairs, but my steps stall when I see Charlie waiting outside my door.

"Jensen," he purrs as he pushes off the wall. "It's about time. I've been waiting for twenty minutes."

"What a creepy thing to say." I stop a good five feet back. As much as I would like to think I could defend myself against him, I'm going to give myself any advantage I can get and distance is my best safety net. "Why are you waiting on me, Charlie?"

The smile that comes to his face turns my stomach in knots. "I got your rent check. Gotta say, I wasn't expecting you to make that change. You know, without going back to work at Tally's. I heard other shops weren't exactly keen on hiring you."

I hold my chin high. "Well, that shouldn't exactly be surprising considering the lies Tally's been spreading, but the first words you said were the most important. You got your rent, so again, why are you waiting on me?"

Charlie takes a small step forward and as much as I want

to match his step back, I stand strong. "There's been another policy change in the apartment complex."

My grip tightens on Dottie's leash and I grit out, "What now?"

It doesn't take much for me to connect the dots when Charlie looks down at Dottie. I take a step back. "You've got to be kidding me."

"Sorry, Jennie, no more dogs." The asshole's smile grows. "I could reconsider for—"

"Of course. Is this still about Tally's? Or are you thinking you can get something out of me? What is you guys' fucking obsession with me?" I take a step forward and meet Charlie head on. "Over my dead body will I get rid of my dog. You think you guys can bully me into doing whatever twisted shit you all want, but you'll be sadly disappointed to know that I don't have to put up with this bullshit." I take another step and this time, Charlie retreats a step. "I won't go back to Tally's. I won't get rid of my dog, and you all can just get used to the fact that the only fuck you're going to get from me is my middle finger."

Charlie's nostrils flare with my final blow. His hand lashes out reaching for Dottie's leash, but I'm faster. I jerk it back, and at that Dottie lets out a low growl. I've had her for two years and never once have I heard her do that, but right now I'm grateful for it.

"I wouldn't suggest trying that again." I slowly start my walk backward, keeping an eye on Charlie, but once I reach the stairs I turn and bolt down them. My heart is beating out of my chest, but when I look back and see Charlie didn't follow, I let out a small breath.

I wait until I reach my car before I reach for my phone. My thumb hovers over Beck's name before I ultimately switch it to call Lucie, knowing Stella's off working with some new PR crisis in Dallas.

It takes two rings before she picks up. "Hey, babes."

I've calmed down a bit, but the adrenaline is battling rage and fear all at the same time. "I need to come over...I have Dottie with me too."

With my tone, Lucie doesn't ask any further questions. "Okay, come on over. Callie and Will are here too, but I can ask them to leave if you need me to?"

"No, it's fine. I just..." I let out a deep breath and start my car. "You know I hate asking for help, but I think I've reached my limit."

"Jensen..." I feel all the concern in the way Lucie says my name.

"I'll explain. I'll be there soon."

A beat of silence passes before Lucie agrees. "Drive safe, see you soon."

I can't find words for much of a response, so I just end the call. I need to calm down, but I want to scream, cry, hit something, *or someone,* all at the same time.

Dottie lets out a whimper in the passenger seat, and before I can say anything she licks the side of my face.

I let out a pained laugh. "Thanks, I needed that." I scratch behind her ear as I keep my eyes on the road. "We'll figure this out. I promise there's no way I'm getting rid of you."

I pull into Dex's parking garage, then punch in the Larsen family code to get in the lobby. It warms my heart a little at that reminder that Dex and Lucie gave all of us a family-specific code so we can come over to visit them anytime without being buzzed in.

My adrenaline has subsided enough but I barely get a

knock on their door before Lucie is swinging it open and pulling me into a hug.

I let out a small grunt as her body hits mine. "Luce, I haven't even stepped inside."

"I know, but it sounds like you need it." Her hold loosens and she steps back. "Come on, we'll put the guys on Dottie duty and we can have girl talk on the deck."

I nod and manage a small smile. "How excited is Dex that I'm bringing a dog over here for Miles to get ideas about?"

Lucie waves her hand over her shoulder. "He'll be fine. Dex is all bark, no bite."

"I don't exactly believe that," I tease. Each step into Lucie's safe space and I'm already feeling better. "Daddy Dex has to bite a little."

Lucie snorts. "Touché."

Once we step into Miles's peripheral, he's bolting over. "Jensen brought her dog!"

Miles rests his hands on his knees as he talks to Dottie. "You're the cutest doggie ever!" He reaches to pet her as her butt wiggles. "Jensen, she looks so much bigger than she does on the phone."

I chuckle. "Yeah, but she's still as sweet as can be." I kneel down next to him. "Think you can take care of Dottie for me? I need to borrow Callie and Lucie for a bit."

Miles jumps up. "Of course I can!"

I smile handing him her leash. "I knew I could count on you."

When I stand, Callie's also getting up from her spot on the couch next to Will, and Miles is bringing Dottie over to show his dad. "Sorry for crashing."

"Don't be." Dex waves me off before turning his attention to Miles.

"Yeah, this is a treat, I think I'm getting ideas for Miles's birthday." Will looks at Callie with a wink.

"No," Lucie snaps immediately as she points to the both of them. "No, I'm serious."

Callie comes up to my side and hooks her arm around my shoulder. "Why don't we head outside and we can talk about that later."

Following Lucie out to the balcony, we sit at the small table off to the side.

"Okay, so, talk to us." Lucie pulls her legs up in her chair. "What's going on?"

I take one deep breath, then exhale it all out. From the issues with Tally's, the raise in rent, then the new "no dogs" policy that led to the awful experience in the hall. By the end of it, Callie's jaws on the floor and Lucie's up from her seat.

"You mean to tell me that he reached for Dottie's leash! That he was waiting on you?" Lucie holds her hands up. "I'm getting Dex."

I grab her hand. "No, Luce, what's he going to do?"

Lucie scrunches her nose. "I don't know..."

Callie huffs. "I know I want to take a baseball bat to his groin, but I guess that doesn't exactly fix the problem."

I let the idea play through in my mind, and it helps to some extent, but it's short lived.

"Makes me feel a little better, but yeah, it doesn't fix the issue." I bury my face in my hands. "Okay, just talk this out with me, please. In reality, there's not much I can do about what happened. A call to the police most likely would result in a warning to Charlie at best. And he still has a right to implement a 'no dogs' rule, so as long as I want to keep

Dottie, I have to leave. At the end of the day, that apartment sucks, I need to move anyway, but my lease isn't up until the end of January."

Lucie claps her hands. "Okay, let Dex buy you out of the lease agreement, please. I'm begging you."

"Luce, no, I can't let you do that. Not to mention, where would I live?"

"You can live with us." Lucie gestures toward their penthouse as if the solution was that simple.

I look to Callie. "Has she forgotten she's about to get married, having a baby, and is raising a five-year-old?"

Callie folds her lips together to stop her laugh. "She has a point, Luce. Let's call your place a last resort. Jen, you know our place is always open, but we run into the same problem, our apartment has a legit no pet policy that isn't complete and utter blackmail."

I lean back in my chair with a sigh. "I know, but...I won't give up Dottie, and frankly, I don't want to go back there."

Lucie sits back down in her chair with a huff. "You're not going back there. End of discussion."

"Okay, Mom, so what do you suggest I do?"

Lucie chews on her lip for a bit, but then Callie speaks up.

"You might not like it, but it's a temporary solution for now."

"We're listening," Lucie says, sitting up. I should have known she'd go full mother hen, but there wasn't exactly any way around it. I'm officially ankle deep in the shit now.

Callie shrugs. "Beck owns his place and dogs are welcomed in that area. They have a dog park right across the street. He's gone for the next week, so it'd be just you and

Dottie. Maybe you could stay there for a bit until we figure out a plan."

Beck's place? No, absolutely not.

I don't even get a chance to say no before Lucie's on board. "Perfect, problem solved."

"No, problem not solved. I can't just crash at his place. Especially not without his permission, and then...just no, the answer is no."

"Jensen," Lucie uses her stern, but freakishly calm mom voice. "I know things are complicated—"

"Pah-ha, Lucie, no."

"Just hear me out." She holds her hand up. "Callie can talk to Beck about it. We all know, without question, that he'd be okay with it, especially given the situation."

"He really would," Callie adds. "But I can talk to him and still leave the details to a minimum. The house is empty, you could just stay there for a day or two until we get a new plan. Will and Dex can also go with us to move you out whenever you need."

I squeeze my eyes shut and run through every single option I can think of, but dammit, I'm running on fumes. "Fine. But only if Beck's okay with it, and we work out a better solution before he comes back."

Callie stands up, pulling her phone out of her pocket. "Deal, I'll go call him now. Do you need one of the guys to help you get some stuff from your place?"

I shake my head. Even the thought of going back there today makes my body feel this weird tingling mixture of rage and exhaustion. "I have my gym-to-work bag in my car. It's got enough to hold me over until tomorrow, and I'll pick up a small thing of dog food for Dottie on my way. I don't think I can handle any more drama today."

Callie nods. "Okay, I'll be right back."

I sit soaking up the silence from Lucie until Callie closes the sliding door. With the barely contained giddy look on her face, I already know what she's about to say. "I know this sucks, but it could have some bright sides."

"*Lucieeee,*" I groan. "No, I'm agreeing to this, just be happy with this solution for now."

Her mouth opens then shuts. "You're right. I'm sorry, I'll stop, I promise."

"Thank you," I huff out, then dial back the attitude. "I know you want me to be happy and want to help. I just can't right now. I love you and I love the idea that we could have the dream of being with guys who are best friends...but I just don't know if it's in the cards for me and Beck. Now, especially, is not the time I want to be thinking about that."

Lucie reaches for my hand. "I know. I promise I'll tone it down."

"Thank you." Holding her hand for a moment, I let another small bit of the weight today has added go. "Let's go back inside. I'd hate to get on Daddy Dex's bad side if I have Dottie overstay her welcome."

Lucie stands from her chair with a smile. "I got Dex to let me move my turtles in before we were together. I think I can handle getting him on board with Dottie."

I snort a laugh. "Does the man ever tell you no?"

"Yes," Lucie states very matter of fact. "Sometimes... when it's needed, at least."

After Callie got Beck's stamp of approval and a few hours of decompressing at Lucie's place, I now stand at the door to Beck's townhouse.

Dottie fidgets in excitement as I stare at the spare key Dex gave me. "Hate to burst your bubble, girl, but Beck's not here."

I swear, she lets out a whine. When she sits and all her wiggles are gone, I take a little offense. "Hey, a little appreciation for me today would be nice."

I shake my head when she decides to lay down on the porch with a huff.

"Thanks, that's perfect."

Turning the key in the deadbolt, Dottie perks back up again. I almost want to laugh at the irony of today's events feeling like my rock-bottom, they've been Dottie's dream come true.

The moment the door opens, Dottie races in, but I freeze in the entryway. Between the amazing smell, the design of this place—I nearly forget to turn the lock before walking in farther.

I honestly can't say I expected Beck's place to be this put together, but somehow couldn't imagine anything different from him. There's exposed brick in the kitchen with a butcher block island. Walking slowly around, I do a double-take, baseball cards are sealed on the wall for his backsplash tile.

I shake my head when I get to the living room; there's one leather couch that Dottie has seemed to claim and then there's a pool table. The whole living room really sells the bar feeling but in a classic Beckham Daines fashion.

The walls have varying sized posters all with pool-related puns like *less talk, more chalk*, a little league baseball jersey in a shadow box, and other framed small details, like baseball tickets and a map of what looks to be Virginia.

"Of course, it's the perfect balance of his humor and damn sentimental side," I mumble to myself—and, I suppose, Dottie.

At the windows, Beck has so many plants that I can't even begin to think of how to keep them alive. I couldn't have more of a brown thumb if I tried.

Turning back, I speak more to Dottie this time. "I sure hope someone else knows what to do with those, I don't have the first clue." I give her small pets on the head. "You probably shouldn't be up here either, Dot. Can't say Beck would appreciate any accidental scratches on his leather couch. Come on, hop down."

I pat my leg with the command, moving back around the living room and stopping at the foot of the stairs. I can't seem to bring myself to take the first step up them. In the past five minutes, I've felt like Beck and I've done an UNO reverse and now I'm the stalker. Being here feels both right and wrong.

Pulling out my phone, there're no messages from him about making myself at home or inappropriate jokes that really shouldn't be funny but are because they come from him.

I click on his contact and hover over the Call button. It feels a little weird to be here and not say anything to him. Callie did say he was okay with this, maybe he just assumed she'd give me the rundown or something.

I know I should probably call and say thank you, but then again, that'll probably be a tomorrow thing. I can't risk any endearing comments or worse, pity from him—not tonight.

Dottie moves around my side to prance her way up the stairs with zero hesitations. Sliding my phone back in my pocket, I let out a deep breath and follow her lead. I really shouldn't be that surprised that when we reach the top she ducks into a room that I know, without even looking, has to be Beck's.

Walking in, I nearly laugh at her already turning circles on his bed and plopping down with a *humph,* as if to say she's not budging. "Dottie, this is getting a little out of hand. So the man goes running with us...what about me? Your owner who's about to be homeless?"

Dottie lets out a little grumbled growl and paws at her face.

"Yeah, yeah, I get it, but we should probably find a guest room."

Dottie repeats her little growled whine before standing up, turning another circle and coiling her body up as she lays down.

"Really?" I huff. How wrong would it be for me to actually sleep in his bed?

I could lie to myself and say it's a guest room...I take another look around, and this laugh bubbles out of me. There are more plants in here, and it's filled with warm greens and soft browns. The comforter looks so cozy I could cry. Not to mention, his whole place smells like a crisp fall day. I'm sure all it would take is my head hitting the pillow for me to pass out.

"Fuck it," I mutter to myself, because Dottie's practically snoring.

Going into the bathroom, I freshen up the best I can with my gym bag essentials, and manage to find a pack of spare toothbrushes under the sink.

I don't slow or stop to snoop further, even though I'm damn tempted to. Marching back in his room, I slide drawers open and close until I land on his T-shirts folded up. Taking the first one I see, I peel off the last reminders of this day and pull his shirt right over my head.

Not smelling it is next to fucking impossible, and with each passing second of being in this perfect house I just find myself getting more pissed... Pissed because Beck's not here. Pissed from the day and I could use his jokes. I could use his "come-ons" that send vibrations down my spine and causes my stomach to flip.

But I also know, good and well, I shouldn't. If he were here...even if he called and wanted to talk about what happened...I'd fold.

Pulling back the comforter, I climb in his bed and curse him. "Alright, Dottie, one night. We cannot stay here again and me keep my sanity."

Dottie doesn't move or even grumble, and it takes me all but a minute to join her in that deep sleep.

Chapter 8
Beck

It's been one week of being home at my parents' and while I'm pretty sure my dad's bitten his tongue off more times than I can count—I think we've come to some sort of acceptance.

Getting a little more one-on-one talks with my mom's nurses has been a great help for my sanity as well. I know there's no stopping what's happening, but they've been encouraging about the whole thing. But deep in my gut, I know we're nearing the end of this, so making her comfortable is my top priority.

Granted, me being here has seemed to cause my mom a little bit of discomfort. I'm not taking it too personally, or, well, trying not to at least. I'm constantly reminding myself that it happens every visit, even if this one seems to be taking a little bit longer for her to feel comfortable around me.

Dad did have a great suggestion of watching some of my games that they have taped. I've gotten to join the past few nights, but the first four nights...I just let that be the bright side of her day, rather than force my inclusion.

Yesterday was probably the best day yet, and I really hoped today would fall into a similar rhythm, but unfortunately that was wishful thinking.

All day I've been nothing but a source of anxiety for her. No matter how many times Dad calmly talks about me or the nurses bring me up as helpful—I can't go in the same room as her without it deeply impacting her.

I've stayed holed up in my room and really don't plan on leaving. It's been raining all day, so I've cracked one of my windows to truly appreciate the sound of it falling.

When a knock comes to my door, there's a clench in my chest.

"Beck, sweetie, it's me, Nurse Jamie."

I let out a small sigh of relief at her normal tone, but even then I open my door cautiously.

The older lady gives me a soft smile. "I wanted to let you know your mom is resting if you wanted to, I don't know, walk around for a bit, make some lunch—up to you. She's usually down for an hour or two."

Clearing my throat, I give her a soft nod. "Alright, I'll make myself a sandwich or something, then come back up here."

Jamie hums. "Whatever floats your boat. At least take your time making it, will ya? You're bumming me out, sitting in here all by your lonesome."

Oh great, if I'm bumming her out, that definitely means my dad's feeling it too. Getting out of here might be damage control more than anything.

"I assure you, I'm fine. I'll take my time, though, if that makes anyone feel better."

She cuts me a look. "Mm-hmm, your dad's in the garage too, if that helps."

It definitely does.

Quietly making my way to the kitchen, I do as Jamie asks. I don't rush and make myself a peanut butter and jelly sandwich like I had planned. I actually take my time rifling through the fridge before deciding on a grilled cheese with chips in the middle of it.

Walking into the dining room, I set my plate down at the spot I claimed as mine growing up and make my way over to crack one of the windows just like I did upstairs.

Sitting in silence provides way too many opportunities for my brain to get carried away, and I try to imagine every single one of my stresses and worries about me being here fall away just as the rain falls from the sky.

Can't say that coping method works every time, but today it does the trick. And as if the universe wants to reward me for that, I get the best video of Dottie turning circles excited to go for a run with Jensen.

Can't say I blame the girl one bit.

> Way to break my heart. Poor girl must miss me so much.

JENNI-CAKES

> It's Monday, she's not expecting to see you today.

> Oh so it's you that misses me?

I expect some variation of "fuck off," middle finger emojis maybe—or flat out no response. What I don't expect is the reply she actually sends.

> Semi-lazy day I guess. Found the tiniest bit of energy for you today.

Shame I'm missing it.

"What's that smile for?" my dad asks, taking the seat across from me.

Well, shit.

"Nothing much, just a friend sent me a video of their dog."

"Oh, a teammate?"

I knew he'd have a follow up. I could lie, end this before it starts but I've already hesitated a second too long. He'd call me on it for sure now.

I look out to the rain with a shrug. "Um, no, just a… friend of a friend really."

"Right," he responds, and I know for a fact he absolutely doesn't believe me.

Okay, I wasn't exactly convincing to begin with. A friend of a friend…what the fuck was that? I should have just said friend but that feels weird to say about Jensen. I think about her in very non-friendly—or, I guess, super-friendly—ways.

I take off my glasses and set them on the table. "We go running together sometimes, it's nothing really."

"Okay," he clips. "I didn't ask another question yet."

Wonderful, wonderful, so this won't be the end of this conversation, and that's my own damn fault.

"Right, well—"

Dad pushes back from his chair. "Why not a game of pool, huh? We haven't got to play all week, and I just cleared it off."

I look down at my half-eaten sandwich. Telling him I'm not done eating won't save me, but maybe the distraction of the game will.

Putting my glasses back on, I nod. "Alright, let's go."

While he heads out, I clean up my lunch and take that opportunity to hype myself up.

It'll just be a conversation. You don't have to go into details.

I'm perfectly happy as is and I can make him believe that.

I step one foot into the garage before the pep talk blows right in my face.

"You're not holding up your end of the deal, son." My dad stares daggers as he rolls the blue chalk on the end of his pool cue.

We're off to a bad start. Shit.

"Seriously, Dad? Couldn't have at least waited until we started the game?"

He shrugs. "You know I'm not one to beat around the bush, but I've held off this week. I've officially maxed out my patience on it now."

"Fucking hell," I mumble. "I'm fine! Today's been a little rough—not gonna lie, but I feel that's warranted."

"Fine," he scoffs. "The deal wasn't 'fine,' it was happy. You're not happy, and it's starting to piss me off. You can act like it's stress about your mom's health all you want, but I see past that. When you talk about Boston, it sounds as if you're simply going through the motions. But then you seem to have the first genuinely happy smile on your face talking to some-one, and then you fucking lie and say it's nothing!"

Ooh, okay, deep breaths. Don't blow up. Don't lose your cool.

"You know what." I wave him off then rack up the balls. "I'd be happy if you would just drop it already and let us play a round."

"How about this deal—"

"Fuck's sake, Dad, what's with you and deals?"

He ignores my question entirely and sets up to break. "I know you, Beck. I know, as your father, that something is going on. I wish you would just talk to me about it, but since that doesn't seem like it's going to happen, I'm resorting to this. I win, and you start talking about what's going on with you. You win, and I shut up."

"Do you know how to shut up? Because you've changed our deal a couple times now, so I don't really know—"

I'm cut off by the sound of the cue ball connecting with the others. Two stripes manage to find their way into pockets.

"I'm stripes," he states.

Motherfucker.

For the most part when I play in Boston with Callie, I take it seriously but still keep it fun. Now I'm locked in. I'm not about to have this fucking argument with him when really, I'm fine. Not entirely sure what vendetta he's got against "fine," but it's true. Why he needs this profound answer of my happiness is starting to piss me off.

Our game is tight, each one of us pulling ahead by one ball each time, but my luck strikes and I'm up to the eight ball first.

"Eight ball, left pocket," I call, then send the ball right where I called it...along with the cue ball. "Fuck!"

"And that's a scratch. I win."

Tossing my pole on the table, I can already feel the start of a headache. "I'm not doing this. I'm fine—why can't you accept that?"

"Say you're happy and I'll drop it."

"What is the hang up on that word?" I huff when his only answer is a blank stare. I pull off my glasses to pinch the bridge of my nose. "I'm happy. There. Said it."

"Say it and *mean it*, Beckham. I don't know why you think you can suddenly start lying to me. You have this tell, you always have."

"You're off your rocker, I don't have—"

"When you're lying you take your glasses off. If you have your contacts in, you look away to avoid eye contact. You've done it since you were a kid. Almost like you don't want to see your own bullshit. You've done it multiple times while talking about Boston, and you did it when you called that 'friend' of yours nothing."

Christ. I put my glasses back on. "That is...you're..." I try to find any sort of comeback. Some reasonable explanation, but dammit. "It's not always that deep, Dad. Maybe my glasses were bothering me."

He *tsks*. "Yeah, and you just looked off to the right. Stop fucking with me, tell me what's going on with you."

"Nothing! Nothing is going on. I'm fine!" I yell, then immediately pull back. "Sorry. Just tell me what you need from me to prove that I'm good. Really, I am."

"Answer my questions. Honestly," he deadpans.

Shit, I'm going to regret this. I give him a nod.

"Why haven't you brought anyone home?"

Yep, instant regret. "Hell. Seriously—"

"Answer the question, son. It's not that hard."

I push off the table. "Well, the answer's not that simple. Maybe I just haven't found the one. Maybe I'm not interested in settling down. I'm thirty, it's not unusual to be single at thirty."

"No, it's not, but you just said maybe more times than necessary. You've brought no one home in the eight years you've been playing. No relationship at all, that I'm aware of.

I got it in the beginning, you were in your early twenties—but now…it's like you're not even trying."

"Why do I have to be trying right now? What is it that has you so caught up on the fact that I'm not in a relationship? What does that have to do with anything?"

My dad stops and stares at me for a moment. He remains deadly silent as he pulls out his wallet, then a piece of paper from one of the folds.

He unfolds it carefully then starts to read words that make my stomach turn. "Dear, Dad, I can't wait to be a dad just like you. I want to have a family just like mine and—"

"Stop. I wrote that when I was, what? Eight?"

"Yeah, eight and fucking happy. Son, you can't tell me you haven't always wanted these things in life. You can act like I'm being ridiculous all you want, but you've always hated the idea of being alone."

"Yeah, well, things change."

"Not like—"

For fuck's sake, I can't take this anymore.

"They do. They do fucking change. They changed for me the first time Mom forgot who you were and I saw my unbreakable dad crumble." I should stop talking, but I can't. "I don't want the person I love to have to go through this. I don't want to put that on them. I don't want to forget the person I love. I don't want my kids to worry about possibly having it when they get older. I don't want them to have to live so long with the memories alone."

My dad's face turns pale. "Dammit, Beckham. You're not seriously saying what I think you're saying. You don't want a relationship because of your mother?"

When I don't say anything, my dad tosses his cue on the table. "Go home."

"W-what? I'm not going—"

"Go home, Beck. I love you more than anything, and I'm saying this in the calmest way I can...but, *fuck*, son, go home, and don't come visit until you figure this shit out."

He starts to walk back in the house, like this is the end of the fucking discussion. I follow him a step behind. "Are you seriously kicking me out the house? Now? You force me to talk about this and now you're telling me to leave? I told you I'm fine, but you can't accept that. It's your turn to tell me fucking why."

My dad stops and turns back around. There's not a hint of anger on his face, just pure hurt. "The fact that you think that your mother is a burden on me...*me?*"

I take a deep breath. He's not understanding what I'm trying to say. "That's not what I said. I just—"

"No, listen to me. You didn't have to say it, but the fact is that you think that's what you'd be if this happens to you, right?"

My silence is all the response he needs.

"I'll gladly live with every single happy memory we have. I'll love her no matter how many days I have left without a thought or hesitation. And I'd fucking relive all of this, knowing everything I know now, I'd do it if it meant being with her and having you. Don't rob yourself of that happiness. Your mother would hate to know you feel this way." My unbreakable father crumples in front of me for the second time. "If she knew this is what has changed your mind... Go home. Figure this shit out."

When he walks back into the house he doesn't slam the door, and that somehow makes me feel worse.

"Fuck!" I shout out some frustration but it doesn't help even a little bit.

My breath starts to feel short so I lean against the pool table. Not now. I can't have a panic attack now.

I take slow, deep breaths, but when that seems to feel pointless I force myself into survival mode. If I'm going to have a panic attack, I can't have it here.

I swallow every emotion. I push every thought to short tasks at hand.

Go get stuff. Get to the airport. Find a flight. Fall the fuck apart at home.

Damn, so this is rock-fucking-bottom. To make matters worse, my phone rings.

Callie's name flashes on the screen, and I send it straight to voicemail. I'm done with today. I cannot possibly handle anything else.

> Today is not the day, so if it can wait then call me tomorrow.

CALLIE BEAR

> Okay talk to you tomorrow.

Now to get back home.

Chapter 9
Beck

Bed. I need my bed.

It took hours to get a flight. Naturally, not a single direct flight was available tonight and because, of course, my fucking luck, I was on standby for four hours before making a flight to New York, where I could take a red-eye to Boston.

At this point I'm too tired to feel anything. I've gone numb and my only thoughts now are sleeping for the next twenty-four hours and kind of hoping I wake up from this nightmare.

Opening the door to my apartment, I don't bother with lights, I don't even wait for the door to close before I abandon my suitcase, rip off my shirt, and walk right out of my sweats. I want to walk up my stairs directly to my bed and crash.

Opening the door to my pitch-black room, I let muscle memory take me to my side. I set my glasses and phone on the nightstand and fall onto the mattress.

There's a sharp bark, and before I can even process what I just heard, the side of my face is wet.

"What the fuck!" I jump off the bed just as there's

another bark and a girlish scream. I hit the lamp on the night-stand and find Dottie on my bed. She barks again as her tail and whole body wiggle in excitement. Pawing her way to the edge, she whines to get more attention.

"What the fuck, Beck!" Jensen yells. "I thought you were supposed to be in Virginia. You scared the shit out of me!"

"Me? Me! This is my fucking house! What the fuck are you doing here?"

I blink a few times as I process what the actual fuck is happening. She might be slightly blurry, but I can tell Jensen looks absolutely horrified right now as she holds her hand over her chest—is she wearing my T-shirt too?

"Callie and Lucie said you were going to be gone for another week! You could have warned me you were coming home after Callie called you!"

Jensen reaches for her pillow and chucks it at me. I catch it despite my exhaustion and toss it back to the top of the bed. None of this is making any sense to me right now. "Oh, I'm sorry I didn't give you a heads-up when I didn't know you were going to be here!"

Jensen holds out a shaky hand. "Wait, you didn't say I could stay? But Callie said..."

The horror on her face is enough to confirm that she was just as blissfully unaware as I was. I mumble several curses and press my palms to my forehead. This day really just won't stop.

"Callie didn't mention anything about you staying here. No one mentioned it at all."

Her jaw drops then she mumbles words in Spanish under her breath and I'm pretty sure I catch "*matar*" some-where in there. Before I can ask her to repeat it, she sighs, going back to English. "I'm going to kill them."

"Get in line." I let out a deep breath and finally scratch Dottie's head as she whimpers for attention. I have a million questions right now, but zero energy to ask them. I glance at my alarm clock: 3:47 a.m.

Jensen still didn't answer why she's staying here and not her apartment. Not to mention sleeping in my bed with one of my T-shirts on. For all that's holy, this is an in-the-morning conversation.

I reach for the covers and have Dottie move back to the middle. "Come on, let's get some sleep. We can talk about this tomorrow."

"What? Have you lost your mind? I'm not sleeping here now. Come on, Dottie, down." Jensen hits the mattress with the command, but her dog doesn't move. Doesn't even flinch. "Dottie, come."

Fucking hell. "Get in the bed, Jen. You clearly had no issues sleeping in my bed even though I have two perfectly good guest rooms." I click off the light, not wanting to argue — I should have known that wouldn't stop her.

"Beck, you're not wearing any clothes—I don't have pants—I'm not sleeping—"

"Jensen! For all that is holy, get your ass in this bed. Despite how many times I've thought about this exact damn thing, I've had an extremely shitty day and I'm exhausted. Please, get in this fucking bed and go to sleep."

There's roughly three seconds of silence before I hear a sigh, then the sound of covers rustling.

"Thank you," I whisper when I feel her settle on the bed. I'm way too tired to open my eyes. Although the light is off, I'm sure the moonlight hits Jensen just perfectly on that side. God, I'm going to kill Callie for not telling me she's here. I can assume the reason for her stay is valid, but a heads-up would have been nice.

I guess that could have been what the phone call was for...she still could have followed up in the text. *Hey, heads-up, Jensen's staying at your place tonight.*

"Beck," Jensen whispers.

"Yeah?" I grumble already halfway lost to sleep.

"I'm sorry you had a shitty day." She pauses. "I did too."

Blindly, my hand finds hers and I give it a soft squeeze before pulling it back. "We'll have a better one tomorrow."

Just as quickly as sleep hits, I swear the morning comes just as fast. Except this time, it comes with another lick to the face.

"What the—" I grumble as Dottie licks me again then lays across my chest with a soft whine. "Alright, I'll take you out, but be quiet."

Sliding out of my bed, I look over to find Jensen still dead to the world. Her long black hair is splayed across the pillow while her tan, inked arms hold on to the comforter tightly.

Man, I've dreamed of having her in my bed countless times, but none of them went down like last night.

Walking into my living room, I grab my trail of clothes to throw them back on and spot Dottie's leash hanging on one of the hooks by the door. She turns in circles as I pick it up.

"Yeah, yeah, I'm hurrying. Hold still." Fighting her for the clip, I take her down the stairs and into the designated dog park area.

Pulling out my phone, I FaceTime Callie. If I have to be up, then so does she.

"Beck?" Callie mumbles. Her eyes can barely stay open as she rolls over on her pillow. "Why are you calling me at seven in the morning?"

"Oh, I thought since I'm taking Dottie out bright and fucking early, that I'd call to find out why *I'm* taking Jensen's dog out at seven in the morning!"

"Dottie?" Callie mumbles again, then she sits straight up with a gasp. "Wait...nooooo. You're home? What are you doing home?"

"Callie Bear, I love you like a sister so I will cuss you out."

"The fuck you will," Will snaps, then joins in on the call.

Great, I'll cuss him out too.

"Why the hell did you not tell me Jensen's staying at my apartment?"

Will looks at Callie, then back to me with a sigh. "Alright, cuss her out."

Callie's jaw drops. "Hey, I had a perfectly good reason not to tell you. It all happened yesterday! You said in your text that if it could wait then to call tomorrow. I didn't think you were coming home early! You left out important details too. I have it in writing."

When I roll my eyes, Callie snaps. "Oh, don't do that. I may not know what happened, but I do know you. I was calling to make sure it was okay for Jensen to crash there, but then you sent that text. Filling you in on Jensen's situation was something I truly thought could wait. I knew you'd let her stay knowing she would never agree to it if it wasn't important.

"Deep in my gut, I know you wouldn't have wanted to

hear what was going on with Jensen yesterday. It seemed you both were having shit days and I, *your friend*, decided to let you have time to just be. I didn't need you calling to check on her, and her, in return, biting your head off for being overbearing when she doesn't know what's going on with your family. I didn't think you would come home early! That's the first night she was there, I swear!"

Shit, I hate that I'm right. I knew Callie would have a valid reason for not telling me. "Cussing you out would have been more fun. Me coming home wasn't exactly my choice."

Callie folds her lips in a thin line, then frowns. "I'm sorry, you can still cuss me out if it'll make you feel better."

"It won't." I let out an aggravated sigh.

"Wanna talk about it? Will's an excellent listener and you know I can talk," Callie says while Will hums a laugh. "No commentary is needed. I know what I said."

I shake my head. "I don't want to talk, but can you tell me now why Jensen's crashing at my place? Or were you waiting to tell me that she's moving in?"

Will makes a cocky grin. "This was so worth the early wake-up call. Go on, Blaze, tell him."

"You hush, go back to sleep." Callie pushes him out of view. "She just needs a place to crash for a bit. She was going to stay here, but we have a no pet policy. I'm all for sneaking around...but from past experiences, we all know Will and I aren't the best at that."

That one gets me. God, this is why we're such good friends. "Good point." I look around the park and spot Dottie sniffing around some of the obstacle courses. "I guess I should get back inside and talk to my squatter?"

"You call her that and she'll chop it right off." Callie

clicks her tongue then makes a slicing hand motion. "Just clean off."

"Yeah, yeah, her threats make my dick hard."

"Gag." Callie snarls her nose then smiles. "I'm glad you're back, ya know, minus all the circumstances you don't want to talk about."

I swallow down a lump in my throat. "Yeah, maybe I'll feel better about it when I kick your ass in pool."

"Keep dreaming, buddy." Callie falls back on her pillow. "Update me later?"

"Will do," I say with a nod, then hang up. Whistling for Dottie, she comes racing over. "So, how mad is your mom about to be at me, huh?" Patting her head, I clip her leash to her collar. "I know you can't respond, but I'm going to keep talking to you anyway."

Making our way up the steps, I barely get in the door before Dottie tugs hard on the leash. I let it go knowing exactly what she's after. "Well, look who's up—my little squatter."

Jensen's eyes cut from her dog to me and the look she gives me supports Callie's "clean off" comment.

With a snicker, I walk over to my island and lean back against the counter. "Come on, let's figure this out."

Jensen sputters a *tsk*. "It's figured out. I'm not staying here."

God, this woman is so stubborn. It's a welcome fucking distraction. "Oh, and you're going where?"

Jensen stands firmly planted at the foot of the stairs. Her face still looks like she wants to absolutely murder me for asking a question that she doesn't have an answer to.

I wait a second longer for her to respond and her glare only intensifies. She's no longer in my shirt, which is so very unfortunate, and is now wearing some green yoga pants and matching long sleeve athletic top. I've seen her running in it before, which reminds me…

"Alright, Jenni-cakes, let's push this conversation off again. How about some normalcy? Give me five minutes."

Pushing back from my chair, I start to walk toward my room to change.

Jensen steps in front of me, her arms crossed and ready to argue now that there's been a subject change. "What do you mean, normalcy? None of what's happened in the last sixteen hours has been normal."

"You're right. So, do you want to sit down and talk about it?" I raise my eyebrows with the question.

Game. Set. Match.

Jensen scrunches her nose in frustration, before cocking her hip. "Do you want to talk about why you're home over a week early?"

Motherfucker.

When I don't answer, Jensen gives me her smirk.

Dottie, however, has zero capabilities to read the tension in the room, so she puts her paws on my side with a whine.

Scratching her head, I look back to Jensen. "It's Tuesday. Let's go run off our shitty day."

Chapter 10
Jensen

I really only have myself to blame here. I should have known that staying at Beck's would bite me in the ass. I just didn't realize it would come from him scaring the absolute shit out of me and seeing him in nothing but underwear.

I may not be able to prove if he's pierced or not, but apparently, he has more tattoos than that fucking thigh tattoo. I couldn't exactly make them out in the dark, but I could see the ink swirled on his skin. I didn't realize that I could be scared then turned on that quickly.

And now, here I am having him kick my ass with a run this morning. Plopping down on one of the spots of grass along the Harborwalk, the icy air fills my lungs and I fight off a cough.

Running outdoors is my personal favorite, but I know I'll be switching to gym treadmills when the snow starts. The salt is way too harsh for Dottie's paws, and frankly, I'm just not a huge fan of running in the snow.

Beck hovers over me with that cocky smirk on his face. "Ah, come on, J. You've got to have more in you."

No. No, I really don't. "We just ran ten miles. I think we're good."

Dottie pants at Beck's feet, I can tell she's got a good workout in, but I swear, she's in love with him. She might not take off after Beck if he kept going, but she'd think about it.

"Alright, Killer." Beck falls dramatically next to me. His hands catching him in a push up position then rolls to his back. "Break it is."

Dottie lays down in between us as we all slow our heart rates down.

I steal a glance at Beck as he rests his arms over his head and his eyes shut. Running with him should not be so damn enjoyable. I hate that he knew this is what we both needed. I didn't anticipate the ten miles, but he's right—this is our normal. Whatever normal is for us, I suppose.

We match each other's speed so well. It never feels like Beck's trying to compete with me either. We just turn off our brains and run. It's the only rational reason I can think of for why I continue to run this route every single Tuesday he's in town. The same one, I hate to admit, that makes me hate the idea of no longer running together over winter.

The corner of his lips turns up, and I know I've stared a moment too long.

"Like what you see?"

I want to point out his eyes are closed, but that straight up admits that I was staring. "I was glaring at you. We usually run five miles on Tuesdays."

Beck looks back up to the clouded sky. "Hey, you're a big girl. Don't act like you didn't want to keep going. If you really wanted to stop at five, you would have said something."

Dammit, he's right. "Maybe I was afraid to say something? Ever think of that?"

Beck lets out a throaty laugh that's every bit of a turn on that it shouldn't be. "Jensen, you're not afraid to tell me anything."

False. Very false.

This time, I choose to ignore him. I look back up to the sky, slowly finding my breath as I recount waking up in Beck's bed this morning. It was so annoyingly comfortable, and every part of me hated that I was alone in it. Even if it was a blessing that I did...walking out to find him wearing glasses is a whole new version of Beck I didn't need to see. It pairs with the reaction of seeing him in his boxer briefs.

"I didn't know you wore glasses." The words tumble out at the memory.

"Don't always wear them. There are these things called contacts, little more practical when playing baseball. I mostly wear my glasses at home, but if you like them then—"

Despite my body still feeling this numbing high, I swat at his arm. "Don't be an ass."

Beck chuckles. "Well, considering you brought up a reminder of this morning, why don't you tell me what happened. Why'd you have to crash at my place?"

I swallow down a bit of my pride, I guess I do owe him an explanation, considering Callie and Lucie didn't give him the heads-up I'd be there.

"My landlord is co-conspiring with my old slimy boss. I can handle myself, but I'm smart enough to know it's better to leave entirely. So, now, I need a new place to live while also finding a new shop to work at...which also seems to be impossible at the moment, but I'll figure it out."

"What the fuck?" Beck snaps. "What do you mean co-

conspiring? I feel like you're glossing over a whole lot of information here."

I feel every muscle in my body tense with frustration. "It's fine, Beck. The apartment isn't exactly worth fighting for when I know I can figure other things out."

"Okay, so you want me to find out the rest of these details on my own. Should I start at your apartment complex? Tally's, maybe?"

"*Ay dios mío!* Look, the guy who did my apprenticeship was a perverted asshat and didn't want me to leave the shop so he could keep ogling me. When I turned his and his wife's job offer down, I could tell that it didn't go over well, but it had to be done.

"I figured, if anything, they would just talk shit about me in the shop, but clearly, I underestimated them. My landlord is one of the asshat's regulars, so I came home to a letter about raised rent that afternoon. When that didn't work because I'm busting my ass at Winedown, they decided to implement a new 'no pet' policy."

"Christ, Jensen, that's why you were working that Tuesday?" Beck doesn't wait for me to respond to that question before asking a new one. "Keep going. What about the other shops?"

Clenching my jaw tight, this is the one I saw coming the least. "Seems I've been put on some form of blacklist for artists. Apparently, asshat's wife is just as big of a cunt and made up a bunch of lies. What's worse is, I'm not sure if she's just bitter that I didn't stay or that her husband didn't get what he wanted. I suppose it was all just an insult to injury."

"I'm going down there." Beck shoots up from lying on the ground.

My body hates me for it, but I match his speed, catching

his arm before he stands. "No. No, you will not. I've already talked Hurricane Callie out of trashing the place and convinced Mama Bear Lucie to stand down. Don't make me fight you on it too—just listen."

Beck looks at me dead in the eyes. "You better start saying better things then, Jen. You're telling me you felt so unsafe that you had to leave your apartment. Don't tell me what lies this bitch is spreading or you won't stop me."

I look at Beck, truly look at him, and he's pissed. Outraged, really. This hyperactive, goofball looks straight up murderous right now and at that I burst out laughing.

Beck tilts his head back. "You think I'm fucking joking? I'm ser—"

"N-no," I stutter in between chuckles. "I believe you. I just—this doesn't fit you. You're—"

"I'm what?" Beck's eyes turn from intense fury to amused in an instant. "What am I to you, Jensen?"

My laugh slows, but doesn't stop. "You're totally a stage-five clinger, but I never thought I'd see that look on your face."

Beck gives me a playful shove. "Yeah, and you're facing homelessness and unemployment if you don't get a handle on this."

"It's fine. I told you, I can handle myself, and I'm not dumb. Staying in that apartment is a choice, one I chose to remove myself from. I needed a place to crash to figure things out. When the solution of an empty place was on the table, I took that one, but I can message Blake from the shop and see—"

"For fuck's sake. You're staying at my place, Jensen. No fucking arguing with me."

"Bec—"

A bit of that murderous look comes back to his face. "I said no arguing. You want to handle this on your own, fine. I can respect that, but you can figure it out at my place. I have two empty rooms, and clearly my bed is big enough for two."

All my amusement dies. "Not happening again. All I had were these clothes from my gym bag and I wasn't about to sleep naked so I stole a shirt. The bed looked comfy...it wasn't that deep."

This time Beck snorts a laugh. "Of course it wasn't."

"Okay, I've shared my shitty day. Your turn."

A new emotion crosses Beck's face—one I've also never seen before. He looks heartbroken.

"Had a fight with my dad." Beck shuffles his knees then scratches at his palm. "My mom...she's sick. Early-onset Alzheimer's. It was a combination of different things, but I— I had to go. He wanted me to go, so cue the hours at one airport, finding a flight to New York so I could get on a red-eye to Boston, then being licked in the face by Dottie."

Dottie perks up at the mention of her name. Her tail wags viciously as she paws her way closer to lick Beck again.

I get it, girl. I get it.

Beck pets her head with a slight tug at the corner of his mouth.

"Seems like you're glossing over some details there, Stalker," I mumble cautiously. The angry version of Beck may have made me laugh, but this...this sad Beck is causing a serious pain in my chest. I want to reach over and hold his hand for comfort, but hold myself back.

Beck looks out to the waterfront with a vacant stare. "I don't have the details in me right now. I know that's not fair of me to say after I made you share, but—"

The instinct to reach over sends a tingle up my forearm.

"You gave what you could. I think it's pretty common knowledge that life's not fair, Beck."

Beck bobs his head with a *humph*. "No, it's really not. You done for today?"

"Yeah," I mutter as I push off the ground. Between the week I've had and the ten miles ran, my legs feel like Jell-O. I want a nap so freaking bad, but then it hits me that I'll have to nap at Beck's place and borrow his clothes again because I abandoned everything yesterday.

With a deep breath, I turn to Beck...my temporary roomie. "Can we go get some things at my place to last me a few days?"

Beck stands with a *tsk*. "We'll get everything."

"That's a lot to—"

Beck holds up his hand. "Stop. Why argue over something that needs to happen?"

I bite my lip. I suppose he has a point, it's the reality of the situation—I'm moving in with Beck—hopefully not for long—but my stuff can't stay in that apartment forever.

"Fine. Come on, Dottie." I pull her leash lightly to get her attention. She's paw over tail for Beck. If she could understand what's happened—I don't think she'd care one bit.

I make one step onto the pavement when Beck's hands find my hips and he yanks my back against his chest and holds me tight.

"Beck!" I fight his grip. "What the hell are you—"

"Chill, Jensen, chill." He continues to hold me tight, but with his voice coming off soft and calm, I relax for a moment. "This might go into that shitty day category, but...uh, I think you started your period while we were running. You have a stain on your pants."

"What!" Oh god, kill me now. What's the date again? I'm usually like clockwork. *Shit, shit, shit.* I've been so stressed and I left yesterday in such a hurry. "I'm going to burn down Tally's. I really think I will."

Beck lets out that raspy laugh and his hands loosen around my waist, but doesn't let go yet. "Ya know, I can't say I wouldn't light the match for ya, Killer, but let's hold off for today. I got you."

I. Got. You.

He lets go and pulls his long sleeve athletic shirt over his head then his arms come back around caging me in between him and the shirt. "Turn around," he commands.

Turning on my heels ever so slowly, I hold my breath until I meet those green eyes. The slight tug up on his lips tells me everything I need to know, he's not one bit deterred by this—completely happy just being able to help.

He ties the sleeves into a tight knot. "There."

I look from the knot to Beck's bare arms as chills appear. "Beck, you didn't—it's cold and you—"

Beck raises an eyebrow and gives me that smirk. "Worrying about me? See, Jennie, I knew you liked me."

Yeah, I do, and that's part of the problem.

He just did one of the sweetest gestures that anyone has ever done for me and he's being so nonchalant about it. Like this wasn't something that has my heart racing.

I push back from him. "No, worried is a bit of a stretch. I feel like we're going to need some ground rules moving forward. I'm using you for a place to stay and not lose my dog. Don't get this confused with anything more."

Beck nods his head slowly. "Right, right. Tell me, Jennie, how is it living in your delusion?"

"It's nice, you're hardly even thought of there." I start walking, not waiting or caring for his response.

Beck jogs up next to me but doesn't speak to me. He looks down at Dottie walking in between us. "Your mom likes me, doesn't she? She just doesn't show it like you do."

Dottie barks and prances at his feet while we walk. Damn dog is a traitor.

"And I'm the delusional one." *I am. I so am.*

I see Beck look over at me from the corner of my eye. I don't have to see more to know he's got that damn smirk on his face. "Oh, I'm definitely delusional. And so desperate."

I bite the inside of my lip to stop the smile. Looking away from him to the waterfront, I mumble. "You forgot stalker."

"That too, but you're so into it."

I pin him with a glare. "Do you want me to hurt your feelings? I will, if that's what it takes."

Beck holds up his hands in surrender. "I get it, you're not ready to admit it. Let's just get your stuff moved into my place, and then you can set those ground rules that *you*, for some reason, need."

My steps slow ever so slightly. Dammit, this is not going to end well.

Chapter 11
Beck

"I still can't get past the fact that you drive a truck," Jensen grumbles as she climbs in the front seat.

"And I still don't understand why. It's a form of transportation." I open the back door for Dottie to jump in. She asked about it on the way here. I get that a lot of athletes have fancy cars, but it's not like this isn't a brand-new truck.

Jensen turns around to scratch Dottie's head. "I know that. I just thought you'd drive something flashier. It's also a normal truck, not something jacked up with tacky lights and obnoxiously loud. You know, something that screams 'I'm overcompensating for my small, pierced dick.'"

Gah, her smart mouth gets me every time. "It's good to know you still think about my dick."

"Yeah, thinking about how tiny it has to be really brings a smile to my face."

I snort a laugh before closing the back door then rounding the truck to get in the driver's seat. I lean over the console and hold Jensen's eyes in a serious stare. "It's not about the size, it's how you use it."

We hold the silence for maybe three seconds before we both start to laugh.

I lean back, satisfied that our moods have lightened. I have a feeling that I might have to do that several more times for Jensen today, but much to her probable disagreement...I make her laugh.

Before pulling out, I shoot off a text to Will and Callie to have them meet us at Jensen's old apartment in about an hour. I want her done with that place today. I'm fine with letting her figure out what's next on her own, but I'm not about to let her continue to have ties to this place so they can hold it over her head.

"Where are we going?" Jensen asks once she realizes I've turned the opposite way of her apartment. I don't answer her and hit my favorites on CarPlay to make my next call.

"Why are you calling Lucie?" Jensen asks before the first ring.

"Impatient, much?" I mumble to her. "You're gonna hear what—"

"Hey, Beck," Lucie answers.

"Hey, Baby Mama, how are you feeling?"

"Tired and nauseous, you know, the usual. How are you feeling about your new roommate?"

"I'm great..." I look at Jensen with a smile, but she's giving Lucie's contact photo the evil eye. "She's hanging in there. Listen, think that kid of yours would want to have a play date with a dog for a couple hours?"

"Beck—" Jensen starts, but Lucie talks over her.

"I think Dex might kill you for it, but I'll help calm him down."

Lucie can't see it, but a devilish smile comes to my face. "So that's how you got pregnant. Every time Dex starts acting like a dick, you *calm him down*. The team was wondering why he's nicer now that he has you."

"Beck!" Lucie squeals, but Jensen...Jensen folds her lips together the best she can, but the corners tilt up ever so slightly. I'll still qualify that as a Jensen smile nonetheless.

"You walked right into that one. Come on, what'd you expect me to say?"

Knowing Lucie, her cheeks are probably bright red right now. "Just bring Dottie over and don't tell that joke to Dex."

"Thank you, we'll be there in about twenty minutes. Oh, and Luce, Jensen needs some clean clothes to change into."

"Okay, see you soon, Jen," Lucie sings.

"Bye, Luce." Jensen hits the End Call button on the screen with a huff. "My hips are not about to fit into Lucie's clothes."

"I'm assuming that's a comment I don't need to respond to, so I'll just tell you the plan instead. We'll take Dottie over to play with Miles for a couple hours, Callie and Will are meeting us at your apartment to get you moved out, where you can put your own clothes on then." And because I can already see the argument about getting so much help all over her face, I lie for her benefit. "I want my shirt back...it's cold as fuck."

Jensen presses her lips into a thin line. "You know, there's most likely a stain on your shirt now."

"I'll survive. Believe me, I've worn dirtier clothes over the years." When I let that statement fully register, I double back. "Not that you're dirty, I meant—"

"I know what you meant, Beck." Jensen's shoulders drop a bit as she sinks farther into the seat. "Thanks," she mutters.

I want to make a smart comment about her looking like she's actually enjoying the truck she was making fun of me for having, but when her eyes fall shut, I'm fighting off the urge to rest my hand on her thigh.

I flex my hand against the steering wheel as the words my father said come back to haunt me.

Don't rob yourself of that happiness. Your mother would hate to know you feel this way.

The look of utter disappointment is something I've never seen from him, but fuck, I can't do it. I won't.

Moving Jensen in with me temporarily is what any good person would do. Giving her my shirt when she needs it is what any good man would do. Me not giving up on our chemistry is more about how great we could make each other feel. But wanting to hear her laugh...resting my hand on her thigh while we drive...not wanting to go get her clothes for a while longer because I'd love to see her walking around in nothing but my T-shirt again...

Maybe we do need some ground rules.

As I park the truck at Dex's, Jensen's eyes flutter open. "Oh, we're here."

"Yeah, if you're tired, I can take Dottie in." At the sound of her name, Dottie places her front paws on the console and goes in for another lick to the face. God, this dog could not be more opposite than her mother if she tried. I pet her head with a soft chuckle. "I don't think she would mind either."

"Yeah, fucking traitor," Jensen grumbles barely above a whisper. "I'll come. I didn't mean to fall asleep. Sorry."

"Don't apologize—it's not a big deal." This weird funk hangs over me and I have to flex my hand again at the mere mental image of her asleep. "Come on, let's head up."

Jensen nods, and what I'm grateful for now is the silence Jensen gives me. Whatever that was on the drive over here is not what we are. Friends with benefits is the most we could be, and the thing is, I think Jensen would agree with me.

I knock on Dex's door and it takes about three seconds before we hear a squeal, then Miles is swinging the door open. "Beck is here with the doggie!"

"Miles, this is Jensen, you know her, she's not a dog," I joke, but it gets flipped around on me when Jensen backhands me in the stomach. "I was kidding," I croak.

"Oh dear." Lucie's voice comes from behind Miles. "What happened?"

Miles places his little hand over his mouth to hide his snicker. "Jensen hit Beck because he was being a meanie."

"Yeah, that sounds about right." Lucie pulls the door open all the way. "Come on in."

"Yeah, I wanna play with Dottie!" Miles cheers and reaches for her leash.

Lucie points to me. "You handle that. Dex is in the living room." Lucie then turns to Jensen, but she stops her.

"Oh, we're definitely about to go talk about your and Callie's lack of communication."

Lucie looks between us with a bright smile. "I actually have no qualms about how this worked out."

"I do," Jensen mutters.

I kind of do now.

I give Lucie a nod. "Good luck with that."

Her smile doesn't falter. "Oh, good luck with Dex."

Yeah, fair.

Making my way to the living room where Miles's laughter is absolutely heartwarming, I find Dex...who's joy is the polar opposite.

"I can't believe you brought the dog back to my house. You know I'll be the bad guy for a week at least now, right?"

"Well, that's because you're a pushover. Miles asked for a sibling and you said no, but look at you now."

Dex fights off a smile the best he can. "Fuck off. How are your folks doing?"

I fall onto the couch next to him. "Well, I'm home a week early...and not by my own free will, unfortunately."

"Beck?" Dex says my name with caution toward Miles, and I know what he's really asking.

The biggest lump forms in my throat, but I swallow it down. "My mom's fine. I don't want to talk about it, just be happy I'm here and brought a puppy over to play with your son."

The look on Dex's face is not at all amused, but given the response I just gave, he doesn't push...on that topic, at least. "Alright, how's the roommate situation working out?"

"It's...something."

Dex sits up a little straighter. "Listen, I'm giving you today, all things considered, but if you think I'm not about to bring this up every opportunity I get, then you have another thing coming."

I should have known this was coming. "That was a completely different—"

"No, don't you fucking say different."

Miles's laughter stops abruptly. "That's a bad word, remember!"

I tilt my head to Dex, biting back my laugh, while he sighs. "We talked about this—they are adult words. Daddy can say adult words."

"Lucie doesn't say *adult* words," Miles retorts.

Dex runs his hands over his face. "Yeah, well, Lucie evens Daddy out, just play with the dog while she's here, bud. Before you get any ideas, she's going back home with Beck later today."

Miles makes a small noise as he goes back to playing with Dottie like she's about to disappear right in front of him if he doesn't.

"Way to turn that around on me, asshole," I whisper.

Dex chuckles. "That's a tactic I got from Lucie. You, Will, and Callie are the go-to bad guys, but back to our original conversation—fuck you, if you think I'm about to let this go."

"You just said you were giving me a pass."

"A day pass—*this is different*—yeah, fuck off."

"It is, actually. You were very clearly in love with Lucie out of the gate."

Dex's eyebrows pull together then he holds out his hand. "Hi, Pot, I'm Kettle."

I smack his hand. "No, no. I want to *sleep* with Jensen. Friends with benefits max—that's it."

Miles cuts in again. "Why do you want to sleep with Jensen? That sounds really boring. And what's friends with benefits?"

Dex mumbles a curse. "Really?"

"Yeah, that's my bad. Welp, this is clearly another conversation for your dad to handle." I jump up from the couch, creating as much distance from Dex as I can. "Jensen!"

I meet her and Lucie at the end of the entry hallway. Lucie's sweatpants hug her curves in the best way, but I don't have time to admire that. I also don't have a death wish. "You ready?"

Jensen quirks an eyebrow. "Yeah?"

"Great, let's go." I look to Lucie. "Miles has a question for you and Dex."

Lucie folds her arms. "What question? It took me an hour conversation to undo the curse words Will taught him."

I don't wait around to answer, I simply take Jensen's hand and walk for the door.

"Beck, what did you do?" Jensen chuckles, but I don't have to answer because then we hear Miles.

"Lucie, what does friends with benefits mean?"

Once we're at her apartment, I get why Jensen said this place isn't worth fighting for—she's practically living in a box. Thirty-five hundred for this place? I think the fuck not.

The entire drive Jensen was quiet, and while I appreciated that she didn't ask for more details on the whole friends-with-benefits comment, I need to see some of that Jensen personality I crave.

I look at the wall closest to her bed and see the thin cloth with a pin-up girl design on it. I nudge her with my elbow. "Oh, hey, a tapestry, who would have guessed?"

Her nostrils flare with a deep huff as she shoves me back. "I told you it was a gift. My sister had it made with one of my drawings when I got my apprenticeship here."

"You drew that?"

It's incredible, so I guess I shouldn't be entirely surprised...Jensen's crazy talented anyone with eyes can see that.

"Yeah, it wouldn't have been my first choice to go on my

wall, but my sister said it was fitting for the situation... thought she would encourage me."

Between the look on Jensen's face and the softer tone in her words, something tells me there's a bit more to that story than she's letting on, but I think I'm pushing her enough today already.

I keep my tone light. "I like it, but for now, it has to come down."

Jensen scrunches her nose then takes a look around. "Beck, this is insane, how are we going to get everything out today? We have zero boxes and getting all my furniture is going to be a pain. Where are we even going to put it?"

It takes me no time at all to answer. "Leave it here."

"What?"

"You got any emotional attachment to the big stuff? The bed, tiny kitchen table, and one love seat?"

"Well...no? But it's my stuff. I don't want to have to buy new things when I find a new place to live."

"I'll buy them."

"Beck, no, that's ridiculous. You are *not* buying me new furniture."

Before I can begin to win this argument with her, there's a knock at the door. "Perfect, Callie and Will are here, more people to back me up on this."

Stepping around Jensen, I open the door, but it's not Callie and Will.

"Can we help you?" I ask the weasel of a man standing in the hall. His salt-and-pepper hair is slicked back, and it takes all my willpower to not punch him in the face when I notice his cut-off shirt that reads WARNING, CHOKING HAZARD with an arrow pointing down.

"Don't believe you're my tenant," he snarls. "Jensen, I

know you're in there. You get rid of the damn dog yet? Or maybe you want to talk about a deal?"

"The fuck?" I mutter as Jensen appears beside me and sighs heavily.

"This is Charlie, my landlord." Her disdain is very clearly written all over her face. "I told you, Charlie, I'm not getting rid of my dog."

Charlie eyes her in a way that has me seeing red. He steps closer as if he were going to just walk right in. I lift my arm to block the door. "I think the fuck not."

"You heard her, this is my place. I can come in if I so please."

"That's where you're wrong. Landlords are required to provide a minimum of twenty-four hours' notice before entering, and not to mention, have a legitimate reason. So, why don't you back the fuck up. You're not coming inside."

Charlie takes two small steps back and huffs an arrogant laugh. "I see when I said no dogs, you didn't get the complete picture. Seems like you have this one on a pretty tight leash."

Jensen looks him dead in the eye. "Yeah, and he'll bite if I tell him to."

I'll bite her, that's for damn sure.

Jensen places her hand on my arm, lowering it so she can step in front of me. "You know what? I'm so done with letting all this bullshit go. Fuck you. Fuck your rent. You want to change policies, be my guest. I'm moving out of this shithole."

Charlie takes a small step forward, and, while I hate him breathing the same air as her, Jensen doesn't flinch, and I'm not about to stop her from standing up for herself. I'll be here if she needs me.

"Go ahead, you want to be this prick's whore instead of

living here? Go for it, but according to our lease agreement, you owe rent through the month of January."

Yep, this one's me. "Consider it paid." When he blanches, I smile. "I bark on command for her too."

Jensen's lips fold tight and her cheeks start to turn bright red. This amazing reaction I get out of her doesn't last long. She seems to force it down then turns back to Charlie. "Now if you'll excuse us."

Charlie looks over at her one more time, then to me before starting his retreat.

"Oh, and Charlie?" Jensen says before he gets too far. "Tell Hank and Tally whatever false narrative they want to spin about me won't make their shitty reality any better."

Charlie opens his mouth, but I'm done hearing his voice. I take one step into the hallway and he spins on his heels and out of eyesight.

"Pussy," I mumble.

"Tip of the iceberg, Beckham," Jensen groans and walks back in this box of an apartment. She folds her hands on top of her and with the click of the door she spins around to me. "I'll pay you back for the rent money."

"The fuck you will."

"Beck—" she starts but I stop her.

"We can argue about it later." Pulling her arms down from her head, I take her hands cautiously in mine. "I told you to call me on a lazy day, but it seems we're stuck in shitty ones, so what do you need?"

"I don't need anything!" Jensen pulls her hands back, a sharp edge in her voice. It takes her a second or two before it really settles in that she does in fact need things. "Dammit! I just need to get out of this place."

"Okay, done. Keep going."

Jensen looks like she wants to fight me, but then she throws her hands up. "I need to find a new place to live, and find a tattoo shop that will hire me after the damage tweedle-dipshit and tweedle-twat did by spreading lies about me."

I swallow my laugh the best I can. "Okay, you're living with me, mark that one off your list. You'll find a solution to the tattoo thing because your drive and work is something they can't even fathom. Keep 'em coming. What else?"

Jensen sighs. "I don't know...those were the main ones. My head is hurting...I just feel like I want a tub of ice cream and to break something."

I nod. Alright, I can handle all this. Walking over to her tiny kitchenette, I pull out one of her plates. "Any emotional attachment to this?"

Jensen pulls her eyebrows together. "What? No? What are—"

"You got a broom and dustpan?" I cut her off.

She huffs. "Yeah, but—"

I step up to her. "Break it."

Jensen looks at me like I have two heads. "I'm not going to break my plate."

"Why not? I have plates, and we already agreed that I'll buy whatever you need for your next apartment."

"I never agreed to that!"

I push the plate in her hand. "Break it, Jen. Now."

Jensen's eyes soften as she looks in mine. She turns slowly, then chucks the plate against the far wall. The sound is way more dramatic than the actual breaking of the ceramic, so I walk back to her cabinet to grab another plate. "Again."

This time there's no hesitation or argument when she

throws. With the shatter, Jensen's shoulders drop. "Okay, you were right, that helped."

I'm too smart of a man to rub in her face the fact that she just willingly admitted I'm right. Gloating isn't the move for today. "Good, now I'm going to clean this up and we'll start getting some of your stuff out."

Jensen doesn't speak, as she gives me a half nod. I'm not about to push her while she processes how she needs to. I find her broom, and Jensen stands like a stone statue until everything is cleaned up.

"You good?" I ask cautiously.

Jensen blinks once then twice before shaking her head like she just came out of a daze. "Yeah, I'm good. Fine, just... a lot."

"A lot, but necessary."

"Right, I know...I know." Jensen takes a deep breath when another knock comes to the door. "That better be Callie and Will, or I might tear this whole place apart."

I hum in amusement. Can't say the idea isn't tempting to do anyway.

I squeeze her shoulder. "Don't worry, Killer, I'll help."

Chapter 12
Jensen

I can't decide what's worse about this entire situation. The fact I'm so deeply indebted to Beck that it's quite ridiculous, or the fact I'm not that upset about it.

Every moment of yesterday should have absolutely sucked, but at each downturn, Beck was there...and made it better.

It didn't take too long between the four of us to pack up my tiny apartment. After the plate throwing, I decided to take Beck's advice and just leave whatever I didn't want.

Unloading everything at Beck's place didn't take long either. I picked the guest bedroom farthest away from him as possible, and thankfully, Beck didn't make any flirty remarks about me sleeping in his bed again.

It had to have been abundantly clear to everyone yesterday that my patience was maxed out. Even Lucie didn't say a teasing word when we picked Dottie up. Although it didn't save me from waking up from messages today in our group chat.

Therapy Dupe

LUCIE

Let's get brunch today. Mandatory girl
time.

CALLIE

I agree! Zenith at 10?

REAGAN

The chef there is hot, you know I'm there.

EMMA

Count me in!

LUCIE

It's a date. See EVERYONE there soon!

I don't bother with a reply and toss my phone to the end
of the bed with a groan. My eyes fall shut again. I swear I
could easily sleep another two hours. I'm not sure what
mattresses Beck buys but they are heaven on earth.

Settling deeper into the covers, I sprawl my legs out,
fully prepared to ditch girls' brunch, but when my legs aren't
immediately met with the weight of my clingy dog, I sit up.

"Dottie?"

I know she slept in here last night, but now she's
nowhere to be seen. Forcing myself out of the cozy bed, I
pull on some sweats then brush my teeth and manage the
tangled mess that is my hair.

Looking in the mirror, I'm tempted to pull myself more
together, but that's silly... This is my new reality—living with
Beck—he might as well get used to the no makeup, messy
bun, no bra look.

With the first step out of my room, I smell the sweet
cinnamon scent and there's a twist in my stomach. At the

stairs, I hear what sounds like an audiobook. Dear god, help me.

I walk into the kitchen just in time to see Beck wearing sweats and spreading the frosting over cinnamon rolls. Dottie sits patiently at his feet, completely oblivious to the fact that I'm here...but Beck notices.

He looks at me with a bright smile and those damn glasses on his face. He taps on his phone pausing whatever book he was listening to. "Good morning."

"Morning," I mutter, walking over to the barstools on the other side of his island. "You stole my dog."

Beck chuckles. "Is it stealing if she came willingly?"

That's not at all surprising. "Thank you for taking her out this morning and letting me sleep."

Beck looks at me then shakes his head. "I guess I'm just roommate of the year." He pulls a cinnamon roll from the rest and plops it on a plate. "You hungry?"

My eyes find the clock on the stove. It's almost ten already and with the looks of this pastry in front of me and the man handing it to me...

Yeah, I'm not going to brunch.

I take the plate from him and do my best to contain my smile. "Thanks."

"So, do you want to eat in silence or do you want to work on those ground rules you mentioned needing?" Beck asks, holding out a fork.

I take it with the click of my tongue. "I can't believe this is actually happening...but after yesterday, it seems it would be smart for us to talk about this *temporary* arrangement."

The corner of Beck's mouth turns up before he takes a bite of his breakfast. As he chews he rolls his hand for me to continue on.

Hell, I guess I do somewhat have to lead this, don't I?

"Okay, well, I'll just be here while I look for a new place. I can pay—"

Beck cuts me off with his best imitation of the Taboo buzzer. "Wrong. I don't need or want your money."

"Beck—"

He cuts me off again. "My first ground rule is that you quit suggesting to give me money. If this were Callie or Lucie, I'd do the exact same thing."

My mouth opens then closes. I guess I hadn't thought of it like that. I kind of hate thinking of it that way, actually. I love Callie and Lucie, and frankly, if their men weren't around, I would expect Beck to do this. But that stupid girlish crush I have on him really only wants me to believe he's doing this for me because I'm special.

Ay, I'm hopeless.

"I guess you're right." I sigh. "If you don't want my money, I can make my peace with that...but no freeloader jokes. I offered to pay and you declined—that's on you now."

Beck chuckles. "Fair. What else you got?"

I'm not entirely sure. I threw out this idea of ground rules when he was flirting with me yesterday, but then Miles said something about friends with benefits as we were leaving.

Yesterday most definitely was a day I'd like to soon forget, but those three words have been sitting in the back of my mind. It had to have come from whatever conversation Dex and Beck were having, but did Dex suggest friends with benefits...or Beck?

I must sit in my ruminating silence a little too long because Beck starts again. "Look, we don't have to make this a big deal. Let's just agree that ground rule number two is to be adults about this. If I do something that pisses you off, then tell me."

"Telling you has never stopped you before."

Beck gives me that smirk of his. "We've never lived together before."

Dammit, those are words I never thought I'd hear coming from Beck—don't hate them—didn't need to hear them. "I guess you're right. We're...*roommates*."

The word hangs with thick tension in the air. Even though it's temporary, all of whatever this is between us feels heavy. I don't know why I said it like that, but with the phrase "friends with benefits" in the back of my mind, and all the pushback I've given him over the past few months—I don't know, roommates feels like the first firm definition of our relationship that I can put out there.

We're not exactly friends, definitely not enemies, and acquaintances feels wrong when it's clear we both want to sleep with each other—at the very least. Or, well, it's clear to me that the attraction is mutual, but the degree of it is not.

I like him, but I also don't want to have to change for him either. That's what my last boyfriend wanted out of me—change—and I refuse to go through that again. Part of me knows Beck isn't like my ex, but according to my plans I'm on a relationship hiatus anyway.

It's not for not knowing who I am or trying to be alone. I simply just want to be a single girl in her twenties.

I cut my cinnamon roll with my fork as I continue to think. Beck's made his interest known and with me now living here...putting it on the table might actually solidify our terminology from roommates to friends and I can get over this crush faster...*or get under it with no strings*.

Stabbing my fork into my first bite, I nearly choose to

stuff my mouth to keep the words from coming out, but then I drop my fork. "Beck...I don't know if this qualifies as a ground rule, or just something I think I need to put out there. It's probably going to make me sound absolutely crazy and random..." I hate this. I hate this. "One thing I don't think I've really said before is that I don't want that traditional, cookie-cutter lifestyle. I'm not looking for a relationship right now. I don't want to ever be pregnant or put my career second to a man's. That's not me, and it will never be me."

Beck studies me and I feel like I want to crawl out of my skin. Deafening silence hangs for two whole seconds before Beck speaks. "Jensen, I—"

Whatever words were going to come out of Beck's mouth get cut off by someone banging on the door, sending Dottie into a barking fit which leads to the clatter of Beck's fork as he drops it from his small jump-scare.

"Beck, open up!" Callie yells through the closed door. "I hate the cold!"

Another knock comes, then I hear Lucie. "Jensen, we know you're still here."

They can't be serious. They actually could not have come at a worse time—what the hell?

Beck mumbles curses and small threats as he walks to the door. He barely gets the handle turned before Callie, Lucie, Reagan, and Emma come barreling into his apartment.

"What the fuck?" Beck stammers, while Dottie beelines around him to greet all the new people. "Dottie, bite this one," he says as Callie kneels down to pet her.

Callie goes into her baby voice. "Oh no, sweet girl would never."

Lucie walks right up to me and hooks her arm around my

shoulder. "We're actually here for this one. I knew she would try and bail on girls' brunch, but alas, today is mandatory."

"Pushing it, Luce," I grit out.

Her smile doesn't waver. "I promise it'll be worth it."

No, no, no. I'd rather not go right now.

Beck must read that thought all over my face. "Guys, seriously? This couldn't have waited a day?"

A chorus of "no" comes from them all. Wonderful.

I let out a deep sigh. "It's fine, just give me ten minutes."

My butt barely leaves the stool before Beck turns bossy. "No, sit down. I made plenty of cinnamon rolls, you all want Jensen for brunch, you can have it here."

I could fake a fight and spare Beck from whatever this brunch is they absolutely could not wait for, but I don't want to leave. I wait for rebuttals from the girls, but with the tone Beck just had, I think they all know it isn't an up-for-debate statement.

"Alright," Lucie says as she unwraps her arm from my shoulders. "I'm still throwing up everything I eat, so it makes no difference to me."

Everyone else shrugs and nods as they all grab a spot around the island.

Beck huffs some words low under his breath that I can't understand then goes to get more plates.

"This place is nice, Beck," Reagan says, looking around. "You might be taking the top spot on my list."

"Your list?" Callie asks with raised eyebrows.

"Yeah, the list of Will's teammates who are worth talking to. You know, Dex is pretty high up there, because, well"—Reagan gestures to Lucie—"but other than that, I want them to impress me. Cool cars, nice homes, and what not."

Lucie scoffs. "Rea, that's terrible. They're all great. You shouldn't rank them on material things."

Gah, these two couldn't be more different if they tried.

"Of course, I can. I'm a material girl, Madonna song and all. Plus, Beck's getting bonuses for all the plants he has and they look good—like he actually knows how to take care of them. As a florist, he's topping the list."

"And *he's* standing right here," Beck says as he hands Reagan a plate then starts around the table. "I do know how to take care of my plants, but I do have to credit my house-keeper some as she helps take care of them during the season."

Reagan looks impressed by his honesty, and if I didn't know she was in a completely loyal and loving relationship with her girlfriend for over a decade...the look she gives him would put a very green complexion on me.

Great, apparently on top of a secret crush, I'm territorial too. I don't remember feeling this way with my ex—surely I did. Those *mine* feelings must have been overshadowed by his controlling, judgmental ones.

I clear my throat. "So, what couldn't wait that we need to talk about?"

Lucie gives a little squeal as she pushes her plate away. "There're two pieces of info that we need to talk about, really. The most prevalent one is that I think Reagan and I have thought of a way to get you your own tattoo shop!"

I blink slowly as I process her words. "I think I'm going to need some more information."

Having my own tattoo shop would be an absolute dream, but that's also a dream I never thought of right out the gate.

Luce spins in her chair to face me. I can see the pure love of this idea written all over her face. "Okay, Reagan found a place that's perfect for her floral storefront, but the catch-22 is that it's essentially broken up in rooms. There's extra space that's really not needed, but the rent price is a whole package deal kind of thing. So, when we were having our family meeting about it, it came to me. Why not have you take some of that space? Essentially, you guys could have a floral-tattoo shop!"

My eyes twitch immediately, wanting to look at Beck for some inkling of how this sounds to him too, but instead, I lean around Lucie to meet Reagan's eyes. "More info from you, actually."

Reagan laughs and sets her fork down. "I know it sounds out there, but the vision could be really cool. I've looked all over Boston, and this storefront is truly spectacular. It's got that signature brownstone and gorgeous bay windows. It'll need a few adjustments to make it work for the floral shop, but it's more space than I need. There's a back section we could renovate into a break room, my freezer, and workshop for big events. For the two street view rooms, it could be really cool to have a walk-in floral shop on one side then a tattoo parlor on the other."

Lucie grabs my arm. "I know it's hard to picture without seeing the space, but this could be the perfect solution."

"I volunteer if you need any wall murals," Emma mumbles as she eats her cinnamon roll. "Beck, these are really good."

"Thanks, I let the oven do the majority of the work." He laughs, then looks at me. "Sounds like a good idea, Jen. Could be a pretty cool set up."

I press my lips in a thin line. I could see it, well, the best I can see is the vision behind it. Having both the plant-floral storefront could pull a different crowd, along with tattoos...

The niches seem so different, but in a way, could be a match made in heaven.

"Okay," I say cautiously. "I'm following the trend of this idea a bit, but it's a huge undertaking."

Callie nods as she finishes her bite of her pastry. "Will's already offered to help Reagan with the rent cost. What you and Reagan pay for, that won't kick in until business is up and running efficiently. And I've volunteered to dust off my master's in finance. I can help lay out a full budget, cost, and expenses plan for when you do start paying."

The hesitation of taking money from Lucie's brother must be written all over my face, because Luce squeezes my hand. "Don't even argue about that. You know my brother, he wants to help, and if it makes you feel better he'd be paying it even if it was just Reagan's business."

I guess that part is true. Will does have a history of spoiling his sisters, not that it's a bad thing, but I'm not one of his sisters, or Callie. I feel like I've been taking a lot of hand-outs lately, and I'm starting to feel a tad guilty about it.

Beck clears his throat. "I know I wasn't invited to girls' brunch, but you guys are getting my two cents anyway. I think it could be a really cool concept, but Jensen's had some crazy days, let her sit on it for a bit."

Lucie's smile turns downright cheesy. This brunch is giving her way too much ammunition to push her whole Beck agenda.

I try to reign her back in. "I definitely am interested, but some time to think about it would be appreciated. What about your other form of news that couldn't wait? What else is going on?"

Callie and Emma perk up for this one. "We're planning a wedding at the Blues stadium!" Emma beams.

"And I'm taking the pictures!" Callie claps her hands.

"Flowers!" Reagan mumbles, now eating her breakfast since we've moved on from shop talk.

Lucie shakes her head. "A small wedding! Between everyone and Miles, I'm afraid this is going to get way too big for what Dex and I want."

Now this is a topic I want to talk about. "Oh, my gosh, Luce! This is so exciting! When is this happening?"

Lucie sighs. "Well, we really just wanted to go down to City Hall, but Miles would be heartbroken if we didn't do something. So when Dex went down to talk to Olsson about playing again, he mentioned turning the team's Thanksgiving dinner into our wedding."

Beck pulls out his phone. "Hold on, when the hell did this all happen? I must have missed my Best Man text."

Lucie holds out her hands. "Look, this all popped up really fast. Dex and I wanted to talk to you two about it, but you know...other things were more important. But I swear we didn't mean to leave you completely out of this."

I squeeze Lucie's hand. "Oh, babe, please, don't worry about us. This is so exciting!"

Beck holds his phone up to his ear. "I have qualms, but not with you, Baby Mama—Dex, what the fuck is this about a wedding?"

Everyone else laughs as Beck walks away from the kitchen yelling at Dex over not immediately sharing this information.

I, however, hang my head as ,yet again, I ask myself, *Really, a crush on this guy?*

Lucie nudges my shoulder. "How are you two doing?"

Callie leans on the butcher block. "Please spare no details. He seemed all guard dog yesterday when we were moving you out. I swear, it was the first time I was semi-attracted to him."

"I'm sorry, did you hear him being bossy earlier?" Reagan asks, holding her hands up. "I sat right down, and I rarely do anything a man tells me to do."

"No, please, not this again. I'm pleading the fifth and guilty tripping you all with reminders of my stressful couple of days. I can't talk about this." I can't talk about how caring he is. I can't talk about his patience or protectiveness, and definitely zero discussions on his random bossy moments. Yeah, that's where the crush is coming from.

"Party pooper," Lucie whispers.

"Come on, Princess Peach, cuss at me if you're going to insult me."

Lucie lifts her chin. "Nope, won't give you the satisfaction."

"I, for one, am still pissed that I haven't heard her cuss." Reagan pushes back her now empty plate. "Her own sister!"

"I might be new here, but I didn't hear it." Emma shrugs.

"Me either, but I heard it was awesome," I say, nudging Luce.

Callie practically beams like she's the chosen one. "I heard it, and all trauma aside, I was so proud."

"And now Dex is the only one who hears it," Lucie says, to everyone's surprise.

"Oh, damn, Daddy Dex gets Naughty Lucie." I nudge her shoulder with props to her.

Lucie's face turns bright red but still laughs. "Enough of that nickname!"

Callie pushes her plate back next. "Oh, I'm so using that when submitting photos of him playing again."

"Don't you dare!" Lucie squeals.

"I feel like that's a nickname Beck would use, honestly," Emma says. "Maybe you two have more in common than it appears."

I don't even know what argument to start with that one. Beck feels like my absolute polar opposite, but then again I don't think it really matters how similar or different we are. There will never be a "we" for it to truly matter.

"Okay, now that that's sorted out," Beck says, coming back into the kitchen.

"Best man spot secured?" Callie lifts an eyebrow with her question.

He scoffs. "Obviously, I will also fully expect a maid of honor offer coming from you when your and Will's day comes."

Callie laughs. "Ha, you're a bridesmaid at best."

For the next twenty minutes, Callie and Beck argue over his role in her wedding, even though she and Will aren't even engaged.

Eventually, everyone hands their plates over to Beck, and while he puts them in the dishwasher, I walk the girls to the door where I'm bombarded with hugs and "love yous."

Before Reagan leaves, she sends me a text with an address. "For the storefront, at least come look at it before you make your final decision."

Sighing, I give her a nod. "Yeah, I can work that out some time this week."

Lucie doubles back even though she was the first one to hug me at the door. Her arms cross around the side of my neck. "It would be such a fun venture, Jen. Maybe I'll even come back for another tattoo, you know, after I pop out this baby."

"If the tattoo isn't *Daddy Dex*, then I'm not doing it."

Chapter 13
Beck

I swear it takes the girls ten minutes to say bye to Jensen and officially leave my house. I could tell that Jensen had zero desire to go out to brunch with them today, so as much as I wanted to just kick them out, I knew this had to be the compromise.

With the dishes loaded, I watch as Jensen finally closes my door and lets out the biggest sigh.

"They don't exactly leave well enough alone, do they?" I say.

Jensen's shoulders tense up. "No, they don't know the word subtle either. Sorry they barged their way in here."

"It's alright, they had good intentions at least." I try to keep my tone casual. "So, you want to do this with Reagan?"

"I don't know." Jensen brushes her hair behind her ears and walks over to my couch with Dottie on her heels. She falls back on the sofa and Dottie jumps up resting her head on Jensen's lap. After a few pets to Dottie's head, Jensen takes another deep breath. "I mean...the idea sounds incredible. Definitely takes out any issues Tally could potentially cause."

Okay, don't scare her away. She seems like she actually wants to talk about it.

I move slowly over to the spot on the couch next to her, but when I look at her I see the stress. I see the want, but also so much fear.

"Alright, then let's do it."

Jensen runs a hand over her face with a groan. "You can't say it like that, Beck."

"Like what?" I deflect. I know how that sounded and part of me wants to take it back, but damn, I want to help her have whatever she wants.

Jensen tosses her hands up. "Like it's a group decision. I don't know how else to say this, because I know you're trying to be supportive, but the choice to go through with this or not doesn't technically concern you."

I get that it doesn't—or, well, it shouldn't—concern me, but...it's Jensen. There's constantly what feels like this pit in my stomach, but when I'm around her it's not that bad. I know her moving in could lead to some dangerous territory, and I really should stop...but again, it's her.

I can't give her a relationship, even if she wanted it, but I can give her this. I don't have to be her knight in shining armor taking over everything, but I can help enough that she doesn't have to feel like it's going to consume her.

I hate that I'm about to use her current situation against her, but it's the card I have to play. "Okay, then what's your plan, Jen? Please fill me in on how you're going to find a new apartment, pay rent, work at Winedown, and figure out this store with Reagan."

Jensen pushes off from the couch, and Dottie jumps up,

becoming her shadow as she paces. "I don't know, Beck! Why do you get an answer, huh? I get that this is a weird situation, and I get that I've needed you a lot more than I normally do these past few days, but I am very capable. I made that insane rent raise work, didn't I? I can figure it all out on my own."

I almost laugh, because of course she can figure it out on her own, but she doesn't have to. Now to trick her into letting me do that.

Don't scare her, I remind myself.

I lean back on the couch, crossing my ankle over my knee. "You're right, you are capable of doing it on your own. You don't have to take my thoughts or input on it. I'm not owed an answer or plan, but what about your questions?"

Jensen stops her pacing. "W-what questions?"

"Your thoughts on this, Jen. Your pros and cons. I'm not saying plan because the plan isn't even on the table right now. Your whys for even wanting to do this. Talk it out with me, let me be your neutral party. I'll play devil's advocate or just listen, if that will be more helpful."

I'm not entirely sure what emotion crosses her face, but when she lets out a breath, she whispers, "That's what I usually call my sister for."

"Do you want to call your sister?" I offer with a shrug. Doesn't have to be me, but I don't want her stressing herself out.

She bites at her lip and shakes her head. "No, I guess you'll work."

I try to maintain my giddy, but it slips through a bit as I pat the spot of the couch she vacated. "Come on, Jenni-cakes, let's get into it."

She groans, but does what I say. "You're going to make me regret this, aren't you?"

"Not my intention, I only want to help." I pat the middle space between us next for Dottie to lie down. "Okay, let's say you want to go in with Reagan, what would you need to do next?"

"Well, a combination of things, I guess." Jensen groans. "A lot of things would need to happen all at once, essentially."

"That's a bit dramatic," I tease, only to spark a bit of that spite in her.

"I'm not being dramatic! I have the required licenses, but I'll have to get with Reagan on the building inspections, get with the health department—not to mention, the things that I would need for it to be a functioning shop. If I went and worked at someone else's place, I would be responsible for my ink, my machine, and other small things, but with this I'm responsible for all of it. Every little detail."

Nodding along as she talks, I work on a mental list. "Okay, so, from the way Reagan talks about her job—she's not fucking around with her side of the business. I imagine she's got the connections and plans for all things the health and state departments could throw at you guys. Cals has you on the financial side, she'd love to use that degree for something she believes in. So, the bright side is, none of those aspects you'll have to navigate alone.

"Now, to play the devil's advocate...Reagan is strong-willed. I don't imagine she'd be the easiest to work with, but you're not exactly a pushover, Killer." I nudge her as she rolls her eyes. "Off the pitch, do you think you could work with Reagan?"

"I can't believe I'm actually talking this out with you."

Jensen pulls her knees up to her chest and sighs. "Yeah, I think we'd be fine. I know Reagan can be a bit of a bitch, but she's also smart and business-minded. Once settled, our roles would be so hands-off on the other's thing, I don't see us not staying in our own lanes moving forward."

"Okay, that solves that problem pretty easily. Now, as for your setup—what do you have already?"

"I have all the basics." She shrugs.

I tilt my head. "Are you this tight-lipped when talking to your sister? I got to say, I may have a new apprec—"

"Okay, fine," Jensen cuts me off while running her hands through her hair. "Okay, let me try to do this without spiraling. Doing this with Reagan means a really high up-front cost. Getting all the furniture, complete set up, not to mention maintaining and growing my ink supply. Then there's a ton of other small things to stay on top of: needles, skin wraps, Vaseline, rubbing alcohol, the list is long. I'll probably need another pen based on design needs. Then there's stuff I would need for piercings."

Jensen takes a deep breath, her spiral clearly starting so I wait.

"There's stuff I would still be responsible for whether I went and worked at an already established place, but I'd owe them rent and have to work with their policies. I'd have a lot more creative freedom and control of how things are run with Reagan, but I'd still technically owe her rent too. The bright side would be, if it grows enough, I could hire more artists and supplement some of that with their booth rent."

"And you don't have to worry about convincing anyone differently about whatever bullshit your old place is spreading."

Jensen nods slowly. "True, they could also try to cause

some sort of stink if they find out I'm opening a place on my own, but I don't foresee that really being a big issue."

Dottie rolls over on her back forcing a small laugh out of Jensen. She scratches her stomach with the slightest smile on her face.

Humph. Smart dog. I was just about to attempt to get the same things out of her.

"Do you want to do it? That's one thing we haven't talked about. Do you even want to do this with Reagan? Once you start there won't be any stopping it."

Jensen's hand slows on Dottie's pets. "I think I do," she whispers.

"Sorry, Jenni-cakes, there can't be a 'think' here. You don't have to know how it will work out, but you have to know if you want it or not."

"It's not that simple, Beck. For you, maybe it is, but for me, there's still that huge upfront cost. If I do this, it means taking out loans and busting my ass a whole lot more at Winedown for all my bills."

"Now, if we're talking money, I can—"

"No, Beck, you said you wanted to talk this out, fine, but I can't accept any more of your money."

I can't help but laugh. "Why not? Please give me one good reason not to."

"Because I'm already so indebted to you."

Jensen hits me when I make a buzzer noise.

"Beck!"

"What? That's not a good reason. Try again."

"It is too a good reason. You said you'd do what you've done for me in the past twenty-four hours for Lucie or Callie if they needed it, but this—essentially funding a whole business—is a step too far."

I open my mouth to argue but quickly shut it. She's got a point, maybe I am taking this all a little too far, but it's something she wants—something she'd be amazing at—and the only real hesitation she has is monetary. I can fix that.

I take a deep breath and think over my next wording carefully. "I see your point, but on the other—"

I don't finish my sentence before Jensen's off the couch. "No, no buts, no other hands or whatever you were going to say. I can figure it out on my own. We're roommates—I've taken enough of your money, any more and that's me walking the line of taking advantage of you."

"Oh, bullshit." Now I'm up. "That's the most ridiculous thing I've ever heard. You are not *taking advantage* of me. Think of this as an opportunity, Jensen, take the fucking opportunity."

She scoffs. "An opportunity? An opportunity for who? Beck, this isn't an 'us' thing, it needs to be me."

"It can be you, you're missing the whole point. I get you want this for yourself. Hell, I want it for you too. If this is about what you brought up earlier..." I can't say for certain why Jensen brought up that she didn't want a cookie-cutter relationship, and I hate that we were interrupted before we could talk more about it anymore. "This is quite literally the opposite of me wanting you to put your career on hold. I want to help start it now."

Jensen's face turns bright red. She holds her hands up. "Okay, that has nothing to do with this. I just wanted to establish...*boundaries*."

I raise an eyebrow. "You don't sound so sure of that."

She throws her hands up. "You know what I mean, Beck."

"Can't say I do. Had we not gotten interrupted I think I

might've figured it out, but now you're going to have to spell it out for me."

Jensen snorts as she shakes her head. "I'm not doing this."

"Great, then you'll take my offer to let me pay for this stuff." I smile as she grits her jaw. "Glad we could come to that agreement."

"You're so full of it. God, would you listen for five seconds? I am not taking more of your money!"

"I don't need five seconds to listen, I've been doing that already. What I'm hearing is no good reason not to. You'll stay here—rent free, because why the hell not? I have empty rooms, use one. I have money to pay for this, so fucking *use it.*"

Jensen threads her hands through her hair, I swear she's about to pull it out and I know she's so close to caving.

"Unless you can give me a legitimate answer then I'm not giving this up."

Jensen lets out a muffled scream. "I can't believe I have a freaking crush on you, you're insufferable!"

Holy shit. Did I hear that right? My smile grows and there's no stopping it. "You have a what on me?"

Jensen seems to replay what she just said through her head. She holds up a finger. "Nope. No way. Forget I said anything. I'm serious."

"You have a *crush* on me?" I take slow steps to her, but she matches with double the number of steps back.

"No, Beck, I don't want to date you."

I want to agree with her, but I'm too happy right now. Perfectly content basking in this confession. "I knew you secretly liked me, I'm too lovable not to."

Jensen retreats all the way to the stairs. "This is done, we're done talking."

I laugh. "Oh, we're far from done."

Jensen clenches her jaw as she takes the first step up. "Follow me up these stairs, Beckham, and I'll push you back down them."

I should stop, I know I should, but this is too big. I can't stop smiling. "I love it when you flirt with me."

Steam practically comes out of Jensen's ears. "Come on, Dottie!" she yells as she hurries up the stairs.

Dottie hops from the couch, pausing at my feet, torn whether to follow or stay. "You fighting this is only hurting her. Be an adult and come kiss and make up with me," I holler after her.

"Fuck you," Jensen yells from the top of the stairs. "Dottie, come," she commands sharply again.

When I give Dottie a nod, she prances up the stairs after Jensen. I wait another ten seconds then hear her bedroom door slam.

Holy hell. Jensen James has a crush on me. I did not see that coming.

I chuckle at the thought like a damn schoolboy, but when my phone starts to buzz on the counter my joy dies at the name on my screen.

Torn between sending it to voicemail and ignoring it completely, I know I would hate myself even more to get a text following this that things have taken a turn.

"Hello," I answer, clipped.

I hold my breath until my dad replies, "Hey, son, everything's fine...I just wanted to check on you."

I let my breath go. Part of me wants to rage at him, but I just can't. "That could've been a text, you know?"

"One you'd answer?" he asks soberly.

"Unsure, I think I'm a little rusty on fighting with you. Was I the weird kid growing up? I hardly remember arguing with you."

A nervous chuckle comes through the phone. "Can't say you were normal, but wouldn't say weird—just a damn good kid."

"Yeah, well, what do we do now, huh?"

Silence hangs, and even through the phone it's palpable. I feel like I'm on the verge of sweating and there's this damn lump forming in my throat. How we left things between us sucks. I hate it, but I need him to at least try to see why I made this decision.

The crush revelation from Jensen felt so good. I know what I feel for her is dangerous, even more than I care to admit. If I think about it, I could see how fun and entertaining a future with her would be. The type of future that I know my dad wants for me, but then I also see the pain and burden I could potentially put on her...it makes me physically ill to think about.

A heavy sigh sounds. "I don't know. I don't like this either. I know it probably seems like an overreaction, but... Beck, come on, why are you doing this to yourself?"

"Dad, not again. I can't do round two of this conversation. It's not like I'm completely alone. I have friends. I have my team. I'll play this game until they force me off the field. I'm good with that, why can't you be too?"

"Could you just try?" he pleads. "Try to find that happiness that I know you deserve. I'm begging you, *please*, just try. If you don't change your mind after, then I'll stop. But I feel like you're giving up on something amazing and it's killing me."

From high highs to low lows.

"Dad—"

"You never give up on things, Beckham, never. Please don't give up on yourself. I can't lose you too."

His pleas send fighting waves of anger and pure agony through me. Is that why he's clinging to this so much? He thinks he's losing me? I don't know what to say, but suddenly my chest feels like it's on fire. That panic attack I pushed off is coming back in full force.

Taking off my glasses, I toss them on the counter then lean on the edge to stay up right. Finding a little bit of composure, I push through. "You're not losing me, Dad."

"Tell me, son, were those your glasses that hit the table?" When I don't answer, he huffs. "Even through the phone, I know your tell."

Dammit, dammit, dammit. The pain in my chest intensifies, and I swear my house is getting smaller. "I can't do this. If you want to check up on me, next time text."

I hang up before he can respond, and immediately go weak in the knees.

I try to steady my breathing, but fuck, I'm practically frozen. There's no stopping the panic, I'm being consumed by it now.

"Beck?"

I'm fairly positive I hear my name, but it also could be a hallucination because I'm sure the ground is going to fall out from under me any second.

And then it does with a blur of black and white, there's something wet assaulting my face then sending me back on my ass.

"Beck," the voice says sharper this time. With the blur

moved away, I feel soft hands resting on mine. "Beckham, hey, it's okay. Take a deep breath."

I try but can't. The hands come to my cheeks and gently lift my head up. Jensen's face suddenly becomes a little bit clearer.

"Jensen?" I croak out between breaths.

"Yeah, it's me. I think you're having a panic attack, so I need you to listen and breathe with me, okay?"

I nod the best I can.

"Okay, I'm going to count through it. Breathe in for one... two...three...four."

I try to follow her directions by holding it for another four then out for four, but fuck, it's hard. Jensen counts through a couple more times before I get a better hang of it and she gets less blurry.

Her hands let go of my face. "Feeling better?"

"Uh, yeah," I whisper. I look around my place, everything as spacious as it could be, even though moments ago I swore it was caving in.

Dottie licks my face again, bringing a very forced laugh out of me.

Jensen pulls her back. "Dot, space, please."

"It's alright." I pet Dottie's head then behind her ear as she tilts her head into my hand. I don't make a single move to get up and neither does Jensen. "Thank you," I say looking up at her. "It came on so fast."

"It's okay." Jensen sits up off her knees then settles right back down crisscross like she's settling in to sit here with me for however long it takes. "Do you usually get panic attacks?"

"I... uh...used to." I clear my throat. I don't think I've ever talked about this with anyone before besides my dad. "They started after my mom's diagnosis, but I haven't had one like that in the past two years."

Jensen hums softly. "Wanna talk about it?"

"No," I blurt out, because I truly don't think I can talk about it. But looking at her, I feel like the biggest hypocrite in the world because I've forced her to talk things out for the past two days.

She nods. "You know I planned on hiding in my room then sneaking out for my shift at Winedown in a couple of hours, but when Dottie started whining and scratching at my door...I don't know, I could just feel something was wrong."

I let out a humph in amusement, the corners of my mouth threaten a smile, but a lot of energy feels drained. "Jensen?"

"Yeah?"

"I know you're supposed to work, but any chance you could get someone to cover? I think we both need a lazy day."

I wait for her to say no, but instead she smiles. "Let me see what I can do."

Chapter 14
Jensen

I'm not entirely sure what willed me out of my room. I slammed the door with such determination to not leave, but then with Dottie whining and scratching at the door—something deep in my gut told me I needed to swallow whatever of my pride was left and go check on Beck.

I could only hear his side and the end of the call, but the moment he went down to his knees my heart broke.

I know I shouldn't take off today, but Beck was strong for me yesterday. Crush confession of this morning aside, I owe it to be here for him today.

Finally getting up from the floor, Beck snaps Dottie's leash on. "I'll take her out real quick."

"I can do that," I protest, but Beck holds a hand up.

"I think some fresh air will do me some good." He raises an eyebrow. "Greet us when we get back?"

Well, at least his flirty side isn't completely lost to me today. "Don't push it."

I stand rooted in my spot until the front door closes

completely. Today has been an absolute ride. Frankly, I have zero clue what's going to happen next.

A lazy day with Beck could be a step toward some very dangerous territory, but I can't think of anything more I want to do today.

That is if I can get off work. Moving over to the couch, I pull out my phone and send a text to Mia.

> I know this isn't a good look considering I took off yesterday, but is there any way someone could cover for me today?

MIA

> I can make it work. No worries, my girl.

> Really? Are you sure?

> Jensen, you've worked here the entire time I've been here and never called out once. I think you're owed some vacation days.

Well, that was easier than expected. Not to mention, a good point made—I do deserve some time off. As tangled up as my stomach feels, I need this lazy day.

Shooting back up from the couch, I march right into Beck's kitchen and start raiding the pantry and fridge. I pull out every possible snack and junk-ish food I can find.

For him being a pro athlete, I'm pleasantly surprised at the findings. An assortment of chips, cookies, a jumbo bag of Sour Patch Kids, Cheez-Its, some beef jerky sticks, Nutella, and the best find...

"No way," I say, just as the front door opens.

"What the hell happened here?" Beck asks, looking at the stuff I've piled up on the island.

I shut the cabinet and hold the jar in my hand.

"Beckham Daines has weed gummies in his kitchen cabinet. What would your coach say about this?" I fake judgment.

Beck laughs as he hangs Dottie's leash on one of the hooks by the door. "He'd say it's legal, and the offseason."

"This is a lazy day essential, right?"

Beck nods with his eyes closed and the corners of his mouth tugging upward. "Oh yeah, it's a necessity at this point. Did you get someone to cover your shift?"

"Yeah, Mia said she's got it."

"Sweet, so get two gummies out, Killer, we're starting our lazy day."

By the end of *The Nightmare Before Christmas* the gummies have officially kicked in. I've completely taken over the majority of the couch. Lying back, I've got my feet up with Dottie sleeping next to my legs. Beck's leaned back on the other side, his glasses are back on and his feet are propped on the coffee table.

"Smash or pass, Jack Skellington?" I say as the credits roll.

Beck doesn't hesitate. "Smash. Sally?"

My eyes stay locked on the screen as I tilt my head side to side, weighing my options. "Yeah, yeah, smash. I'd be their third."

"And who would judge you?" Beck starts to laugh, which in turn makes me laugh.

"I don't know. Some people just don't get it."

A long, drawn-out sigh comes from Beck. "No, they really don't."

The question of why he stopped laughing is on the tip of my tongue, but then my phone rings on the table. "Ah, it's my sister. She's FaceTiming me."

Beck pulls out his phone next. "You answer that, and I'm going to DoorDash us a ridiculous amount of food."

"Oh god, please order chicken tenders."

Beck looks at me like I'm dumb. "Of course I'm going to get chicken tenders and a shit ton of wings."

"Ooo, hot ones, please."

He waves me off. "I know what to do, answer the phone."

Without hesitation, I lift my foot up pushing his bicep before sitting up and answering. "Helloooo, Stella."

And from that alone, my sister is well aware of my predicament. "Jensen James, are you high right now?"

"I..." My mouth opens—and frankly doesn't shut, not even to form a response.

Beck snorts. "Busted."

I kick his side this time. "Shut up, you are too."

My sister sighs. "Who's that?"

Beck reaches over taking my phone. "Hey, I'm Beck, your sister's new roommate," he says, then hands it right back.

A small beat of silence sits, and suddenly I can't remember if I told Stella about anything that's happened over the last two days.

"Roommate? Beck, as in the baseball player is your roommate?"

Okay, yep definitely haven't told her. "So, funny story, well, it feels more funny now, but anyway—Charlie went major creep mode after I made the astronomical rent raise. He told me I had to get rid of Dottie and that sure as shit wasn't happening."

"No, obviously we'd get rid of Dottie over our dead bodies," Stella agrees.

With her name being mentioned, Dottie's head perks up in the middle of Beck and me. Beck leans down to plant a kiss on her head before adding some pets.

"Stella gets it, doesn't she, Dot?"

Stella snorts through the phone. "So, you've moved in with Beck? I'm following this train, right?"

"You're on the right track," Beck says so casually, like this isn't the first time he's talked to my sister. I know we're in a bit of a different state of mind right now, but I don't think Beck would be talking any differently without the gummies.

"Sort of moved in. Temporarily," I add. Shit, are my hands sweating? I feel like I'm on the verge of getting a lecture. Stella is well aware of my *complicated* feelings toward Beck. She's seen this play out before—well, not exactly, but the whole dangerous territory I should be walking away from...yeah, Stella is always the one holding my hand when I'm doing the walk of shame back.

"Right, of course it's temporary." *Yep, she doesn't believe me.*

"Who doesn't want it to be temporary is Dottie." Beck ruffles her back and she barks happily, hopping off the couch to play when Beck pulls out one of her rope toys.

"Jennie," my sister interrupts, taking my attention away from watching them.

"Hmm, yeah?"

"You're smiling," she says with what I can only assume is a bigger smile than mine was.

"I'm impaired, Stel. Not all of us are chill and mellowed out like you."

My sister chuckles. "Okay, sure blame it on the gummy, that's fine."

My eyes flash to Beck, but he's still playing with Dottie.

I'm not entirely sure how much of his attention is sneakily on our conversation, so a topic change needs to be made. "You called forrrr?"

Stella makes a *tsk* sounds, while shaming me with her fingers.

"I'll hang up on you."

"I was just calling to check up on you. Your silence in the family chat makes sense now, all things considered."

I glance at Beck again, I swallow hard. "Yeah, it's been something. Where are Mom and Dad now?"

Stella closes her eyes thinking. "I want to say one of the Dakotas, could be Wyoming...I haven't looked at Mom's location yet today."

Our parents could not be more opposite people if they tried, but the love they have for each other is downright obnoxious. So in love that even though Mom hates all things outdoorsy, she's on a six-month-long road trip with our father because it was his dream to go camping in every state. Granted, she had some stipulations of her own.

"Well, one of us ought to." I swipe up on the screen pulling up our group chat then clicking on the maps. "Wyoming is the winner. I can't believe she agreed to this."

"I can't believe it's lasted a whole month. I was ready to put money down that Dad was pulling an elaborate joke on her."

"Yeah, I think you and Mom both. Neither of you helped while he was planning it. He had maps and red strings connecting the stops. It looked like he was either planning or solving a murder."

Stella snorts a laugh. "Him and maps. They're using a GPS!"

"He's a physical planner person!"

"Like father, like daughter. I guess that entire notebook full of budgeting and life planning you have will need some adjusting, or has it completely gone out the window? Can I do a tarot reading now?"

Beck sits straight up. "Can I see this life planning notebook?"

"No," I say immediately, then send Stella the evil eye. "Thanks for calling, as you can see I'm fine. I'll call you later."

"Noooo," Beck whines. "I'm sorry, I'll stop eaves-dropping."

Of course he was listening, I should have known his nosy ass would.

"Bye, Stel."

"Talk so soon, Jennie," my sister says before her face disappears from the screen.

Dropping my phone on the couch, I huff. Yep, I'll be hearing a lot about this, but she does have a good point about my planner. Maybe mapping out some moves for opening the tattoo shop would help make it easier for me to make decisions on my own.

Definitely don't need to fall into Beck's charms and talk to him about it more. Not that I'm any good at that anyway—clearly.

"I like that your sister calls you Jennie." Beck leans back resting an elbow on the back of the couch. "But I have to say, y'all don't look anything alike."

Not the first time I've heard that, and it won't be the last, I'm sure. Stella's face is full of freckles and has bright blonde hair that she just added lavender highlights to. "Well, she is my adopted sister."

"No shit, really?" Beck asks in an amazed tone that has

me chuckling. He turns his head up to the ceiling. "You know, if I wanted kids, I'd adopt."

My heart pounds in my chest because that is exactly what I want. I don't want to be pregnant, my tokophobia has had me reeling on this since I can remember.

Beck laughs again. "I mean, really, that's my only option since I've had a vasectomy."

Holy shit. Holy shit.

"You've had a what?"

Heart beating louder. Heart might burst out of my chest.

He turns to me with a curious look. "A vasectomy. You know..." He closes his fingers together like scissors, and that dies down the heartbeat a bit.

"I know what a vasectomy is, Beckham. I'm shocked to learn you've had one. Can't say I ever expected to hear you say that."

He shrugs. "I guess it's not something I've ever really talked about before. No regrets on my end."

My mouth opens then shuts. I don't know what to say. My brain is absolutely reeling. Beck doesn't want kids? Or, well, would adopt if he did...

"But you always seem so into kids. Miles adores you, and you're so good with him."

Beck gives me his signature smile. "I knew you liked watching me, Jennie."

I kick his shoulder for the third time.

"So aggressive." He fakes a pout, then smiles again. "I love Miles, and I love the idea of kids. I have other reasons, but kids aren't a guarantee I see in my future. If that changes, then there are other options."

The silence sits between us while I fully let what he's said sink in. Holy shit. He doesn't want to have kids. He can't have kids actually. I could sleep with him and have zero fear of getting pregnant.

Something about that revelation does something to me. I spent years trying to explain my fear of pregnancy to my ex. I don't think there has ever been a time I've truly enjoyed sex because of that fear looming over my head.

"I have tokophobia," I say to him more confidently than I've ever said to anyone. "An extreme fear of childbirth. Stella was actually my best friend growing up. Our moms were best friends, the whole nine yards."

The look on Beck's face nearly has me stopping there but I want to talk to him. I don't know what he's done to me, but every time I'm around him, he brings out something new that I just can't help it.

"We were nine when her mom had a surprise pregnancy. I remember all of it." I swallow down the lump quickly forming in my throat. "Um, neither of them made it through childbirth."

Beck sighs. "Jen—"

I just want to get it all out, so I continue. "The fear started after that, and I know it seems like I had some separation to the situation, but with everything Stella went through... Her dad couldn't cope with the trauma—it was bad, so the fear really solidified with the aftermath."

I prep myself to hear all the sympathies and rationalities that I've been met with before, but again, Beck surprises me.

"I got my vasectomy a year after the doctor told us that there's a chance I could have early-onset too."

"Really?" I try to keep the question more inquisitive than judgmental. I don't need him to rationalize with me and I'm sure he feels the same.

"Yeah." Beck pats the couch for Dottie to hop back up.

He pets her slowly and deep inside something tells me he's never told anyone this before. "I've been told there's never a guarantee. I've been lectured on all the things to do that could help prevent it. I've been to therapy for it, but at the end of the day there is no guarantee, so I made one for myself. If it's genetics, then I can control my future ones. I don't need a kid to have my DNA to love it any differently."

Oh my lord, this freaking man. I relate to so much of what he just said. All the therapy sessions helped me have the tools to cope with the fear—for example, with Lucie—but I also heard countless statistics about women who were fine giving birth. I was told to just get over it by my ex and for a while I tried.

But then here comes Beck Daines with the emotional intelligence of my three-degree holding therapist. I feel seen for the first time and that wasn't even his intention. This is not good. I'm so screwed.

Beck blows out a breath. "Well, that got deep real fast."

This day has been nothing but whiplash and these gummies are not helping...

Or maybe they are.

Beck squeezes my shin. "So, because I *so* wasn't listening...you mentioned something about your parents in Wyoming?"

"I knew you were." I *tsk*. "They're on a six-month-long camping trip. It's my dad's biggest bucket list item for him to complete before he turns sixty. He wants to do a few nights in every state."

"That's pretty cool. I like that." Beck leans deeper into the couch. "Can't say I want to do that, but I like the idea."

"Mom hates the idea, but she's doing it. She had some major stipulations, though."

Beck snorts a laugh. "Oh, yeah?"

"They must travel in an RV, no tent sleeping, and to conclude all fifty states they go to resorts in Alaska and Hawaii."

"Resorts aren't camping."

"That was Dad's argument, but essentially, beggars can't be choosers. I think my parents are the most polar opposite people in the world, but they make it work. Mom sweetened the deal with the RV, promising she'd make all of our Aubela's recipes any time he asked. Mind you, six months in an RV...I think her resort requests are justified."

Beck nods. "Alright, alright, I'm following the compromises. What would you want to do?" Beck's hand lands softly on my thigh, his thumb gliding back and forth slowly.

"W-what?" I nearly choke on the air and my heart beats faster. This isn't fair. Even with the sweatpants separating his skin from mine, I can feel his warmth. It seemed like a mindless movement on his part, and yet the touch vibrates through me.

"What's your big bucket list item? What's in that planner Stella mentioned for before you turn sixty?"

"Oh, um..." I hadn't ever really thought about that before. My plans have changed so much over the past year, let alone the past few days. "I think Stella might be right in throwing the whole plan out. I'm getting a little tired of planning for it to just implode in my face."

"Yeah, maybe that's a good idea." Beck's thumb glides back and forth. It's a small thing, and I never considered myself someone whose love language is touch, but these soft ones Beck gives me make me want more.

Just as the thought crosses my mind, he pulls back. His hand goes to his face lifting his glasses as he pinches the bridge of his nose. "You know, I'm going to take Dottie out again. We'll be back."

"Right," I clip out, pulling my knees up to my chest. I wait for the door to shut before I let out my breath. "I'll be here, I guess."

Chapter 15
Jensen

"I can't believe I'm doing your wedding nails!" Lucie's nail tech pulls her hand in with the brightest gleam in her eyes.

Lucie filled both Elle and Kylie, our nail techs, in the moment we walked in the door. Elle promised Lucie she had a vision for them a couple months ago, and despite Lucie swearing it wouldn't be anytime soon—here we are.

Kylie takes a file to my nail with a snort. "I'm thinking of yours next, practically manifesting baseball babes so we can live vicariously through you both forever."

I raise my free hand flashing Kylie my middle finger. "You know the rules. I already filled you in with what's happened, that's all you're getting."

I set a *no Beck talk* at these appointments months ago. Although they seem to forget and I have to shut it down every time.

I allowed Lucie one joke about me and Beck splitting up the Larsen household. Beck, Dottie, Dex, and Miles all went to the training facility while I met Lucie here for our standing nail appointment. The debrief it led to was more Beck talk than I can handle during girl time.

Kylie scoffs. "I didn't say who—pick anyone else on the team. Hell, you could get with the team photographer if it falls through with the pitcher."

Lucie laughs. "As cute as a couple Jensen and Callie would be, my brother is ring shopping as we speak."

My head whips to Lucie. "Is he really? That's so exciting!"

"Yep, he's already messaged our group chat fifteen times. Apparently, there aren't any rings good enough in the entire city of Boston."

Elle pauses, looking up from Lucie's hand. "Well, that is just adorable."

"Isn't it?" Lucie pulls out her phone, her thumb typing slowly. "God bless him, he brought Adam along, who apparently also agrees that no ring is good enough. I'm going to meet him at one store after this to help before my doctor's appointment."

Why am I not surprised? Adam gives Will hell on the daily, why would he think bringing him shopping for his sister's engagement ring would go smoothly?

"So, when is he going to ask her? Her birthday?"

"No, he's waiting until Opening Day at the stadium. A little rewriting of some bad memories, I suppose." Lucie drops her phone. "I was thinking of throwing them an engagement party after, do you think we could rent out the upstairs bar at Winedown?"

"I'm sure. I can talk to Mia about it."

Even if I'm dreading the idea of working tonight, I have to go. I need space from being around Beck. I don't want it, but it's for the freaking best.

Our lazy day yesterday ended on such a weird note. When he came back in with Dottie we started another movie then ate our food in silence.

The weirdest part was that our silence didn't exactly feel awkward. It wasn't our norm by any means. I definitely wouldn't call it comfortable silence either. It just felt like there was this pink elephant in the corner, and we were a little too impaired to address it.

"Speaking of work—kind of..." Lucie segues. "Have you thought about the offer to do your own shop with Reagan?"

I blow out a breath. "Sort of...now, no one say anything, but I did talk to Beck about it yesterday."

The looks the three of them exchange say enough, but Lucie swallows down her giddy the best she can. "Oh yeah, how'd that go?"

Horrible. Embarrassing. I'm just waiting for my crush confession to be thrown back in my face, but I'm hoping yesterday's talks might overshadow that small part a little bit.

"It was fine. I can't say I can make it work, but Reagan mentioned I could look at the space this week. I might also call Callie and see if she can help me crunch some numbers."

Lucie nods, folding her lips together to fight her smile. "Great. I have no additional questions."

"Good," I say snarkily, knowing she's most definitely lying, but I know her questions are not related to Reagan or Callie at all.

Lucie does her best for the rest of the appointment to let go every mention I make of Beck. That is until we step one foot onto the sidewalk.

"Okay, I have to ask—"

I hold my hand up, cutting her off. "You get one question."

"Four," she counters.

"Luce—"

She grabs my arm. "Okay, three, pleaseeee?"

"Does that count?"

"Nope." She smiles. "First one, are you okay? I know this has been a lot for you, and from what Dex's told me, Beck's not exactly having the easiest time with his family right now. If you need to stay with us, just know our door is always open."

There's a pain in my chest. "Luce, you've been screaming for me to give Beck a chance for months—I didn't think this would be your first question."

Lucie waves her hand. "Oh, I'm still planning our future where we all share a penthouse floor like our own little MLB compound, but I'm always Team Jensen first."

Yeah, this is exactly why I let her get away with all her pestering. "You really are the best, you know that, right?"

Lucie smiles brightly. "Hold on to that feeling."

"Touché." I lock my arm in hers as we walk down the sidewalk. "Honestly, I don't know what I am. I can't decide if I want to pack all my bags and get out of his place as quickly as possible... Or say screw it and just take up his offer to move in more long term while I make things work with Reagan."

"I could see that. Living with someone you're attracted to is rough. I mean, just look at me, I speak from experience."

My laugh comes naturally. I could lie and say I don't find Beck attractive, but Lucie would 100 percent call me out on it.

"It's more than that, though. It's a lot harder to blow him off. He was getting under my skin in passing enough, but..." I trail off, unsure of how to even describe that I feel the most like myself around Beck.

It's like I've reached this threshold of time with him and all my perfectly placed guards have come crumbling down.

"But?" Lucie squeezes my arm.

"If you want me to answer, that counts as one of your questions."

Lucie purses her lips. "Okay, deal."

Ah, hell. I should've known.

I groan softly. "It's just—he does all these things. Especially over the past several days, it's like every interaction with him turns in his favor. He should be annoying, right? He's been obnoxiously hitting on me since we met, but don't freak out when I say this...I think I really like him."

Lucie attempts to not freak—she tries her best not to, at least. Her eyes practically bug out but her squeal is moderately contained. "Okay, great, love to hear that out loud. Totally cool, no biggie. Um, new question, to help me move on, why are you saying that like it's a bad thing?"

"Because it is a bad thing, Luce! I can't—not right now. And that was your last question, so that's all you're going to get for now."

Lucie's eye practically twitches as she squeaks out, "Okay." She swallows hard, and I can only imagine she's trying to think of ways she can trick me into talking more about this. "To recap, we officially have feelings for Beck, but liking him is bad for reasons unknown."

"Reasons I know," I say smugly.

Lucie squeals again except this one has a hint of frustration in it. "Right, right, okay, well, I'm going to go help my brother look at rings, then go to my baby's first doctor's appointment. I probably won't be thinking about this conversation at all."

I pause in front of her car. "Of course you won't. I'll let you have three more questions at your wedding."

"Do I get bonus ones if I send you pictures of the baby?"

I shrug. "Eh, we'll see."

I don't think I've had three days off in a row since I moved to Boston a year ago. Apparently, it's affected me more than I realize because this shift is kicking my ass. With my past call outs, I seemed to have started a bit of a chain reaction. Two of our other bartenders sent Mia a text right as their shift started that they would not be coming in.

I told Mia I could handle it and she's helped where she can, but I'm starting to eat my words.

My feet are killing me, my patience is shot, and if one more person orders a Manhattan, I'm going to lose my marbles.

"Stirred, not shaken," every man in a suit has snapped at me tonight. I don't know what fuckboy finance convention is in town, but that must be the signature drink.

Mia moves around behind me in the bar restocking some of the liquor bottles. "Christ, what is in the air tonight?"

"Apparently, whiskey and a whole lot of bitters," I grumble. "The next finance douchebag that complains he doesn't like the shape of our cocktail glasses is getting his drink poured on his head."

Mia snorts. "Hey, I support women's rights and wrongs. I didn't see anything."

Leaning on the back bar next to her I take a deep breath and try to find my bearings. "Mia, are you seriously wearing heels? Please, tell me you haven't been wearing them all night."

Mia grabs a near-empty bottle of vodka from the mid-shelf, then looks down at her black square-toe heels. "To be honest, I kind of forgot I had them on. I'm pretty sure I lost feeling in my feet years ago. I'm good."

My feet hurt from just the look of them alone. We're a pretty classy bar, so with my white button up and black dress pants I appear polished from the bar, but you best believe I'm wearing comfortable shoes.

"Okay, I'm going to ask a question and your answer could very much piss me off. Are you even remotely tired, sore, any degree of pain really?"

Mia tilts her head up. "Um, not really...I mean—"

"Fuck you." I wave her off at first but then look at those heels again. "What do you mean you don't want to kick those shoes off?"

Mia scrunches her nose. "I don't know what to say! Image is huge to my parents, they had me in suit dresses and heels by the time I was eight. It's my normal!"

"That sounds miserable. I would feel bad for you, but then I remember how much my feet hurt—and I'm wearing appropriate shoes."

Mia steps around me with ease. "Well, how about I make it up to you by helping you cover the bar." Mia points to the other side. "Loverboy's here to see you."

Spinning slowly, I find Beck sitting on a stool with those freaking slutty glasses on his face and a Blues ball cap. Offseason Beck is just next level hot, it's ridiculous.

He sends me a flirty wave as I make my way over to him. "Hi, roomie, miss me today?"

Yes, and no. I tried my absolute damndest to not think about him at all actually. I lucked out by missing him on my way to work. Dottie was the only one to greet me when I got back from the nail salon, and rather than texting, Beck left a note on the counter to let me know he was going to meet up with Adam and Will.

"I didn't realize ring shopping was such a huge group decision."

"I inserted myself." Beck shrugs.

Of course he did. "How long before Will kicked you out?"

"About half an hour. I took Adam and Lucie down with me too. Will was overthinking it, fifteen minutes later and the decision was made. It had to be done."

I *humph* a bit of a laugh. I can see it all playing out now, Beck pestering the shit out of Will until he breaks. It doesn't surprise me at all that Beck knew that was what he needed. Anyone could say whatever they wanted about Beck, but a bad friend is a straight lie.

To prove my point even more, a small s'mores power bar slides across the bar. "I got you that and..." He sets a Red Bull and a bottle of water in front of him. "Lucie said I wasn't allowed to give you the energy drink until you finished the water, but I'm here to enable you." Beck slides my lifeline in a pink can across the bar top then follows it up with the water. "Just drink this at some point to appease her."

"I make no promises." Grabbing the can, I crack it open and take a huge gulp.

"Is it just me or are there a shit ton of guys in suits here tonight? Is it some fraternity reunion or something?"

I nearly spit out the drink, but force it down in a way that burns in my chest. "Not too far off. Our best guess has been a finance convention or some shit, but I like your reunion take. They're all ordering fucking Manhattans, then being real dicks about reminding me to stir it."

"The fuck they are," Beck growls.

I wave him off. "It's fine, I've had worse nights, it's just me and half of Mia manning the bar tonight that's all."

"Want some help?"

I quirk an eyebrow, but don't get a chance to respond with Mia coming up. "Okay, so sorry, but that's all of a break I can give you tonight. I've got someone demanding to speak to a manager, and Alex upstairs is crying over a broken glass."

My eyes nearly roll out of my head. "She breaks a glass every time she gets behind the bar. I swear, she does it on purpose."

Mia shakes her head. "I know, but we had no choice. Someone has to be back there. I'll come back down here when I can."

"I can help Jensen down here," Beck says, causing Mia and myself to whip our heads to him.

"Beck, you don't work here." I get he likes to be helpful, but the offer is kind of ridiculous.

"So?" He shrugs. "I know how to make a drink, and I take directions *really* well." He winks at me, and I can't decide if I want to punch him for doing it in front of Mia or blush.

Mia looks back and forth between me and Beck before biting back a smile. "You know, it would be absolutely insane for you to come back here and help Jensen. As the owner...I couldn't condone such a thing." Mia's tone turns a bit mischievous. "But you know, I am needed upstairs, so I won't be able to see this bar down here."

"Mia, you're not serious."

She scoffs while Beck beams. She takes a step back with her hands up. "I'm not saying he should be back bar, but I'm going upstairs. Also note, that I will not be paying someone I don't see working, and MLB bucks are expected to cover any unforeseen liabilities."

I open my mouth to argue with her, but she waves.

"Bye, good luck."

Beck doesn't waste a second, he's up from his seat and sliding under the gap to get behind the bar. "Put me to work, Jenni-cakes."

"You've lost your fucking mind. You know that right? This"—I point between us—"this is nuts. You can't be back here."

Beck doesn't argue, doesn't make any moves to go back to the other side of the bar. He simply lifts his hat, runs his fingers through his hair then puts his hat back on backward.

Are you kidding me?

"Tell me what to do, Jensen."

Oh, so it only gets hotter.

The string of curses in my head is long, and they only get worse when I hear three different voices calling for the bartender.

"*Ay dios mío*, okay. Fine. Go wash your hands. Get me some more maraschino cherries on toothpicks. And turn your hat back around."

Or else I'm going to tell you to bend me over this bar.

Chapter 16
Beck

Jensen James is a damn powerhouse. Not to mention, runs a tight ship behind the bar.

Coming to see her tonight wasn't exactly planned, and jumping behind the bar to help was definitely not fully thought out. I just knew I didn't want to go back home without her there.

Yesterday was weird as fuck, but the silence today was awful. I tried taking Dottie for a quick run. I tried an audiobook. I tried a game of pool with music cranked arguably too loud. Dottie abandoned me at that point, trotting up the stairs to what I imagine to be my or Jensen's mattress. Her dog bed is mostly a last resort, I've come to learn.

I want so badly to put a finger on why things feel so different between us. I guess, really, we've both had our asses handed to us over the past couple days. Really, it makes sense our dynamic is changing, but that doesn't mean we can't find a new normal... Although I'm not sure we had a normal relationship to begin with.

With any other person, I'd be running at any hint of

them showing more than just a single night interest in me, but Jensen's little slipup has me reeling. It's almost like she hates the fact that she likes me, and I don't really know what to do with that.

Then we both practically put our hearts on our sleeve. For a minute, I thought, why not see what this could be, it'll probably fizzle out, right? But then I realized my hand was resting on her thigh, and I knew I fucked up.

Having her bark orders at me tonight has definitely brought back a bit of what feels like normal for us to some degree, but how seamlessly we've made the night go should come with red flags waving every which way.

With the last customer out the door, one of the bus boys turns the lock with a sigh even we can hear.

"Tonight was insane," he grumbles as he takes one of the seats at the bar. There's not a chance in hell the kid is over twenty-one, but I'd want to come talk to Jensen after a long day too.

Jensen huffs in agreement as she wets a rag at the sink. "You did good, though. We all made it through."

"Hey, what about me? How'd I do?"

Jensen gives me a pointed glare and tosses me the rag. "You don't actually work here, but I suppose you did do a good job too."

"I'm sorry, but this is so fucking cool." The kid stands up from the seat and pulls a hat out of his apron. "I'm a huge fan of the Blues. If it's not too much trouble, could you sign my hat?"

I chuckle. "Yeah, you got a—" I don't even finish my sentence before Jensen slides a Sharpie down the bar. I nod at her. "Thanks."

I scribble my signature where he asks, and then take the selfie with him because they always ask for one.

By the end of it the kid is practically glowing. "Thanks, this means a lot. Jensen, your boyfriend is so cool."

"Oh, he's not—" Jensen starts to correct him, but he's way too focused on his hat to listen.

Jensen sighs as he disappears through the kitchen doors. "I'll correct that later. Come on, let's clean up so we can go home." She picks the rag back up. "You wipe down the bar, I'll start on the taps and bottles. And don't half-ass it either, people working tomorrow will say something to me if it's not done right."

"You sure are a bossy girlfriend," I tease.

Jensen clenches her jaw. "Not funny."

I could disagree, but that terminology is so far from us, so why not laugh at it?

Continuing our rhythm, I let Jensen lead doing all the tasks she asks then trying to fill in where I can. When I finish sweeping, I find her wiping down the bottles.

Grabbing a rag, I walk up next to her. "Where'd you start?"

She lifts her bottle to the right. "From there to here is done. There's really not too much left."

"Great." I step around her and go to the far left side. "Meet you in the middle."

She nods, and an ever-so-slight smile tugs at the corner of her lips. "Hey, want a cherry? I may steal one or two every night." Putting her bottle back, she pulls out two cherries from the container.

"Wouldn't say no to one." Taking it from her, I bite off the sweet fruit, but don't throw away the stem just yet.

Finally meeting Jensen on the bottles, I pop the stem in my mouth. "All done?" I ask.

"Think so," Jensen huffs, but when she looks at me she bites at her lip. Stepping up she takes my hat off and turns it back around to the front. I hadn't even realized I turned it around while cleaning. "Quit doing that," she mumbles under her breath.

"What do you have against my hat being backward?"

Jensen doesn't say anything, doesn't move or break eye contact. I'm unsurprisingly now extremely hard. I practically have a semi around her constantly already, but being in her world tonight... Letting her boss me around, and now this...

Leaning forward, I rest my hands on both sides of her, caging Jensen between myself and the bar. The thought of kissing her crosses my mind when she doesn't push back, but instead, I finish tying off the stem in my mouth then hold it between my teeth.

I mark the rise and fall of her chest. Locking on to her amber eyes, I watch as they run down my face and focus on the tied stem.

After two seconds they flash back up and she smirks. "Find some originality, Beckham." She holds out her tongue showing off her own tied stem.

Holy shit, I could come in my pants from that alone.

"Fuck, Jensen," I rasp out.

Jensen's hands land on my chest, and I'm fully prepared for her to push me back, but she doesn't—she's just touching me.

You know what? Fuck it.

My hands move to the small of her back and I lean—

"So, how'd it go?" Mia's voice registers to the both of us

at the same time. Jensen's touch turns into a push, but I'm already jumping back. "Ope, was I interrupting?"

"No!" Jensen snaps. "I mean, no, we're done closing up."

"Oh, okay." Mia folds her lips together for a moment, looking back and forth between the both of us. "You're good to go. I have everything under control here."

Jensen takes several healthy steps away from me then grabs her coat and bag. "Okay, I'll see you tomorrow. Lock the door behind me?" She nods to Mia but doesn't wait for her acknowledgement.

She makes it halfway to the door, and my brain finally catches up with my dick.

"Jensen," I call after her, but she doesn't stop. She doesn't even slow down.

My feet finally start to move, and I holler for her again.

Mia scrunches her face and mouths, *sorry*, as I pass her by, but I don't waste any time responding.

"Jensen!" I yell again once I hit the sidewalk. "Wait up!"

She doesn't bother stopping. "I'll meet you back at the house, Beck."

Kicking my ass up a gear I finally catch up to her. "Jen, I know you could outrun me if you really wanted to, but ride home with me. We're both going to the same place."

"No, I'm not leaving my car here."

I expect nothing but this stubbornness from her, but she's met her match with me. "Fine, I'm riding with you."

She skids to a stop. "No, you're not."

"Yes, I am."

"You can't just leave your vehicle here, Beck. Just give me a little space, please," she pleads.

The words feel like knives to my chest, and I take a small

step back. I can see the fear written all over her face and it drags the knife in my heart down through my stomach.

What the hell am I doing?

Giving her space won't change anything about our conversation. If anything, she's right—we both need a little time alone to cool down and really think about this.

I know what I want to do, who I want to do it to, and do it multiple times, but this isn't going to be that simple. Whether Jensen wants to or not, we have to talk about this, but it doesn't have to be here on the sidewalk or on the drive home.

"Fine, I'll walk you to your car, then I'll walk back to mine, but you have to promise me we'll talk about this when we get home."

Jensen scoffs. "There's nothing to talk about."

I can't help it...the step I took back is immediately met again. My hands find either side of her face. "Oh, baby, you know that's not true."

Chapter 17
Beck

Getting back to the house, I let out a sigh of relief at the porch light turned on. I knew she'd beat me here, but a small part of me worried she'd sneak off to Lucie's.

By the time I park and get to my stoop, I see Dottie wiggling away. "Hey, Dot, miss me?" I start to pet her head, but Jensen tugs back on her leash with a small scream.

"Christ, Beck, you scared me!"

Stepping closer, I pet Dottie properly this time. "I'm sorry, I didn't mean to. Are you guys going in or out?"

"Back in," Jensen whispers. "I took her out as soon as I got here."

"I could have done that for you." Straightening back up, I lock in on those eyes of hers.

Us living together is a ticking time bomb. We've got to do something. She could tell me to completely fuck off tonight, and not a single part of me would judge her for that. I just hope she hears me out.

Jensen bites at her lower lip and holds out Dottie's leash. "She probably would have preferred that."

"That's not true, right, Dot?"

When Dottie lets out a small bark, Jensen breathes out a laugh.

"See?" I look at her hoping to hold on to this calm-before-the-storm feeling. Jensen's cheeks blush before spinning on her heels to head inside.

With a deep breath, I squat down in front of Dottie to take off her leash. "Wish me luck," I whisper before we head inside.

No part of me knows how this conversation is about to go, and with the way Jensen's on edge, even less so. Hanging Dottie's leash by the door, I hit the lock, then turn to her ready to get this over with, but to my surprise, she speaks first.

"Okay, I know you want to talk about whatever"—she gestures between us—"this is, and I think we just need to get it all out."

I take a cautious step to her. "Agreed. Do you want me to go first?"

Jensen swallows hard then nods.

"Okay, laying it all out there—I don't want a relationship. I don't want love or promises of forever. But I can't say that one time will be enough. I think it's safe to put it out there for both of us that there's this mutual attraction. I can't get you out of my head. I haven't entertained the idea of anyone but you since the night we met."

Jensen stills. "You haven't slept with anyone? No one at all?"

I shake my head. "Haven't in over two years, actually. There's a deeper reasoning for not wanting to have a relationship, so unless it was abundantly clear all the way that it was nothing more than a one-night thing then it wasn't happening."

I can practically see the wheels turning in her head. I dare another step closer. "Jensen, let me be more clear. I didn't sleep with anyone for a year and three months for that reason—I haven't slept with anyone for the past nine months because I met you."

Her eyes widen a bit. "Correct me if I'm wrong, but that makes it sound like our situation is a little more...unclear."

Clear as fucking mud.

"Yeah, you're really fucking with my head, Killer."

"Right back at ya." Jensen folds her arms across her chest with a small sigh. "I can't completely disregard the fact that I do feel something for you, but I don't want a relationship right now either. I know yours seems more of a long-term thing, and eventually I will want to find love. So, for now..."

"Now, we get it out of our system."

"We get it out of our system," Jensen parrots, then purses her lips. "Roommates with benefits, I guess?"

I repeat her this time. "Roommates with benefits. No attachments, and we keep the same ground rule—communicate with each other."

Jensen stands up straighter. "I'm adding a no kissing rule to that."

I quirk an eyebrow, that seemed to have a little bit of thought behind it. "Interesting rule..."

"Other places are fine, but don't kiss me on the lips. I told you, there's a little more for me here. We need to keep this purely sexual. Neither of us want more, right?"

I nod, understanding a bit more of what she's getting at.

"Much to my dismay, I'm a romantic at heart. You kiss me and if it's the slightest bit romantic, I'll be fucked."

I've never considered what it would be like to look my soul in the mirror, but I swear I am right now. I've called Jensen my polar opposite before, but that couldn't be further from the truth.

I get her point. Kissing her at the bar tonight would have been catastrophic, because if I had, I'm not so sure the romantic in me would ever let her go.

"Got it, no romance. No candles or flowers. No fancy dates, just us as we normally are, plus sex."

At that, it's like what we've been talking about registers to her. She lets out a nervous laugh. "I can't believe we're talking about this. This is insane." Jensen holds her hands up and retreats to the living room. "We can't actually do this, can we?"

Following her, I can't find it in me to slow down until my hands are on her waist and spinning her back around to face me. "Jen, we don't have to, if you don't want to. I want to try, but if it's a no for you, then it's a no. I'll still be here for you no matter what you want."

Jensen's eyes pull from mine as she whispers. "Can I think about it?"

"Of course," I answer without a pause. Moving my hands to her face, I bring her back to focus on me. All the struggle is shown in her eyes. I don't ever want to be a form of stress for her.

So, I do the one thing I know to do. Annoy her.

With my signature smile I let go of her face and turn my hat around backward. "Does this help any?"

Her eyes roll immediately, taking the bait. "Beck, don't."

She gives me a quick push back, but I'm not done. "Oh, come on, we still have the classic debate on if I'm pierced or not."

Jensen shakes her head and even though she's starting to walk away I see that smile tugging at her lips. "Good night, Beckham."

I wait for her to hit the stairs before I keep going. "Oh, come on, we can do missionary first so we can still argue. It's perfect for us."

Jensen doesn't say anything until she hits the top of the stairs. She looks back with a smirk. "We'll see, Stalker."

Chapter 18
Jensen

It's officially been one week since moving into Beck's place, and precisely four days, twelve hours, and thirty-seven minutes since our roommates-with-benefits conversation.

I keep going around in circles because one huge part of me wants to do it. Get all our built-up chemistry and sexual tension out. But then I remember how Beck went from being the guy that I found a little annoying and exhausting to a man that I found funny, caring, albeit still a little annoying, but dammit, he's made me like that about him now.

How he has the capability to give serious conversations the depth and attention they require then flip and make me laugh and blush is something I don't think I'll ever understand.

I came to Boston with the intention of not looking for a relationship at all. The rush to find someone and be with them forever was a trap I fell into before. I don't need the pressures a relationship adds right now. I'm allowed to be in my twenties and not be looking for forever right now.

I wasn't even looking for someone I could fall for. But

then, along comes Beck, he really hit that plan out of the ball park.

I can't call my sister or Lucie to talk about this, so I've been stuck playing my own devil's advocate, and the only argument I can make for us doing this friends-with-benefits deal is that maybe it would actually work to help me get past my feelings for him.

He was very clear that he didn't want a relationship, granted he didn't exactly tell me why, but I could cling to that...possibly. Not to mention, I'll move out eventually, then when his season starts back up, he'll be gone all the time with games—really, the deal has potential to fizzle out on its own.

But if it somehow goes insanely wrong, I run the risk of losing the friendships I have now and end up homeless.

However, that feels a bit like a trauma response rooted in me from my ex. With how mature Beck's been about it this week, I've moved this reasoning down a bit on my con list.

Looking out Beck's sliding doors, Dottie lets out a little grumble at my feet. We officially have snow, and she hates it. Between the heavy salt and icy slush, it absolutely tears up her paws if we do long runs.

Squatting down next to her, I scratch at her head and behind her ears. "Sorry, girl. On the bright side, Beck's got a great dog park across the street. You got some energy out there this morning, didn't you?"

"Yeah, she did," Beck says, coming up behind us. He's wearing these jeans I know immediately are Levi's with the way they fit him perfectly. His tan sweater looks so damn comfy that I'm not sure if I want to be wrapped up in it or him wearing it.

He squats down next to me causing Dottie to shift her

whole body around so she can get proper attention from him. *Such a traitor.*

"You ran laps around snooty Mr. Peterson's doodle, didn't you?" Beck ups his tone, which gets Dottie fired up right away. She's wiggling her whole body as he eggs her on until she starts barking.

Pushing back up, I pinch the bridge of my nose. These two.

"Okay, okay." Beck stands back up, now putting his attention on me. "You ready to go?"

"Yep," I say on an exhale.

We're heading out to meet Reagan at the storefront so I can make a final decision on whether I want to go into business with her or start searching for other shops hiring in the area.

Beck slides a small bit of my hair behind my ear. "You only have to be physically ready. Mentally and emotionally can come later."

That right there has my brain screaming *benefits it is,* and my heart begging me to put up walls.

Beck's hand doesn't linger; he simply smiles at me. "Come on, let's go check the place out."

"Wait, tell me again, why am I allowing you to come with me today?"

"Because you're obsessed with me?"

"Beck," I groan, rubbing the back of my neck. I swear he's giving me a crick.

"Because I'm obsessed with you?" he pesters again. My pointed glare only seems to make his smile grow. "I won't bring up me paying for everything. I'm a completely neutral party who has zero interest in seeing you do something you love."

Well, that's a little more embellished than our agreement, but really, I shouldn't expect anything different from him.

"Great, let's go." I nod and start toward the front door where Beck is ever the gentleman helping me with my coat then getting the doors.

When he gestures for me to lead us anywhere, his hand finds the small of my back—again with the touches, they're all small and soft, yet they send waves of warmth through me each time.

"Hey, this place isn't too far off from our running spot," Beck says as we walk up the brick steps. "That's definitely going in the plus column."

"Beck," I groan again, ringing the doorbell for Reagan. "What did we just talk about?"

He holds his hands up. "Hey, that's a plus for me, Jennicakes. I didn't say anything about you."

"As if, that was implied for both of us."

Beck takes a step up, invading my personal space in the best way. It doesn't matter that we're surrounded by snow, Beck always smells like a cozy fall day. "Is it a plus for you too then?"

"I'd say I'm indifferent." I shrug him off but quietly take another inhale of him.

His head tilts back, and I can already tell there's another flirty comeback on the tip of his tongue.

"Hey, you're here." Reagan pops her head out the front door. Her eyes track every bit of the minimal distance between me and Beck. "Come on in."

Beck holds out one hand for me to lead...then the other finds the small of my back. That's on the plus list. Every. Damn. Time.

Taking a few steps into the main hallway, I can immediately see the vision explained in Beck's kitchen brought to life. There's not a single thing in here, but I can see it.

The two rooms on the sides are separated by glass walls while the back wall has this insane art deco tile that I think could easily mold to mine and Reagan's styles. The floors seem to be real hardwood that's in great condition which is a nice plus.

The bay windows have this adorable bench seating underneath them and my immediate thought is how perfect of a waiting area that would be.

"So, whatcha think?" Reagan asks, stepping in front of me.

My mind is running with ideas already, but I try to contain it. No point in letting her see my excitement until I can give a full green light.

"I see what you mean...I could see the execution of us doing this playing out."

Reagan's smile isn't one I typically see this wide, and honestly, it's refreshing. Seeing her genuine excitement for this helps a ton. I know I could make it work with her, but I'd rather us have a good partnership in this, than me simply being someone who helps pay the rent.

Reagan gestures to the room behind me. "For right now, I think this would be the better space to have your set up. I did some research on all the shop requirements and health codes, we'll definitely have to work on some plumbing and electrical for both sides. The floral shop will need it more for the back room, but as far as the front goes, the inspector recommended this side for any adjustments. It has the customer restroom as well."

Nodding, I turn slowly to the right side. I can't explain it, considering both sides look nearly identical, but in my head I saw my set up on this half.

"If you want to take a look around, I have to run out and meet Julie with this check for the landlord. I'll be back in about ten-ish minutes, but if you leave first just press the lock on the keypad."

Beck's hand finds my back again. "Sounds good. I'm sure we'll still be here, but we'll text if not."

Reagan's eyes narrow in on the contact then she immediately bites her lip. Yep, I'm definitely going to be getting a call from Lucie tonight. "Have fun looking around," she chimes before heading out the door.

Beck steps around me to open up the glass door. "Let's start in here, tell me what you're thinking."

With Reagan, I contained it, but with Beck...I don't hesitate. I walk in and start letting all my thoughts out.

"This place is gorgeous. I could see the desk and waiting area there by the windows. I'll definitely get different curtains for the window—these gray ones are horrendous." Spinning around, I walk a few steps back into the room. "Possibly some to break up the room a bit for some more privacy or maybe we could get at least one private room built in for certain piercings and tattoos."

"You could easily get some room dividers too. Do you think you could get some other artists in here too?" Beck asks.

At this point, my brain is running ninety miles an hour and there's no stopping it. I didn't anticipate being this excited over an empty space, but here we are.

"Yeah, I think for sure we could. Eventually maybe two to three chairs along this wall and possibly a room right here for piercings. Oh, and along the glass wall I could have a little snack and water cart. I could get one of those old gumball machines and have like random mini designs in them. And on the glass itself I'm sure Emma could do something really cool, and—" Spinning back around the space, I stop when I see the way Beck's smiling at me.

"You're practically glowing, Jen. Please keep going."

I could probably bounce back into that mode, but with the look he just gave me I feel like my body is sobering up from a high. I don't let a lot of people see this super excited side. Until the girls here the only other person who saw that was my family, but somehow Beck just seems to fit right into those categories.

With a deep breath, I don't go back into my ideas but I'm not done talking about it, and I'm not mad that Beck's here to be the one to listen. "I think I want to do this, Beck."

He chuckles softly, taking a few small steps to me. "You think? Oh, come on, Jenni-cakes, you know you want this."

He's right. *I really freaking do.*

"It's going to be a huge undertaking," I say, reminding myself of the negative one more time.

"It will, but you'll be fine. And I know you said no money talk—"

"Beck," I groan, rubbing the back of my neck again.

Beck pulls my hand away then takes over rubbing my shoulders himself. Good god.

"Hear me out, what about an exchange?"

I raise an eyebrow. "What kind of exchange?"

That cocky smile comes to his face, and for a moment I'm sure he's going to tell me some sort of addendum to our roommates-with-benefits deal.

"I know you're gonna be stubborn and insist on paying

for things on your own so you can still do some of that, but why not let me pay for the tattoos I want in advance."

I take a step back. I can't think this through with his hands massaging me like that. "Wait, what?"

"I want tattoos specifically by you, so why not let me help pay for some of this in exchange for the ink I want."

"Why do I get the feeling you're going to give me more money than the tattoos would actually cost?"

That smile comes back with a small shrug. "Well, I mean, I would have to include the tip."

The laugh wants to come out, but I bite it back. "Beck, I don't know—"

"I'd gladly pay for everything, but—" Beck chuckles when my eyes nearly roll out of my head. "You want this, Jensen. I want this for you. Just think about it, okay?"

I should probably think about it. At least give it as much thought as I'm giving this whole roommate-with-benefits thing, but he's right—I do want this.

I'm standing here in this perfect space, with this incredible man who just wants to help. Maybe he's right, this is an opportunity, but I don't want to take advantage of him either —nor do I want to have him as my crutch.

"Could I have some say on when I use your money? Like, maybe I don't take a lump sum, but allocate it when I need it."

"You can have all the say, as long as you promise to use it." Beck shrugs then closes the distance between us again. "I've got plans, Jenni-cakes. I want free tattoos for life."

I contain my smile the best I can, but I'm sure Beck can see it from my eyes alone. "Alright, deal."

Beck's eyebrows raise. "Really? Just like that?"

My frown comes fast. "Don't make me regret this already."

His hands lift. "I just thought I was going to have to put up more of a fight. Ending on an 'I'll think about it' was the goal."

"Yeah, well, I'm thinking about other things right now," I say then immediately want to take it back.

That smirk of his grows. "Oh yeah? What's on your mind, is it the roommates-with-benefits deal? The piercings? Maybe it's the missionary position? I really think not arguing with you naked is just a missed opportunity for the both of us."

All of the freaking above.

Here we are again. We were just having a serious conversation but he's turned it flirty and carefree. If he hadn't, I'm sure a mental list of price tags would have started appearing in my head, but now I'm just thinking about him.

"I've been thinking about those things." Beck leans in ever so slightly. "I think about doing so many things with, for, and to you."

Beck's spiced autumn scent goes straight to my head and warmth rapidly takes over my body. God, I want to hear all about those things. I want him and fighting it is starting to feel exhausting.

My hands twitch to reach out and pull his clothes off, but instead I let that feeling simmer.

"Tell me one," I whisper. "Tell me something you're thinking about right now."

Beck's eyes flash with a bit of surprise as they flick over to the window before locking back with mine. "I'm thinking that bench seems to be the perfect height for me to get down on my knees and eat that pussy of yours."

His words play out in my head and dammit if it doesn't make my stance a little unsteady.

"Thinking about it too, aren't you?" Beck leans in closer. I don't have to nod or speak for him to know that's exactly what I'm thinking. "I'll tell you what, we don't even have to go full benefits deal. Consider it a trial."

"Reagan's coming back, remember?" I say, more for the disclaimer. Right now, that thought isn't a deal breaker.

Beck leans in with a shrug. "She said ten-ish minutes, we've maybe been here for five, and really, I only need two."

"Always so cocky." I *tsk*.

Beck's arms wrap around my waist with this possessive grip. "Never claimed not to be. So, what are you thinking now, Killer? Do you want to look over at that bench every day and be reminded of the orgasm I gave you?"

I could regret this. With that point in mind it should be a turn off, considering this arrangement isn't long-term... My eyes trail down from his eyes marking every freckle before locking on to his lips.

I can't kiss him, that's my limit, but I need to feel them.

"Fuck it, you better make it a good one then."

It takes maybe a second for my consent to register and Beck snaps. His arms tighten as he carries me back four steps until I feel the edge of the bench on the back of my knees.

"You sure about this?" Beck whispers.

"Don't ask me that." With one last rational thought, I turn around and pull the boring curtains closed then spin back to him. "Just make it worth it."

Throwing our jackets to the side, I quickly kick off my boots while Beck undoes my jeans. He sinks down to his knees as he pulls them down. God, he looks so hot right now.

He looks up at me. "Sit down."

The command sends a thrill up my spine. Hell, I might not last two minutes.

Sitting, Beck brings my knees together to bring me closer to the edge, then peels my pants the rest of the way off.

His fingers glide lightly over the ink on my upper thighs. "I think about the tattoos of yours I haven't seen constantly."

"There's more if you're a good boy. Maybe you'll see them *and* the piercings I have."

Beck spreads my knees wide. "I think you know I love being a good boy." He takes his glasses off and sets them to the side. "A good boy with a healthy appetite."

Beck flattens his tongue as he licks up my center. My head tilts back with his name on the tip of my tongue but it's drowned out by his moan.

He laps me up and down again, each time paired with a whimper like I'm the best meal he's ever tasted. I lean back farther, resting on my hands and using the ledge of the window to hold me up.

"Beckham," I moan as he consumes me.

His head starts to turn as he explores different angles with his mouth—taking careful note of the ones that earn more of a reaction out of me.

When he bites at my clit then licks me through the shock, I know I'm done for. I need more of this. The goal might be to get this out of our system, but first I need to inject him into my veins. I want to feel this man everywhere.

Beck's hands grip on to my hips and just as he starts to flick his tongue up and down my clit rapidly, he makes my hips move. Gliding me back and forth so my body is in perfect tandem with his mouth.

"Fuck, Beck!" Tremors practically light up my body and

every part of me wants to move on my own but I'm completely at his mercy.

His moans seem to match mine and it only makes it hotter. My breath quickens, turning very audible as he continues to rock me back and forth.

"Feels...so...good," I mutter at each hit of his tongue.

I want to close my eyes and let the sensation completely take me, but I can't stand the thought of looking away. "You look so hot right now."

His eyes look up to mine and he winks. Mouth on my pussy, whimpers coming out of the both of us, and he fucking winks.

My orgasm shoots off like a rocket. My scream is surely heard from outside if anyone's on this block, but then they'll probably hear Beck too. He laps up every bit of my orgasm only slowing when my muscles relax.

"Oh my gosh," I breathe out as Beck places a few kisses on my pelvis and thighs.

His hands move around lifting up my ass then licking me up the center one more time. "Worth it?"

I can't even form coherent words for a response. Hell yeah, it was worth it.

Beck reaches for my jeans then helps me get them back on. His hands find my hips when they wobble as I stand back up. "Beck, that was—"

"I know." He runs his hand through the back of my hair. "We should probably head back to the house. I can't promise discreetness since I came in my pants, but I'm not—"

"Hold on, what?" *Did I hear that correctly? He came in his pants?*

Beck tilts his head without a care or hint of embarrassment on that gorgeous face of his. "Oh yeah, Killer, I came from eating that delicious pussy of yours. Are you kidding? I've been thinking of you for nine months, I'm not ashamed to admit I'm probably going to have to work on my stamina if you want to do this again."

All hesitations have officially exploded along with that orgasm. "I want to. Roommates with benefits. Let's get it all out of our system."

The corner of his lips tug up. "Should I ask if you're sure?"

"Never ask that when it comes to you. All I know is that I'm tired of thinking about it. Thinking and fighting are getting me nowhere, so..."

Beck's hand grasps my chin lightly. "Great, then let's stop thinking. Let's just fuck until we're sick of each other."

My smirk matches his. "Fuck each other right out of our systems."

Chapter 19
Beck

Leaving the storefront, I feel fucking amazing. No one pinch me. If this is a dream, I have zero desire to ever wake back up.

Hell, after that I think I just want to live in between Jensen's legs.

I feel alive. I could run a damn marathon right now, no, an Ironman.

Actually, a sexual Ironman, if you will.

Looking over at Jensen in my truck, her knee bounces as she looks aimlessly out the window. I'm so damn eager to get back to my place and go for an actual round...but is she?

I don't want this to turn weird for us. We need to play this smart or it could go south quick. Jensen's so intertwined in our group and I refuse to let this have any impact on her relationships with the girls.

I know she said she wants to do this, but I also told her that we would still be us. Would taking her back to my place and simply having sex feel like that's our only reasoning for being around each other now?

Shit, now I'm overthinking it. We're not a couple. I know we're not romantic, per se, but we can still be us, and there's something we usually do that we skipped.

Reaching over I squeeze her leg quickly. "Hey, it's Tuesday, let's pick up Dottie and go for a run."

Jensen's eyebrows pull together. I know this isn't at all what she's expecting, but then her leg stops bouncing and she seems to relax a bit.

"I'm not saying I don't want to run, but it's actively snowing. I get we have salt and all the plows, but even I have my limits. Not to mention limits for the conditions she runs in."

"I know. But I have a solution for that if you want to go run..." I take a small breath. "Or we can get our heart rates up a different way. It's up to you, Jen. I'm good with either."

Jensen eyes me cautiously and it takes a few seconds but she finally relents. "Maybe we do go for a run."

After picking up Dottie and changing, I take us to our new winter running spot. I may have made quite the case for a new machine to come into the Blues training facility.

"What are we doing here, Beckham?" Jensen asks.

"It's a surprise, Jen." I put my truck in park. "Wait for me to come around, it's still slick."

Jensen lets out a small huff. "I think I can handle a little ice."

I look her dead in the eye. "I know you can, I'm talking to Dottie."

Jensen bites back a smile. "Fair."

Getting inside the lobby, I know the anticipation is eating at both of them. Dottie's turning circles which is only stressing Jensen out more.

"So, do you have, like, an indoor track or something? Are we going to run fake bases a hundred times?"

I chuckle. "No, smart-ass. I have another idea to try first." Making sure the door is locked behind me, I turn to Jensen and tap her nose. "Trust me, Killer."

"Beck," she groans my name as she swats at my hand.

"Follow me."

Picking up Dottie's leash, I lead them both down the hall to our workout room. I honestly can't believe I actually talked Olsson into this. I mean, I'm the one who paid for it, but really, my argument for the team to bring their dogs might actually encourage workouts seemed to help.

Hitting the code to get into the workout room, I hold the door open for Jensen to go in first.

She hesitates for a moment studying my face. Part of me thinks she might actually want to try and guess what I have up my sleeve, or maybe she's thinking of taking Dottie and leaving.

I hold my breath until she walks in. "Head over to the treadmills in the back."

Jensen eyes me curiously, but walks anyway. When she hits the line of machines, she spins around. "What is this?"

"It's Dottie's treadmill."

Jensen's jaw drops. "You bought her a dog treadmill and got it put in a Major League training facility?"

"Hell yeah, I did. Gotta say it's probably a gamble if she'll even like it, but I figured if anyone could get her on it, it's me."

Jensen swats at me first, but her dropped jaw has since turned into a smile. "I cannot believe you did this."

"Believe it." My hands tug her closer by her waist. "I like running with you both, I'm not going to let some snow stop that."

Jensen looks back to the machine then back to me now

biting back her smile. "You could really charm your way into anything, couldn't you?"

"I really could." I tap her ass playfully. "I think the crush you have on me really solidified that statement."

Jensen shoves me back, but that smirk won't leave her face. "You and your ego."

It takes a little convincing to get Dottie comfortable on the machine. Every little adjustment we had to make to ensure her safety while running made her quite apprehensive about it, but once she got going, she absolutely loved it.

Jensen and I stood by on either side for a few minutes to make sure she got the hang of it. It's non-electric, and once she realized she could control the speed, it was game over.

After that, Jen and I hopped on the two next to her and ran our typical five miles. It may not have been our usual route with the views of the Harborwalk, but I'm not complaining.

Dottie's definitely not either. We all but have to pull the emergency brake to get her off.

"Safe to say she likes it." I chuckle, then give Dottie big pets. "Good job, I knew you could do it."

Jensen comes up behind her, ruffling her fur on her back. "Such a good girl. You did so good! Let's find you some water, shall we?"

Straightening my spine, I grab my and Jensen's nearly empty bottles and Dottie's leash. "There's a kitchen, we can refill and get her a bowl."

Walking down the hall, Dottie pants the whole way, but she's got that border collie energy for sure. As much as this was a good excuse to spend time with Jensen, I freaking love this dog.

Grabbing one of the bowls out of a cabinet, I fill it up

with some water. "Here we go, Dot." Patting her head, I make my way over to the small table where Jensen's set us out new water bottles.

"Do you think it's odd how much we talk to her?" Jensen asks, watching Dottie absolutely demolish the water.

"No," I say without a thought. "If someone thinks we shouldn't talk to our dog then I don't want to talk to them."

Jensen shakes her head with a small huff of a laugh. "She's my dog, remember."

"Semantics." I wave her off like that didn't hurt my soul. "So, are you going to be my date to Dex and Lucie's wedding tomorrow?"

Jensen gives me a side-eye. "I'm her best friend. Don't reduce my presence there to being your arm candy."

"Alright, fine, I'll be *your* arm candy. Dex gave me the title of best man in the group chat, that's all the acknowledgement I needed."

"*Dios mío*, you're hopeless."

I take a drink of my water, letting that tension really hang. "I didn't hear a no. It's settled, I'll be your date. Don't worry, I put out."

Jensen shakes her head as she bites her lip. "So, do you have any plans for Thanksgiving?"

Shit, was not exactly looking for that change of topic. Adjusting in my seat, I lean back and look toward Dottie now. "I, uh, guess not really. My dad's messaged a few times, but I haven't responded."

"Beck..." Jensen sighs.

"It's fine, I'm fine. I'll talk to him before Christmas, I just think both of us could use the space."

Jensen's lips fold together. "Well, Stella asked if she

could come down from Salem for dinner. Do you want to join us?"

I should politely pass so Jensen can have quality time with her sister. I should let there be some boundaries for hers and my benefit. Eh, fuck that.

"Okay, Jenni-cakes, I'll take you up on that." I take another sip of water. "How are you feeling about the whole Reagan situation?"

"A little antsy and nervous, but equally excited and a bit relieved." Jensen rolls her shoulders back. "As contradictory as that sounded, it all sort of feels right. I don't fully love that it comes at me spending your money, but the trade and being able to use it when I need it does make it a bit easier to swallow."

There're so many inappropriate jokes I want to tack on, but it's probably not the right moment for that. "I guess this will call for some adjusting in that five-year plan."

Jensen's cheeks pinken, but she holds eye contact as she says, "I think I'm going a bit rogue, and I can't say that I'm regretting it."

Chapter 20
Jensen

Callie has changed the name to Daddy Dex + Baby Mama Day!

CALLIE

HAPPY WEDDING DAY!!!!

EMMA

hehehe I'm so excited. The stadium looks soooo good!

LUCIE

I'm afraid to see what you and Callie have done to the place… is it even a stadium anymore?

CALLIE

Nope we've officially turned it into a wedding venue. All players are now ushers on standby and fake groomsmen when needed.

REAGAN

You know I got to admit it looks pretty good all things considered.

Coming down the stairs, I put my gold hoops in my ears. "You ready to go?"

I make it approximately three steps from the floor when Beck turns around and gives me exactly the reaction I was hoping for.

"Holy shit." Beck fakes going weak in his knees before meeting me halfway. "You look incredible."

I know I do. This is my absolute knock-it-out-of-the-park dress. The red satin hugs me in all the right places, and, if I do say so myself, my tits look amazing in the corset-style top.

I've always felt good in this dress, but I'm not sure if I've fucked up because I didn't think anyone could make me feel better than I do when I wear it—that is until Beck sees me in it.

His eyes are practically eating me up in this thing. His hands find my waist but run up and down the fabric. "I don't think there're words that could do justice to how beautiful you look."

Oh, this is such dangerous territory, but I don't care. I feel way too good inside and out to care about the warning sirens going off in my head.

"Thank you. If it's not too bold, I think I have to agree with you."

"No, don't think that, believe that. Own it. Jen, I'm so tempted to blow this whole thing off, but I want everyone to see me walk in with you."

I shake my head. "I thought I said I wasn't arm candy."

"I didn't say 'see you on my arm.' I'm on your arm. At your side. You could walk me in on a damn leash."

Even though I know my face is now flushed and the temp in here definitely went up a good hundred degrees, Dottie hears the word *leash* and suddenly she's off the couch herding me and Beck.

Taking a small step away from Dottie's spinning, I hold on to the lapels of Beck's suit. "Look what you got started."

"Worth it," he whispers in my ear then places a soft kiss on my shoulder before stepping back. "Alright, Dottie, enough herding. Go upstairs." Brushing my hair back softly, he smiles. "So beautiful...I forgot my watch, then we can go."

The only thing I can do is nod. God, the red lights are flashing. The red flags are being raised and that siren is blaring, but I'm not looking. It'll fizzle out, we haven't even had sex yet to get each other completely out of our systems.

My rose-colored glasses are officially on and I'm no longer listening to the warning that says it's not sex that I need out of my system—it's how Beck makes me feel outside of that.

Yesterday was incredible. On the way home from the best orgasm of my lifetime, I couldn't decide if I made a mistake agreeing to this or was still too wound up to care. But then with what he did for Dottie—again, he took something serious and made it fun. We came home and had a completely normal afternoon eating dinner and watching a movie.

So yeah the rose-colored glasses are on because I trust Beck to not completely destroy me at the end of this.

Grabbing my coat off the rack, Beck's MacBook starts to ring with a FaceTime. When I look and see his dad calling, I mumble some curses. Beck said he had texted...

"Beck," I call, but no answer. "Shit." Didn't he say something about texting only...what if something's wrong?

The laptop rings again, and my lack of impulse control takes over and I'm clicking the Answer button. When an older man with red hair just like Beck's pops up on the screen, I'm holding my breath a little, and then I see the woman on his side.

She's beautiful with her smooth gray hair and kind brown eyes. They both look at me extremely confused and we sit in awkward silence for about two seconds before I find my voice.

"Um, hi, sorry, Beck's upstairs. I'm his...friend, Jensen."

Beck's dad's smile grows. "Hi, Jensen, I'm Rory, his dad, and this is Milicent."

My smile softens and my shoulders fall. Rory doesn't have to say that this is Beck's mom, I can see the resemblance. "Hi, it's nice to meet you both."

"Alright, Jen, Dottie's taken over my bed, so we're—"

Beck stops talking the moment he sees who's on the screen. Yep, that tension in my shoulders is back.

"Sorry, they called and I yelled for you, but—" I start to ramble but then he's at my side with a faint smile.

"It's okay," he whispers. "Hey, what are you guys doing?"

His dad sputters a laugh. "I think the question is what are you guys doing? You look awfully nice in that suit."

Beck's mom speaks up next. "Oh, he does look nice, but look at her, she looks beautiful. You didn't tell me your son had such a pretty girlfriend."

My heart simultaneously feels like it just got a hug and a beating. Beck's never come out and said his mom doesn't remember him. I knew that's most likely the case with the brief details I've gotten from him, but I know that hurts to hear.

Beck lets out a nervous laugh. "Jensen's actually my... roommate. We're going to our mutual friends' wedding."

Rory's eyebrows lift. "Your roommate? That's new."

Clearing my throat, I try to take this one. "Temporary roommate. Beck kindly offered to let me stay here until I find a new place. His home seemed to be the only one in our friend group that allows dogs."

"Oh, you have a dog?" Milicent asks.

"Yes, I do. A border collie named Dottie. She's got a lot of energy."

Rory hums softly. "Well, how lucky Beck's place allows pets."

Beck's shoulders tense as he rocks back and forth slightly on his feet. "It is. Like Jensen mentioned, it's temporary."

Ouch, that hurts a little. I know it's true, and I just said it myself but still, did it have to get reiterated?

I could go out to his truck and wait for him to finish this call to save any more possible comments of our impending end, but I don't want to leave him knowing how much he's struggled with this.

Even though I don't exactly know the details of what happened between him and his dad, I can't leave him. And it's not like Beck's lying—I want this to be temporary too.

I guess my rose-colored glasses do have a few clear spots after all.

Watching Beck and his dad talk with his mom is also amazing. They both word things carefully and answer her questions in ways that have her feeling excited. I'm in complete awe, then again, I shouldn't be surprised the already emotionally well-rounded man in front of me knows what to do.

Beck checks his watch. "I would really love to keep talking, but we do have that wedding to get to."

"I'm sure Dex and Lucie would understand," I say, barely above a whisper.

I can see it written all over Beck's face that he's considering it, but Rory makes the decision for him. "You guys go have fun. Send us some pictures if you want."

Milicent nods slowly. "Pictures would be nice."

Beck's hand finds mine under the counter and squeezes for a moment. "Okay, we can do that. I enjoyed talking to y'all."

It flashes across Rory's face quick, but it seems like he really needed to hear that from Beck. "We loved talking to you. Jensen, it was great meeting you."

I give his parents a quick smile. "It was lovely meeting you both."

"Lovely meeting you, dear." Beck's mom places her hand over her heart. "You look very pretty."

This time I squeeze Beck's hand. "Thank you, that means a lot to me."

"We'll talk later, Beck?" Rory asks, and I hold my smile the best I can until Beck nods. "Good, we'll be waiting on the pictures."

Beck mumbles a "bye" before the call ends.

I wait in the silence still holding Beck's hand for a few seconds. "I'm sorry I answered. I was worried—"

Beck shakes his head. "No, don't apologize. That was nice. I don't get very many of those conversations with her anymore. I'm glad you were here for it."

To think I almost left and missed it. "Me too."

Walking into the Blues stadium, I know Lucie's going to lose her shit. There are lit candles quite literally everywhere. Huge flower arrangements and white rose petals scattered on the floor. There're white drapes covering up the majority of the walls while only allowing glimpses of the snowy stadium.

"Shit. Callie and Emma really went all out," Beck mutters quietly. "Didn't Dex and Lucie say low-key?"

I chuckle at the irony. "They should have known who they put in charge of this. It's their own fault."

Off to the side, a low whistle comes and my other favorite redhead comes walking up. "Damn, Jen, you look hot!"

"I have to agree." Callie looks just as stunning in her fitted royal blue dress. I flash her some flirty eyes. "Look at you, got any plans after this?"

It takes no time at all for Will to wrap his arm around her waist. "She very much does."

"And so do you," Beck whispers in my ear before he steps up to greet Callie with a hug. "Always stunning, Callie Bear. Will—at least you tried."

Callie and I each hit him from the side.

"Hey, I was joking."

"You both look very handsome." Without much thought, I link my arm through Beck's. "I do have to ask about the number of candles you have lit in here, though."

Callie and Will look us both up and down, then look to each other, then back to us.

We probably should have thought this part through a little bit more. I can't say hiding this whole arrangement thing we're starting would go over well—especially with this group, I highly doubt we'd be able to keep it a secret for long anyway.

We maybe should have considered Dex and Lucie's wedding might not be the best place for everyone to see that for the first time. But what was I going to do? Send out a text that says, "Oh, hey, Beck and I are going to try out a roommate-with-benefits situation, everyone be chill about it."

Callie bites back her smile...*let's just see if she can bite back a comment.* "Well, first, I most definitely lost count of how many candles I lit. And second, they're all in hurricane vases, so all fire jokes can stop now." She eyes Will. "I followed Olsson's rules, and I have like three fire extinguishers hidden around."

Will holds up a hand in defeat. "I stopped when my plans for after this were threatened, Blaze. But also, are we just going to ignore what's happening here?"

Beck doesn't miss a beat. "It's Dex and Lucie's wedding, dumbass."

My hand comes to my mouth to stop my laugh. Oh, hell, Will's gonna kill him one of these days, I swear.

Callie's lips fold tightly together as she takes Will's hands. "Okay, come with me, babe. We're gonna walk away."

"Gah, I love pissing him off." Beck chuckles then steps in

front of me. "I think we both know we won't be able to keep this situation a secret, but I'm fine if you want to try."

Keeping it between us does seem like it will be nearly impossible. Not to mention part of what I think will make this work is that it's just us playing into our attraction.

Hiding it from our friends would be the smarter move, but Beck's right. It won't stay a secret, maybe just letting them all know about it will help them get the idea of us out of their system too.

"No, hiding feels redundant, but maybe we don't come out and say it tonight, though."

Beck shrugs off his coat then reaches for mine. "I'm going to hold these for now to keep something in my hands. Dex and Lucie just got here, and anything we do in front of them is going to be called out point blank."

I take a deep breath preparing for that. Lucie's called me on my bullshit about Beck enough. "She's going to hate this arrangement between us, and I'm not entirely sure she'd love my response of beggars can't be choosers."

Beck's smile grows. "Dex is absolutely going to kick my ass over it. Unlike Callie, Lucie won't stop him, will she?"

"Nuh-uh, but hey, this is their wedding, surely they don't care that much about us today?"

Beck gives me a look and I wave him off. "I heard it. Just come on, let's go say hi real quick."

With people already starting to crowd them, I really thought Luce might just wave and move along with whatever Callie and Emma have planned, but no. She breaks away the moment she meets my eyes.

She looks absolutely beautiful in a simple white silk dress, and with what I'm sure was a joint decision—yellow heels.

But before either Lucie or Dex can reach us, Miles is barreling toward Beck. Our coats are dropped onto the floor as Beck scoops Miles right up. "What's up, All-star?"

Miles snickers, holding his hand over his mouth. "I have a secret. Daddy says I can't tell *anyone*."

That's all the challenge Beck needs.

He feigns his hand over his heart. "But Miles, you can tell me—"

"Miles, don't, baby," Lucie chastises in the sweetest voice before pulling me into a hug. "Jensen, you look so beautiful."

Her hug hits me right in my soul. "Me? Luce, you look breathtaking."

Dex comes up behind her pulling her into his arms. "Yeah, she does."

"Isn't it bad luck or something for the groom to see his bride?" I tease Lucie.

She rolls her eyes. "I think we'll survive. We actually have some news to share." She turns to Dex. "Which, we should probably go ahead and get out of the way before you-know-who spills the beans again."

Lucie doesn't even get a nod to Miles before Dex is stealing him back from Beck. "Come on, bud. Let's get this party started."

As Lucie starts to follow behind, she gives me a scrunched nose smile. "I bet he doesn't make it all the way through."

I raise an eyebrow to Beck. "Do you know anything about this?"

Beck shakes his head. "Can't say I do." Picking up our coats, he drapes them over one forearm then slides his hand to the small of my back. "Come on, it seems like we're in for a little surprise."

At the back of the entryway, Dex lets out an ever-classic dad whistle to get everyone's attention. "You know, when Olsson said we could turn the team's Thanksgiving dinner into a wedding, I was thinking a few flowers, maybe we dressed up just a little. Mine and Lucie's families would tag along...nothing too crazy. I should have known you fuckers have no chill."

"I think the commissioner's trophy should have reminded you of that," Adam yells, which gets him a good laugh and agreements from the team.

Dex shakes his head. "Needless to say, when Emma and Callie showed up to our house with a damn binder, compromises had to start being made. Lucie and I did officially get married at City Hall this morning to save everyone from sitting through a ceremony."

A few people start to boo, and Beck and I join in. Lucie flashes me a smart-ass look, but I just stick my tongue out at her.

Dex holds up his hand. "I get it, I get it. Relax, we still want to celebrate with you guys. I've got one better for you if you'd all just be quiet for the first time in your lives." Tugging Lucie closer to him, she places one hand on him and the other on Miles. "Luce and I couldn't be more grateful for you all. When this past season started, I didn't know what to expect, and if we're being honest I wasn't too excited for it. But then these fuckers from Seattle get traded—"

"You're fucking welcome," Will yells.

Beck leans close and whispers, "Wait for it."

"I don't want to hear it," Adam adds.

"So predictable," I whisper back.

Lucie's face starts to turn bright red as she shakes her head.

Miles's hands go up and yells, "That's too many curse words! The babies can hear you!"

Wait...what?

I lean in to Beck and whisper, "Did he just say babies?"

"I think he did, but he's also five." Beck seems just as confused as I am and holds a finger up.

Dex lets out a heavy sigh. "As grateful as I am for this team and to be playing with you all again, I can't wait to see my beautiful wife in the crowd with Miles and our twins."

Holy shit.

Lucie pulls some sonogram pictures out from Dex's pocket.

"Holy fucking shit," Beck mutters next to me.

My hands rub my temples. "Oh there are so many Daddy Dex jokes coming to me."

At least twenty of us all start to close in on them to get a look at the photos and to celebrate, but then Miles holds out his hands again. "Red light!"

You best believe we all freeze at that very moment.

Lucie starts to laugh. "We'll be here all night. Everyone will get to look at the photos, and I can assure you there's two." She looks at Dex. "We asked for confirmation...a lot."

Olsson comes up to clap Dex's back. "Well, we're all so happy for you. We could always use some more kiddos in the stands. Now, things we didn't let Dex compromise on, open bar and dancing after we eat. Everyone, take your seats, you can congratulate the couple after."

While everyone else seems to follow Olsson's request, I'm pretty sure us girls are on our own wavelength.

I reach for Lucie's hand first. "Two babies?"

Slight fear might be showing in both of our eyes, but there's an overabundance of happiness there too. I know deep in my gut that Lucie is meant to be a mom, twins somehow only feels fitting.

"Two babies." She nods, handing me the sonogram.

Callie and Emma come to each side of me.

"Oh my word, two little Larsens!" Callie squeals.

"Are they identical or fraternal?" Emma asks next, leaning deeper into me to get a better look.

Lucie laughs. "Fraternal. It's way too early for the genders. Well, I could do the blood test in a few weeks, but right now, I'm still wrapping my head around there being two of them."

Reagan reaches for the pictures next with tears in her eyes. "Twins? Lucie, I have got to be prepped for these types of announcements! Here Will and I are, saying no to kids and you're going to have two!"

Callie claps her hands. "Oh, I can't wait to spoil the shit out of these kids. All of them, whoever has them. This is my and Will's official start of competition to be the favorite aunt and uncle."

"Will's going to have to fight Beck on that one." I say it. I hear it. I know what I've started.

Lucie takes my hands. "We're in the same room as him but I don't care. I need details. I could barely focus on the announcement with you two whispering in each other's ears."

"They've had small touches since they got here," Callie adds.

"Non-sexual touches, let's get some perspective."

Reagan doesn't look up from the picture or lower her voice even a smidge when she says, "They hooked up in the store yesterday."

Oh. My. Fuck.

Emma, Callie, and Lucie don't let that slide by quietly.

"They what?" Lucie squeals.

Callie hits Emma's arm. "I told you something was up."

My heart's beating out my damn chest. I didn't think about cameras there...I swore she didn't come in at all... during it, but I guess I was distracted.

"For all that's holy, be quiet. Also, how did you know that?"

Reagan snorts a laugh. "I didn't until just now. But I had a hunch, you two reeked of sexual tension."

Fuck my life.

Lucie squeezes my hand. "So it's true? Why didn't you tell me?"

I take a quick glance around the room and while most people aren't truly paying much attention to us, my eyes find Beck's. He tips his drink to me with a wink.

Yeah, he knows exactly what we're talking about right now.

"Now's really not the time to get into the details, but we're sort of trying this roommates-with-benefits thing. It's not a big deal—"

"*Not a big deal,*" Lucie parrots. "You're out of your mind. I may not be as shocked as when I heard two heartbeats in my stomach but this is pretty high up there."

Callie scrunches her nose. "Just roommates with bene-fits? Nothing more?"

"It's a tale as old as time," Emma sing-songs, and I smack at her side.

Reagan finally releases the sonogram back to Lucie. "Oh, come on, let her live. So what if he's not her forever. A girl's got to eat."

Lucie lets out an exasperated sigh bringing her fingers to

the bridge of her nose. "Well, I get that, but—okay, you know what? I'm on board."

I raise an eyebrow. "Just like that? This is a temporary thing between us, Luce, you get that right?"

She nods with a forced smile. "Whatever happens, happens." She takes a small step back. "I'm going to go process this information really quickly then we'll come back to it."

Callie chuckles softly. "You broke poor Lucie."

Emma sighs. "She had you and Beck on her vision board."

I turn my head to her with a smirk. "Think she'll replace me with you and Tripp?"

Emma's face sours. "Rude."

Reagan snorts a laugh. "She'll be fine. I'm just glad whatever you two did got you to agree to our little joint venture. I'm having a contractor come in sometime next week, let me know your days off from Winedown and we can make a plan on what needs to be done in your room."

"I'm off Tuesday and most mornings."

"Okay, cool, I'll text you." Reagan nods then steps over to her girlfriend before taking their seats.

I can practically feel Callie and Emma's anticipation.

"I've got to ask," Callie starts, "Is he really pierced?"

"If so, where exactly is it? Is there more than one?" Emma adds on.

Christ, these two.

I can't say I blame them for their curiosity, even though I'd prefer they didn't ask them in a room full of his teammates, but unfortunately, I'm still asking myself the same questions.

I'm already backing away from them as I hold my hands up. "I'm so not talking about this right now."

"Party pooper," Callie scolds.

I simply give her a shrug. "Sorry. Girls' brunch topic—if you're lucky."

Emma laughs but still doesn't lower her voice. "You mean if *you're lucky*."

Ah, hell, I walked right into that one.

Spinning around, I march right over to the empty seat next to Beck and try not to notice any of the players now looking my way after Emma's comment.

"How much shit did they give you, Killer?" Beck pulls my chair closer to his.

"Enough," I huff out. "I'd say the conversation isn't over by a long shot either."

Beck takes a sip of his drink with that cocky smirk on his face. 'I'm sure I'll be up next."

"Oh yeah, I'm sure the guys will be a lot more relentless than the girls," I say sarcastically.

Beck snorts. "Fair. Dex will be the worst about it, but then you have Lucie to deal with." Beck carefully brushes some of my hair behind my back then trails his hand softly down my spine. "Does your 'don't ask me if I'm sure' remark still stand?"

My eyes cut to him with a smirk. "It still stands."

Chapter 21
Beck

We make it through dinner and three songs before Lucie's pulling Jensen out to dance and the guys surround me at our table.

"So, you and Jensen?" Dex asks, taking the seat next to me.

"So, twins?" I match his tone with a cocky grin then turn to Will who's now sitting on my other side. "Has it really sunk in yet? All the baby making—"

"Fucking hell," he mutters. "Yeah, then I feel better when I remember that Adam has to experience it too."

Adam holds his hands up across from me. "At least I got to guilt trip the fuck out of you. Had you running miles with you trying to sneak back in her apartment."

Tripp laughs. "Gah, that was the best story, but we're getting off topic. The girls sent us with a purpose."

Yeah, I'm not surprised.

"Look, guys, it's plain and simple. We're not dating, we're just doing no-strings attached while we live together. If you could all go ahead and accept it and move on, that would be great."

Adam starts to laugh. "This is going to blow up in your face."

"Lucie's going to murder you." Dex leans back in his chair. "Truly, if you make Jensen cry, she will."

Tripp shrugs. "That will save us from having to pick sides when this all goes to shit."

"It's not going to go to shit or blow up in my face. Jensen and I are both on the same page here. Now can we all be grown-ups and stop acting like this is high school?"

Will shakes my shoulder. "I almost feel bad for you, but then again, no, I don't. The girls will eat you alive if this goes south. I get you and Callie have this friendship, but she will help Lucie bury your body."

Dex perks up. "Actually, you know what? With all the pushing you did with me and Lucie, keep doing what you're doing. Have your little benefits—whatever the fuck it is. You remember that pass I gave you? Yeah, it's over now. I'll be sure to point out all your bullshit and will say I told you so at the end of this."

I honestly shouldn't have expected anything less with the pestering I gave him about Lucie, but hell. Shutting my eyes, I pinch the bridge of my nose and grit out, "It's not like that between us, just drop it."

Dex snorts. "Hey, déjà vu."

Adam picks up his beer. "Alright, who wants to be in the pool this time?"

"I put a hundred that they crack within the month," Tripp tosses out his bet.

Then Will. "I'll put my money on New Year's."

Dex throws up his hand. "They won't make it two weeks."

And with that, I'm out of my chair. "Oh, fuck off."

Walking away from this conversation might only encourage them more, but I don't have to convince them. I'd love to tell them it's none of their business, but that means jack shit to this group.

I barely make it past the tables before Jensen's breaking away from the girls dancing in the middle.

Her smile tells me she was watching all that unfold. "How much shit did they give you, Stalker?"

I chuckle, stepping closer to her I already feel ten times better. My shoulders fall from being pinned up. "Enough. Our friends have lots of opinions."

"And questions. They'll get over it." She sweeps her hair behind her shoulder. "Should I ask you if you're sure, or are you going to come dance with me? Give them something else to have opinions on."

Her hands reach for mine and every comment, bet, even the people around us seem to disappear.

"I have a better idea."

"Oh, yeah?" A spark lights in her eyes as I pull her to me.

"If we're going to give them something to have opinions on, might as well go all out."

"Lead the way, Beckham." One of Jensen's hands trails up my shirt then slides her fingers in between the gaps of the buttons.

Any and every fuck to give in my body leaves at her touch. I'm damn near tempted to toss her over my shoulder and carry her—just for good measure—but I'm sure anyone looking at us right now will get the picture just fine.

My grip on her hand tightens slightly as I weave us

through the table set up then slip through one of the curtains.

Jensen doesn't ask any questions about where we're going. She definitely doesn't ask what we're going to do when we get there either.

Pulling open the door to Dex's former office, I prop the door with my foot and haul Jensen to me. Her legs wrap around my waist as I carry her in and set her right on top of the desk.

My lips hover an inch or so away from hers. "In the spirit of communication, I really want to kiss you."

Jensen hums while her fingers find their way back in between the gaps of my shirt. "Put that energy someplace else, Beckham, and don't you dare rip this dress either."

A small groan comes out at the thought, but then again, I have to agree with her. "No, I want to fuck you in it." I place a kiss on her shoulder. "Have your legs shaking in it." A kiss to the marigold on her collarbone then up her neck to her ear. "I want to fuck you so good that whenever you wear this dress it reminds you of me."

Jensen's whole body quivers and her hands latch on to my biceps to steady herself. "You're stealing a lot of my memories, Beck. First the window, now the dress..." Jensen lets out a breathy moan as I kiss her neck. "What's next?"

"Let's find out," I whisper against her skin.

Jensen's head tilts back and she arches her back. If I can't kiss her lips, then I'll happily cover her body with them. Trace every single tattoo she has with my tongue.

"Beck, for my sanity—remind me that you had a vasectomy."

My body stills. My knee-jerk reaction is to be a little hurt that she thinks I'd lie about something like that, but when I lean back to meet her eyes I know that's not what she meant.

"It's done. Snipped. Doctor cleared, Jen. I swear." She nods her head slowly and her hands reach out for my belt, but I capture her face with mine. "We don't have to have sex. I can have your legs shaking and leave you with an orgasm to ruin this dress without it."

"Always so cocky." Jensen's eyes nearly roll out of her head before she undoes my belt. "I want to. I want to find out what piercings you've got down there." She pushes me back then sinks down to her knees. "And after I'm done showing you how good of a girl I can be, you can fuck me against that window."

"Fuck..." I groan. My hands tangle in her hair as she pulls my pants down.

Her smirk grows as she sees the ring I have at the base of my shaft then a Prince Albert at the tip. "Please tell me a man did these."

"You jealous, Jennie?"

Her eyes flash up. "Maybe."

Oh, she is—I can see it—and fuck if I don't want more of it. "Can't say only women have touched my dick like you're about to, Killer."

Jensen smirks as her hand wraps tightly around my shaft. "Yeah? Well, I'm the only one who gets to touch it now."

Before I can agree she has me in her mouth. "Fuck, Jensen." My hips pulse forward ever so slightly and my grip tightens in her hair. "It's only yours..." I grit out, and for some reason I can't seem to add that it's hers for now.

We might be temporary, but with a sweet moan from her as she takes me deeper, my dick might belong to Jensen forever after this.

My hips move a little more at the thought. My head tilts back when it draws more moans from her.

I can already feel my balls tightening and that tell of a tingle at the base of my spine with Jensen's mouth taking me like the good girl she said she is, but then her hand slips back from my balls and lightly rims my ass.

I immediately pick her up from the floor and carry her back until I've got her fully pressed against the window. The look on her face tells me she got the reaction she wanted out of me.

"Got to work on that stamina, Mr. Pro Athlete."

"You're right." I lift her dress slowly, letting my fingers tease her soft skin until I reach the lace of her underwear to slide it just as painfully slow back down. "You said you were a good girl, but that's a lie." My hands lift the back of her thighs. "You're lethal, baby."

Lining up with her entrance, I pause.

"I've never had sex without a condom. Never would have even considered it, but with you—"

"Beck..." she cuts me off, my name hushed as her hands hold tightly on my shoulders. "I'll already think of you every time I put this dress on...make me feel you."

Good god. I'm deep inside her before I can think twice. Both our heads tilt back with a moan as the sensation works its way through our bodies.

"Oh my god, that ring is right on my clit."

My smirk grows as I lift her body then bring her back down. Her nails dig into my shoulders, and I start to move her in quicker pulses.

"Fuck, Beck, that feels amazing."

Her walls start to squeeze me like a vise and that tingly feeling from her mouth around my cock is now an electric shock. We've barely even started, and while I could blame my lack of control from it being a while since I've had sex, I don't think that's the case—it's her.

Something about us feels so deep and connected, even though we both see an eventual end to whatever this is...the thought is enough to have my heart pounding and my grip on her tighten like I don't want to let her go.

Fuck, I'm feeling way too much. This is supposed to be just sex...

"Deeper." Jensen tugs at my shoulders bringing me back to the moment. "I need to feel more of you."

Shit, the word feel is starting to lose all meaning.

I press her harder up against the window so my entire body is in line with hers. "Are you going to come all over this cock, baby?"

Jensen's eyes lock with mine, this wicked grin on her lips. "Maybe, unless you come first again."

Shit, she's everything. Fuck all the overthinking, I just need to focus on this—on her and why we're doing this in the first place.

My dick is absolutely raging as I slow down my thrusts. I move tortuously slow so that she feels every inch going in and out. All while that ring on my base teases her clit. Her eyes squeeze shut and her nails claw into my shoulders.

"We may not be in the typical missionary position, but I'll still argue with you, Jen. So, go ahead, lie and say you aren't going to come on this cock."

Jensen's head tilts back with a moan when I reach the hilt, but curses when I slowly pull back out. Her eyes latch back onto mine as her hands move to my face. "If I say it, will you go faster?"

"Maybe." *Fuck yes, I will.* "I can see it in your eyes, baby.

I can feel it in the way you're squeezing me like a fist. Say it and we'll both get that orgasm we're wanting."

"I'm going to come—" A moan of my name immediately comes as I thrust hard and fast into her. Her arms twist back around my neck. "You feel so damn good...I knew you would."

All my sanity snaps, relentlessly pounding into her. There's this feral need to consume her fully and while my first thought is to taste her lips on mine, I at least find enough sense to hold back.

Her head arches a bit and my mouth finds her neck to satisfy the need. I nip and suck at her neck until I'm positive there will be a mark left.

The sounds coming out of us both are nowhere near quiet but I don't fucking care. It isn't until Jensen's sounds pause for two thrusts that I pull back, because on the third thrust her red lips form a nice O shape and her walls pulse around my shaft.

"That's my girl." I nip at the top of her tits and let myself go at the sound and feel of her release.

My hips slow in tandem with our plateau, then I slowly set her legs back down. Keeping my body pressed against hers until our breath evens out, I caress her cheek softly.

"You owe me a new dress," she whispers in an exasperated breath.

I tuck a strand of her hair behind her ear then place a kiss on her quickly forming hickey. "No way. I'm throwing out any other dresses you have actually, so you have to wear this one."

Jensen giggles then rests her head on my shoulder. "Does sneaking off during Dex and Lucie's big day make us bad friends?"

"Fuck no. Do you know how many times I've entertained Miles for Dex to do this exact thing? Asshole owes me."

"Good." Jensen lifts her head back up and this freshly fucked glint shines in her eyes. "Even if it did, I wouldn't regret it."

My heart pounds loudly in my chest. "I don't think I'll ever regret a single second with you."

I'm terrified I might regret losing you.

Chapter 22
Jensen

"Okay, so I'm not allowed to let your sister do her tarot cards?" Beck asks as we unload our Thanksgiving to-go feast. One thing I'm grateful for today is the fact that not a single one of us even brought up the idea of cooking.

"Right, and don't you dare tell her your birthday unless you want us to know all about your zodiac and star chart."

"What if I do, huh? It could be interesting. And it's something your sister likes, I'm just trying to be supportive of your family," Beck teases.

With the last to-go box spread out on the island, I turn to him, hip cocked. "I don't need you to be supportive. I have other needs for you and not one of them include you getting all buddy-buddy with my sister."

Beck steps to me, his hands lean against the wood as his eyes level with mine. "Tell your sister Thanksgiving is canceled, let me fulfill all those needs for you right now."

That is oh so tempting, especially with the memories of yesterday still fresh in my mind. Not to mention the marks. I had to throw on a turtleneck for the hickey he gave me.

I knew sex with him was going to be good, but it's more than good—the only word I can truly think to describe it is Beck. It was every part of him that made me fall for the guy.

It was just as spontaneous and fun as he always is, but again he had me feeling everything. All the possessiveness and want for him.

When my high truly came down, I kept waiting to feel this wave of impending doom. This need to run for the hills and salvage what I can of my heart—but it never came.

I'm not sure if my rose-colored glasses are firmly back on and my mind is purely set on being in the moment, or if I'm just majorly delusional, but I'm going with the former. Beck makes being in the moment easy, so why not roll with it?

I glide my finger from the buttons of his Henley down his sternum then push hard until he relents.

"Damn, woman, you could have said move."

"Oh, you're fine." I brush him off but his hand captures mine pulling me to him.

"No, I'm not, kiss it and make it better."

My laugh comes with ease, and for a moment I press deeper into him. Soak in the warmth of his body against mine and let all the tension pent up in my muscles go.

I love that he's wearing his glasses today. Something about him in them just feeds my soul. It's like the Superman effect, except it's not a disguise from anyone—it's like a different side that feels more mine than anyone else's.

I'm going to have to be a little more on guard when Stella gets here. And not because of the roommates-with-benefits deal, because Stella will see the feelings behind it. I'm not exactly sure how she's going to feel about me working through them instead of burying them, but it's too late to go back now.

Beck's hands move around my waist, then he drags his lips up my neck to my ear. "I see you covered up that hickey I gave you."

A small tingle slides down my spine. "Sure did. Don't worry, I can still feel you."

A low growl comes from Beck as he backs me up against the island. His hold on my body tightens and just as he nips at my ear, Dottie starts to bark. His grip flexes and neither of us move until the knock comes to the door.

Perfect freaking timing, Stella.

Beck places one more quick kiss on my neck before letting me go. "No tarot cards and no zodiac talk."

My hands trail down from his shoulder to his pecks. "Good boy."

This smile comes to his face and a playful smack comes to my ass. "Go answer the door."

With a bit of a skip in my step, I answer the door with what my sister can tell right away is too damn happy.

My greeting is lost when her jaw drops and her head tilts to the side. "Oh my god, you're practically glowing. Are you high again?"

I fold my lips together tightly. "No, can't I be excited to see my sister?"

Stella steps inside, setting her bag down then pulling her snow-clad coat off. "See, I believe that to some degree, because of course you're excited to see me, but also I don't think I've ever described you as glowing."

I pinch my eyebrows at her. "Okay, that's a bit rude."

Dottie prances up to Stella as she takes her boots off. Her voice goes up at least four octaves as she pets her. "There's my sweetie! Have you missed me?"

"And somehow my greeting was too happy."

Stella snaps up. "I'm always this much of a delight."

Ah, yes, and she's humble too. A smart remark is on the tip of my tongue when Beck walks up beside me. Stella's smile grows the size of a coat hanger.

Beck barely gets his hello out before Stella says, "So, you must be the one who cracked my sister like a glow stick."

"Stella! ¿*Por qué dirías eso?*" Why would you say that?

She waves me off with a *tsk*, then holds her hand out for Beck. "I know we met briefly on FaceTime, but it's nice to officially meet you."

Beck shakes her hand but he looks at me with a smile on his face. "This is about to be fun, isn't it?"

"Oh, it so is." Stella reaches into her bag and pulls out two bottles of wine. "Boozy Thanksgiving!"

Beck's laugh warms my body, but when he takes the bottles and Stella pulls out two more, I can feel the headache already forming.

"Stella." I sigh, bringing my hand up applying a bit of pressure.

My sister walks right past us to the kitchen, ready to make herself completely at home. "We'll pour your glass first, sis."

Beck steps to me, bottles still in hand. "Come on, Killer. I'm even more adorable when I'm tipsy."

I give him my best side-eye for entertaining this, but that smile he has melts me. I try to keep some of my bite in my tone. "I will call Lucie to come get me."

"No, you won't." Beck moves so quick I don't even register the kiss to my forehead until he's turning, walking back to the kitchen.

Stella hovers over the to-go boxes, lifting the lids at a few to see everything we got. "Cheeseburgers, wings, tacos...and no cooking on our end. Must say, this was a fabulous idea."

"I have to agree. I had Jen pick out the spread and I came in with the credit card." Beck sets down three wineglasses then a bottle opener. "Which one are we opening first?"

Stella slides the bottle of Cabernet to him. "I say we open 'em all, but I know this one is Jennie's favorite."

Beck flashes me a grin. "Perfect, we'll start with this one then."

"Yeah, I bet you will," Stella whispers. The smile on her face is a bit more smug than Beck's.

I'm honestly waiting for her to outright ask what's going on between us. Unlike Lucie, Stella isn't afraid to cuss me out like a sailor without blinking an eye...all lovingly, of course.

Making my way over to them slowly, Beck hands me a glass and I take a big gulp. "Anyway, how's work going, Stel? You ready to be flying out this weekend for whatever inevitable scandal happens today?"

Stella groans and slides the bottle of Zinfandel to Beck. "Just put a straw in that bottle for me. I'm already hating the phone call I'm sure to be getting tomorrow for whichever sleazy public figure has their side piece fuck up Thanksgiving."

While Beck doesn't hand her back the bottle with a straw, he does give her a very generous pour. "So, what is it you do exactly?"

"I work for a PR company." Stella plops down on one of the stools around the island. "Primarily, I clean up messes and scandals."

"That puts it lightly." My sister is *the* PR girl with the company she works for. "Stella lives to make grown men cry while she puts out their fires. People have started requesting her by name with how good of a job she does."

Stella waves a hand for me to stop, but the look on her face says otherwise. "I am pretty good at it. However, I would love to stop having to deal with random fires and flying out all the time."

I make my way over to the seat next to her. "What? I thought you loved your job?"

"I do. I really do love coming in looking like a bubblegum princess with my pretty dresses and purple streaks in my hair for everyone to doubt my capabilities then completely blow them away. And yes, make a few grown men cry in the process." Stella shrugs. "But I also want some good fires and puzzles to solve. I want to work with a place and nurture it, not come in only for crises."

"Have you looked at some of the places around here?" Beck asks. "I'm sure there are plenty of companies that could use someone on deck."

Stella weighs her head back and forth. "I've looked some, but haven't really had a ton of time to dig too deep into it, but I suppose if I moved here"—Stella spins to face me—"we could find a place together. I could probably swing moving here with the company I'm with now too."

Hi, heart, meet my stomach.

"I...uh...I guess we could." My eyes seek out Beck but he hides his reaction to my sister's suggestion by taking a sip of his wine. I guess he could have zero feelings about the situation.

Stella follows my gaze. "Unless this isn't as temporary as mentioned before?"

Yep, my heart is definitely deep in my stomach now.

Beck clears his throat but keeps his eyes down at the

wine in his hand. "It's temporary, but no hard move-out date."

Stella reaches over to squeeze my leg. "Well, it was just an idea. One that doesn't have to be entertained today."

She's right, it doesn't. But Beck's right too—we're in the moment, but the moment will eventually pass.

"We can talk about it over the next few weeks. I know Reagan is wanting to get the ball rolling on our building so worrying about apartments is a little low on my list."

Stella thankfully takes my bait and her eyes light up. "Oh, tell me more about that. What are we thinking? Do you get to have your own name? Can I pick it? I'll be your PR girl, and you'll get the family discount."

"No, I get the sister discount—which is free." I take a sip of my wine really hoping a buzz takes that lingering pain of moving out of Beck's place eventually off my mind. "I would imagine I'll get to name my business..." I look to Beck. "That actually does seem like something Reagan might be anal about."

A bit of a smirk finally tugs at the corner of his lips again. "I could see that, but at the same time, I assume she'll want to keep the business separate to some extent. Let's just come up with a name for shits and giggles at least."

Stella squeals. "Ooo, okay, this is going to be so fun. But also I need a burger to think clearly."

"That's fair," Beck says and immediately turns to grab some plates. When he sets them down, he pulls his phone out of his pocket. "You guys dig in, I'm going to call my dad real quick."

I'm out of my seat before I even realize it. "Is everything—"

"Everything's fine, baby," Beck cuts me off. "He just wants to check in. I'll be back, you eat."

I let out a small sigh in relief. "Okay, tell them I said hi."

Beck nods then holds his phone up to his ear before heading up the stairs. I watch and wait for him to disappear then Dottie's up and chasing after him.

A smack comes to my arm. "Jensen James. You better start talking."

I look at my sister, eyes wide. "Okay, first, ow, and second, what the hell was that for?"

"Oh, don't you dare. I knew something had to be going on with how damn happy you look, but that man just called you *baby*, and you want to gloss over it."

I sputter a laugh. "What? No, he didn't."

"Yeah, he did. I know it just happened but I'm replaying it in my head because I'm pretty sure I almost fell out of my seat with a swoon."

Wait...he did say baby. I hadn't even really registered it, it just felt natural to hear.

Stella's voice turns to a whisper. "Jensen, you like him."

"Well, duh, you are one of the few who actually knows how I feel about him." I take a deep breath. "But it's not—"

"No, Jennie, it is like that. Try again."

I sit back down next to her. "It is, but it isn't at the same time. Can you just trust me? This isn't anything like what happened with Travis. We're not even really dating, just roommates with benefits."

Stella hums softly. I know she's leery, but that's simply from my past experience, not her lack of trust.

When she doesn't say anything, I add, "I told him he's not allowed to kiss me. I know in my gut that it would be the end of me. I have boundaries set and so does he."

"Good, and listen, I'm never here to judge you. If you want to date Beck, then date Beck. He seems really great."

"We're not dating, Stel. Just...getting it out of our system."

Stella's eyebrows raise up high. "O-*kay!* If you say so."

"We're not dating. I'm serious."

Stella holds her hand up to count. "You live together, the man calls you 'baby,' I'm imagining you both are exclusively fooling around with each other during this time...a.k.a dating."

Well, shit, when she puts it like that...

"But we don't kiss, we don't go on dates, per se...we just happen to enjoy each other's company." Alright, not helping myself too much here. "And there's a definite end, remember? He may have called me baby, but he also said it was temporary."

Stella stands up with a smug smile and grabs a plate. "Temporary, my ass."

I reach for my glass and send the remainder of my wine straight down my throat. Come on alcohol, help me out here.

Stella stops filling up her plate and pours more in my glass. "You might as well take the bottle, Sis. It makes the delusion easier to swallow."

The evil eye I give her doesn't faze her, and for that, I drink some more.

"You know, you didn't want me to do a reading last time we were on the phone but I did one for you anyway. Want to know what I learned?"

"No," I answer immediately. "I'm begging you, please."

Stella shakes her head as she digs through the food boxes. "Fine, fine, I won't say anything. However—"

"Stella!" I snap, but she just laughs me off.

"Relax, I'm moving on from you and loverboy." When she's satisfied with her choices on her plate, she comes back to sit next to me. "I was going to say, I think you should have your business named something witchy and powerful."

"Of course you do," I mumble with another sip of my wine. Rounding the island, I grab my plate and start getting my own food.

Stella's mom loved doing tarot readings, crystals, and star charts. I remember every full moon we would have these big sleepovers where her mom would do all these rituals.

After she passed, my mom really made an effort to keep them going. Even though Dad and I weren't exactly big into it, it was always the thing we did as a family every single month until Stella and I moved out.

"What would you name it? And put a little bit of your PR brain into it," I tease her.

She scoffs. "I always use my PR brain!"

Before I can give her another smart-ass remark, Beck walks back down the stairs and gives one for me. "Was that the same brain that told you to bring four bottles of wine to our Thanksgiving meal?"

"As a matter of fact, it was." Stella scrunches her nose taking another sip. "It is also telling me I'll be crashing in Jensen's bed tonight as well."

Humph. "You think?"

Stella simply sticks her tongue out at me so I retort with my middle finger.

"Alright, alright, no sister fights." Beck makes his way over to my side, his hand briefly landing on my back as he steps around to grab his own plate.

Butterflies flutter in my stomach. "You have a good talk?" I ask cautiously. I still really want to know what happened between him and his dad, and with the way they talked to each other last night I'm even more curious.

Beck gives a small nod. "Yeah, we did, my parents said hi back to you."

Well, that seems like it's all I'm going to get on that front. I swallow down any other questions.

"What about something with angel numbers?" Stella blurts out. Gah, I love her. "For the name of your tattoo shop. I know you and Dad don't really get into all of it like me and Mom, but we all have angel number tattoos."

"Okay...I do like that." I give Stella a grateful smile.

Beck gives me a small nudge with his elbow. "Are the angel numbers the 222 on your arm?"

"Yeah, I have twos for alignment—"

Stella snorts a laugh. "Your guardian angel was shoving that number down your throat when you were..." She trails off when she catches the look on my face. She holds up her glass. "Sorry, wine makes the PR brain work less."

Beck steps around me again to fill up his plate. "When you were what?"

I'm itching to send Stella my middle finger again, but you know what, Beck gets to be vague about whatever happened with his dad, I can be vague about this. "When I lived at home. I had some things that weren't exactly in *alignment.*"

Beck's mouth opens but Stella tries to recover her fumble. "But now you are with your shop, so why not something like Tattoo 222 or Ink 222...maybe—"

"You could do Tinta 222," Beck says, earning both a stunned look from me and an impressed one from Stella.

"Since when do you know Spanish?" I ask.

Beck shrugs. "I don't know a lot, but you mumble

Spanish when I annoy you sometimes...I wanted to know what you were saying."

My heart feels like it skips a beat. I don't know what to say, honestly.

Stella takes this one for me. "I like Tinta 222, I think you should go with that, Jennie."

I clear my throat. Shit, Beck really is going to steal everything from me.

"Yeah, I think I will."

I foresaw the headache today, but I didn't quite realize how much of a bitch she would be.

Rolling over, Stella doesn't budge. She's always slept like the dead, but with a wine hangover, there will be no waking her until she's ready.

I quickly get ready for my double today, only bothering to be somewhat quiet for my own headache.

Agreeing to a double shift at Winedown might not have been the best move, but money still has to be made. I want to be able to control when I use Beck's money so there are many more doubles in my future.

I barely make it five feet down the hall before I know, without a doubt, that Beck's not here. It's entirely too quiet in this house for him or Dottie to still be here.

Part of me hoped they might be across the street at the dog park but when I see the notepad on the counter with a glass of water and a bottle of Advil I know that's not the case.

Morning Jenni-cakes,

Dot and I are headed to the training facility for a run, then

Dex and Miles meeting us there. Red Bull is in the fridge, and medicine on the table if you need it.

P.S. If I were to take Dottie to one of those groomers that do cool styles and temp dye their fur... How mad would you be?

Shaking my head, I shake out two pills and gulp them down with some water before picking up the pen.

If you plan on stalking me later, I'll be at Winedown all day.

P.S. Very mad. My dog is cool enough on her own.

Raiding the cabinets, I grab a couple of the varying power and granola bars that Beck ordered with groceries last week, then snag the Red Bull from the fridge.

Before I can bring myself to walk out the door, my eye catches on the glass of water Beck left out. Picking it up, I drink it all, and the reasoning in my head is that Lucie would be proud, and my slight hangover demands it...not because it could earn me a good girl comment from the man who set it out.

When I get to work, I shoot off a text to Stella to let her know where I'll be. Thankfully, Stella didn't bring up the topic of me and Beck again. After finding out that Beck's secretly been learning Spanish, I think Stella knew I couldn't handle any mentions of him when we retreated back to my room for a sister sleepover. My feelings for him were written so clearly on my face that she didn't have to bring it up.

Sliding my phone in my back pocket, I turn around ready to get things open and find Mia beaming at the bar.

"Hi, I'm here for my daily Beck update." Her chin rests on her hand as she leans on the bar top, like she's ready to eat up every word I'm about to say.

No, no, no. I refuse to talk about this again. Why do I have such nosy friends?

"You know I think maybe we should start with a shift update...are we out of anything important? Anyone call out that I need to know about?" I try some leading, a.k.a. avoiding questions, but Mia's not falling for it.

"Winedown is completely amazing now that I've taken it over, nothing is out of stock, everyone's working who's supposed to be, and I want to know about you and Beck. You've given me nothing for a whole week! You had three days off, and I demand to know if they were well spent."

"Okay, they were well spent." I shrug her off and tie my apron around my waist. "Can I start opening the bar now?"

Mia's eyes roll, but given the professional she is, she shrugs me off. "I shall find out how it's going on my own then. I'll cut you first tonight, my girl."

Thank god.

I let out a sigh as Mia gets up from the barstool, then says, "Nice hickey."

"Dammit." My hand covers my neck. I swore the collar on my button-up covered it fairly decently. "Hey, I said they were well spent."

"It seems like it." She laughs. "Have a good shift, I'm going to step out for lunch with my parents but then I'll be back. Text me if you need me."

"Sounds good," I say, but then remember something. "Oh, Mia, you know Will and Callie with the Blues?"

"Yeah, Callie's the redhead right? And Will is the one who doesn't drink?"

"Right." I nod. "Will's going to ask her to marry him, so we're wanting to throw them an engagement party after

Opening Day. Her brother is going to plan it mostly, but wanted to know if he could rent out the place."

Mia raises an eyebrow. "Rent out the entire restaurant, or just upstairs?"

"Lucie mentioned upstairs, but Adam said the whole place if possible. I can give you his number if you want to talk it out."

Mia comes back to the bar, waving her hands. "Wait, wait. Is Adam the really big one? Super hot, but always looks serious?"

I can't stop my laugh. "That would be him. He's not always serious, he's actually pretty fun, gives teddy bear energy when you get to know him."

Mia cocks her head. "If you say so. Just give him my email. If it's business related it should stay in my inbox. That's what my parents would say, at least."

"I'll pass it along. Oh, and whatever date he gives, go ahead and mark me off."

Mia spins on her heels with a wave. "I know, I know. Have a good shift, Jensen."

And you know, I actually do. We're busy but not slammed. I'm working with competent people today which was a major surprise, considering it's the day after a national holiday.

It isn't until about two in the afternoon that my sister finally shows up at the bar with a few shopping bags in hand.

"Excuse me," she says very overdramatically as I make my way to her. "I'm in need of a drink after fighting off the Black Friday shoppers."

"Oh, you poor soul, what can I get you to revive you?" I joke.

"Hit me with the hard stuff. Coke on the rocks, don't you dare get me a diet."

"Coming right up." Getting her drink, I decide to pop a cherry on top just for the fun of it. "Here you are."

She picks up the stem. "Ah, *gracias*. Nice hickey, by the way. Now I get why you had on a turtleneck."

Shit, has everyone noticed it today?

"Moving on. What are you doing out shopping?"

Stella smirks, but doesn't pester anymore. "I picked up a new power suit. Flying out to New Jersey tonight. Did you know that having your mistress show up with a turkey for a company Thanksgiving is not a good look?"

I fake disbelief. "I bet they didn't even get to break the wishbone."

Stella fights her laugh as she swallows the cherry. "The wife threw the turkey through the conference room wall."

"As she should."

"As she should," Stella parrots in agreement before taking a sip of her drink. "I'll be there for a bit, and again, no need to further discuss at this time, but I am down to get a place here together if you want."

My stomach turns, and Stella can see it all over my face.

"It's just an option on the table, Jennie. I'm thinking of making the move whether you want to or not, so don't think this is something you have to be a part of, or that you'll be leaving me high and dry."

"Thanks, I'll keep it in mind."

Stella's smile grows again. "Good, and P.S. I wrote a very inappropriate note on yours and Beck's little pad on the counter."

My eyes shut as I grumble, "How inappropriate?"

Chapter 23
Beck

If you plan on stalking me later, I'll be at Winedown all day.

P.S. Very mad. My dog is cool enough on her own.

P.P.S. This is so cute I could just...gag. Thanks for letting me crash. Beck, if you get this before Jensen throws it away—please continue to make her shine like a glow stick. She deserves nothing less. Xoxo Stella.

P.P.P.S? I stole some Advil too.

I chuckle at the notepad in my hand. It would probably be a smart move for me to stay home tonight. I got more than enough shit from Dex at the training facility, and the pure hate I felt yesterday when Stella brought up Jensen moving out came with red flashing lights in my head.

Then I slipped up and called her baby in front of her sister, which I know did not go unnoticed by Stella. I then got many well-worded questions from my father when I called him asking about Jensen.

Everything in my brain is yelling at me to stop this. Walk away while I still can, but I can't. I'm drowning in my feelings for her now and being around her seems to be my only life preserver.

I know I can't be what she wants. I care way too much about her to put her through loving me. I know this could blow up in my face, but I didn't expect it to happen this quickly.

Yet, here I am, picking up my keys again after dropping Dottie off at the house so I can go reach for my life preserver.

Walking into Winedown, I find Jensen's eyes immediately. She flashes me a quick smile before helping the person in front of her.

Weaving through the tables and people, I grab the first empty seat I see at the bar.

Once the other bartender registers who I am, she simply nods and nudges Jensen. I must have made my intentions very clear the past few times I've been here.

Jensen leans around the other girl and shakes her head at me. I can tell from that look alone that she's about to make me wait. Not that I mind, I'll gladly sit here all night and watch her.

A few people come and go from the bar while Jensen occasionally looks my way. I simply give her a smile or wink. I don't know how much time passes as I watch her, but finally the bar seems to steady a bit and she makes her way in front of me.

"Hey, Stalker."

"Is it really stalking if you begged me to come find you?"

Jensen's jaw drops a tad. "Begged is an awfully strong word for me, Beck. You, on the other hand..."

"Oh, don't start with me, Jenni-cakes, I'll have you begging in the supply closet."

Jensen's cheeks redden a bit, and I mark the rise and fall of her chest.

"You thinking about it?"

"Maybe," she whispers.

Leaning on the bar, I pitch my voice lower. "I like that my mark is on display today."

And at that, her blush dies and her hand goes to her neck. "*Nunca más*. Have you learned that one yet?"

"Yes, I have, and yes, it is happening again. I may not be great at speaking it yet, but I mostly started learning to understand what you whisper to yourself about me."

Jensen leans to meet me halfway on the bar. "Get ready to hear about all the things you do that piss me off."

I don't miss my opportunity. "You know I love when you flirt with me."

Jensen's blush comes right back, and oh, how I adore it.

I'm so completely wrapped up in it that I don't register the person moving into the seat next to me until they're saying Jensen's name.

"Hey, Jensen, long time no see." The guy looks about my age with tattoos down his arms. I can't say he's necessarily looking at Jensen in any sort of way, but it doesn't matter.

This pain comes to my chest when Jensen gives him a smile. "Hey, what are you doing here?"

The guy gives her a nonchalant shrug. "Well, you haven't responded to any of my proof of life texts so I thought I'd check in."

The fuck? I shouldn't care that he sent her texts, especially if she's leaving them on read, but fuck that, I do care. I care a whole fucking lot.

Jensen holds her hands up in defense. "My bad. As you can see, I'm alive. Been a little busy, but alive nonetheless."

Jensen eyes land on me. I don't know what she's about to introduce me as, but I know I'm going to fucking hate to hear the word friend. "This is Beck. My roommate. Beck, this is Blake, he works at Tally's."

Blake? I think she's mentioned that name before…I think that's the name she threw out as another option of whose house to crash at. The pain in my chest only gets worse and my stomach turns in knots.

"Worked," Blake corrects. "Officially quit two days ago."

Jensen's eyes go wide, and I hate both myself right now and hate the fact that this is nowhere the end of this conversation.

"Wait, really? How'd that go?"

"Not quite as bad as your exit, but not pretty, either. Did you know I too am a slut and a thief?"

My blood boils. I know I told Jensen not to tell me the lies they were saying about her, and apparently that was a good call. "Jensen, what the fuck is he talking about?"

Her eyes lock on mine and her face softens. "Beck, it's fine. I told you they were saying things, and we handled what we could in that situation. It's over now."

Blake shifts in the seat. "Sorry, I didn't mean—"

"No, it's fine." Jensen turns her attention back to him and it takes all my willpower to not reach over the bar and take it back. "So, what are you doing now?"

"Eh, I'll let them get their hissy fit out, same as I told you to do. But in light of how they treated you, I may have clued the health department in on a few glaring violations along with a copy of Hank's license that, surprise, surprise, he forgot to renew."

Jensen's eyes light up in a way that has my stomach turning in knots. "You didn't…"

"Damn right I did. We'll see what comes of it, but in the meantime, I'm going to go visit my sister for a bit. She runs a bed and breakfast and usually needs extra hands over the holidays. After that I'll come back here and look for a new place to work."

Don't say it. Don't say it.

"Well, if you're interested I'm going to be opening my own place. Wouldn't mind renting a spot—"

Fuck.

"Jensen." Her name is out of my mouth before I can stop it. I'm overstepping. I'm well aware I'm being a total dick right now. I need to stop before I make it worse.

Jensen tilts her head. She's rightfully pissed at me. I can see it all over her face. "Got something to add to that interruption, Beckham?"

I stand from my seat. "Nope, I'm gonna go actually. It's your thing, I know you can handle it. I'm just—" *I'm making it worse. Holy shit, I'm making this so much worse.* "I'll see you at the house."

Jensen huffs a small breath. "Yeah, maybe."

I feel that "maybe" all the way home. I hate it, and myself. I can't explain it.

I know I don't own her, but in some fucked up way, it bothered me that I couldn't put this claim on her either. Jensen said someday down the road she did want that forever type of love...

After taking Dottie across the street, I stare at my empty living room with a sigh. I wanted to stay on that damn barstool until Jensen could come home with me, but here I am, stewing in my own downfall.

Dottie jumps up on the couch to turn a few circles before lying down with a humph.

"I know...I wish she was here too. Surely, her 'maybe' was an empty threat..."

Dottie lifts her eyes to me, and I swear if she could talk she would tell me not to put it past her mom to let me sweat it out.

Sighing, I do the only thing I can bring myself to do, which is play a round of pool. I don't turn on an audiobook or music, I let the silence be my punishment.

Nearing hour two, my anxiety is starting to feel a bit like something clawing inside my chest. Calling Jensen would most likely go to voicemail, and calling Winedown would only piss her off more.

Another half hour passes and I'm about to grab my keys again to head to the bar but then the front door opens.

Dottie jumps up from the couch and races to greet Jensen the moment she steps through the door.

Jensen squats down to give her a big greeting, but when she stands back up and her eyes lock onto mine, she softens. "Hey."

"Hey," I breathe out, stepping to her slowly. "I'm sorry for being a dick at the bar."

Jensen bobs her head as she chews on her bottom lip. "Want to tell me why? I know we didn't say it, but exclusivity felt pretty implied on my end for this whole roommates-with-benefits situation."

"No, I know. But I was jealous, Jen. There's no point in me denying it, I was fucking jealous."

Jensen takes a deep breath as she takes a step toward me. "Beck, it's fine to be jealous. Do you honestly think I've never been jealous? I hated watching Mia flirt with you, I know I pushed her on you, but I hated it. What I don't get is why you thought that needed to cross over into me mentioning my shop then run away in the middle of it."

I tug her to me, resting my forehead on hers. "I left because I don't know how to make sense of us, baby."

"And you think I do?" Jensen pushes me back slightly. Her eyes locking onto mine while she waits for an actual explanation.

"No, it's—" Complicated? Fuck, that's putting what we are lightly. "I don't know how to make sense of how I wanted so badly to show everyone in that bar that you were mine. I wanted to get up and take my bat to Tally's for even thinking poorly of you. I hated the idea of Blake working with you because I was so fucking jealous that he might get to have you longer in his life than me."

Jensen swallows hard. "Beck, I came here not wanting to entertain the idea of any relationship. You said yourself that you don't want love or a relationship...is that still true?"

Her question hits me like a ton of bricks. My hands flinch to reach for my glasses but instead I pull her back again and rest my forehead back on hers.

Taking a deep breath, I can't look at her when I whisper, "It's still true."

Jensen's hands glide up my arms to rest on my shoulders. "That's okay. It's what we agreed on. And if it helps, I hated calling you my roommate, but I didn't know what else to say —I know we're not more, but you aren't just a roommate or a friend to me either."

Pulling her flush against me, I kiss the top of her head. "We're clear as mud, baby."

Jensen hums in amusement. "It definitely seems that way."

Holding her tightly, I rub her back slowly. "I'm sorry again for being a jealous asshole."

"I don't care that you were jealous." Jensen rests her chin on my chest and looks up. "You're really hot when you're all possessive and bossy."

My eyebrows raise. "That's good to know."

"Yeah, but then you ran away in the middle of interrupting me and that brought your hotness down to scale. It did not give pierced-dick energy."

Fuck, I love her bratty mouth. Picking her up, I toss her over my shoulder.

She lets out a little yelp. "Beck, what are you doing?"

Carrying her up the stairs, I smack her ass. "Reminding you how much you love my pierced dick."

And with that, I get no smart-ass remark or fight to put her down. I carry her all the way to her bathroom and turn on the shower before setting her down on the counter.

I trail my finger from the mark on her neck down the cleavage of her shirt. "Do you have another shirt for work tomorrow?"

Breathlessly, she says, "I do, but—"

That's all I need to hear. I rip her shirt off and buttons fly every direction.

"Beck!"

"I'll buy you more." I kiss her neck as I pull the shirt off then unclasp her bra. "I find it extremely annoying that I've gotten two orgasms from you, but still haven't gotten you naked yet."

Jensen's hands push me back and I can already see the fire in her eyes as she grips on the V of my shirt then rips it apart. "Feeling's very mutual."

Peeling off the rest of our clothes, I walk her back into

the shower and watch as the hot water cascades over her body.

I watch as droplets of water fall down her skin that is marked so beautifully with black and red ink. Reaching for her waist to bring her out of the water slightly, I then glide my hands up to her pierced tits.

"You did say you had piercings of your own, didn't you?"

Jensen smirks. "I did. You going to keep looking at them or put 'em in your mouth?"

Fuck, she doesn't have to ask me twice. Steadying her body against mine, I dip my head taking the bud of her nipple in my mouth, teasing the barbells with my tongue.

Jensen glides a hand through my hair and arches her back. "Yes, more."

I earn a throaty moan from her when I palm the other one lightly with one hand then glide the other hand slowly down her back to grip her ass.

With one more flick of my tongue, I turn her around, backing her up against the tile wall. "I'm not done, but I have to ask...I don't mind your hands or mouth *exploring* down there, but how do you feel about it?"

Jensen's hand wraps around my cock, stroking me slowly. "I get to play with yours, I think it's only fair you can—"

That's all I need to hear. I take her nipple back in my mouth then the hand around her back glides lower, teasing her hole with my finger.

Jensen pulls at my hair and her whole body melts. "God, Beck."

My name on her lips has my dick twitching. I swear, all I need to come is her moaning my name. That's all it would take.

"Do you want to come like this, baby?"

Jensen writhes against me as I suck the piercing in my mouth hard and push my finger a little deeper in her tight hole. "I could," she says breathlessly. "But I want to come on your dick."

Shit. I want that too, but I'm not leaving this shower until I get two out of her.

Spinning her around, my hands tug at her hips. "I'm nowhere done with this ass of yours. Hands on the wall, Jensen."

"Thank fuck for that," she says as her hands go up and her ass pushes back.

Fuck, that mouth of hers. Everything about her. I just love it.

Kneeling down, I lick her from her entrance to her ass as I stand back up. When her moan comes, I push deep into her.

One of her hands reaches back, seeking out my hips as I glide in and out of her.

Taking her wrist, I pin it behind her back. "I didn't say your hand could leave the wall, Killer."

A wicked smile comes to her face as she bounces her hips to meet my thrusts. "I want to argue with you in every position. You're not my boss, Beckham Daines."

"Fuck," I groan, letting go of her wrist. "Jen, baby, I don't want to come early, but I will if you keep flirting with me like that."

Her hand goes back to the wall. "I come first, and then you can."

I smack her ass. "I want you to come twice." We might be wet from the shower but I spit on her ass for good measure before teasing her tight hole again. "I want you to come for me now."

My thrusts come hard and fast while I tease and stretch her ass. "Has anyone ever touched you here, baby?"

Jensen's head tilts back with a curse. Her hips leaning farther back to meet my touch.

"Answer me, Jen."

Her moan turns into a muffled scream and her walls clench around my cock. "No, only you."

"That's right, baby. Only me." I spit on her ass again, working her more and more with my finger.

Her moans turn into soft pants and just as she did in the office, her sounds stop right as she's on the brink of her orgasm. With one, two more thrusts of my hips and finger, her mouth makes an O and she's falling over the edge.

Fuck, she's so beautiful when she comes. How I hold it together is a miracle in itself, but hell, I want to see her make that face again tonight and that's more than enough motivation to hold it together.

Easing out of her slowly, I pull her back against me. "I want another one, but first...catch your breath." Jensen's head falls back onto my shoulder and she takes a deep breath in through her nose and out her mouth. "Good girl."

She does it a few more times before reaching up to touch my face. "That pierced dick is making its impression again."

A soft chuckle comes out. Spinning her around again, I let the water soak her hair completely before turning us around. Taking some of her shampoo, I pour some in my hands.

"Are you going to wash my hair?" Jensen asks with a cautious smirk. "That's awfully romantic."

"It is." I look her dead in the eyes. "Get on your knees."

Jensen's grin grows a little wider on her way down. Her

hand wraps around my shaft as she teases my piercing with her tongue.

Lathering up the soap I run my fingers gently through her hair all while taking control of her head for her to take me deeper into her mouth. "You won't be down there long, baby. I'm not strong enough to handle much more." Jensen looks up with my dick halfway in her mouth. "Fuck, you're killing me."

Bending slightly, I run my fingers through the base of her head and bring it forward until I hear her gagging on my dick. Pulling back, she takes a few deep breaths.

"So that's why you said to catch my breath." She laughs. When she leans back in, her tongue licks my piercing before I'm pulling her back up. "Hey, I didn't get to explore," she pouts.

I turn her back around to let the soap wash out of her hair. "There's plenty of time for that another night, I promise." Gliding my hands through her hair softly, I help get the last of the soap out. "I told you, I want two and you're so damn hot that I want to come at just the sight of you."

Jensen wraps her arms around my neck. "I assure you, you can get another one if you fuck me like you did in Dex's office."

I'm picking her up in an instant. This time turning us against the glass wall of the shower. Lining her up, I glide in slowly at first to make sure my ring at the top hits her right where she wants it to.

When I'm all the way in, I take a second just to look at her swallowing me up perfectly. My head tilts back with a moan. "Fuck, give it to me, baby, because you've made me a weak..." *Thrust.* "Weak." *Thrust.* "Man."

"All the good boys are weak for their partners." Jensen

tightens her arms around my neck. "And you, Beckham, are so fucking good for me."

"Fuck," I rasp, then lose all control. I'm pounding into her with no real rhythm, just pure need. Her body must feel as desperate as mine. Within a few strokes, she's squeezing the hell out of me. "Come for me now. No arguments, come."

"Beck, fuck." Her nails dig into my back and that silence comes for two beats and we're both lost in our climaxes, riding out each other's pleasure until our bodies feel boneless.

Or at least mine does.

Setting her down slowly, I place a kiss on her shoulder. "Maybe I should get jealous more often."

Jensen's smile brings this twitch to my own and I want to kiss her so fucking badly. But I know what that would mean to her...I need it to mean that to me, if I ever do.

Chapter 24
Beck

After drying off, we make our way back downstairs where we heat up some leftovers from yesterday and take them to the couch.

Jensen pulls her legs up criss-cross, then pulls a throw over her lap. "So, your other tattoos...I know what the thigh tattoo was, but I didn't get a good look at them the night this whole thing got started."

"I'm sorry, you're going to have to always refer to it as my slutty thigh tattoo."

Jensen snorts a laugh. "Slutty tattoos. Slutty dick. Slutty glasses, and a very slutty ego."

I tilt my head to her to watch that blush creep up her cheeks. "What can I say, I'm a slut for you too, Jenni-cakes."

"We're getting off topic, Beckham. I was talking about your tattoos."

"Right, right. What do you want to know about them?"

Jensen shuffles on the couch to face me slightly. "What do they mean to you?"

"Tattoos don't always have to have a meaning. I was sure you'd agree with that, Miss Tattoo Artist."

"Okay, first, lose the attitude. Second, not every tattoo has to have 'deep, profound' meanings, but I think all tattoos have them whether the person realizes it or not." She holds out her arm. "My cherries, for example, there's no big meaning or story behind it. I love cherries, that's about it. But it was the first tattoo I got when I moved here. It made me happy to get something so simple, but for me at the same time."

Reaching over, I take her arm in my hand, rubbing my thumb over the red ink. "I'll never be able to see a cherry and not think of you."

"Same here." Jensen pulls her arm back. "But lastly, I know you, Beck, your tattoos have a story. Tell me 'em."

"Okay, you got me." I take a deep breath before speaking. I've never actually told anyone about why I got my tattoos, but I know I want to share it with Jensen. "The lightning on my leg was the first one I got. It was a few months after my mom started forgetting things and we had just gotten started on her diagnosis.

"She was a physics teacher at my high school, which probably would have been a nightmare for a lot of teenagers, but not me. I've always been close with my parents, can't really explain it, but I am."

Jensen places her hand on my leg. "I know I've only talked to them once, but I can see that. You don't have to explain that part to me."

The moment it fully registers that her hand is touching me, I take our plates and move them to the coffee table and pull her into my arms.

I need more of her—not sexually, but more of her touch, her comfort.

I let out a small breath when she adjusts cuddling deeper into my body instead of pulling away. "Keep going," she whispers.

"Naturally, she was everyone's favorite teacher. She always made it fun and had the best experiments. She had one of those generators that she would set up to make your hair stand straight up. If someone got frustrated or an argument broke out in her class, she had this ball where the electricity would follow your finger—if anything needed to be worked out, you had to hold your finger to it until the issue was resolved. If it was something someone didn't understand she'd sit there touching it too while they talked it out."

Jensen laughs. "Oh my gosh, that's so sweet."

"I didn't always get it, but it worked every time. She said something about how it made them stop focusing on what the problem was and focus on the electricity following their finger that they'd calm down enough to actually be able to understand. So, one day when I got really fucking sad, I thought about that and got the lightning tattoo the same day."

Jensen looks up, this pained look in her eyes. "Beck."

I brush my fingers lightly through her hair. "It's okay, it's not the exact same thing, but every time I look at it I do feel a little better."

Jensen lays her head back down on my chest. "I'm not calling it slutty anymore. That's the sweetest thing I've ever heard."

I chuckle and place a light kiss to the top of her head. "After that I got the eight ball as a baseball because it combined both my mom and dad. Pool was always my dad's favorite, he taught me the moment I could stand over the table. But then Mom said I needed to have an actual appropriate hobby as an eight-year-old, so she put me in little league."

Jensen runs her hand over my shirt right where the tattoo is on my ribs. "Now you're in the major leagues and have a pool table in your living room."

"I think it's safe to say both of them stuck with me. I got my piercings after my vasectomy, can't really say why, seemed fun at the time."

"Very fun. That's all the reasoning needed." Jensen's hand moves south, and I catch it before she can tease me.

"Watch it, Killer. You tease me, I tease you back."

"What a threat," she mumbles, tugging her hand away, it wraps back around my waist. "You've got one more, Beck, what does the brain and heart tattoo on your chest mean to you?"

I take a deep breath for this one. "It was something the therapist told Dad and me when all this started, her mind might not be able to place us, but we'd always be in her heart and there's nothing anyone or any disease could do to change that."

Jensen's hold tightens around me. "I love that. I imagine your head has a hard time rationalizing it too."

Fuck. I swear Jensen's the missing part of my soul because that's exactly why I got it. I still don't understand why this is happening to my mother. The most amazing person I know, and I want nothing more than for her to remember me. To take this illness away from her, but the only thing I can do is keep the memory of her in my heart.

My anxiety starts to claw at my chest again, but unlike earlier I'm not sure if I can stop it from taking over.

Jensen's hand moves up to my pounding heart. "When we lost Stella's mom, the grief felt so immeasurable. I couldn't understand it...I didn't want to. The woman I loved like an aunt was gone—my mom couldn't leave her room for days, I stopped speaking entirely, and Stella was so angry, she started pulling her hair out.

"My dad saw it unfolding with all of us. He got us all into therapy, even though we didn't want to. A month after that he signed up to take Spanish classes so he could work on being a bit more fluent in Spanish so he could talk to mom's family about how she was doing and not have to have my mom feel like she had to slow down or translate while she was grieving. While he did that, he took Stella to MMA and me to an art class."

Jensen shifts around so she's straddling my lap. Her hands rest softly on my chest.

"Stella hated it at first, and I didn't care enough to fight him. Neither of us participated in the beginning, we half-assed whatever we could to appease my dad, but then somewhere in that, I started talking about what I was drawing with my therapist. Stella stopped losing her temper and hurting herself.

"A few years ago, Stella and I were joking about how it felt like he should have put me in MMA and her in art. I'll never forget the look of amusement on his face, as if it was ridiculous that we should have been switched... He told us that we both needed to feel something with our hearts instead of letting our minds control the things around us. Our own lightning if you will. Stella needed an outlet that let her feel her pain and express aggression in a controlled environment while finding her strength again. When she was in class, her sole focus was just that class. I needed to actually feel something and express it, instead of letting it consume me. I poured my heart into sketches. Drawing Stella's crystals and copying her tarot cards."

Jensen holds out her arm again. "The hand fan was my redrawing of Stella's mom's. My cheetah is something I drew during one of Stella's MMA tournaments." She chuckles. "She was so fast on her feet, but I had to put stars around it because she said if she couldn't beat them physically, she'd hex them."

All the pressure in my chest has completely vanished. I chuckle even at the thought of Stella saying that to Jensen when they were younger. Something tells me she still thinks the same way now.

Jensen runs a finger over my chest. "So, yeah, I like this one the best. I want to know the reasoning behind all the ones you have me work on too."

"I'll tell you every single one." Leaning up, I run my fingers through her hair, pulling it back to place a kiss on her inked collarbone. She's right, the reasons behind the tattoos mean something no matter if it's the marigolds or the cherries. I want to know every single thought behind ink on her skin and hell, I want her to know about mine.

She lets a soft moan of my name escape her lips as I start to softly kiss her neck. "Can—can I ask you one more question?" she asks in a soft whisper.

"Anything," I answer, never letting my mouth leave her skin.

She doesn't say a word for a moment, but with an exhale, she asks, "Why no relationship?"

The question takes me by surprise and I freeze in the crook of her neck.

Jensen picks up on my hesitation quickly. "Beck, I'm not

asking so I can rationalize with you. I'm never here to judge you. I just want to understand." She takes a deep breath. "I *need* to understand."

Fuck, that ache is back in my chest. I swear it's never going to leave me alone, and to make matters worse—it doesn't feel like a panic attack simmering...I think it's heartbreak.

Leaning back against the couch, I want to find a way out of this conversation, but this was a part of our deal. We communicate.

"I don't want a relationship because I don't want to forget my family. Nor do I want the person I love the most to have to live with the memories of who I was. Yes, I love my team, I love my friends...but if I do start to forget then Dex will have Lucie. Callie will have Will. Adam will surely find somebody. Tripp and Emma will hopefully figure their shit out, and you..."

My words die off because I don't want to say that she could have someone else. I hate that fucking thought even though it's the reality of the situation. The fantasy is that she would have me.

When I open my mouth again, Jensen stops me. "Please don't say it. I don't want to hear you say what you see for my future."

My whole chest is now on fire. "Good, because I don't want to say it either."

Jensen's eyes turn cold and distant. "Is that what your and your dad's argument was about?"

I give her a slow nod and mumble a curse at the look on her face. "Jensen, I'm sorry."

Her eyes blink rapidly and a soft smile comes to her lips. "You don't have to apologize."

Her hands find my face in a soft caress. "Like I said, I'm not going to rationalize with you. We don't have to talk about it anymore. I know what we agreed to at the start of this, Beck. I just needed to understand why."

"You know it has nothing to do with you, right? It's just, I can't—" Sitting back up, I meet her eyes. There's no pull to take off my glasses. No need to look away from her beautiful face. "I wish it could be me." *I want it to be me.* "But I can't, and won't, ask that of you."

"Beck, honey." Jensen shakes my shoulders lightly. "I came here because all my ex did was ask me to change. He wants a stay-at-home wife and four plus kids. Now, I commend every woman who does that. This is no diss to them at all, but I never want to be pregnant, that part about me has never even wavered. When I tried to discuss adoption as an option—because it wasn't that I didn't want kids, period—he told me no. I put getting my tattoo license on hold because he said it was a waste because I wouldn't be able to do it after we had kids. He started leaving baby books and pamphlets about women's health through ovulation and pregnancy around our apartment.

"He made so many snide comments about what I should want out of my life as a woman. Pushed so many of my girl 'friends' on the same agenda that I started believing I was the problem. I can't even begin to explain how great it was to learn that Callie doesn't want to have kids at all. All I was told for three years was this is what I should want, and I was apparently behind on this race that I never even wanted to run. I went back to therapy to try to find some sort of peace about this life he wanted me to live."

Anger radiates through my entire body. "Jen, you know

that's not true, right? You weren't the problem then, and you're not now."

The corners of her mouth tug upward. "I know that. I swear, it took therapy and a hex from Stella for me to, but I do. And, honey, you're not the problem either. I swear, me asking wasn't to try to make you feel bad about your reasoning."

I take a deep breath. "I know, but—"

"No, no buts, just understanding. If there's a but later then we'll talk about it then. For now, there's simply under-standing each other."

Nodding back is all my brain can manage. There's a baseball-sized lump in my throat stopping every single piece of my heart that I want to give to her.

Jensen places a small kiss to my forehead. "Get some sleep, Beck."

My hands flinch against her skin, nearly finding the strength to keep her here with me, but then she gets up and I can't stop her from going upstairs with Dottie following behind her.

Chapter 25
Jensen

I slept terribly last night. All I can think about is my and Beck's talk. It's playing over and over in my head.

I don't want to ask him to change, but also I've never felt like I understand him more. I get that fear. I believe his reasoning because I've lived it.

All my ex did was practically force change on me. I don't want to do that to Beck, but the thing I can't seem to let go of is what he said before I talked about why I moved here. *"I wish it could be me, but I can't, and won't, ask that of you."*

What if I want it? If the decision is completely his, then I could accept that. Not having kids through getting pregnant —that's my decision, but kids are never off the table for me.

The only way I can rationalize it, is the same way. Does Beck feel about a relationship the way I do about getting pregnant? *I wish it could be me...* If he thinks not being in a relationship is a favor to me, then that's bullshit. That decision should be left for me to decide. If he were to ask me...I think being the one to love him is the actual favor.

When that thought gets my heart racing, I try to sober it

with the reminder that he also said it wasn't about me. If this truly is something he feels without a doubt, no exceptions, zero chances of regret, then I'll walk away without a word of what he means to me.

I won't try to change his mind or make him feel bad for his choice. It's his to make and one that we agreed to.

With barely five hours of sleep, I've decided to put all my feelings into some sketches of some tattoos that for some reason remind me of Beck. I went ahead and just dedicated the whole file to him.

I've got a cherry blossom tree that I think would be pretty great on his ribs. I've got "stalker" written out in my handwriting. Clipped the trail we take running every Tuesday then added some electricity around it to make it look charged.

By the time I finish it, my itch to draw still hasn't been scratched and I need to get more out. This really might be crossing a line but I add Emma and Callie to a group chat and ask anyway.

> Okay, I don't need follow up questions or commentary... Could either of you get Beck's dad's number for me?
>
> Everything is okay, just no follow ups.

After hitting send, I roll out of bed to pull myself together somewhat. I can't imagine I'll be hearing from either of them for a bit considering it's not even eight in the morning.

Walking down to the kitchen, I'm honestly a little surprised I'm up before Beck. Granted, I can't say what time he normally gets up because I'm the one who is usually dead to the world until at least nine.

I grab Dottie's leash and snap it quick before her zoomies start.

"Hey, I got that," Beck's voice comes from the stairs.

Butterflies erupt in my stomach, because that's what this man's presence has done to me now. But as quickly as they come, they all sort of die when I realize he's looking ready for the day, and for more than just a normal lazy morning.

His hand covers mine softly as he takes the leash. "Dex called and we're gonna go to the training facility. I'll take Dottie with me."

"Oh." Yep, all flutters are dead. Shaking off the weird dread coming over me, I force a smile. "Okay, she'd love that."

Beck's eyes trace up and down my face. "Do you want to come with us?"

Maybe, if that was his first question then I probably would have, but now, that feels like a pity ask. "No, I'm good. I'll call Reagan and see if she wants to go over some stuff for the storefront."

I truly do my best to keep any attitude hidden, but Beck has become this safe space for me, and apparently I don't hide my feelings all that well after I feel safe.

His hand caresses my face softly. "Jen, come—"

"I'm fine, Beck. Really." I take a step back from his touch and move toward the kitchen. "I need to get something set up with Reagan and—"

My words stop as Beck grabs my wrist and pulls me into his arms holding me tightly. It takes me a second to even compute what's happening, he's just holding me in a hug. His head nestles into my neck and as he takes a deep breath in and out, I finally let some tension go.

I wrap my arms around his back and his hands flinch,

tightening around my body. We don't say anything, but I can tell it's helping us both feel better. Beck continues to make slow deep breaths like he did when he had his panic attack.

I start matching my breaths with his until he pulls back. His lips pressed against my forehead, and he holds there for a few seconds before Dottie decides enough is enough as she wraps us up in her leash.

"Dottie." I chuckle. Reaching for a part of her leash I tug her back around while Beck holds me close to keep me steady.

When we're untangled, I go to step back already feeling better, but Beck captures my chin, willing me to meet his eyes. "I'll see you tonight."

"I work—"

"I know when you work," he cuts me off. "I'll see you tonight. It wasn't a question, but a statement."

I nod when he lets go of my face. "Don't run away from me this time."

A smirk finally touches his lips. "Only plans I have are to sit on the barstool and watch you work."

"That's a good stalker."

Beck's smile grows, and in an instant his arms come back around my waist pulling me up for another hug. My feet leave the floor with a small giggle. "Beck, let me go."

He leans his head back. "I don't know if I can."

The butterflies seem to find a revival. I can't stop the blush from coming to my face, but I can try to mask it with a bit of an eye roll. "You can. Now, go give Dex hell for the fun of it."

"Always do." Beck lowers me down slowly, before letting me go. "See you later, Killer."

"Yeah, yeah, now go." I move to Dottie to give her some

goodbye pets, and make my way over to the kitchen. If he pulls me in one more time, I'm canceling on his behalf and we'll spend the morning naked.

Which really sounds like the better plan, but alas he walks out with a wink before shutting the door behind them.

Picking up my phone, I send a text to Reagan to see if she can meet me at the storefront, then I get my reply from Callie and Emma. Here we go.

CALLIE

But I have so many follow ups.

EMMA

Second ^ How are we not allowed at least one question? I mean if we're going to violate some rules…

JENSEN

Pretty sure you're doing a form of blackmail already, Ems.

CALLIE

Your point?

JENSEN

… Guys, come on, please?

EMMA

Fine. Hold please.

Now, ALLEGEDLY, if I were to have Beck's emergency contact pulled up on my screen. And by chance took a picture of my drink to show you what I'm drinking while "working" you'd probably find what you're looking for in the middle section.

CALLIE

Allegedly.

JENSEN

THANK YOU.

Before I can second-guess myself, I call Beck's dad. If I'm going to have Callie and Emma break some rules, I suppose I better follow through.

It rings a few times, and I nearly hang up before he answers with a cautious, "Hello?"

Shit, here goes nothing.

"Hi, Mr. Daines? It's Jensen, uh, Beck's friend."

"Hi, Jensen." His dad's voice still holds this wariness to it. "Is Beck okay?"

Shit, I probably should have led with that too. "Yes, he's great—I mean, he's fine… Listen, this probably sounds nuts, but I had my friends break what I'm sure is a confidentiality law or something to get me your number." Oh my god, I'm rambling like Callie. Get to the point, Jen. "Anyway, I'm a tattoo artist, and I wanted to draw up some tattoos for Beck as a thank you for helping me. I want them to be a surprise, so I was wondering if I could ask a favor."

A pause comes through the line and I hold my breath until I hear his dad chuckle softly. "Ask me anything. Also, it's Rory, not Mr. Daines. That makes me feel way too old."

Gah, something tells me I'm about to see where Beck gets a bit of his personality.

"Alright. Rory it is. I was wondering if you could send me some pictures of Beck growing up. Some of his favorite moments, especially with you and his mom. I'm a bit of an inspiration drawer and I think some images would help spark some creative ideas."

"I can do that. I have to say, I really appreciate you doing this for him. As his dad, and with what he's been going through over the past few years...it just really makes me happy to hear."

An ache comes to my chest. I know they've been talking somewhat more since I answered that FaceTime, but based on our talk last night, I think it's safe to say neither of them are completely over their argument.

"Mr. Da—sorry, Rory, you have an amazing son. I'm sure you're aware of that, but I wanted to say it anyway."

Rory lets out a breath. "I know I do. Now, if we could just get him to see that, we'd be golden. I've seen glimpses of the real him with the last few phone calls and texts. You seem to bring something out in him that I haven't seen in a while."

My heart starts beating rapidly. "Oh?" is all I can manage to voice.

"That picture he sent of you two at the wedding had to be the first real smile I've seen him have outside of a ballfield in years."

A nervous laugh bubbles out of me. "Beck always has a genuine smile."

Rory snorts. "Guess you're a common denominator there. For everyone else, he fakes it really well. Straight up lying he has a tell, but faking it so you don't ask him something he has to lie about—he's mastered."

There's no air in my lungs at this point. "Tell?" I feel like his dad might be a man on a mission now with this conversation, but he's got me hook, line, and sinker.

"Oh yeah, the boy's never been able to tell a lie with his glasses on or make eye contact. His mother and I caught on to it quickly, it never faltered from what I can still see."

And just like that these past few days start a montage in my head.

When Stella brought up it being temporary...he kept his eyes on his wineglass...he looked me in the eyes when he said he wished it was him...and didn't when I asked him if not being in a relationship was still what he wanted.

But then again he said he would take off his glasses, he didn't completely do that. But he wasn't looking at me either.

"Jensen?" Rory asks amidst my spiral. "You're trying to figure out all the times he's lied, aren't you?"

Shaking my head, I try to pull myself out of it. "Um, you know, I haven't exactly..." Shit. "I called for the pictures."

"You're right, I'll work on getting those. I'm sorry, I didn't mean to start something."

Yeah, right. I honestly can't stop the smart-ass remark. "Yeah, you did."

Rory hums in amusement. "Guilty. I love my son, I want him to be happy and he seems hell-bent on living his life alone, when I know that's not what he wants."

Chills run through my body. This phone call was a mistake. I try to find some level of a calm tone. "With all due respect, people are allowed to change."

Another breath of amusement. "They are. Beck said the same thing himself. But he hasn't changed, he's lying to himself, and that's the difference."

His words vibrate through me. Is he right? It's what's kept me up most of the night and now Beck's dad is only making my spiral worse...or better, if he's actually right about this tell of his.

"I'll get you the pictures, Jensen. I saw an opportunity so I took it on the other stuff."

Even though my brain feels like it's spinning, I have to admit I did expect to get a glimpse of why Beck is the way he is. "Like father, like son, it seems."

Rory laughs. "Beck is the best parts of me and his mom. I just want him to be happy, and if I truly believed being alone is what he wanted then I'd find peace in that. But I hope you know it's not your responsibility either. I've overstepped enough for today, but I'll leave you with that. Everyone deserves to be happy, and if it's not Beck then I hope you find it too."

I take a deep breath then swallow hard. I won't force Beck to want me, and if I can't tell him then at least someone will know. "I think he's been my happiness for longer than I'd care to admit."

"So, I'm thinking an extra sink here. Maybe get you a small private room in this corner, and maybe some—Jensen, are you listening?" Reagan asks.

My nod is slow at first but then my brain catches up. I blink rapidly out of my daze. "Yes, sink sounds great, the room will be appreciated, and if I could finish that sentence for you, it would be extra outlets if possible."

I flash her some half-assed smile. I was listening to her, but I get why it seems like I wasn't. I'm officially in a funk. So deep in my funk that even pulling out my tried-and-true sketch book hasn't helped.

Part of me hoped Reagan wouldn't be able to make today work, but she said she'd meet me here at ten. While getting ready, I messaged Lucie to meet me there and us get some brunch after.

I have to talk to someone. I have to get this out or I might go insane.

I know Reagan can tell something's up, but as nosy as she is, she also knows I won't spill my heart out to her here in our new business space.

A happy squeak comes up behind us and we both turn to find Lucie walking in. "I'm so excited for this!"

Now, Lucie...Lucie will care deeply about my attitude, so I plaster a smile on my face. I'll spill my guts to her later. "You were right, Princess Peach. I think this will turn out really cool."

Lucie tilts her head. "Actually, I said it would be the perfect solution, Beck was the one who said it could be a cool concept."

I roll my eyes. "To-may-to, to-mah-to. You ready to get some food?"

"Considering I actually feel like I could eat something today? Yes, I'm very ready, but I did get here early so no rush if you aren't done."

Reagan steps to her sister for a hug then a small pat to her belly. "Well, if these babies are calling for food, then we're done."

Lucie scrunches her nose. "I swear if we get there and I start to feel nauseous I will cry. I cried this morning at literally nothing. The sunrise looked so pretty from our balcony, I just started bawling."

I snort a bit of a laugh. "And Daddy Dex still left your side to go workout with the guys? I'm shocked."

Lucie lets out a heavy sigh. "Well, he tried canceling. He's tried saying he'll just back out of pitching again and coach so he can help—"

"I bet that went over like a ton of bricks," I say.

Lucie's been so happy about him pitching again. Honestly, brave move on Dex's part.

"I did not take it well." Lucie folds her lips together for a moment before admitting, "I may have told him that if I have to grow two babies in my stomach, he could throw some effing balls. But I actually said the F word."

Reagan huffs. "Well, if you're not going to repeat it correctly then why repeat it at all."

Lucie's jaw clenches. God bless her, I think she's a bit hormonal, and I know Reagan is not about to help at all.

I reach for Lucie's hand and pull her a step away from her sister. "I bet Dex was impressed you actually cursed. Plus, he has to pitch again, all the guys would stand with you on that statement."

Instantly, her shoulders relax a bit. "I still felt bad, but you're right, he was impressed."

"See, no feeling bad. Let's head out before your appetite changes." And I have to referee a sister fight—that's Will's job, not mine. It also probably wouldn't help that I'd take Lucie's side no matter what.

Reagan pulls out her phone, typing her thumbs on her screen quickly before my phone vibrates in my pocket. "I sent you some screenshots of some things the health inspector emailed me, and a list of the new codes to get in and out of here anytime you want. We're getting new locks and security cameras outside and in the back room put in today, so might want to keep that in mind in case you bring Beck with you next time."

The comeback that it didn't happen in the backroom is on the tip of my tongue but thankfully I have enough forethought to stop it. "Thank you, I'm going to start looking at some furniture so I'll probably come measure out some stuff later this week."

And I can't say whether Beck will be with me or not.

Honestly, I don't know if this roommates-with-benefits thing can go much longer.

My heart keeps going up and down because I feel for him so much that I would never want to push a relationship if he truly didn't want it. I'd walk away, but my soul feels so deeply entwined with his.

Walking out of the shop, Lucie links her arm in mine. "There's a cute place a block up. Want to go there?"

I snort a laugh. It's freaking freezing outside, but I guess she did say she's actually hungry. "Did you look for the closest place to the shop before you got here?"

"Oh yeah!" Lucie tugs at my arm as she starts down the sidewalk. "I haven't been able to hold down food in weeks, Jen. Weeks!"

"Poor Princess Peach."

"Don't poor princess me, I'm about to start what will borderline be an interrogation on your whole roommate situation. You have until our butts hit the seats. No arguments or taking Beck talk off the table. It's not happening."

I find a laugh. "This may shock you, but I have no arguments. Talking about Beck was why I called you."

Lucie hums, intrigued. "Shall I sit down now?"

"On the salt and slush sidewalk? No, I think you can hold out until we get to the restaurant."

Lucie grumbles under her breath, but when the wind picks up, she leans into me. "Alright, fair."

And whether it's the conversation we're looking forward to or getting out of the cold, we pick up our pace.

The moment Lucie's butt hits her side of the booth, she shakes out a chill and rubs her hands together. "Okay, spill."

"Can't we order—"

"Nope," Lucie pops the *p* for good measure. "Come on,

Jen, you know there's no point in stalling. That's not very you."

I *tsk* at first, but of course, Lucie's got a point. "Alright, so I like Beck. At the sake of sounding very immature, I like, *like* him."

Lucie blows a raspberry at me. "Try again, I already know that. Tell me about the reasons you're hesitant to make it more than this silly roommates-with-benefits deal."

"It wasn't a 'silly' deal, Luce. There were, and frankly still are, deeper reasons with that. When we first made this agreement, neither of us wanted it to turn into a relationship. And the real kicker is Beck is the one who I think still wants to stand on that."

"Wait." Lucie's eyebrows pull together. "Beck doesn't want a relationship? With you?" I can see what little anger lives in Lucie stirring. "I might cuss again."

"Relax, it's not about me...I don't feel completely comfortable disclosing his reasons, but in his defense, it is valid if he truly doesn't want a relationship."

Lucie shuffles in her seat. "Okay, my pregnancy brain is really trying to dig into what you're saying. So, you think they are valid, but you're not sure if he means it or not?"

I nod. "Correct, and add in a conversation with his dad about it, and you'll be about just as confused as I am."

Lucie's lips fold together, and I see she's holding back a laugh.

"Lucie!"

Her arms go up. "I'm sorry, but this is...I don't know. I'm working with breadcrumbs here, and my two eyeballs that see how much you two care about each other. I'm sorry, I'm just not getting it."

"Again, neither am I! Luce, I think I'm in love with this

man and I've only lived with him for just over a month and been his friend with benefits for a whole week. That is insane! Why do I fall in love with the men I'm involved with? I was sure I was stronger this time."

Lucie's smile turns Joker-like, despite my dread.

"Well, then why are you smiling like the Joker? This is serious."

"You're right, it very much is. Jen, you love him. Think about your ex for a second, he constantly made you feel less-than right? You had to mold into his lifestyle and expectations. Does Beck do that? Has any part of moving in felt uncomfortable? You know, minus the extreme levels of sexual tension."

I see the point she's about to make, and dammit, I'm going to let her make it. "No to both."

"You know Beck's completely incomparable to your ex. I don't even have to say it, you believe that deep in your gut, that's freaking surface-level knowledge. Stop diminishing what you feel."

"But what if what I feel isn't valid?"

"Your feelings are always valid. They are valid to you because they are yours. What you and Beck agreed to was made with valid feelings. You telling him that you can't continue with the only benefits aspect because of your feelings for him, is valid. No matter the time frame you developed them. And I hate it, but whatever his response is will also be valid."

This pit forms deep in my stomach. Shit, now I'm the nauseous one.

"Luce—"

Her hand reaches over to take mine. "You also get to control when that happens, so trust your gut, and I swear on everything—no matter what happens, you will still be my best friend. Nothing will ever change that."

I squeeze her hand. "Good, I'd hate to kidnap you, Princess Peach."

Her smile grows again. "Is it kidnapping if I come willingly?"

Chapter 26
Beck

I'm at a fucking loss. Ever since Jensen got up from the couch last night there has been this elephant on my chest. I can't breathe properly and this dark cloud is looming over me. I slept like shit. I've practiced with the guys like shit.

When Dex sent out a text for anyone available to meet him here to practice and workout, I thought it might be nice to get out, move my body, and find any sort of joy from the game I love. But that didn't happen, because all I've been able to think about is Jensen.

Tossing my dirty clothes in my gym bag, I let out a heavy sigh and close my eyes. I need to get a grip, but...shit, if my hands don't feel weak.

The one bit of reprieve I got this morning was from simply holding Jensen in the doorway. There's this peace in having her at my side. I've been forcing this *faking it* mentality and fighting off my anxieties so no one would question what I'm feeling for so long, but now I find it exhausting.

Even before we slept together, when she helped me

through that first panic attack...I just felt safe with her. Every discussion we have, I feel safe because I actually get to express what I'm feeling for the first time with someone who might not have the same experience, but can relate to what I'm feeling.

I don't know how long we can keep this arrangement going. And I have zero clue how I could ever let her go. I'm so tired of fighting my anxieties, but the fear of what our future could look like has me in a chokehold.

Even the thought of having Jensen experience what my dad is going through fills my entire body with fear... I start to see spots when I think a second too long about it. There're no what ifs in my head, only the worst possible outcomes. The thing is I can't decide which one is worse, forgetting her or losing her.

We were supposed to get each other out of our systems but instead she is my new system. She's the other part of my soul that I didn't even know was missing.

I can't stop thinking about this. How I managed to make it through this unofficial practice with the guys is a miracle in itself. It's like I'm here, but I'm not. I'm stuck in the death spiral of panic and if I wanted to be honest, I'm fucking sad.

At some point, in this mental panic attack, my muscle memory must have started box breathing. Finally finding some strength, I blink my eyes open. My hands are gripped so hard on the edges of the cubby walls my knuckles are white.

Leaning up, I let my grasp go and shake out my hands.

"Beckkkk!" Miles bursts into the clubhouse with Dottie following behind him. "I have a question."

Turning around slowly, I sit on my cubby because I'm not sure how much longer I can keep standing. Dottie makes her way between my knees and rests her head on my leg. Giving her soft pets, I find a little bit more composure. "Alright, All-star, what's up?"

Miles's smile immediately gives him away. The boy is about to do some scheming. "I was thinking that Dottie could come home with me for a little bit. Mommy got so sad this morning, she said the babies make her *motional*. I think Dottie could cheer her up."

My heart warms a bit at him calling Lucie his mom now. When Dex texted us this morning, he mentioned Miles had started doing it but to act normal about it.

Which I get, but frankly, I don't think the warning had to be given, Lucie is the mom Miles deserves. I'm not going to question that.

"You know, I love your thinking, but something tells me your dad has either already told you no, or you're looking for forgiveness instead of permission."

Miles's mouth opens then shuts. His eyes narrow in on Dottie. "Well..."

"Miles, you better not be asking Beck about the dog," Dex scolds lightly as he walks in the clubhouse. "I already told you no, we're not bringing the dog back home."

Miles's shoulders fall practically to his ankles. "But Mommy would love to see Dottie."

Dex shakes his head. "Mom wants to see Dottie's owner, Jensen, not the dog."

My heart rate kicks back up at the mention of Jensen. "Lucie went to see Jen?"

Dex gets this cocky smirk on his face. "Yeah, she's home now, but they got brunch together. Want to fill me in on your side? Luce and I can compare notes later."

I know it's a joke I should play into. Blow him off or give

him the finger so I don't actually cuss at him in front of Miles, but none of that is in me today.

Dex steps up to Miles. "We're going to leave in ten minutes. Why don't you and Dottie go play on the turf, I think Tripp and Adam are still in the batting cages. I'll be there in a bit."

"Okie!" Miles bounces on his feet before running to the door. "Come on, Dottie!"

Her big brown eyes look up to me and she doesn't move until I pat her chest. "Go on."

I get the three seconds of silence from Dex as he waits for the door to close behind them. He moves to sit in the cubby next to me. "That dog really seems to mind you, given the fact you're not her owner."

I glare at him. "First, way to kick me when I'm down. Second, the dog has a name, you know what it is so call her by it."

Dex lets out a *humph*. "That didn't take long. Should I tell you I told you so now...or?"

"Fuck off." I *tsk*, but Dex simply laughs.

"Oh, so much déjà vu. Please say something dickish now to really sell the whole thing."

My mind immediately goes back to when Dex was an extreme asshole when Lucie got started and hell if that doesn't make me feel a little bit better.

"Nah, I think I'll take the high road on this one."

"Motherfucker, way to ruin it," Dex mumbles with a chuckle. "Want to talk about it?"

I tilt my head to him. "Would it matter if I said not really?"

"It would, I'll walk the high road with you, drop it completely."

Oh, bullshit.

I barely get my head shake out before Dex starts. "I actually want to talk about myself. Do you realize how much happier I am with Lucie? I'm married to the most beautiful woman I've ever seen—she's carrying my children. She loves my son like her own, arguably loves him more than she loves me."

Resting my elbows on my knees, I pinch the bridge of my nose. "You're so subtle."

"And not done. Whatever you and Jensen have doesn't have to look like mine and Lucie's. I don't know what's going on, but I can't say it's good with how shitty you did today."

I blink with my glare. "Again, with the kicking."

Dex shrugs. "Hey, you don't want to talk about it, I won't ask for details. All I'm saying is...thank you. I've said it to you before, and I'll keep saying it. You pushed me to look past my hang-ups about what a life with Lucie could look like, and now I get to wake up with the woman of my dreams at my side. I look forward to coming home every single day. I'm genuinely happy for the first time in a *very* long time, so thank you."

I swallow hard. "What if I can't push myself? You can say 'thank you' but my encouragement really had little to do with it. I was simply pointing out the obvious."

"I could point out the obvious, but it'd be a waste of breath. You know what Jensen means to you, so decide on what you're going to do about it." Dex pushes off his knees and stands back up. "Now, I've been here throwing pitches that already have my shoulder hurting and working out with you assholes for hours. I want to go home and spend time with my wife. Will's already gone because he wants to be with Callie. What do you want to do? You can get some batting practice in..."

This fucker.

Standing up, I let out a heavy sigh. "I'm going to go home and see Jensen."

Dex's smile grows. "Good, you should go do that then. And, for all that's fucking holy, take Dottie with you."

"Of course, I'm taking *my* dog home. I'll fight Miles for her, I'm not afraid."

"You seem to be afraid of something," Dex mumbles under his breath.

"You know, maybe I will let Miles take Dottie home for the afternoon."

Dex pauses before walking out the door. "I'll take Dottie if you plan on sorting your shit out with Jensen tonight."

My whole body goes rigid. "I..." I clear my throat, unsure how to answer him.

Dex gets this smug look on his face. "Next time, I'm not taking the high road."

"Fair," I mumble as we go to get his son and my dog separated, which wasn't exactly the easiest of feats.

Dottie may listen to me, but with some encouragement from Miles and further encouragement from Adam and Tripp...Dex and I got stuck playing a fun little game of hide-and-seek. Dex thought it less fun than me, which I feel slightly bad for since talking to him did give me a bit of clarity.

There's a peace in knowing that coming home means Jensen's there and I get to grab ahold of my life-preserver for a bit. However, I have to be sure that this is what we both want now. Neither of us wanted more at the start of this, and

I won't force her to change her mind just as much as I know she wouldn't force me to either.

Walking in the house, I hang up Dottie's leash then kick off my shoes by the door. The house feels entirely too quiet so I yell, "Jen, we're back!"

But unfortunately there's no answer.

Damn. Pulling out my phone, I send her a text.

> You know, as your stalker, I feel I need to have your location on my phone.

JENSEN

Now why would I make it that easy for you? I want you to work for it.

> You know I love a challenge.

I'll be home soon. Had to swing by Winedown to help Mia for a bit.

> Drive safe.

Sliding my phone back in my pocket, I look down at Dottie. "She said she'll be here soon. How does the couch and some TV sound in the meantime?"

Dottie lets out a soft bark, which I take as her approval. Plopping down on the couch I wait as Dottie snags one of her toys from her dog bed because that's all it is now...her toy storage area, then hops up next to me.

"I see we went with the bear." I pet her back as she lies on her one singular toy that she doesn't chew. "Too tired to murder any other toys?"

I chuckle when she lets out a huff, but I know this dog could get up and go run another several miles if she knew that was an option.

I go for the remote the moment my phone starts to buzz in my pocket. Pulling it back out, I fully expect to see Jensen calling, but it's my dad with a FaceTime call.

My heart kicks up a bit on impulse, but I answer the call and prop my phone against this random decor thing on my coffee table.

I'm fully expecting Dad to speak first, but then my mom does. "Oh, Beck, honey, hi! I didn't know what your dad meant by...oh, what did you call it?"

"FaceTime," Dad answers, tears already quietly falling down his face. "It's an interesting little trick, isn't it?"

My mother's face lights up. "It is, it's like you're here with us."

I've never really thought about being thankful for furniture, but right now I'm so fucking glad I'm sitting for this. "Mom?" I croak.

Am I hearing things? Does she actually remember me right now?

I'm damn near holding my breath as Mom holds up a picture of me at one of my little league games. "Look at you. I remember this team, I did not like that coach of yours."

It's official, I'm dreaming. I have to be. But then Dottie turns on the couch nudging her head in my lap and I feel this jolt run through my body. "You did. Said he was too crass and didn't know a thing about baseball."

She keeps her eyes on the photo. "I tried to explain the rules, but he didn't want to listen. More men really should listen to me."

"Yes, they should," I answer. I want to ask a question to keep the conversation going, but don't know what to say. I just need her to keep talking. I need to talk to my mom again.

She flips through several more in her hands, not speaking

for a minute, but then she sets them down. "I'm just so proud of you."

I can't stop the tears. I wanted to keep it together and not cause any worry or fear, but I can't help it. Dammit, I need to pull it together.

"Oh, Beck, why are you crying? Your dad was getting all emotional too," Mom says in her sweetest tone.

"I'm fine, really." But I'm not. Shit. I wipe at my face and pull it together the best I can, and when it seems like I can't the front door opens.

"Beck, I'm—" Jensen doesn't finish her sentence when she realizes I'm not holding it together.

She's at my side in an instant and doesn't even see the FaceTime until she hears my mom.

"Oh, who's this?" my mom asks, acknowledging Jensen now in frame.

Too many emotions are hitting me right now for me to speak. My mom remembers me. I want to tell her so many things. Tell her about Jensen and what she means to me, but don't want to overwhelm her.

I clear my throat the best I can then wipe at my face. "T-this—"

Jensen's hand runs down my back softly. "Hi, I'm Jensen, a friend of Beck's."

My mother's eyes turn soft. "You're so beautiful, and is that a dog I saw too?"

"It is," Jensen replies with a smile, not even batting an eye after walking into this. "Her name is Dottie."

"Hi, Jensen," my dad adds, but his eyes immediately meet mine after. "We were looking at some pictures, should we show Jensen some of the really good ones?"

I find a bit of a smile when my mom's eyes light up. "I

love this one." She holds up a photo of me standing on Dad's pool table, I couldn't have been older than four in it. "You know, Rory told me he wanted Beck to become a professional billiard player, but I wanted him to play baseball so badly."

Jensen's hand moves to hold mine as it registers that Mom actually remembers me right now.

Dad takes the response on this one, thank goodness. "You sure did. He agreed with you too, considering he plays in the major leagues now."

Mom's eyebrows pull together as she tries to place this information, and I almost attempt to change the subject but then Dad hands her something else. "Here's his first baseball card. Jensen might see it better if you hold it up."

Mom takes the card cautiously, but as she looks at it she nods. "That's right, he did." She holds the picture out with a proud grin. "See what happens when you listen to me?"

Swallowing the lump in my throat, I finally find some words. "I could listen all day."

Jensen's hand squeezes mine, and while part of me is thankful that it's out of frame the other part wants to pull it in frame. To tell my mother what Jensen means to me, but spilling all my feelings now would be unfair to Jensen in this moment when we haven't even talked about it ourselves.

We spend the next ten minutes talking with my mom about memories of my childhood and a few slipups happen when some pictures of me and my grandfather come up.

Dad was quick to switch it up with some other pictures, but after a while we know we've kept her talking long enough.

"I'm so happy you called," I say as my dad starts to collect the photos.

"Me too." My mom's smile isn't as bright as it was at the start, and then it turns into a wince. "My head is really hurting now. Beck, will you help your dad with dinner? I know you both love breakfast for dinner, maybe you can do that? And don't forget to pack your bag for baseball practice tomorrow."

Shit, she's getting lost in another time.

I take a deep breath. "Yeah, breakfast for dinner sounds great, and don't worry, I'll make sure it's ready to go. I won't forget."

"Good." Her head nods and her eyes stare off into another moment in time. "I'll see you in the morning."

I make a nod to Dad that I hope he understands is to get her down to rest immediately, and he nods back. He stands and slowly comes to her side. "Let me help you get settled, then I'll come help Beck."

Jensen and I wait, not moving a muscle until I'm sure they're no longer in the room. Leaning forward, I end the call. My heart rate picking back up again.

She remembered me. She told me she was proud of me.

Jensen's hand slides on my back in another soft caress. "Beck—"

She gets my name out, but then I'm pulling her in my arms and I lose it.

Chapter 27
Jensen

Shifting as Beck pulls me to him, I throw my other leg around his lap and hold him tight as he lets out all the emotions he was holding back from that call.

"She remembered me, she hasn't recognized me in two years," he cries and his arms pull me in tighter. "Part of me made peace that she never would again..."

My heart falls down to my stomach. "Beck, honey..." My words die off because what do I say? It's okay? It's not, here he is already mourning his mom for years—there's not much to say in this grief to make someone feel better.

Taking a few deep breaths, Beck pulls back to wipe at his face. "Fuck, I'm sorry."

Pulling his hands away I replace them with my own. "There's no need to apologize."

Beck's glossy eyes lock with mine. "I just...that was a lot. Amazing, and I'm grateful for every moment of clarity I get from her, but...I think it might have been easier had she not remembered me." Beck retreats farther back on the couch and runs his hands over his face. "Dammit, that's a horrible thing to say."

"No, no, it's not." I reach for him again, pulling his arms back to my waist and forcing him to look at me. "Listen to me, that's not horrible. You've been grieving your mom for so long, you're allowed to have mixed emotions about it."

He lets out another deep breath. "I just wish this wasn't happening to her."

My heart breaks. Leaning in, I hug him tight. I know exactly what he means because there were so many times that I thought the same exact thing for Stella, for my mom, for myself. His arms squeeze my back, and I whisper, "I wish that too."

Neither of us move for several minutes. I try to keep my breathing in line with his, in hopes it encourages a panic attack to stay at bay. I can't tell for sure if one's even stirring in him, but it doesn't matter, I want to be here. I want to be his comfort in this moment.

Eventually, Beck's arms move to my shoulders. Sitting back up, his hands glide my hair softly behind my ears. "Thank you."

I find a soft smile. "Of course, what do you think about us having a lazy day?"

His eyebrows pull together. "Don't you work tonight?"

"I took it off. That's why I was at Winedown. I helped Mia with some restocking and asked her if I could get the afternoon off."

Beck breaths out an amused *humph*. "Did you get this gut feeling that I was going to be in need of some emotional support?"

I chuckle. "Something like that."

Something in my gut was telling me to take off work this

morning. Something in my gut is telling me that there's no moving on from Beck, and as much as I'd love to lay it all out there, I know today probably isn't the best time for that.

"What should we do then, Killer?"

"How does breakfast for dinner and some pool sound?"

Beck sits up and places a kiss on my neck. "Sounds pretty amazing."

Getting up from the couch, we make our way to the kitchen, taking note of all the things Beck has in his kitchen then the stuff we need from the store. All it took was one whine from Dottie to convince Beck to bring her along for the ride.

We had a bit of a debate on whether we were going sweet or savory for our breakfast dinner. To which Beck ultimately declared tonight would be savory with bacon, chorizo, eggs, and diced potatoes, then he was going to make pancakes in the morning.

Beck pops the potatoes in the air fryer while I crack the eggs in a bowl. "You know, we didn't have time for me to make it today, but next time let me know when you want to make breakfast for dinner and I'm going to make my mother's menudo."

The sentence comes out, and when it registers at how that sounded I grimace a bit. We've had such a normal couple of hours, following a very heavy moment. The idea that we might not do this again is one I don't love, but could be our reality.

Beck thankfully seems unfazed by it as he moves around pulling out different pans for the stove. "Oh yeah, why not tonight?"

"Didn't have enough time. Typically, you need about three-ish hours, but my mom would cook it on low overnight." A smile comes to my face as the memory itself practically has the smell along with it.

"Overnight?" Beck asks with a raised eyebrow.

"Yes, overnight." I chuckle. "My dad asked her the same question the first time she made it for him. She loves to bring up because she still makes fun of him for asking that to this day."

This smile comes to his face, and I nearly ask what it's for, but don't.

"I've always loved breakfast for dinner because my mom was a firm believer that it didn't matter what time of day it was, you should just eat food. In the morning, if she made anything non-traditional for breakfast, she would always joke that it was to spite my dad. Apparently, he had some questions when she would be eating pasta for breakfast."

I snort. "Pasta for breakfast actually sounds pretty good."

Beck's smile only grows as he starts to cut open the meats we bought. "It became this whole thing. 'Breakfast' food was practically only eaten at dinner time in our house, unless that's just what you were craving in the morning."

"I love that." I move my eggs over to the stove. "And only solidifies my idea of menudo more. It's typically served as a breakfast or brunch food, but it's a soup so especially in the winter, it would hit the spot any time of the day."

Beck slides in beside me and places two pans on the stove. He plants a quick kiss to the side of my head. "I look forward to trying it. And maybe you can teach me how to make it."

Warmth fills my body. This has gone entirely too far, so fast. I love this man. And it wasn't the sex that started it, it was just him. He hasn't done anything inherently romantic, no candles, flowers, or fancy dates. Or, really, I don't think I realized what type of romantic I was until Beck.

With my ex, I did get all the things. The basic romance of the same exact expensive restaurant for dates and gorgeous flowers but the kicker is they came with condescending remarks and judgment. But that's not Beck. He could do all those things, but the difference is the partner, and I want Beck to be mine.

I won't judge Beck if he says he doesn't see more for us, but I have to put us on the table for him to actually do that. Moving on from him will hurt so much worse, but I have to know if this is truly what he wants before letting him go.

The question is, when do I tell him?

"How was brunch with Lucie?" Beck asks, pulling me back to the moment.

"Oh, uh, it was good." Shaking off the wave of emotions that just hit me, I put my focus back on scrambling our eggs. "I went to meet Reagan first. She's having a contractor come in to get some more outlets, a room, and an extra sink added."

"That's great, whenever you want to call in our deal, just let me know."

We've got two deals going, but I want to call in on the other one.

When I don't answer, Beck nudges me with his elbow. "You okay? If you want to talk about that more—"

I shake my head again. *Come on, Jensen, pull yourself together.*

"No, no, we're fine, I was just thinking of where to start that's all." Technically, not a lie. "I also talked to Luce today about having Emma paint some murals. Apparently, Reagan asked about that too, so we'll be talking to her about some things later. I have a feeling her payment request will either be monetary or florals for life."

Beck snorts. "Yeah, Emma doesn't exactly scream tattoos, does she?"

I give him a side-eye.

His shoulders drop. "Jen, come on? You said—"

I wave him off. "I know. I'm just giving you a hard time." Keeping this playful moment going, I look at him again. "I think we just talked about jealousy being okay. Don't be thinking about what Emma screams."

Beck's head tilts back with a genuine laugh. He sets down his spatula and his hands find either side of my face. "You are the only girl I ever want."

I suck in a breath. His smile is cheesy and seemingly appears carefree, but if his dad was telling the truth about his tell...then Beck actually means that.

I sit with that all through finishing our dinner. I know Beck can tell something's off. I try my best to mask it with the excuse that I'm just hungry, but now our plates are empty and I'm racking the balls on the pool table looking for some sort of distraction.

"Are you sure you want to play?" Beck asks, handing me my cue.

"Yeah," I say, turning my eyes back to the table. "I don't think we've played together since that time you tricked everyone into a pool tournament for Callie and Will."

Beck lets out a soft chuckle. "You mean the night I became obsessed with you."

My shoulders relax slightly and I want to joke about him being my stalker or how delusional he was, but they all get stuck in my throat. "I'll break."

Beck opens his mouth to speak, but I move to line up

with the cue ball. As I lean down, my phone dings twice back-to-back and then another follows.

"Want me to get that?" Beck asks cautiously.

Another ding comes. and I let out a sigh. "Yeah, I think my phone's on the counter. I'm sure it's the girls' group chat."

I line back up and send the ball right down the middle. Can't say I got the spread that Beck usually does, but I'm pretty proud of it.

Leaning back up, I look at Beck as he comes back to the pool table. He looks white as a sheet. "Jen, why is my dad texting you?"

Oh, fuck, fuck, fuck.

Abandoning my cue on the table, I walk to him quickly. "Okay, hear me out, I swear I had good intentions."

I reach for my phone, and Beck doesn't pull away or demand for me to open it.

"Okay," he mumbles.

My phone dings a few more times, I switch it to silent. Opening my phone, several pictures are being sent one to two at a time.

"Are those the pictures my mom was looking at earlier?" Beck's voice is barely above a whisper and my heart is in my stomach.

Taking a deep breath, I look in his deep green eyes. "Yes, I may have asked Callie and Emma to get your dad's number for me. After our talk last night, I couldn't sleep, so I started sketching some ideas for tattoos you might want... It seemed like a good idea at the time, so I asked your dad to send me some pictures of you from your childhood for inspiration. I didn't—"

Beck steps in toward me. "So, you asked my dad for

pictures, and because of that my mom started looking through them too...and then remembered who I was."

I hadn't thought about that. Shit. "Beck, I'm so sorry."

His hands move before I even register what's happening, he's sitting me on the edge of the pool table and his hands cradle my face softly.

"Jensen, you said not to kiss you because it means more to you. What if I want to kiss you? What if I want to kiss you, knowing it means something to me?"

My heart is pounding so loud that I swear he has to be able to hear it. I want to lean in and kiss him first, but I have to know.

I search his face, looking for any hint of hesitation or clarity that this is about to actually happen.

He's not wearing his glasses today since he went out with the guys. I guess the tell I'm hanging on to is if he can answer me without looking away.

"And if I asked you about your reasoning for not wanting more? You said you wouldn't ask me to live with the fear of you forgetting me. What if I want to be with you no matter what the future looks like?"

His hands glide back through my hair. His eyes stay locked on mine. "I'd say fuck what I said before. Fuck what I thought I wanted. I only want you."

The pounding of my heart stops. Everything stops actually. There's just Beck.

"Then kiss me."

Chapter 28
Beck

"Then kiss me," Jensen whispers, and my whole world explodes.

My lips capture hers and in a fucking instant, everything becomes crystal clear. No more mud mucking whatever this is between us.

I love her. Can't imagine my life with-fucking-out her type of love. The worst-case scenario is wasting another second of not actually being hers.

My tongue explores her mouth as our kiss turns demanding. Her hands lock around my shoulders and I lean her farther back deepening the kiss.

When I feel her soft moan against my mouth, my knees threaten to give out on me. I need her, with every fiber of my being, I need all of her. Forever.

Hoisting her back into my arms, I carry her up the stairs and straight to my room.

This isn't our roommates-with-benefits deal anymore. It's not just fucking her in a public place or in the shower. It's her and I genuinely giving this an actual chance. I don't want there to even be a thought of this being temporary. Every-thing is different this time, and I want that to be abundantly clear.

Our kiss never wavers, and with every pass of my lips, I'm begging, promising, demanding that she knows she has me.

Standing at the foot of my bed, I finally set her down and truly look at her. I am fucking mesmerized. "You're so beau-tiful, Jen."

Her blush comes with a smile, but I can see the concern written all over her face. I know everything I said about my reasoning for not wanting this is lingering in her head.

And for that I can't blame her. I know a kiss isn't going to be enough to reassure her. I want to tell her every part of me belongs to her. That I'll never love someone other than her, but the words get stuck in my chest.

Her hand presses softly on my chest. "Beck..." Anything she might have wanted to follow up with doesn't come out.

I brush her hair behind her back and rest my forehead against hers. So many words are still sitting on my chest. The weight of them physically hurts. Letting out a deep breath, I need to say something, but what comes out isn't nearly as poetic as I hoped.

"I'm with you, Jensen."

Those deep amber eyes lock with mine. Lust might be fighting to take over, but I can still see the small hints of fear.

She takes a small step back and her hands rest on my waist. "Beckham." My full name comes out as a plea this time.

I pull her back in, I can't let her get in her head. They're valid fears, I know that, but I need her to know I want us. I press a soft kiss to her lips again. "I promise."

Her hands find either side of my face and she lets out a soft sigh. The smile on her face tells me enough that I haven't completely fucked this up already. "I know—now, show me."

She leans in and her kiss sends shockwaves through my body. She's right, words can wait because loving her isn't just confessions and promises—she deserves those things, but for right now, I need to prove to her that I'm right here with her. I'm in this with all the passion and love she's giving me.

Picking her body up closer to mine, I hold her to where her toes barely touch the ground. "I need your clothes off."

She chuckles softly. "You're going to have to let me go for me to do that."

"I don't want to." I grab a chunk of her hair, kissing her deeper. When her tongue tangles with mine, I nearly come in my pants. Shit, not that again. Not this time at least.

Breaking away from her the best I can, I try to find any form of self-control and grit out. "Clothes off, or I rip them off."

Jensen's smirk turns wicked as she pulls her shirt over her head. "Maybe next time."

My shirt follows. "Oh, definitely."

We pull off the rest of our clothes, but once she reaches for her underwear, I grip her wrist. "Allow me."

Gliding them down slowly, I lower to my knees. Placing soft kisses to her hips, the tops of her thighs, and right on that perfect cunt of hers.

Her hands grip on to my hair and her head falls back with my name coming out at barely a whisper.

I pepper a few more kisses along her inked skin then take advantage as she steps out of her underwear by sliding my tongue from her center then sucking her clit into my mouth. A curse comes and her grip tightens. I'm tempted to stay down here all night and be perfectly happy with that, but this time is different.

Rising up slowly, I trail more kisses on her skin. When I reach her face, I grip her chin and pull her flush against me. Her eyes stay shut, but her arms wrap around my back. "Stay with me, baby, please. Open your eyes."

As they slowly open, I have my thumb glide across her lips. "We've fucked before, but that's not this."

I feel her swallow against my hand. "Good, make love to me, Beck. I'm right here with you."

"Fuck," I groan, spinning her around and laying her back down on my bed.

Hovering over her again, I note every line and swirl of ink on her skin lit only by the moonlight streaming in through the blinds.

God, I could look at her all night.

Looking at her and committing every inch of her body to memory would be more than enough for me, but if I get to touch her...kiss her...make her all mine, I'm going to do that.

My fingers trail slow from her chin down her collarbone, then the valley of her chest.

Biting back a smile the best she can, I nearly lean in to bite her bottom lip myself, but I'm not done taking in this view.

Jensen's hands pull at my torso. "God, Beck, get down here."

I love her.

Our kiss fuels my soul a little more.

I. Love. Her.

Rocking back and forth ever so slightly, I know my piercing is giving her quite the tease. I know she's wanting me to move, but it wouldn't be us if I didn't edge her a little.

"Beckham," she groans in warning against my mouth as she hooks her ankles around my ass.

I pepper a few kisses on her face. "You're going to have to give me a second. Kissing you is about to send me over the edge."

Jensen's nails dig into my back with a soft moan. "Believe me, I'm hanging on by a thread, Beck."

I capture her mouth again as I slide all the way in with ease. My thrusts start slow, but nowhere near lazy. Each drive into her carries the promises I can't voice right now.

I wish I could fucking say them. I want to, and part of me is terrified that not getting them out will be my downfall, but praying with each second that she can feel what she means to me.

Jensen's nails continue to claw at my back and she loses the rhythm of our kiss. I know my ring is right where she likes it on her clit and with the way she's squeezing my cock she's close.

Wrapping my arms under her, I pull her tighter against me and kiss her neck, letting every moan of hers come out crystal clear. The force of my thrusts increase but I don't dare change our pace.

"Come with me, Beck," she whispers.

I nip at her ear. "I'm always coming with you, Jen."

Every time. Everywhere. In bed. In life. Just with her.

It doesn't take but a few more strokes in and out before we're both falling over the edge.

I want to take that as a good sign, but as our highs come down I'm afraid it won't be enough.

Her legs unhook and entangle in mine. I place one then two kisses on her collarbone before going up her neck, and giving one more sensual kiss to her lips.

She hums softly. "I knew if I kissed you I'd be fucked."

My head goes back with a laugh. Rolling off to the side I pull Jensen to me. Her head rests perfectly on my chest as I brush my fingers through her hair softly. For the first time in years, I'm not afraid of what my future will look like. I just see her.

Jensen and I spent the rest of the night in my bed with a lazy naked make-out session to make up for lost time. When Dottie whines outside our door, I throw on some sweats to take her out one more time before bringing her back up with me and falling asleep with Jensen in my arms.

Everything feels so right when I shut my eyes, but then that bubble pops.

I know I couldn't have slept for more than an hour, and Jensen's still cuddled close to me when Dottie starts pawing at my leg.

"Dot, go back to bed. I already took you out," I grumble, snuggling deeper into Jensen.

Dottie paws at my legs again, but then I hear it: my phone ringing from downstairs. Getting up to answer my phone is the very last thing I want to do, but know I have to look at who's calling.

Sliding out of the bed, I pull my sweatpants back on, then pat Dottie's head.

Once I make it downstairs the ringing stops, and for a second I pray it doesn't ring again, but then it lights back up and my stomach drops.

Racing over, I see the name I really didn't want to see.

Answering, I can't even get a hello out before I hear everything in my dad's voice.

"Beck, your mom—"

"I'm on my way. I'll call you on my way to the airport." I feel the panic attack coming on immediately, I shove it back as best I can.

I'm both grateful and absolutely hate that he doesn't argue because fuck this means that it's it. I'm going to have to say goodbye and I'm not ready to.

I clench my fists as an unimaginable pain sweeps through me. My throat tightens and I swear I'm choking on air. This panic attack is going to take me down, but I can't let it. I have to get back home.

Grabbing a sweatshirt from the top of the laundry, I just move with that one thought in mind. I slide my shoes on at the door then snatch up my keys—except they're not mine, they're Jensen's.

The pain in my chest comes back in full force. "Fuck, fuck, fuck," I whisper-shout. I should wake her up. Every muscle and instinct is begging me to go wake her up and bring her with me.

I stumble over to the island and brace myself against the wood. All that fear comes racing back tenfold and I'm seconds away from passing out but I can't afford that. Whatever's happened, I need to get back home.

I know what I'm about to do might be unforgivable, but I feel like I'm dying. What if this is too much? What if she actually sees what could happen and I lose her too? Why can't I fathom the idea of walking up the stairs?

Waking her up feels like it will seal every fear I have. And then what words would even come out of my mouth? My mom is...

I can't breathe. Fuck. I can't breathe.

I try everything to get my breathing under control, and even with a few deep breaths, I know I won't be able to. My eyes latch on to our notepad. A small bit of clarity hits me. Grabbing it and a pen, I write down every word I wanted to tell Jensen earlier.

It's nowhere close to what she deserves. I promise this is the last thing I ever want to do without her, even though I wish I had enough courage to go back up those stairs and wake her up.

As I drop the pen and grab my keys I've never hated myself more, but I walk out the door and head to say my final goodbye.

Chapter 29
Jensen

Falling asleep in Beck's arms is a peace I didn't know existed. But maybe it only does in my dreams because a chill vibrates through my body. I roll reaching for Beck aimlessly seeking out that peace again, but, when I reach the edge of the bed and find no one, my eyes fly open.

Alone. I'm in this bed alone.

Looking around the room hoping to find any clue as to Beck just being in the bathroom, any sound of him and Dottie just had a midnight craving, but the bathroom light is off. Dottie is asleep on my side of the bed and the clock reads just before five in the morning.

This pit forms deep in my stomach and then I hear the faint sound of a phone vibrating. I swing my legs off the bed. I think I lost it on the floor somewhere...I don't really remember much other than Beck. Beck's kiss. Beck's touch. The promises of more.

Rifling through the pile of our clothes on the floor, I try to use that for a reminder that last night did actually happen. I don't know where Beck is, but my phone is still ringing and my mind is racing. I need this to be him calling...but it's his dad?

Crumbling to the floor, the pit in my stomach turns into knots as I answer on a shaky breath. "Hello?"

"Jensen," he answers in a panic. "I'm sorry to call at this hour, but it's important."

A wave of nausea hits me and no words come out. Deep in my gut, I already know what he's about to say.

"We're going to have to say goodbye tonight, and as much as Beck thinks he has to do it alone, he's wrong. I'm sorry to ask this of you, but I know he won't—he needs you."

Tears prick my eyes at the strain in Rory's voice.

"He's stubborn and so headstrong that I know he left without a word. I'm not looking to make this—"

"He left?" The words tumble out as what he said registers. "When?" I croak.

He left? A wave of hurt and anger hits me. In light of the situation, I hate it, it feels selfish...but I feel so betrayed. Why wouldn't he wake me up? Let me be there for him and not have to wake up this way.

A heavy sigh comes through the line. "He said he's on the way from the airport to the house now. I know I'm biased but I beg you to give him a little grace. He's the best person I know...right after his mother. Losing her is going to destroy him—he's not thinking clearly."

Forget my stomach being in knots, I've been punched in the gut and shot through the heart. As angry as I am that he didn't wake me when he left, I know what Beck's mom means to him.

But I can't seem to let go of why didn't he wake me? I know I want to be there for him during this. Had he woken me, I would have gone with him without a second thought.

Hell, if he had said *I'm going, can you meet me there later*, I would have made peace with it, but to just leave? Not a single word said, and now I have to hear about it from his dad?

"Rory, if he left without me—"

"Jensen," he cuts me off before I can finish the sentence I honestly didn't want to say. "You don't have to come. I meant what I told you earlier, you deserve to be happy. He shouldn't have left. I won't defend him more than I already have. You are not wrong in not wanting to come, but you will be welcomed in my home if you do."

Tears well in my eyes and it takes everything in me to not let them fall. I want to be there for Beck, I really truly do. It's not that I owe it to him to hear him out, but I want to know why he left. I want to know if he feels like what we have is worth fighting for.

I can fight on my own for a few days if I need to, but I won't forever.

I force the lump in my throat down. "I'll be there, just tell me—"

"I already got you a flight. I'm not going to have you pay for that."

A surprising pained laugh comes out as one tear makes its way down my cheek. "Of course you did—like father, like son."

"I'll send over all the information. And, Jensen?"

"Yeah?"

"Thank you."

My chest is on fire. I want to thank him, considering he's calling me and paying for my travel down to them. I want to tell him that I love his idiotic son, who never lets me do anything alone even though he's the one so hell-bent on being alone. But instead, I say, "See you soon."

I feel Dottie come up beside me as I hang up. She licks my face as she nudges into my lap. It's then I decide I've held back my tears long enough. I cry out every emotion—all the anger and pain.

When my phone lights up again with my flight info, I know I have to swallow it all down. I don't want to lose Beck after this, but god, he's got to let me all the way in.

With a deep breath, I get up off the floor and freaking move. One foot in front of the other, one suitcase haphazardly thrown together, step into my jeans one foot at a time—all of it, just one thing at a time.

Dottie whines anxiously as I zip up the suitcase and I let out a small curse. "Sorry, girl, I don't think you're coming with me."

Pulling out my phone, I call Dex, hoping he'd appreciate me not calling his pregnant wife at five in the morning.

He answers with a groan. "Hello?"

My mouth opens and boy do all those emotions threaten to come back up. "Dex...I'm sorry, it's Beck's—"

Thankfully, I don't have to finish my sentence. "Don't say anymore, what do you need from me?" His voice is calm and alert now.

Taking a deep breath, I find my steady, one thing at a time mentality. "Can I bring Dottie to you? I'm about to head to the airport."

"Done. Text me on your way up. I'll meet you at the door."

"Thank you, and please don't wake Luce. I'm trying really hard to be strong and I think I'll crumble if she hugs me."

"I can hold her off for now, but I can't make any promises after that."

I almost find the slightest laugh. "Yeah, I'll need her later, but not now. I'll be there in twenty minutes."

With that done, I lug my suitcase down the stairs and immediately fill a Ziploc bag of kibble for Dottie but that's when I catch a glimpse of it...the freaking notepad on the counter. I need it to be blank and need to have something written on it at the same time.

Taking two steps closer, I can see the paper full of words in his handwriting. I can't read it, not now. Ripping it off, I carefully fold it and shove it in my back pocket.

"Deep breaths, Jensen. You can do this."

Putting Dottie's leash on, I grab my things and I'm out the door. One foot in front of the other. One drive to Dex's place and then the airport. By the time my butt hits my seat, I feel like I've gone completely robotic.

I pull out the note from Beck, but still can't find the strength to read it. I can't have it say that he regrets last night. I can't know coming into this if last night meant something to him or not. His dad said he needed me, so that's enough for now. The heartbreak can come after if that's what's meant to be.

Chapter 30
Beck

I'm in hell. That has to be the only logical explanation. My panic attack has reached new levels of drowning. I can feel the weight of the pain of knowing I won't see my mom again waiting to finally crash down and simply end me.

The lump in my throat is astronomical. All I can do is stare off into the void as I listen to the nurses as they do their jobs.

The headache she mentioned last night only got worse and worse. They did everything to keep her as comfortable as possible, but about two hours after I got here, she passed in her sleep.

Her head nurse, Jamie, assured me that because of the care I was able to provide, she truly believes my mom had one of the most peaceful final stages of early-onset that she's ever worked. Not that it makes me feel anything other than this immeasurable pain in my chest—it's the least I could have done for her.

When they started work on her postmortem care, I somehow ended up in her spot on the couch.

"Here." My dad holds out a cup of coffee. I don't even think about reaching out and taking it, but my disinterest only spurs him on. "It wasn't a question, son. I'll get you anything else if that's it, but you're fucking drinking something."

"I feel like I'll throw up anything I drink, Dad, just... please—not right now."

The sigh he lets out tells me more than enough. "Fine, then humor me and hold it."

There's zero energy in me to argue so I take it.

He takes the seat next to me.

He leans back in the seat with a sigh as he shuts his eyes. I know he's got to be exhausted, I'm fucking drained myself but he seems to be holding it together way better than I am and it's starting to piss me off.

"Dad, I don't think I've taken a full breath since you called. I'm losing my fucking mind. How the fuck are you so calm right now?"

He doesn't move, doesn't even open his eyes when he says. "I'm just thinking of your mother. The first time we met. Our first date. The time she got us busted for making out in her car in a random field."

I nearly laugh but it comes out more of a choked cry.

Dad finally sits back up, his hand lands on my shoulder. "I'm an absolute wreck, but you know her, Beck, she'd hate this. When your grandfather passed, all your mother did was talk and think of him the way he was before his diagnosis. And she made me promise if this very thing happened that I would do the same.

"Beck, I'm going to miss her so much, but with the memories of her—having you—I can live for the both of us.

She will always be with me, and I refuse to disappoint her by not continuing to be the husband and father she made me to be."

"Fuck, Dad." I hang my head. I know deep down he's right. I hate that it's taken me to this point to realize that I haven't been the person she raised me to be. "I think I've disappointed her. I know she said she was proud of me earlier, but if she knew how I've felt—"

"No, you could never, she was always so proud of you. We both are."

Setting the coffee down on the side table, I run my hands over my face. It's more than that, and he knows it. "I should have brought Jensen here. She was home and I just...left."

My dad lets out a slow breath. "Yeah, I'm not going to lie to you...Mom would hit you over the head right now for not bringing her with you, but she's not disappointed in you."

The memory of every tap to mine or Dad's head every time we did something she deemed dumb plays in my head and this time I actually manage some form of a laugh. "Jensen would have loved her. I wanted to tell Mom about her today, but didn't."

"Mom would have loved her too, but more importantly, *you* love her. Want to tell me why you didn't bring her with you?"

My knee starts to bounce with every excuse I think of, because I'm an idiot? Because it's not her grief to deal with? But then I decide on the truth.

"I was so fucking terrified." The lump in my throat comes up almost immediately. "You were right," I choke out. "All I had to do was try. I didn't even realize I was...until it was too far gone. I don't see a life without her. I love my friends, my team, the game, but there has never been a love that compared to my family until her."

Dad lets out a soft tsk. "You can't be scared of love, Beck—"

"No, I'm not scared of loving her, it's not that. I'm terrified of what loving me could mean for her. The moment I decided I was going to let that fear go...you called and then all of it came back...I couldn't even tell her how I felt, Dad. She deserves more than that."

Sitting up straight, I can't decide if getting that out in the open has lifted some of this weight off my shoulder or made my looming panic attack worse.

"Beckham, you can't always have this total control over your life. I don't know how to help you see this, but you deserve more too. I'm not saying more from her, but you deserve the life you want. I won't say you should've left the way you did, but you have to let go of this fear and guilt."

I want to believe him, I really do. I've never thought I didn't deserve my career or my friends, but my family is a whole other story. It's more than not seeing a life without her, it's not being able to live without her. But I was too fucking scared to tell her that, so I walked out the door because that felt easier.

Dad shakes my shoulder. "Life is unpredictable as is. It's not always fair or forgiving, but you've found something incredible. Do you think I deserved your mother? Deserved to have this incredible son with her? I didn't. I could hold on to that thinking if I wanted, but instead I count my fucking blessings. It doesn't matter if I truly deserved them or not, I got those decades with her. I have you. So stop giving up on yourself. Just live your life like your mother would have wanted."

I bury my face in my hands, letting out muffled curses. Here I was about to place my anger on him for being calm and now I don't even know how to explain what I'm feeling. A small, pained laugh comes out when her voice from earlier comes in my head. "She did say more men should listen to her, didn't she?"

"Never heard truer words. My life was better when I listened and did what she said." Dad's laugh comes out sounding slightly lighter than mine. "I wasn't always perfect at it, and it took me a minute to really figure that out. Loving her is the easiest thing I ever did, but getting to have a life with her—even now, I'm still the luckiest guy in the world, all because of her."

I let out a breath with a heavy heart. "I'm going to miss her so fucking much."

The hug he wraps me in nearly sends me over the edge. "I know, son, I will too, but you won't have to go through this alone."

I grip on to his arm trying to find any sort of grounding, and then there's a knock at the door.

I swallow hard and finally find the strength to open my eyes. "That must be someone with the coroner's office."

With one more tight squeeze, Dad lets me go and we're both on our feet. "I'll go get it, you wait here."

I should probably go with him, but I can't seem to move to follow him. I can't move, period. Can't find the will to sit back down or take the step to actually be there for my dad.

That is, until I hear, "Beck?"

I'm not sure if I'm hallucinating or what, but at the sound of Jensen's voice, I'm turning.

At the sight of her my feet move instantly. I wrap her in my arms and this still feels like a dream. It's not until her sweet cherry blossom shampoo registers in my brain and her arms finally wrap around my back that it feels real.

"You're here. You're really here."

"I'm here," she whispers. "I'm here."

I hold onto her, letting her presence fully consume me. For how long, I'm not sure, and eventually, I have to lean back to look at her face because some part of me still doesn't believe it.

"You're here," I repeat.

Tears pool in her beautiful eyes and the softest smile comes to her face. "I'm here." Reaching up, her thumb glides across my cheek wiping at the tears I didn't even know we're falling.

My dad claps my back before reaching to hug Jensen. "Thank you for coming."

Her eyes flash to me, and I see all the pain I caused in them for the briefest second, but then it's gone. "Of course, thank you for getting me here."

"You did this?" I look to my dad—and he thinks he's the luckiest man in the world...

"I told you, I won't lose you too. I won't let you self-destruct," he says, so matter-of-fact that I feel the punch in the gut that it was meant to be. "I'll let you two have a minute."

I pull Jensen to me and give him a small nod. "Thank you...for everything."

He drops his head with a small smile, then looks to Jensen. "Just so you know, his mom would not want you to let him get away with this easily. Give him hell, it'd make her proud."

I feel Jensen's muscles tense in my arms. She's not going

to want to do that, she's going to let me get by without talking about this.

I wait for my dad to disappear into the kitchen then take a few short seconds more of holding her close. I press a kiss to her head. "He's right, you know."

"Beck," she whispers. "Now's not—"

I cut her off cradling her face in my hands. "No, now is just fine. Don't tell me it's okay. Force me to talk about this, like I do with you."

I can practically see her thinking it through and god, am I so glad that I see that fight in her win. She pushes back out of my hold. "You said you were with me, Beck!"

Running her hands through her hair, she takes a slow breath. "I don't know how to have this fight with you right now. And you know what, maybe I won't. I won't force you to talk about why you left. Don't tell me your apologies or reasons, not now. I just want you to listen to me."

Yep, Mom would have absolutely loved her.

Tears pool in her eyes, but they don't fall. My strong, stubborn girl knows I don't deserve them, not right now. "I love you, Beck. I know that wasn't a part of our plan, but I do. Coming here—after waking up alone—I have no regrets. I've given this my all. You have me on every molecular level, but I won't take your half. I deserve more."

"Jen—" I want to agree with her, because I know she does, but she holds her hand up.

"I know you can't give that right now, so I'll make up for it because that's what loving you has taught me. I'm here because I want to be by your side through this..." She pauses and pulls a folded piece of paper from her back pocket. "But I can't know what this says until we're back in Boston."

Taking the note, I know she's right. Even though I want

to tell her everything—lay it all out there for her to know—I know why she wants to wait.

I dare a step closer and she doesn't push back when I pull her back in. "Okay, Jen, I won't say anything else, but I *am* sorry for leaving." Placing a kiss to the top of her head, we stay there, wrapped up in each other's arms until my dad comes back in, and it's time for our final goodbyes.

Chapter 31
Jensen

I haven't left Beck's side for two days. I held his hand through their final goodbyes and fell asleep in his arms each night. Not that either of us has actually gotten any quality sleep.

It's been nonstop people calling, dropping by, and all things planning for the funeral arrangements. Or, well, reception.

The one bittersweet part of all this is getting this better understanding of Beck. From the stories I've been told of his mother to the requests she's made for her passing—after her father passed, she made sure it was written in her will that she wanted zero sad music, no mournful preaching, or to have an actual funeral.

Rory recounted the whole story with this smile on his face. Said he remembers bickering over that with her until they finally agreed that he could have a reception in her honor. His love for her radiates from him every second he speaks of her. Every time someone mentions her name, it's clear.

Beck managed a small chuckle when he got to the part where she also insisted no one was allowed to make long-winded eulogies and the game Beck's most proud of had to be played the entire time.

So, with that in mind, they decided to have an open gathering at the chapel they got married in, and have this last World Series game playing on the projector.

Every now and then, I find Beck looking up at it with the slightest tug at the corners of his mouth. Otherwise, he's practically running on autopilot at this point. Not that I blame him, he's been making the best small talk he can and nodding along with people's condolences.

I hold his hand tightly each time. He's exhausted from this grief and all the decisions that had to be made. I can practically feel Beck's pain—I just want to help him carry that weight, and I'm trying to.

I've been holding it together the best I can, being whatever he and his dad need, but I'm still so hurt over how he left. I feel so incredibly selfish for it, given the situation. I all but spiral when I start thinking about us.

I've considered asking for the note countless times, just to know how he feels about us because I don't want to be here if my presence is hurting him. But then it turns back into me feeling selfish because I'm not ready to let him go yet. Then how can I even think about asking any of these questions while he's grieving... The emotional carousel is killing me slowly and I don't know how to make the ride stop.

Beck's hand tugs me back a step as someone starts talking to his dad. "Hey, why don't you go take a break? There're some water and snacks in the kitchen."

Rolling my shoulders back, I feign a soft smile. "I'm okay, but I can get you both water if you want."

Beck lets go of my hand to cradle my face. The small touches haven't stopped and I'm all but clinging to them for my sanity.

"I'm good, but if I can't make you take a break, then I know someone who can."

I follow Beck's eyes as he looks behind me with the slightest smile tugging at the corners of his lips. I'm so exhausted that it takes me a second to register the reality of Lucie, Callie, and Emma headed our way with Dex, Will, Adam, and Tripp following behind them.

The weight of stress that falls off my shoulders is instant when Lucie wraps me up in her arms. Tears well in my eyes, and I do my best to hold them back, but I'm the first person Lucie goes for. I'm the person she wanted to check on first. As selfish as it makes me feel, I really needed it.

She told me they were all coming, but without her physically here I pushed it to the back of my head to keep Beck my focus.

"You look exhausted," she mumbles, still holding me tight.

"Thanks, I really fucking am," I whisper, hoping only she hears me. I really don't want to let go, but I can hear everyone else giving their condolences to Beck and his dad, and I know I can't lose it just yet. Lucie will be the first person I run to when I get back to Boston.

Beck rests one hand on my back, but looks to Lucie. "Please, make her go take a break."

I don't even have time to open my mouth to argue before Lucie steps to him giving a tight hug then takes my hand. "I've got her. We'll be back in a bit."

I look over my shoulder. "Beck, I'm—"

"We've got him," Dex cuts me off, appearing right beside him.

Callie takes the next opportunity to step in between us. "Lucie's orders."

Emma takes my other hand tugging me along with Lucie. "Five minutes tops."

With the first step all arguments die. I follow their lead, when Lucie completely bypasses the kitchen and pulls us into a private room I know I'm about to let out the cry I've been dying to have.

With the click of the door, Lucie turns, giving me that soft smile. "Let it out, Jen."

If she insists.

I let out all the stress, all the hurt, the emotional turmoil I've felt because I know without a shadow of a doubt that they won't judge me for it.

Lucie hugs me head on, while Callie wraps around my back, and Emma comes to the side.

"I was holding it together so well." I laugh slightly through the tears. "I don't know what I'm doing here, but I know I can't leave him. And I feel like the worst person in the world because I want to know how he feels so bad, then I think about how he left in the middle of the night without a word, and I feel physically sick."

I hadn't had the time to fully explain what happened, but with the call to Dex in the middle of the night and one very brief text to Lucie from the plane I'm sure they've all made the assumption.

They probably saw this coming from a mile away. Some part of me saw it too, but I was sure it had changed.

Lucie leans back. "Okay, first off, you're not the worst—

you're human, Jensen. Of course you're having mixed emotions right now, in any other situation I'd be tearing Beck a new one."

"Agreed," Callie adds. "Give yourself a little bit of credit, babe."

Emma runs her hand up and down my back. "Did he mention why he left?"

I shake my head. "Not one that I've let him say. He did leave a note, but I've been too scared to open it. I'm terrified to know what it says. None of this is what we agreed to—I honestly don't know what I'm doing here. I just know I can't leave, but I can't make this about us either. Now I'm in here falling apart. I've been stuck in this death spiral of sadness, guilt, and hurt."

"You're putting way too much pressure on yourself." Lucie dabs her sleeve on my cheeks. "Have you eaten anything? Drank water?"

The look I give her is answer enough.

"Okay." She looks to Callie and Emma. "Can you guys get her something small to eat and some water?"

I don't waste my breath arguing, I just let them do whatever. The idea of food makes me feel sick, but that excuse will mean nothing to Lucie.

"Jensen." Lucie shakes my shoulders slightly when it's only us left in the room. "Listen to me, I truly am so sorry for Beck and his family. I hate this situation, but I want you to hear me when I say I'm here for you. I'm not about to let you tell yourself you're the worst. I don't want you to feel guilty. I'm not saying don't be sad, but if no one's putting you first right now, let that person be me."

I let out a pained laugh as another tear falls. I don't know how I got so lucky to have Lucie.

"I'm serious, Jen, we'll leave right now if you want to. I'll be that girl. I don't care."

I swipe at my cheek and for the first time in days I don't have a forced smile. "Say what you actually want to be."

The corners of Lucie's mouth turn up. "I'll be that bitch if it means you get some rest and a chance to actually breathe."

"Hearing you say that is more than enough." I give her the biggest hug. "I love you, Princess Peach."

She chuckles. "I love you too."

Lucie doesn't let me leave the room until I drink the entirety of the glass of water and the dinner roll Callie and Emma brought.

Walking back out, I hold Lucie's hand for every ounce of courage I can steal from her.

Beck's eyes find me the moment we enter back through the chapel doors. In spite of everything, I can see that longing still in his eyes. I don't want to give up on us, I just hope that longing isn't rooted in him already accepting the fact that he'll let me go.

Lucie's hand squeezes mine. "I'm obviously not the one you need to be hearing this from, but he loves you."

I attempt to swallow the lump that is all but taking up a permanent residency in my throat. "I know that to some degree," I whisper, watching as Beck weaves through the people to get to me. "It just can't be about that right now."

Chapter 32
Beck

I've all but drained Jensen over these past few days. There were things that had to be done and my attention was pulled elsewhere that I didn't see how bad until Dex showed us pictures of Miles and Dottie together. Her eyes barely lifted and her smile was faint.

I know I've hurt her and so much of me has wanted to fix that every chance I get, but I get why she said wait.

I want to give my mom the goodbye she deserves. I want to be the son my dad needs. But I think I needed these few days to really let all the hurt, anger, and resentment go.

I'm going to miss my mom so fucking much. I'll think about her every single day, but I'm so happy to have Jensen. I want to start living again. I need to know my mom's looking down to see the man she remembers me to be.

As the reception comes to a close, I watch as Lucie attempts to revive Jensen as much as she can.

Dex falls in line next to me, this slight smile on his face. "I've got to warn you, Luce is about to kidnap Jensen."

"I'd expect nothing less from her." I huff out a small laugh. "Don't you have something to tell me anyway?"

Dex *humphs*, and for a moment I think he might let it slide, but I want to hear him say it.

"I told you so."

Thank fuck. "Yeah, you did."

Dex's hand lands on my shoulder. "I know you don't want to hear any more apologies, so just know that I'll keep Dottie in my house until you both come home. However, I can only hold back my wife for so long."

And there's a little more of a real laugh. "You can promise Lucie that I've got it under control. We'll be home in a few days."

"Take your time." Dex squeezes my shoulder. "We love you, man."

"I love y'all too. Thanks for coming down."

"Of course." Dex nods, then looks back to our girls. "I'll take mine, you get yours."

"Thank god, yours is scary."

Dex's smile grows obnoxiously. "Tell me about it."

When we get within ear shot, I can hear Lucie's pleas. "Are you sure you don't want to come home with us? You can get some actual rest and I'll make you whatever food you want."

Jensen's head tilts back and her eyes shut. I want to take the opportunity to answer for her and say no, she stays with me, but I wouldn't fault Jensen if she decides to go. Honestly, it makes me kind of happy to know that Lucie loves my girl this much.

I want to fix my fuckup first. I want Jensen to stay so I can tell her what she means to me. But I suppose if she leaves I'll go too.

Jensen lets out a heavy breath. "I'll be home in a few days, Luce. I promise."

I reach for Jensen, careful not to startle her then pull her back against my chest. "I've got her Luce, I swear."

Lucie doesn't seem entirely convinced. Dex was right, she would definitely kidnap Jensen right now if she could.

Dex pulls Lucie a step back. "It's okay baby. You can mother her when she gets back."

Only then do I see Lucie relax a bit. Her eyes move between Jensen and mine. "Promise you'll both get some rest? I'm sorry, I can't turn it off."

"We'd never ask you to do that, Luce." I place a small kiss on Jensen's head and hold her tighter. "We will get some rest later."

I don't think either of us can truly rest until we talk. I actually refuse to rest myself until I can tell her how much I love her.

Jensen reaches a hand out for Lucie. "It's okay. Text me when you get home?"

Lucie manages a half-smile then nods. She pulls Jensen away from me for one more hug, then we say our goodbyes to the rest of the group.

Callie hugs me from the side. "Round of pool when you get back?"

I find a small laugh. "Game night at our place."

Will's hand lands on my shoulder. "We'll be there. Call us if you need anything, okay?"

I give him a nod then get our goodbyes out as they all load into the car to take them to the airport.

My hold tightens around Jensen and I press a small kiss to her temple. "I want to take you somewhere."

Jensen tilts her head back. "Beck, you need rest, you're exhausted."

Spinning her around slowly, I bring her body against mine. "No more of that. I appreciate all you've done for me these past few days, baby, but please, no more. If you're exhausted, I'll take you back to the house and we'll sleep with no alarm. Just sleep as long as we need."

Leaning slightly, I meet her eyes. "But if you're up for it, I'd love to take you somewhere."

Jensen's eyes fall closed as she lets out a deep exhale. When her eyes open again, I can see that bite in her coming back just a bit. "Where are we going?"

Taking her hand, I start to pull her to my rental car. "It's a surprise."

Her steps drag a bit. "Don't we need to say something to your dad?"

"Nope, I talked to him already. This is for just us, Jen."

Her feet drag for a few more steps until I finally feel her hand relax in mine and her steps lighten.

Opening her door, she slides into the passenger seat. Rounding the car, I take my seat, and the moment I put the car in drive my hand finds her thigh. There's not a single hesitation. No pull to bring it back. It stays there firmly until we pull into the parking lot of my high school.

Jensen sits up in her seat. "Beck..." Her tone weak. "What are we doing?"

"Come on, Killer, we have something to work out. There's only one place that I know delivers every time."

Getting out of the car, I take her hand in mine then send a text with the other. When Lucie took Jensen for a break, my old principal walked in and I knew what needed to happen.

He meets us at the door, still in his suit from the reception. "Beckham," he greets with a soft smile. "I think you know where to go. Mrs. Henry hasn't moved it."

I give him a nod. "Thank you, I appreciate this."

"Of course, take your time." When he goes back into his office, I take Jensen up the stairs then down to the back hall where my mom's old classroom was.

Jensen stays quiet, but by now I'm sure she knows what we're doing. When I hit the lights in the classroom, we see it at the same time—my mom's electricity ball.

"I had to bring out the big guns, Jen. I can't risk it."

Jensen squeezes my hand and as she turns a tear glides down her cheek meeting this smile on her beautiful face. "Well, come on then, let's work it out."

Moving to the little ball, I flip it on then set my finger on one side. I watch as the electricity links to my finger then watch as Jensen puts hers on the other side.

At that moment, I know that everything I'm about to say to her will hold no fear, no anxieties for what our future will look like. I want that love my parents have with her. I didn't get to tell my mom about Jensen, but right here, right now, I'm changing that.

I pull out the note I left her a few days ago and drop it on the table. "Instead of reading this, can I say it?"

Jensen pulls her eyes from her finger to meet my eyes. "I think that would be better, yes."

"Growing up, I always wanted the life my parents had... the love that they had, but when she got sick—it was like nothing made sense anymore. I was so heartbroken for my mom, my dad...myself. I started mourning her before she was even truly gone, and with that, the life I thought I wanted.

"It wasn't until you walked into that bar ten months

ago that I felt this spark to want to have someone in my life again. With everyone, I kept this mask up of this happy, carefree guy, but with you it didn't feel forced. You challenged me. You blew me off countless times, but it didn't deter me because I had convinced myself that being around you was okay. You didn't want me as much as I didn't want a relationship so why not seek you out? Why not put all my energy into being around the person who made me actually feel something real? Even if I was lying to myself about it, I knew somewhere deep down that I couldn't let you go."

Tears fall silently down her cheeks and she sputters a small laugh. "I can't call you my stalker ever again."

"Please, never stop. Jensen, I want you to call me everything. I want you to call me on my bullshit. Call when you need me, and just call me yours. I want our back-and-forth. I want to fight with you. I want to apologize with you. I want you. I'm sorry I left the way I did. I wish I could go back and change what I did, but I know I can't. I can't undo the pain I've caused you and I'm so sorry."

Jensen's shoulders fall a bit as she takes a small step to me. "Beck, it's okay" she whispers, but I hold up my hand.

"Don't make any excuses for me. After the night we had, it was unfair to do that to you. The only thing I can say is that I swear it will be the last time. Jen, I don't want to spend a day of my life without you. I love you. I love you so much that those words don't even do it justice. You're the part of my soul I swear I threw away when I was mourning. I want to be the man my mother raised me to be, and *fuck* if I don't want to be that man for you."

I don't register Jensen stepping to me until her lips are on mine. My hand falls off the little ball as I lean into her embrace. My hands capture her face and I kiss her knowing every bit of anxiety I have will be met with her.

Whatever time I have with her will be filled with a love that I can't say I deserve, but will cherish with every single breath I take.

Jensen leans back and I glide my thumb across her cheek in a soft caress. "You asked me in the office how many memories I planned on stealing, baby, I want to steal all of them. Make up for all the time I've wasted and steal every bit of you if you'll let me. I love you."

"I love you too," she whispers. "Thank you for keeping eye contact during that speech."

This laugh bubbles out of me. "Fucking Dad. Ratted out my tell, didn't he?"

For the first time in three days, I see a genuine smile on Jensen's face. "He sure did. I can't wait to call you on it for a very long time."

I place a lingering kiss on her forehead. "I can't wait either, Jenni-cakes."

After leaving the school, we pick up food from one of my favorite places in town then sleep well into the next day. It's so nice waking up to see Jensen's eyes no longer red and a bit of color back in her face.

It's nice waking up next to her in general, though. There's still this pang in my chest, knowing a vital part of my life is missing, but when that feels a bit too much, I'll reach for Jensen then recall the best moments of my mother just like my dad said.

This grief feels different than I ever expected it too, but I can't say that I'm alone in it anymore. I'm no longer afraid that the pain will consume me.

Sitting down at the kitchen table, Dad made a huge spread of pancakes for lunch all with different toppings mixed in. Some with chocolate chips, some with strawberries, some with both, then some with blueberries.

"Dad, were you craving pancakes?" I ask with a bit of humor in my tone.

He lets out a hum as he takes his seat across the table. "Seems pretty obvious to me that I was. Jensen, I'm not sure if Beck told you, but his mom always insisted that there were no time rules for food."

Jensen takes her seat then looks up at me. "He told me all about it. I think pancakes sound great."

I place my hand on her back as I take the seat next to her. Reaching for the seat of her chair, I pull her closer to me. "I didn't say they didn't sound good. Was more noting the extreme amount."

"I can freeze them," Dad says with a shrug. "So, you two good now?"

"Dad," I chastise, while Jensen tries to stifle a laugh.

Meeting my dad with a complete dumbfounded look he simply shrugs. "What? I've never beat around the bush before. Don't plan on starting anytime soon. Besides, I meddled, I need to know how it worked out."

I place a hand on Jensen's thigh and tilt my head back with a small groan. "Fuck's sake. Yeah, Dad, we're good. No more meddling is needed."

Dad looks at Jensen with a smirk. "We'll see about the meddling."

"No, no, I promise I got it under control." I make sure to

hold eye contact with my dad for a solid few seconds before looking at Jen.

Jen's head shakes and she mumbles, *"Ya sé que sí."* I know you do.

Squeezing her thigh, I relax a bit at her trust in me. That's all I need.

"Well, that's good to hear. I can find some peace knowing you won't screw it up completely when you head back to Boston," Dad says pouring syrup over his pancakes.

That small twist in my chest comes back. I know we have to go back, but leaving him here all alone has me feeling a bit uneasy.

Dad sets down the bottle with a sigh. "You do know you have to go back to Boston, right?"

Oh, sometimes he—I huff a breath. "Yes, I'm aware of that."

"Good, 'cause I was thinking—possibly—I could find a place up in Boston," he says, picking up his fork. "I don't plan on getting rid of this house, but I meant what I said—I will keep living for myself and your mother. I want to be at more of your games, travel to some of the away games too when I can. I'm not jumping to any conclusion on what's happening here, but you know...I want to be around for it."

Jensen's hand finds mine on her leg as I'm sure she can see the mix of emotions written all over my face.

"Yeah, Dad, we'd love that."

Chapter 33
Jensen
A month later

"I think it looks perfect, Ems."

I watch as Emma tilts her head side to side looking at her work on my wall. With the contractor finishing all our renovations, I decided to let Emma loose on my wall next.

She painted "Tinta 222" in an old-school tattoo font and took my sketch from the tapestry Stella got me when I moved here and repainted it behind the logo.

I had planned on simply hanging the tapestry here, but Beck insisted it go up in our room.

"Are you sure you like it? I feel like this one line—"

"Emma, it's perfect!" I cut her off. "I get it—you think you see a crooked line or small imperfection but you've been looking at it for hours. You did this with the side room, remember? Take a few days and come back."

Emma scrunches her nose as she looks over to the small designs she did for the piercing room. We wanted it to stand out without it being overwhelming so she painted some stars and witchy elements that my sister sent over. Beck, naturally, had to add cherries, the pool balls, and baseballs to the mix.

Emma was sure it was going to come out to be this chaotic mess of a pattern on the wall, but it turned out so fucking cool.

Her shoulders drop as she lets out a sigh. "You're right, I know. Paint brushes down and step away."

I snort a laugh. "Good girl."

Emma whips one of her braids back behind her shoulder. "I am, aren't I?"

"Just not as good as my girl," Beck says, walking through the door with Dottie in tow. He's at my side in an instant and planting a kiss to my lips.

Emma sticks her tongue out. "It was funny at first, but now I'm afraid this will turn gross."

Beck looks her dead in the eye. "I was referring to Dottie, Emma. Geez, relax. Jensen's not a good girl, she's—"

"Ah, stop it," Emma squeals and plugs her ears. "I knew you'd make it gross."

Shaking my head, I lean back onto Beck's chest and his arms come around my waist. "Anyway, you're coming to our place tonight, right? Reagan and Julie can't make it, and Blake's still out of town. Mia has to work so I've got you paired up with my sister Stella as your partner for the pool tournament.

Emma throws her canvas bag over her shoulder. "Yeah, I'll be there. Need me to bring anything? I think Tripp is picking me up, and we can get something on our way."

"You'll get something of his up," Beck mumbles, to which I quickly send my elbow back to his stomach. "Dammit, Jennie."

Emma's face goes flat. "What'd he say?"

"Nothing," I reassure her.

Emma's quickly gotten over any comments that have to

do with her and Tripp being anything but friends. She's stood strong on her stance that they missed their opportunity to be more, so being friends is all she's interested in now.

"You don't have to bring anything—we've got it covered."

"Alrighty, sounds good to me." Emma walks over to her case of paints and supplies then wheels it to the door. "I'll see you all tonight." She raises her hand over her head with a wave.

"See you la-*ter*!" I squeal on the last syllable as Beck immediately spins my body around to face him before I could finish the sentence.

His hands go up and thread through my hair. "Hi, I missed you."

I may roll my eyes, but this warmth fills my body. "You were only at practice for two hours, Stalker. How are you going to survive away games?"

"Horribly," Beck states, then places a quick kiss to my lips. "I'm going to tell Reagan that her business partner has a high probability of being kidnapped, so don't be alarmed if you go missing."

I link my hands behind his neck, pulling him down slightly. "Zero concerns needed. I'm sure I'll be right where I want to be."

A smile tugs at the corner of Beck's mouth until it lands on mine. He kisses me slowly but the passion behind it sends shockwaves through my body.

Beck lets out a low hum when my tongue slides against his. "Where did Reagan say she put cameras again?"

"There are some at the doors and in the back room. There're a few up here, but we made sure my room is pretty much out of view for client privacy."

Client privacy with a little perk, in my opinion at least.

Beck, however, lifts me up and brings my legs around my waist. "Dottie, stay here," he commands before carrying me out of my room.

"Beck, what are you doing?" I laugh.

This sexy glint comes to his eyes. "Oh, we're going to find a camera. I want to watch back how good I fuck you."

A thrill sends sparks down my spine. I know Reagan hardly looks at the app to view the cameras, but I'll be sure to send her girlfriend, Julie, a little warning just to be safe. I've gotten a few of those texts myself from her so I'm not worried —just turned on.

"I think I'd rather watch it back and see you come in your pants again."

This wicked smile comes to Beck's face. "There's my lethal girl."

"So the teams are: Will and Callie, Dex and Lucie, Stella and Emma, Tripp and Adam...and lastly, your future winners, me and Beck."

A chorus of boos come from the group, naturally. I pull two pieces of paper from Beck's hat with a shake of my head. "Alright, relax. First up is apparently a couples battle with Callie and Will versus Dex and Lucie."

Dex tilts his head back. He was pretty much over this whole tournament idea before he even walked in the door, but there was no way Beck was letting him off the hook. "Alright, Luce, let's get this over with so we can just hang out for the rest of the night."

Lucie runs a hand over her already showing belly.

"Sounds good to me, the babies are dying for one of those cinnamon rolls."

I step to her. "I'll go get you one, Princess Peach. Everyone else is free to eat too after this."

Lucie's hand catches mine before I walk off. "Ooo, can you get me some of the sausage balls too? I've got a baby girl demanding sweet and a baby boy demanding salty."

My smile comes easily. "I'll get you a variety."

"Thank you." She blows me a kiss as I walk away.

Rounding the island, I start loading up Lucie's plate when Adam files in beside me. He stalls before picking up a plate to look at his phone and then laughs before his thumbs start tapping across his screen.

I cut an eyebrow up to him. "Did you just giggle at your phone?"

"What? I don't giggle." Adam jumps, like he completely forgot I was even next to him. But I was indeed next to him and I happened to see a three-letter name at the top of his screen.

"You're texting Mia?"

The question is asked, and I swear this burly man blushes.

"We're talking about the party." He shakes his head, shoving his phone back in his pocket.

I hum softly. "I thought Mia only kept her business talks to emails. My mistake."

Adam keeps his voice low. "Please keep this between us. We're just texting, it's no big deal."

"Okay," I say, then fold my lips in a thin line. Must say, not a match-up I necessarily saw, but seems like Adam isn't quite sure of it either. "I saw nothing."

"Thank you." He nods, but as I walk away I notice he pulls his phone right back out.

Dropping off Lucie's plate, Callie has already sunk half of their balls in. Granted, I'm not too sure Dex and Lucie are putting up too much of a fight. It was technically Lucie's shot but the moment she saw me hand Dex her plate she just shot it randomly around the table.

She passes her cue stick off to Will. "Here, it's your turn."

With a laugh, I make my way around to the couch where Beck sits talking to Stella. "So, is this everything you hoped it would be?" I tease.

Beck pulls me into his lap and places a kiss to my temple. "It's so much more."

"I'm assuming that my idea of you and I living together is now officially off the table, correct?" Stella asks with a snarky smile.

I don't even get my mouth open to respond before Beck's hold on me tightens. "That's correct. I've tricked her, she's here to stay."

"*Dios mío, estás loco*," I say, and Beck doesn't miss a beat.

"*Loco por ti*." Crazy for you.

"My god," Stella cries. "It's too sweet. My tarot reading a few months ago was so freaking right."

Beck's hold tightens again. "Now that Jensen is officially stuck with me—I'm going to have to know about the tarot cards."

I tilt my head back with a slight groan. "Here we go."

Stella scoffs. "Well, if she had asked months ago, she would have known my reading pulled the Tower card, which obviously supported her decision to move here and break away from her old life."

"Ay, move on from that one." I give her a little shove. "You should have pulled the Death card for all that stuff."

Stella's eyes roll. "That's not how it works and you know that."

Beck playfully puts his hand over my mouth, to which I, 100 percent, bite him for. "Ah, dammit, I don't know how it works. Hush, I'm learning."

Stella sticks her tongue out at me. "See, your boyfriend cares."

Leaning my head on Beck's shoulder, he places a quick kiss on my forehead. Yeah, my boyfriend does care.

I let Stella finish her spiel on how she also pulled the Wheel of Fortune card, which she contributes to how everything has been playing out with me running my own shop. And lastly, the Lovers card, which, out of all the cards that have to do with relationships, I have to admit I can't deny she got the one for soulmates perfectly right.

By the time Stella's wrapped up the gist of her reading, Lucie makes her way into the living room, plate nearly empty. "We're out."

Beck laughs. "That's got to go down as one of the fastest losses I've seen."

Dex rounds the couch next. "I want to hang out with my wife and friends. Why must it always involve a game night?"

Callie leans over the couch with another boo. "Don't be a sad loser, or I'll tell Miles on you."

Lucie tries to stifle her laugh with a sausage ball, but the look Dex gives her says he's not amused for a total of five seconds before he breaks into a chuckle himself. "Alright, fair. Who's up next against these two assholes now? I need someone to bring them down a peg."

I look around to where Beck's hat sits on the counter in

front of Tripp and Emma. "Hey, Ems, will you pull a paper out of the hat?"

Tripp takes the hat and holds it out for Emma to pull from. She gets a bit of a smile as she unfolds it. "Beck and Jensen's turn."

Beck stands up taking me with him. "Come on, baby, let's show 'em how it's done."

Callie chuckles. "Hey, it's the first night you met all over again."

When Beck lets me go once we reach the table, I look up to him with a smile. "Rack 'em up, honey."

Epilogue – Jensen
A year and a half later

"Okay, are you ready to go now?" I ask as Beck continues to stretch in the grass. It's the first Tuesday we've had since the season started to run now that it's officially spring again here in Boston.

"Jen, baby, can I not stretch first?" Beck pulls his foot behind his back.

On one hand, yes, the man can stretch— he looks damn good while he does. We're coming up on a year and a half of us officially being together, and during that time I've given Beck so many tattoos.

I've added to his slutty thigh tattoo by continuing the lightning strikes all the way down his leg. He's got the cherry blossom tree spreading across his ribs. And his left arm has been my most recent playground for his patchwork sleeve. The latest one I did was a rendition of the pinup girl that's on my tapestry in our home, but, at Beck's request, the legs had to mimic mine.

He was hot to begin with, but with even more tattoos? He has me freaking drooling sometimes. However, right now,

I'm pretty sure he's stalling for something and it's pissing me off.

Dottie's even circling him in anticipation at this point.

"*Ay dios mío*, Beck." I tilt my head back with a slight groan when he simply pulls his arm across his chest. "I'm about to start running without you and you can catch up."

Beck chuckles. "Okay, Killer, relax. I'm ready."

"Great," I clip, but with one step forward to start, Beck's grabbing my wrist.

"Hold on, you're missing something."

I pinch my eyebrows together. "No, what are you talking about? I'm not missing anything."

He tilts his head then proceeds to look up and down my body. Is he trying to get thrown in the harbor today or something? "Beckham Daines, I'm going to start running without you."

His head goes back. "Oh yeah, I remember. Dottie, come here." Bending down, Beck unclips her leash, then puts it back on. I can't tell what he's doing, but he's really pushing it.

"You've got five seconds," I warn, but as Beck turns to me, he doesn't stand up...no, he stays down on one knee and holds up a gold engagement ring.

"I think this is what you're missing, Jenni-cakes."

My jaw drops and my sour attitude disappears, but I know this fucker was egging me on, on purpose. "Beck, w-what are you doing?"

"Before I ask you to marry me, I had to make sure I could still get under your skin. I had to hear a little bit of Spanish, and really, I would have loved a threat but I think you might have been saying those in your head."

My laugh comes through with happy tears. "I was so about to throw you into the harbor."

"Thank god." This heart-stopping smile comes to Beck's face. "Jensen James, would you do me the absolute honor of marr—"

"Yes," I answer before he can even get the question out. "Yes, I'll marry you."

The moment Beck slides the ring on my finger, he's up and pulling me into his arms. Dottie starts to bark and the crowd that's formed around us starts to clap and cheer, but the moment Beck's lips meet mine everything fades away.

Beck cups my face. "You ready now, baby?"

I sputter a laugh. "You expect me to run...now?" I pull back a step to fully admire the ring now on my finger. At Callie and Will's engagement party, I tattooed a J on Beck's finger and a B on my own, but I have to say the ring looks pretty amazing along with it.

"Yeah, Killer, we're still going on a run." Beck gives me this devilish grin. "You can chase after me, though, if you want."

"Oh, my sweet, delusional stalker."

"So possessive with that little 'my.'" Beck pulls me in again. "But I want the title this time, it's your soon-to-be delusional husband."

"You're damn right." I wrap my arms around his shoulders. "You're gonna get three miles at best out of me now."

Beck scoffs and places a kiss on my forehead. "We'll see about that. You know how it usually goes. You never want to stop running with me."

"Yeah, but now I know I get it for life." I wiggle my ring finger. "How about, in offseason we elope in Vegas?"

"I love when you flirt with me."

Epilogue – Beck

Five years later

"Dad! Grandpa keeps beating me at pool!" Isaac yells as he scoots his stool around to the top of the table. "Will you come help me?"

My dad waves my six-year-old off. "He's not going to help you. I can beat him too."

I shake my head as I pull the cinnamon rolls out of the oven. It's been almost three years since Jensen and I adopted Isaac and his older brother Declan, who's nine. We fostered them for maybe a year, after their parents passed in a freak car accident.

"You know, I would love to help, but Mom and Dec are almost home, and you guys are going over to Aunt Cals and Uncle Will's house for the weekend."

My sweet blond curly-haired, blue-eyed boy all but leaps off the stool and races to the kitchen. The movement, of course, has Dottie up and off the couch chasing after him.

As he rounds the island, Dottie's at his side licking his face. He giggles and pushes her back. "I have two questions."

I give a quick glance to my dad because Isaac always has more questions than he says. "I can't wait to hear 'em."

"First, can Dottie come with us this weekend?"

"Nope, sorry, kiddo. No dogs allowed, you know that."

Isaac gives his best attempt at a growl. "Why not? I just don't understand why, though."

"The building they live in doesn't allow dogs. I think we should maybe focus on the fact that Aunt Cals wants all her nieces and nephews under her roof so you can all get so insanely hyped up on sugar and be maniacs with no rules for two whole days."

Isaac's eyes light up as he raises his finger. "But if she wants us to have no rules then I should be able to bring Dottie."

I blink. *Fuck.*

"Kid's got you there, son," my dad says.

"Not helping." I sigh. "What was your other question going to be?"

Isaac folds his arms over his chest. "Are those my cinnamon rolls to bring Thea?"

My heart does a full flip. It's safe to say myself, Jensen, and Lucie are all very happy that Isaac and Thea seem to have this close friendship. Dex is only pretending to hate it right now, and I get it, she's his little girl. However, Luce and I specifically might be already planning their wedding.

"Yeah, those are for you to bring to Thea."

His arms drop in relief. "Thank goodness, she loves it when I bring her cinnamon rolls."

I ruffle his hair with a chuckle. "Yeah, I admire your game, kid. Now, why don't you go ahead and bring down any blankets, pillow, whatever you want to sleep with down here. I've already got your bag packed."

Isaac peers up at me. "Can Dottie come help me?"

Oh, great, he's scheming something. "Considering you know it's okay for Dottie to come with you, I'm slightly afraid to ask what your plan is...but you know, I'll have Mom be the bad guy."

Isaac simply shrugs. "Come on, Dottie."

When he hightails it up the stairs my dad chuckles. "You know he's about to try to get that dog wrapped up in his blanket or something."

"I wouldn't put the attempt past him. Are you sure you're good to go for this season?"

Dad doesn't say "Oh, I'm good." No, he sends me the finger. "Quit asking me that. I've helped with the boys for the past three years during the season. Just assume I'm good unless I tell you otherwise."

I hold my hands up in defense. "Geez, okay. Consider that my last attempt of letting you not have practically nine months of travel."

"Thank god," he grumbles as he stands up from the barstool. "I will, however, be taking this weekend off since the boys will be with Callie and Will."

"Oh, you mean, I actually get the weekend alone with my wife?" I send him a snarky smile. "Thank god."

"Keep the attitude up and maybe I'll decide to pop by randomly."

"Do it at your own risk, old man."

I get another bird sent my way, but there's always a *happy for me* smile that comes with it.

Just as quickly as the door closes, I barely get the frosting on Isaac's cinnamon rolls before it opens again.

"Dad, we're back!" Declan hollers as he walks in. Now, with Declan being older, it's taken him a bit of time to heal from his loss, but within the past year, it's been amazing to see him come out of his shell.

Jensen and I both practically had to swallow our tears the first time he referred to us as his mom and dad.

Stepping to greet them, I always seek out my beautiful wife first. I give Jensen a quick kiss to avoid any gag noises the kids will make. "Hi, baby, how was work?"

Her smile fills my entire chest with warmth. "Great. Dec's got something really cool to show you."

"It's really not that cool." Declan slides onto one of the barstools. "I think I could do it better."

"I think I should be the judge of that. What is it?"

Jensen's hand touches my arm, then hands me her iPad. "He knows how to pull it up. Where's Isaac?"

"Upstairs trying to figure out how to sneak Dottie into Callie and Will's place."

Jensen nods slowly. "Ay, okay, I'll go take care of that."

I dare another quick kiss, then turn to go take the other stool next to Declan. "Okay, show me."

Dec spins the stool back and forth. While his hair is darker than his brother's, he has the same piercing blue eyes, except right now I can see the nerves showing through them. "It's really nothing, I—'

"Hey, Dec." I place my hand on his shoulder, stilling his anxious movement. "It could be the alphabet—out of order—with just simple lines, and I'm still going to want to look at it."

Declan's lips fold together, and for a moment, I think I might have to give a lame pep talk, but he takes Jensen's iPad and pulls up what he's been working on.

"Okay, I think it might need to be cleaned up a bit, but

you know how Mom has that tattoo of the hands linked together with a string?"

I nod. I am very aware of every tattoo on that woman's body.

"Well, I tried to copy it at first, but then it sort of morphed into something a little different."

Spinning the screen around, Declan shows me a drawing of four hands in line art, all reaching toward each other and a red string looping them all together.

"It's all our hands. Yours and Mom's, then mine and Isaac's with the string looping through. But what's really cool is that I did it as an infinite line, so there're no breaks. Each of our hands links to each other in the circle."

I'm not going to cry. I'm going to hold it together.

"Dec, this is amazing."

"I wanna see! I wanna see!" Isaac yells running back into the kitchen with Jensen and Dottie right behind him.

I pull Issac into my lap while Declan shows him all four of our hands linked together. Jensen comes up behind me and places a hand to my back.

"Holding up good, honey?" she whispers.

Tilting my head back, I meet her eyes. "I couldn't be better, Jen."

Also by Mollie Goins

Thank you for reading Stealing You, I hope you enjoyed reading Beck and Jensen's story!

The Boston Blues aren't finished yet though, Adam and Mia's story is next in Catching Mine for an accidental pregnancy and marriage of connivence!

Pitcher Us

Coach Me

Stealing You

Catching Mine - Adam

Scoring Her - Tripp

Aster Creek - Small town series

Feel It All

Bring It All

Despite It All

Acknowledgments

Well, well, well, here we are again writing acknowledgements. I always find myself not wanting to write these as they are one of the very last things I do during my publication process. Reflecting on that I truly believe it's because I'm in the fourth stage of grief and I'm so sad to officially be hands off from this story.

Beck and Jensen were unexpected story that I poured my entire heart into. I knew their plots and knew their characters, but what I didn't expect was for their story to be my favorite book written to date. I suppose I may feel this way after a few other books, but this one just hit me right in my soul.

So, thank you to Beck and Jensen for being the FMC I strive to be and the MMC that reminds me to feel all my emotions.

To my husband. What a crazy year we've had. Dare I say we knocked it out the park with both of us solidifying our dream jobs. You will forever be my inspiration and partner in crime. I love you immensely.

To Page. You know how I said that escalated quickly, yeah we are lightyears ahead of that now. You are incredible, an inspiration, and a fucking mastermind. I will forever jump when you say to, and always be by your side.

To Courtney. The strongest mother I know. The

marketing queen. The time, care, and love you put into your job is incredible. The example of a badass boss babe you show your kids in unmatched.

To Brittany, hehehehe. To be honest I was nervous when I handed Beck and Jensen over to you, but boy, I'm forever grateful to have you on my alpha team. Thank you for being my fiercely loving reader. Here's to me constantly making you love tropes that you don't like.

Thank you to each and every alpha/sensitivity/beta reader. Courtney, Page, Brittany, Isabella, Kelsey, and Molly. I appreciate each and every one of you. Thank you for making Jensen and Beck all they could be!

Thank you to everyone who had a hand in bringing Stealing You to it's final draft and building up the Mollieverse:

Cover design: Kimberly Sable - KBG Designs
Dev & Proof edits: Lauren Sakowski - Author's Best Friend
Line edits: Caroline Palmier: Love & Edits
Marketing/Publicist: Courtney + Page
Literary Agent: Amanda Wooden

To my readers. It's because of you that I get to have my dream job. You are incredible. I want each and every person reading this right now to know that it's because of you that I get to do this. I'm eternally grateful.

From the bottom of my heart, thank you for being you. Love, Mollie.

About the Author

Mollie Goins is a contemporary romance author, with books in the sub genre of small town and sports. With swoon worthy men and strong women, each book delivers on all the sweet, spicy, and emotional moments that you can escape in.

Residing in a small town in Tennessee with her high school sweetheart, Mollie is also a mother to two adorable but wild kids who always keep her on her toes.

Mollie is a chronic out of order reader, so while her books are in a series, each book can be read as a standalone. However, Mollie also loves a good Easter egg, so be looking for callbacks from book to book.

For more information visit molliegoins.com